FOR KING AND COMPANY

by

Ellis K. Meacham

THUNDERCHILD PUBLISHING
Huntsville, Alabama

This is a work of fiction. All of the characters, organizations, and events portrayed in this novel are either products of the author's imagination or are used fictitiously.

FOR KING AND COMPANY

Published by arrangement with Jon Meacham.

ISBN-13: 978-1542877602
ISBN-10: 1542877601

Published by Thunderchild Publishing.
Find us at http://www.ourworlds.net/thunderchild/

Table of Contents

Dedication

To Jon and Arthur

PART I

Combined Operations

The continuous thunder of the guns from the frigates grinding against the port and starboard sides reached a crescendo too painful for the human ear to tolerate. Merewether wiped away the blood that trickled into his eyes and peered forward through clouds of smoke, seeing only shattered spars, masses of tangled cordage and windrows of smoldering canvas, punctuated by bloody ragged heaps that had been British seamen only a few minutes before. The frigate no longer heaved with the recoil of her own broadsides. She was a dying ship, already low in the water. But the colors of the Bombay Marine still sparkled at the peak.

There was a flicker of movement on deck. The figure ran to the flag halyards, loosened the turns about the pins, and began to haul down the ensign.

"No!" shouted Merewether. "No! No! No!" The flag was fluttering to the deck. "Don't strike! We'll go down with colors flying!

The stocky figure turned, calmly folding the bunting, and looked back at him. The features were indistinguishable in the gloom. Only staring china blue eyes and an incredibly broad cleft chin were visible. A dead silence fell; the cannonading on either hand had ceased.

"Hoist our colors!" Merewether shouted, then realized that no sound had come from his lips. He made a mighty effort to move forward to the halyards, and came full awake, shaking uncontrollably. Grey light was in the room, with a chill drizzle of rain to welcome the New Year outside. Caroline slept peacefully beside him. Merewether had had another nightmare.

He lay still, forcing his muscles to relax. It was time to rise and report to the dockyard again after these past two weeks of leave, but he felt a lassitude that numbed his limbs and overwhelmed his resolution for the moment. This last dream had been more horrifyingly real than the one he had had last week. In the first he had been confronted by a huge black spider that unaccountably wore the ivory face of a beautiful woman who spoke seductively to him, then slashed razor sharp claws at his throat. He had felt the sudden pain, the gout of life's blood rising to strangle him, and had awakened in a paroxysm of coughing that aroused Caroline.

He marshaled his energies, forcing himself to rise and face the morning in these shabby lodgings here in Calcutta, seeing the unfamiliar bulk of his dear pregnant Caroline under the sheet, and wondered again if he had contracted some distemper along the Persian Road last fall. He and Caroline had remained at home the evening before, regretting invitations to any of the watch parties since Caroline was again feeling queasy in her pregnancy. The dockyard had not declared the holiday; with the flagship, *Pitt*, careened and *Rapid* waiting her turn, all hands would turn to today in regular routine. He was again in command of *Rapid,* but she was out of commission, slated for extensive refitting before she would be ready for sea.

Sir John Waldron, Commandant of the Naval Service of the Honorable East India Company, had refused to take the flagship back to Bombay. The ship's bottom was so foul with weed from the cruise in the eastern seas that her speed was diminished by half. Instead, he had taken passage in *Gazelle* last month. And Captain Bridges, *Pitt's* commanding officer, had come back to Calcutta a sick man. He was still in the hospital at Fort William, and soon to be invalided out of the service. Not for the first time Merewether wondered who might get that plum, a thirty-six gun frigate. He set out to walk through the drizzle to the dockyard, leaving Caroline asleep.

He stopped at the warehouse by the ropewalk where *Rapid's* crew was housed ashore and took the morning report from Lieutenant MacCamy. The other officers would return from leave today, but the hands had been kept busy in the ropewalk laying up cordage of hemp to replace the worn-out standing rigging, while the sailmaker and his mates overhauled sails and sewed new canvas in the loft. As he left the warehouse, he saw *Gazelle* coming up to the anchorage. She must have made a fast turnaround at Bombay.

"Commodore wants to see you, sir," the chief clerk told him. Merewether hung up his wet hat and boat cloak and went into Land's office.

"Ah, Merewether. *Gazelle* dropped off the mailbags at Budge-Budge last night and there seems to be an official communication for you." He handed over the oilskin-wrapped packet. "And our friends have been lucky, MacLellan and MacRae both selected to be captains, and Larkin to be a first lieutenant. Tollett promoted to commodore."

Merewether slit the wrapper, his fingers trembling a bit as he remembered his fiasco on Mauritius last year, wondering if retribution had come at last. "Well, I'm damned! Relieved as captain of *Rapid!"* Merewether felt a sense of shock; he had commanded the sloop for two years almost to the day. He pulled a second sheet from the cover.

"Well, I'm damned!" he said again. "Ordered as Master and Commandant into *Pitt!"*

Land showed surprise. "My congratulations," he said at last. "I thought it certain that one of Campbell's pets at Bombay would get the command. Of course, with her captain sick almost the whole of the cruise down to Java, her crew has got a bit out of hand. Waldron was able to hold them in check as long as he had his flag in her, but Whaley, her first, is a little too handy with the cat for my taste, and last I heard twenty-six seamen and two petty officers had run."

"Run! Where to?"

"Sixteen turned up enlisted in the Royal Navy. We sent a petition to Pellew, but he refuses to release them. Says any British citizen has a right to serve in the Navy, regardless of his enlistment in the Marine." Land shook his head, and continued. "He did promise to take the matter up with the Admiralty, and that will be the last anyone hears of it."

"I can see his point of view." Merewether nodded. "Now, when do I read myself in?"

We will refloat *Pitt* on the spring tide tonight, and commence loading her equipment and guns tomorrow. Time enough then," said Land. "And since we expect to careen *Rapid* tomorrow, I think it best that you retain command until that operation is completed. Larkin may then relieve you."

Merewether thanked Land and took his leave. There was much to be done.

Rapid was a dead ship, riding high out of the water. Her upper masts had been struck and her rigging removed in preparation for the careening on the bar across the Hooghly tomorrow. As the gig hooked on to the gangway, Merewether heard the sound of the pumps and saw a solid stream of water gushing from the scuppers.

"We're pumping a half hour out of four, sir," explained Tompkins. "She has a bad leak about midships. Wells up through the deadwood and keelson like a spring. The carpenter thinks it's damage to the keel, but I know she has not touched bottom since I've been in her."

Merewether went aft to the cabin and looked about the bare room. Sangh had delivered his personal belongings to his lodgings two weeks ago, and other furnishings, including the brass bed, desk, blunderbusses, truncheons and chairs were locked in a storeroom ashore. On an impulse, he opened the strongbox. It was empty, as was the strongroom beneath the deck. The barren cabin depressed him, and he went forward to find the boatswain and complete his inspection.

"I think everything is in order, Tompkins. The dockyard hands will handle her for the heaving down tomorrow." The gig came back to the dockyard, and Merewether went to find *Rapid's* papers, the articles of enlistment of the crew, and lists of the myriad items he would have to account for when he turned over command.

The initial enlistments of the crew for two years had expired last week. Two-thirds of the ordinary seamen and all but two of the petty officers had extended for another year, he was pleased to learn. He wished he might take the officers and men from *Rapid* to *Pitt,* but it was impossible.

Merewether turned to the reports of the Board of Survey, checking off against the allowance lists those articles worn out, expended, or lost in service. It was dull, tedious work, but he wanted no surcharges filed against his pay for shortages. He encountered a report of two blunderbusses expended last February 17th, and realized that they must be the two he had issued to Eldridge and Webster when they boarded the *Duchy of Lancaster.* He remembered that Eldridge had reported he had brought them back when he appeared before the promotion board last summer, and four, all with the brass nameplate, "Rapid", set in their stocks were stacked in the corner. Well, for once in his life he had a surplus. He was over ordnance allowance by two blunderbusses.

Merewether came to the bottom of the stack, made the last deletion, initialed the page and sat back, the onerous task completed. He could turn over the ship to Larkin and accept his receipt with a clear conscience now. He looked at his time piece — not yet eleven o'clock — and reviewed the events of the morning. His elation had subsided, and doubt intruded as he considered the greater responsibilities of commanding a thirty-six gun flagship frigate. Merewether had no inkling of what duty she might be destined to perform. He knew Whaley, her first lieutenant, only by sight, but Land had spoken somewhat critically of Whaley this morning. Merewether shrugged the matter off. The man would conform to his policies and orders given, or be sacked, he told himself.

The surge of confidence reminded Merewether that he had two years' seniority in the Captain's List of the Marine, and was far from being the junior captain now. That episode in the first few weeks of his marriage six months or so ago came suddenly to mind. He had told Caroline that after ten years of commissioned service in the Marine he would be entitled to three years' leave with pay. She had accounted it a promise, and he realized with a sense of shock that the service would be completed next September. Eighteen years of service to the Company and its Marine, commencing as a scullery boy at twelve — he was now thirty — entering middle age, and soon to be a father. That three years' leave was not so remote or unthinkable now, even at the outrageous cost of passage to London for Caroline and himself. He clapped on his hat, locked the door to the grimy little room, and walked across to the arsenal.

MacLellan was at his desk. Two almost empty bottles of Scotch whisky and an accumulation of dirty glasses were set before him. Evidently there already had been toasts proposed and drunk on account of his promotion to captain.

"Ah, Captain," MacLellan said, coming around the desk, hand extended. "Happy birthday and a prosperous New Year!"

"And my congratulations for a well deserved promotion!"

"Will ye have a wee drop, sir?"

"Just a finger." It was too early in the day for much heavy liquor, but he drank to MacLellan's health. "What duty do you forecast?" he inquired, setting down the glass.

"It will no longer be Calcutta, Captain. Commodore Waldron said last month that he wanted me to succeed West — he retires this year — as Fleet Ordnance Officer for the Marine, and my billet will be Bombay Castle."

When they parted two hours later from the officers' club, MacLellan said, "Of course, I'll see you here tonight . . ." He stopped short with a rueful expression, then muttered, "The Devil take me, I've spilled the porridge," and fled.

Merewether was puzzled a moment at MacLellan's behavior, then recalled the three visits in the past two days by Sangh, his steward; each time he had been closeted with Caroline. Light dawned. There must be some sort of birthday entertainment in the wind. The thought touched him. His birthday had not been remembered since, as a child, he had been given a slice of cake and sugared tea by his mother in a corner of the kitchen in Bell Flower House. He must simulate the surprise, he decided, as he came back to the dockyard.

It was a gay affair, planned by Caroline and executed by Sangh with a host of assistants. There were Sir Thomas and Lady Jeffrey; Commodore Land escorting a sprightly recent widow; MacLellan; all the officers from *Rapid* and *Comet;* and a group of young lady acquaintances of Caroline. It commenced sedately enough with a toast to Merewether, and the presentation of a silver whistle in celebration of his birthday, but quickly developed into a lively wetting-down party for the new commissions of MacLellan, MacRae and Larkin. Merewether felt relaxed and happy as he made the rounds of the guests, and thought of the love that had inspired this party.

It was close to midnight and dessert was on the table, when Sangh tiptoed up to whisper in the ear of Commodore Land. He frowned, muttered an apology and went out. Merewether wondered briefly at the intrusion — possibly some dispatch to be receipted for in person — and harked back to the droll tale being told by Lieutenant Dillon. The gale of laughter at the conclusion of the story subsided as Land re-entered to stand beside Merewether at the head of the table.

"Gentlemen," he said tightly. "Delightful as this occasion has been, duty calls. *Pitt's* gone adrift on a bore in the Hooghly!"

There was a babble of comment and concern from the officers as chairs scraped back. Caroline appeared distressed at the abrupt ending of the party, but managed to dissemble. He saw MacLellan delay a moment in earnest conversation with plain little Miss Mary Wilkins, the daughter of their landlady, and then join the others in a mad dash for the dockyard.

He was not legally in command of *Pitt,* he told himself, but if the flagship of the Bombay Marine were lost now, another such command might never come his way. The horses galloped through the deserted streets, and Land, Merewether and MacLellan swayed with the motion of the tonga.

What could have gone wrong? The superintendent of the dockyard, the sailing master, and his senior boatswain were in charge of the evolution, with skilled seamen in two anchor hoys and a picked crew under Lieutenant Whaley in *Pitt.* Merewether had watched the quick efficient operation in times past, the two hoys alternately holding the refloated hulk with their anchors, while the other moved across the stream to drop its berth, where it would be furnished with its own cables and anchors.

Still, a tidal bore was a frightening and dangerous phenomenon — rare, but by no means unknown at this time of the year, particularly with the full moon and spring tide. The bed of the Hooghly was simply too shallow and restricted to accommodate the huge volume of water forced upstream against the seaward flow of the river. Thus the incoming tide tended to roll up and over the downstream current until it became an irresistible tidal wave, five or six feet high, racing upstream, snapping moorings, capsizing or swamping small craft, and causing ships to drag their anchors unless spring lines had been rigged and precautions taken. Bores had been known to run over thirty miles above Calcutta, and *Pitt* was light, no burden of armament, supplies or even ballast in her. She might ride the bore like a chip in a mill race until she smashed into another vessel or drove ashore.

Horses pulled up with a clatter of hooves on the same pavement at the dockyard gate.

"Where is she?" demanded Land of the anxious second-lieutenant on duty.

"I canna say, sir. Here's Carr, he brought the word." A grizzled boatswain's mate rolled forward, knuckling his forehead.

"Sor, we had just got the lines aboard from the hoys . . ."

"Speak up, man, where's *Pitt?"*

"Went out of sight upstream is all I know."

"Hellfire!" said Land, turning to the duty officer. "What's the high water interval tonight?" The officer looked at the slate hung in the guardhouse window.

"One hour, fifty-five minutes, sir, commencing at eleven ten," he read off. Land pulled out his watch.

"Less than an hour of slack water, Merewether. We have to hand her before the ebb sets in, or she'll go down faster than she went up!" He turned to MacRae. "Get *Comet* ready."

"Aye, sir, but the wind is almost dead foul."

"I know, but I want you prepared to intercept her if she comes downstream, grapple, anything to get a line on her!" MacRae and his officers departed for the landing at a trot. "And Merewether, turn out your crew and man the dockyard launches."

Larkin turned to go as Merewether called after him, "Bring two muskets, cartridges and a half dozen iron ramrods." Larkin waved his hand in acknowledgment as he disappeared into the darkness.

"We'll require grapnels heaving lines and towing cable in the launches," Merewether told the duty officer. "Better bring a half dozen balls of small stuff too."

The launches were under way a few minutes later, pulling across towards the careening bar. Land and Merewether were seated in the sternsheets, Hamlyn at the tiller. The damp wind blowing the light drizzle at twelve to fifteen knots chilled them to the bone. The temperature must be under fifty degrees, and Merewether soon wished he had an oar himself to pull. There was a momentary break in the scudding clouds allowing the full moon to illuminate the river. *Pitt* was not in sight, but there were other vessels, anchored close to the west bank of the river. Merewether doubted the ship had been carried more than two or three miles even by the onrushing bore. It was entirely possible the frigate had capsized and sunk, so light she was. They passed the bar where she had been careened, seeing lanterns moving about on shore, and then made out a light upstream.

"Steer for the hoy," Land told Hamlyn. "Hail her."

A voice answered the hail. "She be gone upstream. We was nearly capsized in the bore, and the other hoy did." There was a pause, and then, "Six men drowned, they say."

The moon reappeared and Merewether could see the small vessel, disproportionately broad for her length, double ended, the single mast stepped right amidships, a large capstan mounted forward from her bow, a cable running through its block to disappear in the water.

"Do you still have your cable?"

"Yes, sir. *Pitt* hadn't got the bitter end secured when the bore struck."

"Very well, stand by." The launch pulled away upstream, the second boat following and making good speed in the slack water.

It seemed an eternity before lights were sighted. They could be on shore, or on an anchored vessel, but they appeared to be almost in midstream. The moon broke through again and it was possible to make out the mastless hulk riding high out of the water. A hail brought an instant reply.

"We lost our lines," came the shout. "Can you get one on board?"

"It's your ship, Merewether," said Land. "Godspeed."

The heaving line pulled the light towing cable aboard, and a shout announced that it was secured. Another line went forward to the second launch, and the two boats took a strain. Merewether looked back towards the west bank and saw it begin to slide by. The interval of slack water had passed and the ebb was beginning to run.

The two launches had an insensate beast by the tail, a creature at the mercy of the wind and current. He had no solid object to which he could moor, and only the feeble strokes of the oars as they ploughed ineffectively through the water to try to hold the ship. He might be able to influence the vessel's drift to some extent, but it was impossible to check her with the steady pressure of the wind against her inordinate freeboard and the inexorable flow towards the sea of the huge volume of water forced upstream by the bore, now emptying from the narrow channels and creeks.

The sky had cleared. The drizzle stopped. But the wind cut like a knife through wet clothing. The moon now lighted the surface of the water in contrast to the dark lines of vegetation on either bank. *Pitt* was a little nearer the west bank now, an occasional light on shore sliding by at an alarming pace. There was no profit in wearing the hands out in a futile effort to check the drift, Merewether decided. Downstream there was the anchor hoy and *Comet* standing poised to attempt the interception. it was preferable to make the contact with the hoy, rather than risk a collision that might send both ships to the bottom.

"Larkin!" he shouted. "Double-bank the oars and pull for the west bank." There was a bustle in both boats as the hands took their new positions.

"Give way."

If the pulling boats could influence *Pitt* to the westward, there was a chance of bringing her down close enough aboard the hoy to pass a messenger attached to her cable. Even then, there was doubt as to whether it would hold against the enormous strain of the rampaging hulk.

The light line tightened, rising rigidly to the fairleads as the hands put their backs into the double-banked oars. The combination of tide and wind must be moving her at a good seven knots, and both boats headed northwestwardly at an angle to her bow pulling with little visible effect. Merewether knelt in the sternsheets as *Pitt* came around a slight bend, and he could see the cluster of lights that marked the hoy, possibly a mile downstream. If he could give the ship another hundred yards or so westing, she might pass close aboard for the hoy to pass a heaving line and get the cable secured in time.

It was a backbreaking seven or eight minutes, the launches rowing desperately while they were dragged stern first through the water. Merewether could hear the stentorious breathing of the oarsmen rasping above the sound of the wind, now beginning to raise whitecaps on the river. It was hard to gauge the effects of the pulling boats — and the wind was helping too — but the hoy's anchor lights were barely visible along the port side of *Pitt.* She should pass close enough now.

Merewether pulled the new silver whistle from his breast pocket and blew on it. The shrill note cut through the sound of the wind, and attracted instant attention. “Way enough!” he shouted. The oars were lifted out of the water. “Now, I want you to sing out, ‘Aboard the hoy! Pass a line! Pass a line!’ ” He set the cadence himself, and in a moment the two boatloads of seamen had settled into a powerful chant that must be audible far down wind. He heard a thinner echo from *Pitt* joining in, and saw lanterns being swung from her poop. There was a chance.

The monkey’s fist of the heaving line arched up over the stern in the lantern light, and frantic hands snaked in the messenger and the heavy anchor cable that followed. There was a rush to the forward bitts, and then a soft but carrying voice shouted, “Secured!” from the forecastle.

“Cast off,” Merewether told the sternhook. “Give way. Come to starboard.” The launches pulled clear towards mid-stream as the cable from the hoy took the strain of checking and holding a twelve-hundred-ton ship running stern-to at seven knots.

For a moment she was dragged at an angle to the current, one end out of water, the other forced under he thought the hoy would be capsized. He could hear the cable groaning on the bitts as it tightened and water snapped from the rigid hemp. The cable certainly would have parted but the hoy’s anchor began to drag through the muddy bottom of the Hooghly a few yards at a time, relieving the pressure, then holding, then dragging again. *Pitt* finally came to a halt.

“God bless me” said Land. “It is more than I can credit”

There were lights moving downstream and Merewether realized that *Comet* was under way, prepared to risk sudden destruction to get a line on the frigate. “Larkin,” he called. “Go down and tell MacRae she’s secured for the present.” He turned to Land and said, “And with your permission sir, I think we should board her and I shall read myself in.”

“It’s damned foolish, Merewether, but I have no objection.” There was no doubt as Land saw it. Merewether should wait for the ship to be warped across the river and safely moored in her berth. If she were lost or damaged now, Merewether would be responsible.

But Merewether felt a cross-grained determination to assume the risk; it was impossible for him to leave the obligation longer to her disabled captain, or even with Lieutenant Whaley.

It was broad daylight when the two launches came back to the dockyard. Merewether was legally in command of *Pitt,* and Larkin had relieved him as Master and Commandant in *Rapid.* The frigate seemed secure enough for the present, though it would be a day or so before she could take on board her own anchors and cables and refit the windlass in preparation for warping her across the Hooghly. With two anchor hoys alternately moving and holding her, the maneuver would have been quick and easy. With only one available, *Pitt* must use her own anchor to hold herself in place as the hoy shifted position. He saw the muskets, a packet of cartridges and a bundle of ramrods glistening with moisture in the bottom of the boat. He had not required them to shoot a line aboard *Pitt,* he was thankful to remember, as he told the coxswain to return them to the gunner.

In the dockyard office, Merewether looked down at the soggy wrinkled ruin of his dress uniform and up at Land. "I'll go home and change, sir," he said. He realized that he was suffering again the familiar, nagging compulsion of a commander to stay in sight of his ship, and wished for a moment that the responsibility was not his.

"As you wish," said Land, "but there's no need to hurry. I intend to breakfast and take a nap before I return."

Caroline had, of course, been concerned. Merewether had to give her a full account of the mishap while he sponged off and shaved, and then ate the breakfast the maid brought in.

"Oh," said Caroline over a second cup of tea. "Mary Wilkins came in for a bit last night after Doctor Buttram saw us home from the club. She was quite curious as to Captain MacLellan. It seems he's asked to be allowed to call on her."

Merewether recalled the slight delay last night as MacLellan had a word with Miss Wilkins before he joined the exodus for the dockyard. "Tell her to nourish no false hopes," he said lightly. "The man is posted for Bombay." He kissed Caroline, and went out into the bright hot morning.

Merewether sat back in the chair in the office he had borrowed for use during *Pitt's* fitting-out period. Yesterday had seen the frigate safely warped across the Hooghly and she was now moored to her own anchors, bow and stem. Her silhouette had altered. Even the few tons of stone ballast now being stowed and secured under the critical eyes of Mister Hobday, the dockyard sailing master, Boatswain Caldwell and Carpenter Owens, had reduced her freeboard and restored a semblance of the graceful lines she sailed on. The water casks, guns and stores, together with her spars and rigging, would complete the metamorphosis and make her a live ship again. He looked back at Whaley sitting quietly across the desk, round hat held in square, stubby hands, the fingers rough and stained with tar, pale blue eyes fixed on some object in the far left corner of the room.

"And you do not know the reasons that moved four lieutenants and four midshipmen to request transfer to another ship or station?"

Whaley's eyes shifted briefly to Merewether, then resumed their inspection of the corner. Whaley was a stocky, roundish man, not fat, but heavily muscled. "No, sir. Except that I consider them to be namby-pambies, not a backbone or bit of enterprise in the lot."

The thing had come as a surprise in Merewether's third day of command of *Pitt.* Jarvis the second lieutenant, and Lawing, the senior midshipman, had evidently been elected as emissaries to wait on him this morning. They had solemnly delivered formal requests addressed to the Commandant of the Marine by way of Merewether and Land for transfer and reassignment to other duties. Under regulations, Merewether was bound to forward the requests, no matter what recommendation he might endorse on them. This development, coupled with the desertions, now numbering almost thirty ratings, was disquieting. He could be left a captain without sufficient force to sail or fight his ship.

Merewether fought down the impulse to cross-examine Whaley and demand particulars. He kept his face impassive, studying the man opposite him. Whaley's hair was light brown, worn short, but with a tendency for the forelock to fall over his eyes. The mouth protruded a bit, lips set in a horizontal line, and the cleft chin gave the impression of being almost as broad as the cheek bones. Not so much a cruel or ruthless face as an insensitive one, he decided. The eyes flicked back and met Merewether's squarely.

"Of course, you may talk to the gentlemen if you wish, sir. I've only stated my private opinion of them." Once again Whaley transferred his gaze to the corner.

From the dossiers laid out on the desk, it appeared that these officers were no recent recruits in *Pitt:* even the most junior midshipman had joined her at Bombay over ten months ago, There was no evidence of disciplinary action, not even a letter of admonition and reprimand, in the records of any of the officers to explain the requests for transfer. Whaley's own dossier had revealed his age to be thirty-three, original appointment as second lieutenant, 1795, and to rank as first lieutenant from 1802. He was senior in commissioned service in the Marine to Merewether himself.

Merewether made a further inquiry.

"Has any officer required disciplinary action during this cruise?"

Whaley uncrossed his legs and his gaze shifted to the opposite corner of the room. "Why, yes, from time to time; entirely informal, you know. I don't hold with cluttering up an officer's record with such matters."

"Such as?"

"Small matters, sir. Confinement to quarters, deprivation of shore leave, extra duty looking out at the masthead, writing an essay on shiphandling — nothing worthy of note, sir." He looked squarely at Merewether. "You know, Captain Bridges was sick this whole commission, and with the flag in her I was the commander, as well as first. It wasn't easy to make *Pitt* as smart a ship as Commodore wanted her, but I did it." Whaley looked past Merewether out of the window towards the anchorage, the firm lips parted a little and quivering, then said almost inaudibly, "After all that, I'm passed over . . ."

The matter suddenly came clear. Merewether could read the bitter conviction in Whaley that slack performance by his subordinates had ruined his prospects for promotion to captain. The officers, fully aware of his disappointments in not being selected, were seeking to escape further retribution, deserved or not. There was no need to prolong the interview.

"Very well, Mister Whaley, you've been most enlightening." Whaley left the room in his short brisk gait.

Merewether pondered the situation briefly, then concluded that he would not endorse the requests just now. Let the matter simmer a few hours, time enough in the morning. He certainly could not release these officers now. He despised himself a moment for the procrastination, then put the matter out of his mind and turned his attention to the tentative watch, quarter and station bill for *Pitt.* She required some four hundred men to fill her complement, and by death, disease and desertion during her last commission, she was close to a hundred men short. Waldron must know this, and there might already be a draft of ratings on its way from Bombay, but he wrote an urgent request for the men and left it with the Master Attendant's chief clerk as he left for lunch at the Calcutta Club.

Boatswain Tompkins's face was mottled red and white with anger. He was almost incoherent as he pointed out the narrow section midships along the keel. Larkin stood looking unbelievingly at the timbers exposed by the removal of marine growth from *Rapid's* bottom. Somehow a twenty-foot strip of copper plates was missing, and the teredo worm had almost consumed the exposed wood. Here, Merewether realized, was the source of the leak Tompkins had mentioned to him last week.

"Damn that thieving, lazy Fowlke!" sputtered the boatswain. "I know just when it happened too. I took three days' leave when my son and his bride came to London . . ."

"When was this?"

"Why, just before the Company bought the ship," replied Tompkins. "She was nearly finished in the graving dock when I took the leave, and Fowlke promised to put that last copper on the next morning." He paused and thought a moment. "She was out of the dock when I came back, and the thought never crossed my mind again."

"Of course, the contract was with the former owners, but the Company's solicitors might look into the matter, Commodore," said Merewether. He turned to the carpenter. "And what do you think, Mr. Svensen?"

"Why, sir, you can see the keel is riddled. The planking can be replaced, but in a seaway, 'twould be a constant worry."

"There is some kind of drydock here in Calcutta . . ." began Larkin hopefully.

"Nonsense," growled Land. "It would almost be rebuilding her to replace that keel section, and I would have to get orders from Bombay for putting the ship in a private dock."

"Sir, I can pour boiling pitch into the keel and then replace the planking. If we put some braces in the hold, with good weather and a bit of luck, you might get her around to Bombay," interposed Svensen.

"Impossible," decided Land abruptly. "She'd have to leave her battery and most of her supplies here, and I won't risk the men to sail her, Larkin. Bad luck on you, your first command, and unseaworthy. But I'll ask Waldron for authority to have the repairs made here, subject to an estimate of the cost."

Two days later, Merewether congratulated himself upon his procrastination in action on the requests for transfer by the officers in *Pitt,* since he was now able to endorse them "approved" with a clear conscience. Land had ordered *Rapid's* officers and crew into *Pitt* to fill her watch, quarter and station bill to overflowing. Only Boatswain Tompkins was left to supervise the shipkeepers from the dockyard stationed in *Rapid* as she awaited her fate.

"I know it's hard lines," he told Larkin a few days later over lunch at the Calcutta Club. "You are a captain one day and the second lieutenant in *Pitt* the next. But, consider with the appointment in your record, you'll get another command soon enough." He thought of Whaley, and continued, "This fellow is my senior in commissioned service in the Marine, so try to get along with him."

Larkin laughed shortly. "I admit it is a disappointment, but I'll survive. And I am looking forward to working with thirty-two-pounder guns and carronades. Be a bit different from those nine-pounders we've had."

They left the club and came back to the dockyard to see the water casks being hoisted in, while the boatswain's mates and topmen spun the intricate web of stays and standing rigging. The topmasts were now set up and in place. Merewether thought of the problems he had encountered in fitting together two crews with the conflicts of seniority and authority of petty officers. Most of the conflicts he had solved by the simple expedient of putting the men in separate watches: Pitt's men under the cold blue eye of Larkin, and the port watch under MacCamy with steady young Dobbs as his assistant. Still, there had been half a dozen cases among the artisans that would require further resolution — possibly even a change of rate or so. The life of a commander was never serene, Merewether concluded, as he turned to go into the dockyard office. Another two weeks, and *Pitt* might be ready for sea — time to give consideration to the quantity and variety of cabin supplies he would require for the forthcoming commission, where ever it might take him.

Caroline was bubbling with gossip at dinner. Mary Wilkins had confided that MacLellan had called upon her four times since the New Year, and would be her escort tonight to a small private dinner planned by the Houghtons.

"She thinks he is becoming serious," she concluded. "By the bye, how old is Mister MacLellan?"

"Almost forty, I think. How old is she?"

"Thirty-five, I should guess. Mary is a dear little person, and I do hope something develops. Of course, he is under orders to Bombay, but not until June."

"It's hard to picture Mac on his knees asking for her hand," laughed Merewether, and the conversation turned to other matters.

After dinner, he fought down the impulse to go back to the dockyard, and turned his attention to the latest edition of the signal book. With seven months' absence from the quarterdeck, his recollection was hazy, but in a quarter of an hour, the print had blurred, his mind was again focused upon his new commission, and Whaley in particular.

The first lieutenant was certainly energetic. He had demonstrated faultless seamanship in the ballasting of the ship, and setting up her standing rigging thus far. Still, there would have been a flogging this morning but for Merewether's intervention yesterday afternoon. The man was one of *Rapid's,* a gangling half-wit named Braden, whose sole accomplishment was the ability to make perfect splices. Tompkins had reserved him for this one duty, as his weight was of no consequence in tailing on a brace. The petty officers had come to understand the man's limitations.

A stay awaiting an eye splice in its bitter end, secured to the bulwarks with a bit of twine, had come adrift and was flying in the breeze. Braden was close beside it, his long slender fingers pulling hempen strands through the loops held open in another line by a fid, as he completed his splice. The stay could cause no harm; it was merely an Irish pennant to annoy an officer with a passion for seamanship such as Whaley.

"Here, you," Whaley said in his soft voice. Braden had paid no attention, intent now on pulling out all the strands even. "You! said Whaley again. "Secure that line!"

Braden, mouth open, had looked up and about, blankly right past Whaley, and then continued his single-minded attention to the splice.

Merewether had seen the glint in Whaley's eye as he stepped towards Braden with the evident intent of putting the half-wit on report for deliberate disobedience to a direct order, a flogging offence.

"Oh, Mister Whaley!" Merewether had called. Whaley paused momentarily, glanced towards Merewether, then looked back at Braden as though he would finish with that business before responding to the summons. "Mister Whaley!" Whaley had then turned reluctantly.

"Yes, sir?"

"I should like to see you a moment at your convenience, please." Whaley had stepped briskly over, to be drawn out of earshot, and Braden explained. At the mast, he certainly would have mitigated the charge, but it would have put Whaley in a bad light to have brought such a complaint, and then be overruled in a public hearing.

With an effort, Merewether turned his attention back to the signal instructions, but it was impossible to concentrate on them. His eyelids were heavy. He was tired. He had not regained the weight lost last year in the ride across Persia. No use to fight it, he decided, and went to bed, closely followed by Caroline. Just before he dropped off to sleep, he wondered again if he might have contracted the distemper.

It must have been only a few minutes when Merewether came awake with a start, and then found himself quite unable to sleep again. A sense of doom settled over him. He racked his brain. Had he overlooked some essential in the refitting and commissioning of *Pitt?* Was he in default in his reports to Bombay Castle? Was there something yet undone in settling his accounts for the trip last fall to Teheran? The thought of Persia reminded him of the diplomat he had accompanied on the mission last year, Alfred Robert Percy, a man polished hard as a diamond, Caroline had said. He no longer felt the sense of shame, the fear of discovery of his bastardy, that had haunted his adult life. He realized that without conscious logic he had accepted the fact that he was Percy's son, was tacitly recognized as such. He felt an inner confidence, even a sense of pride, that he'd never experienced before.

Caroline moved restlessly beside him and turned to him in the coolness of the night. The depression of a moment ago vanished as she welcomed his attentions gladly and with spirit.

The Earl of Minto (Gibby Elliott, Percy had familiarly called him) was an affable, outgoing man who spoke in slow rounded sentences, quite different from the quick, incisive style of Sir George Barlow. The new Governor-General of India presided over the small gathering in his chamber with an air of great goodwill, almost brushing aside the formal deference accorded him. Commodore Land had taken Merewether in to present him a few minutes before the arrival of the other conferees.

"Ah, yes, Merewether, I read your report a few weeks back. Interesting. And Rob Percy's too. He thinks the peril of Bonaparte's invasion through Persia is ended, but Boy Malcolm will yet attempt to see the Shah. And how was Rob when last you saw him? I heard a rumor that he was painfully wounded."

"Yes, Your Excellency, he lost a leg by reason of gangrene setting in after a bullet wound."

"A pity. Rob so loved to ride to the hounds. He was most complimentary of your services in the mission, said it would have failed but for your enterprise. And now, I think our party has gathered." He tinkled the bell on his desk.

In the momentary interval before the secretary opened the door, Merewether wondered what reward he might receive if Percy expected a barony out of the affair. He then decided that speculation was futile.

The secretary held the door as the officers filed in, led by Vice-Admiral Sir Edward Pellew, Commander-in-Chief of the India Station. Merewether had met him briefly two years ago, after the French frigate sent to supply Tipu Sultan was taken off Ceylon. He saw with astonishment that Pellew had become grossly fat, with a vast belly, and pendulous jowls lapping over his collar. The sedentary life of an admiral seldom now at sea, and the rich drink and provender had betrayed the energetic Pellew.

The introductions were brief, Merewether was flattered when Pellew remembered the occasion of their previous meeting and shook his hand. The others were General Sir John Stanley, commanding Fort William; Colonel Lionel Smith, commanding HM 65th Regiment; Major Eric Abbott, commanding the first battalion of the 47th Infantry; Captain Ian Dunbar of the Royal Navy; and Captain Richard Seton of the Bombay Marine. Chairs were already ringed about the large desk that had replaced the table Sir George had used. Merewether slid into the one at the left end of the ring beside Land.

"Gentlemen," began Minto, looking left, then right, "it is a most felicitous occasion that brings together so many distinguished officers of our military forces to plan what promises to be a challenging operation." He paused to pick up a sheaf of notes on foolscap, looked at them, and continued, "It involves a place called 'Ras ul Khymah', if I pronounce it correctly, a fortified town on the south coast of the Persian Gulf, and the seat of Sheik Hassan Bin Rahma, who commands the Joasmi pirate fleet."

It was inevitable, Merewether thought bitterly. He had spent most of his first three years in the Marine cruising against those Arab cut-throats who delighted in executing captured infidels to the last man, and had hoped never again to enter the Persian Gulf after last autumn. Still, if the presence of the Commander-in-Chief of the India Station and the general commanding Fort William betokened anything, it promised to be a well-planned and well-mounted affair. He gave his full attention as Minto continued.

"This office is in receipt of the most urgent representations from the Government of the Bombay Presidency, supplemented by a report from Mr. Bruce, the political agent at Bushire, and transmitting a formal request for assistance from our ally, the Imam of Muscat, against whom this Hassan Bin Rahma seems to be leading the Wahabees in revolt." Minto looked at Captain Seton. "You had concluded a treaty with the then leaders of the Joasmis only some two years ago?"

"Yes, Your Excellency," replied Seton, a tall fair man with prominent nose and chin. "February 6th, 1806, to be exact."

"The Wahabees are reported to be a dissident sect of the Moslem religion, and in addition to their piracies they seek to convert their captives on pain of having their throats cut," Minto continued. "They have taken more than a score of country ships, and those of our friends in Muscat and Persia this past year. Only a few weeks ago a squadron of their ships over-powered the Company packet, *Minerva,* in the Gulf, hacked her master into bits, and then killed every man in her, save only one mate and the carpenter. Then, last week, we had another report of an attack by these same pirates on a country ship just north of Bombay, but they were frightened off by the appearance of a Marine cruiser."

Merewether listened to the measured cadence of Minto's voice, visualizing for himself the bloody actuality of the events mentioned. The Joasmis had only come to be a serious problem about the time that he had entered the Marine, but in the half dozen brushes he had had with them, they had proved to be very fair seamen and ferocious fighters, seeking first to cripple and surround their prey, then carry her by boarding.

"In light of all the circumstances, the Governor-General and Council is constrained to grant the relief sought by the Imam and the Bombay Government. These facts have previously been communicated to Admiral Pellew and General Stanley, with the request that the Navy mount this operation in combination with the Army and the Bombay Marine. Do you have a report, Sir Edward?"

"Yes, Your Excellency," said Pellew briskly. "Captain Seton is in possession of fresh intelligence. He is of the opinion that a destruction of the fortified town of Ras ul Khymah — is that the pronunciation — will deny the pirate fleet a base, and we can then sweep up their vessels in the Gulf at leisure. Commodore Dunbar, Colonel Smith and Captain Seton have drawn the actual operation order, of which we have copies for all concerned." He laid a slender packet before Minto, and fair copies were passed around the circle of officers.

Merewether felt a twinge of resentment. Apparently he was to be a part of the expedition, but Seton had not seen fit to consult with him. He suppressed his pique, and looked at the order, much briefer than the one he had drafted with so many doubts last year for his Bengal Squadron. The names leaped out: Dunbar, with the temporary rank of commodore, to be in command of the combined naval forces; Smith, colonel of the 65th, with his pockmarked face, to command the military forces and siege operations; and Seton to have political charge of the expedition, including the use and deployment of troops to be supplied by the Imam of Muscat. Hell's bells, the order created a three-headed monster! He could foresee endless confusion and friction with the authority and responsibility for the mission thus divided. Merewether read on.

His name finally appeared in one of the concluding paragraphs: Commodore Dunbar would exercise direct military command over all ships present, but Captain Percival Merewether, HCS, was designated Senior Officer Present in the Marine ships for liaison and administrative purposes only. Hell's bells, he thought again, all the onus and headaches of the operation, and no real authority to deal with them. He felt Land stir restlessly beside him, clearing his throat, but Land did not say anything.

Appended to the order was a list of ships and forces to be embarked: HMS *Chiffone,* 36, and *Caroline,* 32, both no better than fifth rates, and four transports to be furnished by the Royal Navy; there were eleven Company cruisers, with *Pitt* heading the list. The Marine had again drawn the heavy end of the operation, Merewether thought sourly. He turned the page.

The flank companies of His Majesty's 65th Infantry, a detachment from the 47th, mostly sappers and engineers, a battery from the Bombay Artillery Regiment, and a thousand Sepoy Marines completed the list. The Company was furnishing two-thirds of the ships and forces, but had no control over them. Merewether sat back again awaiting the discussion. To his surprise there was none.

Outside, the army officers mounted horses held by troopers and cantered off towards Fort William with their escort.

"Sirs," said Land to Pellew, Dunbar and Seton, "I would be honored if you would join us for lunch."

"I cannot, Commodore, but I thank you. I have a previous engagement. But perhaps these gentlemen will keep you company." They uncovered as a footman assisted Pellew to hoist his ponderous weight through the door of his carriage.

"Of course."

The two parties each mounted their tongas, and trotted around to the Calcutta Club.

Land, Seton and Merewether had gin, Dunbar chose Madeira, glasses clinked, and each officer sat back to assess the others. Dunbar was a rarity, a lowland Scot who had achieved high rank in the Royal Navy, which tended to draw a majority of its officers from the sons of landed gentry in the southern counties of England. He was of moderate stature with a square ruddy face wearing a perpetual expression of great good humor. Yet his eyes were hot and brown. Merewether speculated whether he might be easily inflamed to anger.

Seton he had known casually from his earliest days in the Marine. The man was two years Merewether's senior in the Captain's List, but he had not seen active service for a long time, his linguistic accomplishments in Arabic making him far too valuable as a political agent and diplomat to risk at sea.

"Well, Merewether," said Dunbar suddenly. "I saw you frowning at the operation order. What displeases you?"

The direct question took Merewether by surprise. Dunbar's expression of good humor had not altered, but there was a hard glint in his eyes. Merewether took a sip of gin and tasted the half lemon before he made his reply.

"I suppose, Commodore, I was surprised that there is no commander-in-chief designated."

Dunbar looked hard at him for a moment, then sat back and glanced away. "Oh, that. Simple enough. Pellew wouldn't have the army in command or Stanley the navy, and, of course neither would accept a Bombay Marine officer." He smiled. "I thought mayhap you questioned the strategy or tactics."

"No, not at all," said Merewether, despising himself the while for his insincerity. Dunbar had a temper with a short fuse, he concluded, and also pride of authorship in the operation order. Merewether resolved to govern himself accordingly in his future dealings with the man.

Now Land led the conversation into other fields. Seton appeared to be a man of reserve, pleasant enough but taciturn, painfully slender with thin graying hair. The few remarks he interposed were penetrating, even witty. Land called for another round of drinks after he had placed their orders with the waiter. Halfway through the second gin Seton's reserve dissolved, and he suddenly intruded into the chitchat, cutting Dunbar off in midsentence.

"The Imam of Muscat trusts and relies upon me implicitly," he said in a loud carrying tone, causing heads to turn across the room. "He has promised . . ."

"Hold fast Seton," said Land. "No cause to tell all Calcutta . . ."

Seton continued as though he had not heard the interruption, a hectic flush blossoming on either cheek, ". . . ten thousand men, forty guns, and the transports to move them. He never . . ." Land shook him by the shoulder. "Quiet, man!"

Seton looked at the commodore for a moment, mouth open, then tossed off the remainder of the gin, and subsided in his chair staring into space. The waiter appeared with his retinue of assistants bringing the first course, and Seton revived as he was served. Merewether wondered at the reaction. He had a time or so before encountered a man to whom alcohol was poison, but never one so suddenly afflicted as Seton had been.

Merewether came away with a confusion of impressions; Dunbar, straightforward, but a man not to be crossed, quick and violent in temper. Seton, quiet reserved and intellectual, but susceptible to spirits in astonishingly small quantities. Of Colonel Lionel Smith, he had formed no impression beyond the hard pocked face; Smith had made no comment during the council of war, but few rose to his rank in a line regiment without ability and influence.

"I don't like the thing at all," complained Land as they drove back to the dockyard. "A three-headed monster, and they'll be at one another's throats before they are over the horizon."

Merewether was a little surprised at Land's use of the very phrase that had entered his mind when he read the order. It was mid-afternoon, hot and sultry, and the gin had imparted a lassitude that threatened to overwhelm him. He forced himself to go out to *Pitt* and observe her progress. Less than a week, he concluded, and she would be ready for sea.

Merewether had moved his furnishings aboard *Pitt* two days ago — his sea chest, a few odd belongings, and the shelf of books Caroline had assembled for his further education and entertainment during this commission remained in his lodgings. The quarters were spacious, but by no means as well arranged or comfortably fitted as *Rapid's,* since this ship had been built as a ship of war with flimsy bulkheads designed to be knocked down in a trice when she cleared for action. His sleeping cabin on the starboard side was crowded by two thirty-two-pounder carronades that crouched at either end of the cot bolted to the cabin floor. He would have preferred the brass bed from *Rapid,* but there was no space for it. He had been able to indent on the dockyard as custodian of *Rapid's* allowance for her desk and chairs to furnish the day cabin and had boldly walked off with the rack of four blunderbusses and truncheons, daring Land or the yard gunner to challenge this bit of petty larceny. The flag cabin on the port side was a mirror image of this one, but locked and empty, completely unfurnished. Merewether hoped it would remain so this cruise.

There was a knock, and Whaley entered with the morning report. Whaley laid the slip on the desk and looked downstream through the stern lights with a smug expression. "Four more hands have run, sir, two of them petty officers from *Rapid."*

Who?" demanded Merewether. This was a shock. The men had extended their enlistments only last month.

"Carson and Butterweck."

Carson had been a gunner's mate and Butterweck the senior cooper's mate in *Rapid.* Merewether had been in the process of solving their problems of seniority with *Pitt's* petty officers by the expedient of making Carson a master at arms and transferring Butterweck to the carpenter's crew. Now they had incurred all the penalties of desertion.

"You have notified the dockyard and the sheriff of Calcutta, I am sure, Mister Whaley. At least we are not shorthanded for the nonce." Whaley's satisfaction in making the announcement galled him, and he turned back to the manifest he had been reading in dismissal. Still, the matter was disturbing.

Only yesterday, Ames, a promising mizzen topman in *Rapid,* had almost fallen to his death from the royal yard when a footrope parted. He had managed to catch a backstay with one hand and divert his hurtling body head-first into the starboard shrouds to survive. The parted line showed wear, but there were particles of grit, possibly from a fragment of holystone in the fiber. Ames was rope-burned, sore, shaken and apprehensive. Merewether sighed, laid aside the manifest, and wrote a chit to transfer him to a billet with the master at arms while the matter was fresh in his mind, taking the place of the deserter, Carson.

His assignment to this ship had been ill-starred from the first day when she went adrift on the tidal bore. Then all of her officers save Whaley and her surgeon, Mefford, had requested transfer and reassignments, though that now appeared to be a blessing in disguise since he was able to replace them with *Rapid's* contingent. Now, two reliable petty officers who had served him well for more than two years had apparently found their condition intolerable, and another was convinced that an attempt had been made on his life.

Merewether blamed himself for not acting sooner and with more vigor to suppress the hazing by *Pitt's* old hands. There was an almost continuous hammering just above his head pounding in his ears as the carpenter and gunner installed their mounts for the lone nine-pivot gun he had removed from *Rapid,* He could stand it no longer, and escaped ashore.

All he could see was the top of Caroline's head gleaming the lamplight as she bent over the table on which her selection of books was laid out. Some were from her own small travelling library, but most had come from the bookseller at Fort William.

"Since you follow the profession of arms," she said with an upward glance, "this translation of the Iliad should engross you. And I've managed to find the *Decline and Fall* in a good octavo edition. I have the collected works of Goldsmith and Pope, and Johnson's *Rasselas,* as well as the works of the Bard. You should not want for entertainment on your voyage."

Merewether thought of the day's events and wondered if he would have time or inclination to while away the days and nights at sea absorbing the contents of his bookshelf. With the conflict in his crew, his compelling need to direct the men into an effective whole to work and fight the ship, and his responsibility to keep the peace between the Marine forces, the Royal Navy and the Army, he could foresee few idle hours.

"Thank you, my dear, I shall try to further my education. And now shouldn't we be on our way?"

Caroline picked up the blue cape she had devised, and Merewether held it as she draped it over her shoulders and arranged it so as to conceal her ungainly figure. They went out to the waiting tonga and rode through the cooling evening the short distance to the town house of Mister Andrew Salisbury, a senior Company official, and uncle by marriage to Miss Mary Wilkins. MacLellan had said nothing, but the reason for the affair was obvious. It promised to be a long night.

Here on Friday, the first week in February, all the repairs, refitting and victualing of *Pitt* had been accomplished. She awaited only the arrival of the hoy from far upstream, filled with clear water from an uncontaminated spring, before reporting ready for sea. MacLellan had asked Merewether to stand up with him at the wedding to be solemnized Saturday afternoon at St. John's Church. Caroline in her condition had demurred to serving as an attendant to Mary Wilkins, but she would preside at the tea table at the reception afterwards.

Frivolous distractions, Merewether decided, as he thought of the sullen crew in *Pitt.* Even *Rapid's* men appeared to have become infected with the general discontent. If there was the remotest possibility of mutiny, he had the absolute duty not to get the ship underway, but Larkin, MacCamy and Dobbs, together with Boatswain Caldwell, insisted the air would clear once the regular routine at sea resumed. The master at arms reported no leader inflaming the hands, and the consensus was that the present temper was the result of an arduous tropical operation last year, followed by the past weeks of back-breaking labor in refitting the ship. He hoped their judgment was sound.

It would be more than a week before the transports and Royal Navy would be ready to embark the troops. They had ample force to escort the convoy without *Pitt,* and Merewether felt that he required at least a week of general and special drills at sea to re-establish the skills and teamwork of his crew so that they would respond with the correct action in the heat of battle without direct orders.

"I am dubious, Merewether," said Land. "I'd have to get consent from both Pellew and General Stanley for you to proceed independently . . ."

"Only to Bombay, sir," urged Merewether. "Lord knows I need the time to shake the crew down, find out the mismatches in the station bill and, and I must learn the sailing qualities and handling characteristics of *Pitt* for myself."

"I can't believe you'll find that much difference. But I shall ask. When do you want to sail?"

"Monday, sir, if the water is on board."

The water hoy came in sight while church services were being conducted by Purser Davis on Sunday morning. Doctors Mefford and Buttram took their samples, pronounced it potable, and the cooper with his mates took charge of the watering operation. Merewether seized the opportunity to call a meeting of his officers to ascertain their state of readiness. He still had no word from Land.

As he waited in the day cabin for the messenger to deliver the summons, he drank his fourth cup of coffee — tea simply did not possess authority enough this morning — and ate a slice of toasted bread, his first solid refreshment of the day. It had indeed been a gay affair, the nuptials celebrated with fitting solemnity, the bride radiant but entirely self-possessed, and big MacLellan pale and tremulous. Once the ceremony was over and the party had adjourned to the reception, Caroline at the tea table found little custom. This was a hard drinking array of officers and civilians, one toast after another offered and drunk. Larkin, Dobbs and Buttram had determined that this would be an event their old shipmate would remember, and their exuberance had lifted and carried Merewether along in spite of his resolve to abstain. The party had continued long after MacLellan and his bride had stolen away, and he hoped that those gentlemen were nursing heads as sore this morning as his. Sangh slid in the door, coffee pot in hand.

"Not now. Be sure you have enough for the officers," he told the steward. "I think they will appreciate it." He was beginning to feel human again, enough so that the nagging worry that had possessed him these past weeks escaped him for the moment.

The order to proceed independently to Bombay came out to the ship during the first dog watch. Merewether hoped no word of it would reach the port watch on shore leave, since he intended to drop down the Hooghly on the ebb tomorrow morning, and he wanted no more desertions. This was his last night ashore with Caroline for some indeterminate period, and he felt a flush of tenderness for his wife who must now cope alone with her pregnancy.

MacLellan and his bride, both glowing with self-consciousness, were guests for dinner. They were boarding with Mrs. Wilkins here in the other half of the bungalow, until MacLellan's orders for Bombay should be executed. There was a ceremonial round of toasts drunk in Madeira, then dinner, and an early parting.

Later Merewether and Lady Caroline sat in companionable silence in the yellow lamplight, engrossed in their private thoughts. Merewether's mind inexorably turned back to *Pitt,* and he found himself stiff and tense at the prospect of taking her down the river tomorrow, even with the counsel of the Indian pilot who had brought her up. Foolishness, he decided. She might have her quirks, but she should handle as well as any other ship. He relaxed, poured another brandy, and invited Caroline to bed.

Two days later *Pitt* dropped the pilot at the Sandheads in the late afternoon. It was too late to commence any drills and Merewether was in no mood for such after the trying descent of the Hooghly. *Pitt* was more than three feet deeper in draught than *Rapid,* and must needs stay exactly in mid-channel. With the launch and cutter towing alongside, prepared instantly to pull bow or stern about, two anchors ready for letting go, and only topsails, headsail and spanker set, he found her momentum frightening in these swift, narrow waters. He had anchored last night with the great sense of relief at the few hours of surcease from the constant tension of being alert for hazards, no matter who had the deck. He had broken one of his own most cherished precepts, and drunk two gins before Sangh served his dinner. Now in the open waters of the Bay of Bengal, he felt a wave of relief as the special sea details were relieved by the underway watch, all plain sail was set, and the ship steered south southwest towards Ceylon under the vigilant eye of Lieutenant Dobbs.

"The first two days will be almost entirely drills on seamanship, tacking, wearing, reefing taking-in and setting sail" Merewether told the assembled officers and warrant officers the next morning. "I want every man to know what his duty is under every conceivable condition at sea. Indeed, we may surprise you with a fire, collision or man overboard drill at random, to add spice to our affairs. The balance of our time will be spent at gun drills and then at target practice. I intend to burn up those kegs of stale powder in your magazines at targets, Mister Vance," he said in an aside to the fat little gunner who grinned in approval. "Now, are there any questions?"

There was a restive movement among the officers ranged about the bulkheads of the day cabin anticipating their dismissal. They understood only too well, he knew, a week of backbreaking exertion for all hands, of driving men until they had mastered every detail of their duties in this ship and were able to perform them in darkness or gale or with round shot whistling past their ears. He heard another throat cleared, and Whaley spoke up.

"Now I demand that each of you gentlemen bear a hand, no lollygagging or sightseeing about the decks, no Irish pennants or gear adrift, pipes knocked out in the kits, and I want every idler on report, whether he is in your department or not. We'll have no namby-pambies in this ship!"

"Very well, gentlemen," said Merewether after a pause, seeing the expressions of irritation on the faces of Larkin, Dobbs and Hamlyn. "I think you understand the necessity of these drills, and you may be excused." Whaley's gratuitous admonition had left a sour taste with these officers, the feeling that they were under more of a compulsion than the implicit demands of their professional duty. He wished that the first lieutenant had remained silent.

The first three days of shiphandling and seamanship exercises went well enough. Most of the hands were practiced seamen, the weather was fine and comfortably cool. Merewether soon discovered that *Pitt* handled nearly as well as *Rapid.* Despite her size, her underwater lines were finely drawn, and she would sail within a quarter point as close to the wind. His confidence was restored and he looked forward to the gunnery drills and target practice with the thirty-two-pounder main batteries of short guns and carronades. Some of the sullen disposition in the crew seemed to have evaporated and the spirit of teamwork became more evident as the evolutions were repeated.

Masts and yards had been sent back up, and sails bent on for the third time this cruise. *Pitt* settled on the starboard tack, as closehauled as she would lie, and the hands came pouring out of the rigging, down ratlines and stays for a well deserved breather.

"Man overboard!"

The hail came from far forward, and for a moment it crossed his mind that Whaley had staged an impromptu drill on his own initiative. Then he saw hands peering over the starboard bulwarks, and realized it was a live emergency. Hamlyn pulled loose the lifebuoy at the break of the poop and sent it spinning down as Merewether reached the rail. He saw a white face in the water, eyes staring up blindly, arms and legs thrashing in mad panic, oblivious of the buoy bobbing only a few feet away.

"Hands to the braces!" Dobbs shouted forward. "Wear ship!" Over his shoulder, he tossed the command to the wheel, "Starboard your helm." It was entirely the correct reaction, much quicker than going about, and a course of a point or so to the left of the reciprocal of the ship's track should bring *Pitt* back through the same waters it had just traversed.

"Away quarterboat!" shouted Hamlyn, and there was a rush to man the falls of the boat maintained on davits on the starboard quarter in readiness for just such a duty.

Yet something was inexplicably wrong. The bow was swinging to starboard. Dobbs and Merewether realized almost simultaneously that the quartermaster had erred, either misunderstood the command, or had a mental lapse and put the helm hard over to port. It would still be all right to come to the wind and go about, though not as fast as wearing, and the ship had sufficient way on to carry her bow past the eye of the wind and settle on the port tack. It was then that Dobbs made the first error of judgment in a matter of seamanship that Merewether had noticed in a year and a half.

"Shift your helm!" shouted Dobbs, fairly dancing with rage.

"As you were!" shouted Merewether, but it was too late. The quartermaster suddenly conscious of his initial error had already reacted, the shifted rudder had halted the swing of the bow, her way was insufficient to carry her now past the eye of the wind, and the ship was in stays, caught dead aback, helpless for the moment.

To compound the matter, there was a horrendous crash on the deck aft, and the quarterboat rested at an angle on its stern, a wooden block split cleanly through dangling from the after falls to explain the casualty.

Dobbs had regained his composure. He let *Pitt* gather stem way, then put the rudder over, the hands hauled around on the braces and the sails filled as the ship settled on the port tack. There was yet a chance of recovering the man if he had overcome his panic sufficiently to see and reach the lifebuoy. They sighted the buoy ten minutes later, but there was no head in the water beside it. The man was lost.

"Who was he?" inquired Merewether of Whaley.

"Why, a young lad named Rush, I'm told. I didn't know him, he was out of *Rapid.*"

"Rush?" An image of a bony homeless waif of fifteen, articled as a ship's boy at Bombay Castle over a year ago, appeared in Merewether's mind. He had served in the galley and as a powder monkey at quarters last winter during the cruise of the Bengal Squadron. Only yesterday the lad had re-identified himself, grown five inches taller, heavier thirty pounds, beginning to sprout a sandy beard, and proud that the boatswain had accepted him as a striker in the deck force. It might have been himself fifteen years ago, Merewether thought.

"Poor fellow," he said to Whaley. "But few men would drown if they would only keep their heads. In blind panic he could not see the buoy right in front of his nose. Well, enter him in the log, inventory his sea-bag, though I doubt he had a family, and have the purser cast an account of his pay." The vision of the white face and staring eyes haunted him, but the exercises continued while a crest-fallen Hamlyn oversaw the reeving of a new fall for the quarterboat davit. It was apparent to Merewether that sheer panic, not the failure of the tackle or the mental lapse allowing the ship to be taken aback, was responsible for the loss of a life, but it seemed an ill omen to lose a man so uselessly so early in the commission.

The gunnery drills commencing the next morning had degenerated into a shambles by the end of the second day. Experienced hands performed poorly, and some did not even go through the motions. Larkin and Gunner Vance cajoled, threatened and shamed the crews without visible improvement. The sullen atmosphere of a few days ago had been replaced by a muttering undertone, defiant eyes and reluctant movements. By the end of the day, Larkin had sacked three gun captains for inefficiency. The breaking point came when a seaman let go the gun tackle he was heaving on, turned and spat between Larkin's feet, splattering his shoes and stockings with tobacco juice.

"Put that man in irons!"

Two masters at arms stepped forward, billy clubs at the ready, as the man retreated among his mates. The masters at arms pressed into the group seeking to reach the offender, then found themselves jostled, their clubs snatched from their hands and thrown over the side. Boatswain Caldwell came up on the double with four more masters at arms, moving in with practiced authority to scatter the crowd and seize the culprit. In short order, three men were frog-marched forward to the brig.

Merewether had been below when the mêlée erupted and arrived on deck only in time to see the end of the affair.

"Bloody filthy swine!" Larkin raved, wiping the stains from his shoes with a wad of oakum. "I've never held with the cat, but this time it's the only answer." His pale blue eyes glinted and his face was suffused with fury.

"Bring these three and the other members of the gun crew to the mast in the morning," Merewether said. "Do you intend to conduct target practice tomorrow?" There had not been a case meriting a flogging in Merewether's crew in over two years, and he shrank from the prospect.

"Yes, sir, though I'm afraid some of these donkeys may blow themselves or the ship up, what with the way they've performed so far."

"Very well." Merewether turned to go aft, and became aware that he was the subject of an intense scrutiny by three men lounging at the break of the forecastle. They were Batts, Sublett and Osborne, captains of the fore, main and mizzen tops respectively, all lithe, agile, slender men as befitted highly skilled seamen who performed their duty in a web of hemp and canvas far above the deck. Batts and Sublett turned away, but Osborne's feral yellow eyes stared into his for an insolent moment before he too moved forward. This was the man mentioned by Ames, the topman he had transferred to the master at arms force after he had almost fallen from the mizzen top a week or so ago. Merewether wondered for a moment if the man might still be vindictive; Ames had been in the party that came to the aid of the disarmed masters at arms. Unlikely. Yet unaccountably two lines from the Bard popped into his mind:

Yon Cassius has a lean and hungry look;
He thinks too much: such men are dangerous.

Merewether shrugged off the thought as he went aft, but he slept ill with the thought of the flogging in his mind.

The mast he convened at the commencement of the forenoon watch was brief. Larkin made his statement, and the masters at arms identified the two men in the gun crew who had disarmed them. Actually, Merewether considered as he listened to the character given each of the prisoners by the leading petty officer, the offence committed by the man who splashed Larkin with spittle was minor by comparison with the disarming of the masters at arms. A breach of discipline and a personal affront to Larkin deserved punishment, but the action of the other hands in protecting him was symptomatic of a far more dangerous spirit of unrest in the crew.

"Is there anything further you have to say in your defense?" he demanded. "No? Then I find the charges proved in each case. Step forward, Bell." Bell, the spitter, took a pace forward. "I sentence you to six lashes with the cat to be administered by the leading master at arms." Bell hung his head as he stepped back into ranks. "Step forward, Carter and Phillips." They took the step and looked defiantly at Merewether. "Carter and Phillips, your offence is most serious. I have considered convening a Court of Inquiry which might very well sentence you to hang. I prefer, however, to settle this matter within my own ship. I therefore sentence each of you to receive twelve lashes with the cat to be administered by the leading master at arms."

He realized instantly that he had made no impression on the two men. "As for the nine other men of the gun crew who failed to give assistance to the masters at arms, extra duty for thirty days, and deprivation of shore leave at the next port."

* * *

The boatswain's mates passed the word throughout the ship, down hatches and scuttles to the very bowels of the vessel, bringing up pale-skinned holders and storekeepers who rarely saw the light of day on deck.

"All hands to witness punishment! All hands! All hands!"

The response of the crew was sluggish, but finally the hands were in ranks, mustered by divisions. Bell was led to the starboard main shrouds, stripped to the waist, and triced by the wrists. Samuels, the leading master at arms, a short-legged man with the torso of a giant, took position behind and to the left of the man. He wore a leather glove on his right hand to reinforce his grip on the cat, while he held the nine leather tendrils gathered in his left hand. Merewether steeled himself. "Carry out punishment," he commanded.

Samuels brought the cat back, then forward in one fluid movement. Red welts erupted across Bell's back from shoulder to waist, and he threw back his head, mouth opening soundlessly.

"One," said the boatswain.

"God!" said Buttram, turning away. Samuels stroked the tails of the cat back into alignment with his left hand, using his fingers as a comb.

"Two." By the sixth blow, blood was trickling down Bell's back to soak his waistband. The masters at arms disengaged his wrists, threw his shirt over his shoulders, and led him forward to the sick bay where the loblolly boys would minister to him. He had not uttered a sound during the flogging, but now he walked unsteadily, wracked by dry sobs.

"Carter. Carry out punishment." The man twisted between the masters at arms to look over his shoulder and smirk at the hands. There was a mutter in the ranks, instantly silenced by the petty officers.

Samuels was truly an artist with the cat. He laid a criss-cross pattern on Carter's back that was almost exactly symmetrical, completing the design with the twelfth lash. Carter stood rigid, refusing to cry out or wince. Nine times twelve, thought Merewether, one hundred and eight welts. When Carter was released, the masters at arms had to carry him below.

"Phillips. Carry out punishment."

The man was very fair with milk-white skin. He cried out hoarsely at each blow after the third. The twelfth lash to complete Samuels' design was high on the back. One of the tails flew loose above his shoulder, and the weighted knot in its end curled around his head to strike Phillips squarely in the eye. It was entirely unintentional, but punishment had been inflicted far in excess of the sentence.

"See to him, Buttram!" Merewether went below, sick and trembling. Sangh brought tea and then brandy. It was nearly an hour before Buttram knocked and entered.

"Blinded," he said. "The eyeball was ruptured. Nothing I can do but apply medications and give him enough laudanum to make him sleep the rest of the day. Truth to tell, sir, I could use a bit of that brandy too."

"Useless," said Merewether. "Of course it was an accident, but the man is maimed. Here, have some brandy." He thought of the young seaman lost overboard, and continued, "An unlucky cruise . . ."

Merewether was diverted by the knock and entrance of the messenger from the office of the watch bringing a request for permission to exercise at quarters: target practice. "I'll come," he told the man.

The target raft was ready to be hoisted over the side when he reached the deck. "Send the hands to quarters," he told Dobbs, seeing Whaley going forward to his battle station on the forecastle.

The practice went surprisingly well, considering the reluctant conduct of the gun crews during the drills yesterday. It was more interesting of course: the men could hear the guns speak and see for themselves the results of their aim. By the conclusion of the drill, the raft had been reduced to splinters.

"An excellent practice," he was able to tell the perspiring Whaley and Larkin in the late afternoon. "I begin to entertain some hope that we may hold our own in an engagement." He watched the chattering hands skylarking as they dispersed from quarters with the words "Up spirits" ringing in their ears, and told himself that morale was on the mend. The smoking lamp had been relighted in the forecastle and several members of the watch below clustered on deck forward in the twilight puffing on their pipes.

Whaley, Larkin, the gunner, and Merewether could only attempt a reconstruction from the scanty evidence that remained after the event. Hamlyn had passed the word for the second dogwatch to relieve, and one of the pipe smokers moved over to knock the dottle out in one of the spitkits placed about the decks for that purpose. They were simply clay pots fitted with a metal lid with a hole in its centre, designed to hold ashes and sparks from pipes or cigars and prevent them from blowing about the deck. Their use was relentlessly enforced by the petty officers under the direction of Whaley, both to keep *Pitt* shipshape and reduce the danger of fire.

Hamlyn's evidence was explicit. As the man rapped the bowl of his pipe on the metal edge, an orange ball of fire erupted, accompanied by a low-order explosion, and engulfed three of the four seamen standing near the pot. The deck was blackened and scorched, but there was no fire. The metal cover flew high in the air, glanced off a stay, and sailed into the sea. There were only minute shards of the pot to be found, interspersed with charred fragments of serge from a thirty-two-pounder carronade cartridge.

Some person or persons unknown had concealed the gunpowder in the spitkit with the intent that just such a casualty as this would result. Two of the men survived less than an hour. (Their lungs were seared, Doctors Mefford and Buttram reported, by breathing in the fiery gas.) The third had burns on face and hands, but would recover. The pot with its removable lid had not sufficiently contained the powder to cause a full-scale explosion.

Merewether made an entry in the log appointing Whaley, Larkin and Boatswain Caldwell as a Board of Investigation, and they spent the better part of the night cross-examining witnesses.

"Sirs," Gunner Vance testified, "Mister Larkin told me he would fire five shots each from the main battery thirty-two-pounder guns and carronades. I used the oldest powder in the magazine to make up two hundred cartridges. I still have twenty of them. I made only ten nine-pounder cartridges, and you saw them fired."

"What about your regular supply?" demanded Whaley.

"It tallies exactly with my ordnance inventory, sir," the gunner insisted. "And the bale of empty cartridges we took on at Calcutta is under lock and key. Never been opened, sir."

A stream of gun captains, powder monkeys, and even the Sepoy Marines stationed during general quarters as sentries at each hatch and companionway, denied that any cartridge brought on deck had not been expended. The smoking lamp and galley fires had been out from the time the gunnery drill commenced, so the cartridge might have been placed in the pot at any time during the day with the expectation that no spark would reach it until late afternoon. The investigation ended with a close interrogation of the masters at arms, who could name no suspects.

Merewether shook his head as he read the report. It had been a senseless, vicious act, aimed not at any particular person, but only at the first man who might casually drop a spark into the kit. *Pitt* had lost two able seamen, another was painfully burned, and the madman remained at large within the ship.

"Copy your report into the log," he told Whaley the next afternoon. "Caldwell understands that his masters-at-arms are to continue the investigation and report any inkling, no matter how trivial, that may point to the culprit?"

"Yes, sir. And you know I was within a dozen feet of that kit all day yesterday. I don't remember a soul approaching it after the word for quarters was passed, but a number knocked out their pipes in it just before the drill commenced, so the powder must not have been in it then."

"Possibly, but the ways of gunpowder are chancy. In the serge cartridge, no spark may have been hot enough to penetrate."

Merewether went on deck to stand with Dobbs and Hamlyn as they took the evening star sights. The ship was making a good six knots by the log under all plain sail, and by their reckoning should be off Palk Strait, separating Ceylon from India, by dawn. He noted in his night order book the possibility that *Pitt* would be challenged by a Royal Navy picket ship by morning, and made sure the watch had the current recognition signal before he went below to dine.

Merewether never knew what caused him to wake. It was dark, entirely silent except for the continuous background creak and sigh of the ship, and he knew it must be some time in the middle watch. He could smell the hot metal of the dark lantern mounted overhead with its tiny aperture open to focus a beam of light on the tell-tale compass above him. The course was south by west, entirely steady, not even a quarter point off. Dobbs, he knew, had the watch.

The northeast breeze came pleasantly cool through the sternlights at this hour, though *Pitt* was now only ten degrees north of the Equator. The door to the day cabin had been hooked open to increase the circulation of air, and he sleepily resolved again to have the carpenter cut a vent for a windsail over his bed for more comfort. A shaded dim night-light was mounted on the bulkhead in the day cabin beside the door to the passageway to light the way of the messenger should he come.

There was an audible thump on the deck below him, followed by something that could have been an inarticulate cry muffled by three inches of teak planking. Whaley? He occupied quarters immediately below the sleeping cabin. A nightmare? Merewether's eyes flicked up to the tell-tale compass again. The ship was swinging slowly to starboard, almost two points and still moving, but he had not heard the usual squeal of the blocks as the tiller ropes strained through them. On this course with the wind over *Pitt's* port quarter, the helmsman customarily carried a few degrees of starboard helm to balance her tendency to sag off before the wind. The wheel must be unattended!

Merewether was off the cot in an instant and had started into the day cabin in his shirt when he heard faint sounds in the passageway beyond the cabin door. From time immemorial in King's ships a marine sentry was posted outside the entrance to the captain's quarters, but this was a precaution the Bombay Marine had rarely found necessary in its ships. He saw the latch on the door lift, snatched a blunderbuss from the rack on the bulkhead and retreated into the darkness of the sleeping cabin to shelter behind the door jamb.

The door to the passageway eased ajar, a head peered in, then it was pushed fully open and three barefoot men carrying billy clubs came silently across the cabin towards him.

"Hold!" said Merewether, stepping through the door and drawing the hammer on the gun to fall cock with an audible click. "Drop those clubs!" The three men froze. "Drop them!" he insisted, swinging the muzzle from side to side. Only then did the clubs rattle on to the deck. "Hands behind your heads!" In the dim illumination furnished by the night light he recognized them: Batts, Sublett and Osborne.

He realized suddenly how vulnerable he was. He had allowed these quick agile men much too close, and at this range the charge of shot in the gun would be a solid mass. At least two could reach him in a leap and kill him with their bare hands.

"Turn around and keep quiet!" They hesitated for what seemed an eternity while Merewether read their thoughts, and he moved the gaping belled snout of the blunderbuss left, then right. They decided by common consent not to chance it, uncertain which of them might die, and turned about.

There were three oak stanchions along, but separated from, the inboard bulkhead, placed there last month to brace the deck beams when the long nine-pounder pivot gun was mounted as a stern chaser. It was worth the clutter and inconvenience in the cabin to have an accurate and effective gun there, Merewether had decided. Now he had found a use for them.

"Each step forward slowly and stand against those stanchions," he told the men. Once against them, he looked about for a line, an unlikely article of cabin furnishings, then saw the cords supporting the curtains over the stern lights. He picked up the penknife from his desk, eased sidewise and cut the cord loose. It was laid up out of linen thread, waxed smooth and hard, strong for its size.

"Now, Batts and Sublett, turn around. Put your hands behind you on either side of the stanchions. Osborne, I want a slipknot about one wrist, then four turns around the other as tight as you can pull, and finished off with a square knot. A square knot, I say. No thief's knot." A thief knot superficially resembled a square knot, but its bitter ends came out on opposite sides of the loops, and it slid apart without holding a strain. A seaman suspecting that a shipmate might be rummaging his bag and helping himself to tobacco frequently tied such a knot. If he found a square knot on the sea-bag when he returned, he knew it had been opened. Osborne carried out the order, yellow eyes glinting in the glow of the night light. Merewether watched him closely.

"Now, you do the same." He secured the wrists, working carefully with one hand until he was ready for the knot. He then tore a curtain into strips and gagged each man.

There was only a moment to take stock of the situation. Any second another mutineer might come into the cabin to see what was detaining the three men. Evidently the off-watch officers had been surprised in their quarters, and Dobbs overcome on deck. They must have control of the ship, he decided, she was back on course according to the tell-tale compass.

Merewether could not guess how many were involved, but there must be many more than these three. He had no chance to overcome them singlehanded. Although he might kill some, the others would surely overwhelm him, and they undoubtedly were armed by now with at least the officers' personal weapons. His one salvation was to get Gunny and his marines on deck, seal all hands below and recapture the helm, then retake the ship a section at a time. The thought of Caroline and their unborn child crossed his mind. If the mutiny succeeded he would die; if by some chance he survived but lost the ship, his career was ended in disgrace. His future surely depended upon the course of action he took in the next few moments. He slid home the inside bolt on the cabin door; it should delay entry. Any delay would be to the good.

The marines were quartered forward on the main deck, but aft of the crew's quarters. He sought a route by which he could reach them without hindrance. He had prowled this ship, but there were areas yet he had not explored. He tried to visualize the compartments and passageways from the stern forward, from the keelson to the weather deck. There was no way below except from the passage outside his door, and certainly the mutineers would have posted guards by now at every companion, hatch or ladder. He forced himself to concentrate on the problem, oblivious of the hate-filled gaze of the three top-men.

He thought of Sangh, irrelevantly wondering where he might be at this juncture, and saw in his mind's eye Sangh bringing a laden tray up to the pantry through the scuttle from the cabin galley below. It was in the forward inboard corner of the pantry, a convenience installed by those Parsee shipwrights at Bombay in this frigate to insure that the captain's meals would be piping hot, served without delay from the stove to the table. The cover came up easily, he laid down the blunderbuss as an encumbrance, put his legs into the narrow opening and lowered himself into darkness, smelling the odors of tea and spices as he dropped the short distance to the deck. The galley gave him no more access to the forward part of the ship without risk of discovery than the passage above, but the lazaret filled with cabin stores and spirits was below it, and there was a hatch in the corner. He went through it gingerly into utter darkness, stumbling over casks and boxes and dunnage, fumbling for the door. The bolt was inside, thank God; it moved stiffly, but came free.

There was a cask right in front of the door with only a narrow space over it to the deck beams. Merewether slithered through and began to crawl forward. The casks contained fresh water with heavy dunnage to hold them secure against any pitch or roll *Pitt* might take. Merewether made detours, blindly feeling his way across the tops of the barrels, hearing the scurry and squeal of an occasional rat, but pressing forward to leave the water and smell the beef casks. He must be almost to the forward waist hatch where there was a ladder. Here far below the waterline he could hear the surge and splash as the ship ploughed through the sea, a background to the continuous sigh and creak of the vessel and its cargo. He came to the end of the tier of casks and dropped to the deck.

The hatch was in place, but not secured. He pushed it up, and with a Herculean effort slid it back a foot. The storeroom in which he emerged contained by the smell of it biscuit, flour, peas, spices, all dry stores. On the deck above were the Sepoy Marine quarters. He tried the hatch, then found the manhole in it, and emerged in the passage just aft of the marine quarters. Sheikh Gunny, the senior Jemadar of the detachment, had a private cubicle on the starboard side. He awoke instantly in full possession of his faculties.

"Gunny, I need you! We've a mutiny! All your men — don't bother to dress!"

The marines came to life. There was barely a rustle and patter of bare feet on the deck, not a clink as bayonets were fixed. Gunny told off two parties, one to take control of the helm and weather decks, the other he led himself with Merewether at his side, armed now with a cutlass and pistol from the marine armory, but still wearing only his shirt.

At the aft companionway to the wardroom and officer's quarters, a lantern shed yellow light to outline a figure lounging at the top of the ladder, a pistol dangling carelessly in his hand. Gunny stepped noiselessly forward and was at the top in a single bound. The man lay suddenly senseless on the deck.

They found another guard in the wardroom who instantly threw down his pistol and surrendered when they appeared. Whaley was tied unconscious in a chair, a great knot on the side of his head. Larkin was conscious, a bloody bruise on his jaw. MacCamy, Hamlyn, Buttram and Mefford were conscious and unmarked, while Sangh squatted unharmed in a corner.

"And now on deck!"

There was a brief mêlée aft, and two pistol shots forward, wounding a marine. After the round-up in the grey dawn, thirteen men, all petty officers from *Pitt's* old crew, were in irons. Some may have escaped, melted into the puzzled unaffected hands locked below in ignorance of the event but as to the prisoners in custody, there was no doubt as to guilt. Dobbs, the quartermaster, boatswain's mate, and messenger of the watch were found trussed and gagged in the quarter boat. A guard had been posted in the warrant officers' quarters, but they had not been aroused.

A cooper's mate was the first to break, a fair young man with a button of a nose, trembling uncontrollably with tears running down his plump cheeks, the very antithesis of a mutineer. "Yes, sir, I thought at first they was only lollygagging' talk, yamin', don't ye know, about this King's ship what set their officers adrift, loaded her with lassies from an island, and never been seen again . . ."

Bligh and the *Bounty.* Merewether knew the story had been often enough repeated in the forecastles of the Marine. It was bound to appeal to the young sailor, who now stood in handcuffs, flanked by two masters at arms before his desk in the cabin with Whaley, head bandaged, Larkin, Dobbs and Boatswain Caldwell seated on either side.

"How many more hands than you thirteen were in this?" demanded Merewether. "Speak up, man, you know you stand in a mighty slippery place with the noose about your neck!"

"I don't rightly know, sir, I never told anybody . . ."

"Who recruited you?" asked Whaley thickly. He yet appeared half stunned, suffering a mild concussion by Buttram's diagnosis.

"Osborne, I guess, sir. He said it was too much hazing last cruise, and starting again this one. He was to be the captain, and Batts and Sublett the mates. There was others, I heard, said they wouldn't come in, but they wouldn't peach or pike . . ." Merewether was sure there were others, but he tended to believe this contrite and terrified lad.

"All right, Plunkett." He decided to terminate the interview. "You have to stand trial with the rest, but if your testimony is the same as it was here, I will intercede with the Court of Inquiry and ask mercy for you. Now lock him up, separate from the rest." The masters-at-arms led the weeping cooper's mate out.

"Bligh!" said Caldwell. "He were First in *Jupiter* when I were coxswain of her gig in '84. A hard un, he were, and we all laughed fit to kill when the word came back he'd been set adrift!" He laughed again at the recollection, then sobered suddenly to return to the business at hand.

"Very well, gentlemen. We were lucky, and came off without serious casualties." Merewether felt the lassitude of reaction setting in, and while it was almost more than he could face, he felt compelled to address the crew. "I have the authority to convene a court on board this ship since we are on detached service, try and execute them, but I would have to certify that the ship would be endangered otherwise. I prefer to transport them to Bombay Castle for that purpose. And now, I want all hands on deck, mustered by divisions." He despised himself for his squeamishness. Nearly any other Captain in the Marine would have had the mutineers dancing on thin air below the yardarm by now, he told himself. He could read disapproval in Whaley's face as the meeting adjourned to the deck.

It had been a well planned and coordinated operation: the helm, deck watch party, wardroom and warrant officers all struck simultaneously, and only Whaley had been able to offer resistance. It was the blow and the muffled outcry that had warned Merewether. He felt a little more warmth for the man — who was no poltroon — but could not bring himself to like him.

Pitt crawled sluggishly up the latitudes, clawing her way against unfavorable winds, past Portuguese Goa, finally to come in sight of Bombay. The wind here was dead foul, but Merewether put the launch and two cutters with double-banked oars over the side to tow her in to an anchorage off Bombay Castle.

It had been an unhappy and tedious voyage, men needlessly lost and injured, a determined effort made to take the ship, foiled mostly by luck. And yet the performance of the crew had improved, he told himself cynically, not because of his silver-tongued oratory the morning after the mutiny, but more likely in an effort to convince the officers that they had had no part in it. Merewether combed his hair, adjusted his hat and belted on his sword to make the official call. The gig was waiting at the starboard gangway.

Commodore Waldron was away in the frigate *Bombay,* accompanied by the sloops *Prince of Wales* and *Mercury,* he discovered, scouting to the south in preparation for the oft-postponed operation against Mauritius. Commodore Tollett was acting in the absence of the Commandant, visibly chafing at the inactivity his recent promotion to flag rank had imposed upon him. He took the report and replied to Merewether's query.

"No, Merewether, we have no report of the convoy from Calcutta. You are the first to arrive. I presume you had orders to proceed independently?"

"I did, sir. I needed to shake down *Pitt* after we transferred *Rapid's* crew into her. And now I have thirteen prisoners to be handed over for trial by a Court of Inquiry."

"For what?"

"Mutiny, sir. My report speaks of it."

"Well, I'm damned! Tell me about it."

Merewether felt a flush of embarrassment as he made a bald report of the events leading up to the night of the attempt, conscious of the fact that it was the first such incident in a Marine ship in more than sixty years. "So, after the three ringleaders were secured, I managed to get forward through the hold and alert Gunny. There was no trouble after that, though I am sure some of the mutineers escaped and are still on board."

"This fellow Whaley . . ." began Tollett.

"Oh, he did very well. In fact it was his resistance and outcry that warned me."

"I didn't mean that. It was just that during the time I was with Waldon in *Pitt* before *Rapid* joined us, it seemed that every day it was, "All hands to witness punishment". Of course poor Bridges was sick during most of the commission, and Whaley had a heavy responsibility, but I never thought the cat served a very useful purpose, and certainly not every day." Tollett paused and looked out over the harbor with *Pitt* swinging to her anchor in the foreground. "You expect more trouble?"

"No, sir. Morale seems to have improved, and liberty in Bombay should help."

"Very well. You might consider adopting the custom of the Royal Navy, and post a marine sentry at your door for a time."

"I don't believe it is necessary. He would serve little purpose if a determined move was made, and it would complicate matters for Gunny."

"Very well. Deliver your mutineers to the prison marshal in the morning. But I'm afraid we must wait for the convoy to find enough officers for a court of inquiry. It is, after all, a capital offence." Tollett started to rise in dismissal, then checked himself and looked narrowly at Merewether. "This affair hasn't shaken you, robbed you of your confidence, has it?"

It was a disquieting question. The thought had not crossed Merewether's mind, and for a moment he was not sure himself.

But it would never do to admit the slightest doubt. Even a hesitation in denial could be fatal; he might be relieved as a commander and his career would be at a dead end, one of the listless officers growing old in the service, waiting out their pensions, puttering about at routine duties on some backwater station.

"Not at all, sir," he told Tollett sharply. "I would not take *Pitt* to sea if I had the slightest doubt!"

"No offence, Percival," said Tollett smiling as he rose. "It's just that I have seen a loss of confidence cripple otherwise excellent officers. I shall see you tonight at the Governor's reception."

Merewether was quickly at a loose end. There were few old acquaintances to renew here at Bombay Castle just now, and these were soon visited. It was only early afternoon, liberty for the starboard watch would have commenced, and he did not yet feel the compelling necessity to return to *Pitt* to see if all was well. He decided to go over to the bazaar in the town where he had bought Caroline's emerald ring the previous autumn, and at least try to find another gift for her. In his boredom he even looked forward with unaccustomed anticipation to the social affair tonight.

Customs varied considerably between the Presidencies. The overpowering formality of Calcutta under George Barlow, and only slightly less of Penang, did not hold here at Bombay under Governor

Jonathan Duncan's regime. He led his contingent of officers into the foyer of the Governor's Residence, and was quietly directed without announcement to the ballroom for dancing and an adjacent salon for refreshments. He soon encountered Tollett and his wife, made the introductions, and a young staff second-lieutenant was told to acquaint the younger officers with their contemporaries, while Merewether was drawn aside to be presented to His Excellency.

"Yes, Merewether, it has been three years this month since last I saw you here. You were first in *Sir John Shore,* sailing for Calcutta, and I have heard good things of you since."

Merewether was not surprised at the accuracy of the recollection. Duncan was famous in the Company for his memory, this plain solid man in late middle age, upright, incorruptible and just, a veteran of thirty-six years with the Company, and governor of Bombay these last thirteen. He was popular with the Marine. No matter how parsimonious the Court of Directors might be, Duncan could find the powder and victuals for its ships, and Cornwallis had relied implicitly upon his fiscal advice during his first administration. He felt a flush of satisfaction at being remembered so favorably.

"Thank you, Your Excellency." They moved on to the tables.

Most of those in Tollett's party he had met at one time or another, two captains and three senior lieutenants with their wives. Mrs. Tollett was a small Yorkshire woman who did her best to conceal a sense of insecurity. She had married a penniless young second-lieutenant with no inkling that he would rise to Commodore in the Marine, and her social obligations had increased accordingly. Merewether was greeted, introduced to two of the wives he had not previously met, and then to another woman, apparently unattached.

"And Mrs. Hale, wife of Captain Hale . . ." Hale, he knew, was in command of the frigate *Bombay,* now south in the Indian Ocean flying Waldron's flag during the reconnaissance of Mauritius. Merewether bowed and murmured in response, and then found himself seated beside her, but she was turned half away from him.

"Gin and lemon," he told the hovering servant.

"And tell him to bring one for me," said Mrs. Hale over her shoulder in an unexpectedly strong voice. Merewether amended the order, and tried to take another look at the woman.

The last time he had seen Hale on a social occasion was some three years ago in this very room. His wife then had been fair, fat and forty, but this woman from what he could see of her was of olive complexion, slender with black hair piled high on her head, and no more than twenty-five. He could only assume that Hale's first wife had died and he had married this woman some twenty years his junior. She was perfectly aware of his appraisal, and her dark eyes snapped as she spoke over her shoulder again.

"Yes, I'm the second wife, married less than a year, and half Portuguese to boot!" Mrs. Hale said sharply. "My father was in the marine and married my mother right here at Bombay. I came back from England last year to see my cousins, and stayed to marry back into the Marine, worst luck!"

Merewether was embarrassed. He had intended no offence. He looked about the table, but no one appeared to have noticed the woman's outburst except Mrs. Tollett across the table, who was looking at him with a curious expression of concern. His thoughts were interrupted by the approach of the Indian waiter, followed by his assistant bearing a tray with the two glasses of gin and a plate of quartered lemons. The waiter served them with a flourish, then withdrew with a salaam.

"Well," said Merewether brightly to the woman's back. "First today. Cheers!" He lifted his glass to Mrs. Hale, and she turned in her chair to respond with a perfunctory wave of the glass, then drank off the gin neat without lowering it from her lips.

"Order me another," she said, now facing him. She was a beauty, he saw, white teeth, red lips, straight nose and bold, challenging brown eyes. Her shoulders were bare and her torso was encased in a skin-tight jade bodice that exposed the upper half of her breasts. No other woman present was dressed in such fashion. "I suppose you're like the rest of these Marine heroes, fearless at sea, but timorous as a mouse when the husband is a captain?"

Merewether managed to mask his astonishment by signaling the hovering servant and giving him her order, then taking a sip of gin and a taste of lemon. He looked across the table to see the barely perceptible shake of her head from Mrs. Toilet, and realized that the music had commenced again. Commodore Tollett was off on some mission with the Governor's party and as the unattached male he conceived it to be his duty to lead the Commodore's lady out for a dance.

He excused himself, rose hastily, and moved around the table to proffer his invitation to Mrs. Tollett.

Safely in the ballroom Mrs. Tollett shook her head at him again, and said, "A sad affair — poor Captain Hale, him with grown children and grandchildren. Fair cast a spell over him she did, bewitched the man into a panting love-sick moon-calf, so that he married her two months after Emma died!" They parted in the evolutions of the dance, but when they came back together, she continued as though there had been no interruption. "The captain has only been gone two months, but the gossip is that she's betrayed him with three different men none of them in the Marine thank God! Her family has quite disowned her. They're old Portuguese merchants, here in Bombay near two hundred years. And Captain Hale is a jealous man. If he learns of these affairs, he will call them out. You're a married man yourself, Captain?"

The question caught Merewether by surprise, he certainly had entertained no notion of dalliance with the woman since she had been so obvious, and a drunken woman presented distasteful problems, but he realized in shame that the thought of Caroline had not crossed his mind during the episode.

The music stopped and they went back towards their table. Just before they reached the door, he saw Mrs. Hale again clinging possessively to the arm of a tall handsome man in civilian dress. They went towards another table, well away from the commodore's, both apparently convulsed with laughter, the woman almost doubling over with mirth at every other step, and then pressing herself against the man as he whispered in her ear.

"A disgrace!" breathed Mrs. Tollett. "And that is Mister Conroy, the Company's agent to the court of the Mughul. He has a lovely wife and two children in Yorkshire. Shame!"

"He's a long way from home," said Merewether. He had intended the remark lightly. The circumstances of enforced bachelorhood out here for many of the Company's servants were so common as to occasion little concern. Some of the bluest blood of England ran in the veins of half-castes around the older establishment, though they were recognized only as Indians by the British. He saw the couple reach their table, servants pulling back their chairs for them, when by apparent common consent the pair embraced in a passionate public kiss. There was a titter of laughter from the tables near by as they disengaged and took their seats. Such a display by a half English, half Portuguese wife of a senior Marine officer was, Merewether realized, a bit more than even Bombay society was willing to accept, particularly at the Governor's Ball. Tollett rose as they rejoined the group.

Mrs. Tollett soon acquainted the commodore with the scandal. He raised his eyebrows in half humorous resignation, and departed to find the second secretary who was managing the affair. Twenty minutes later, Merewether saw Mrs. Hale, still escorted by a red-faced, angry Conroy, hurry past the doorway, her chin in the air, but her gait unsteady. Evidently the pair had been invited to leave the entertainment.

It was two hours after midnight when the affair broke up. A long line of carriages plodded under the porte-cochère to load their passengers. Merewether had no transportation. He could find none of his officers, and decided the walk to the landing would do him good after the gin and rich provender. Here at the end of February there was a bit of a tingle in the air at this hour. The streets were well lighted and many of the night watch were about, since so many distinguished personages were aboard.

Only a short distance from the main gate to the naval establishment was a public house operated by a former purser in the Company's maritime service. It did a thriving business and had three large public rooms, one restricted to officers, another to warrant officers, and the third for enlisted men. In addition, at the back, opening off the side street were several private rooms available for officers to rent for lodging, drinking, dining or the discreet entertainment of a female friend. Merewether had often enough patronized the establishment in former years, but he had no intention of stopping tonight, though by its lights and the sound of voices, the evening was by no means over. He passed by, glancing over the half door into the enlisted men's bar to see the clouds of tobacco smoke hanging over the happy faces of the patrons and catch a whiff of the aromatic spirits. He had almost reached the corner where the narrow lane intersected the broader street when he heard running footsteps, a wordless shout, and the sound of a blow on flesh. A brawl, he surmised, as he cleared the corner of the building, prepared to dodge sidewise if necessary.

Within the entrance to the lane a curious tableau met his eye. There were two struggling figures illuminated by the glow of a lantern mounted on the wall. A woman's shapely back was presented to him, naked from the waist up, bare arms flailing the air striking at a barefooted man clad only in a shirt. The ripped ruin of a jade green bodice dangled below her waist, and Merewether recognized the pair.

"Here now!" he commenced just as Conroy managed to capture both of the woman's wrists, transfer them to the grip of his left hand, and strike her a heavy blow across the side of the face.

Merewether was aware that several persons had emerged from the public house behind him attracted by the shout. Evidently the blow had stunned the woman, for she commenced to slump, and Conroy caught her about the waist with the evident intention of carrying her back through a door that stood ajar a dozen paces down the alley.

It was a private matter. He was certainly under no obligation to the woman. He had no desire to make a powerful enemy in the Company hierarchy. But the blow had been brutal. Once back in the room, worse might follow. The little group from the bar stood aside as sightseers only. Merewether decided that he must intervene.

"Loose her!" he said urgently. Conroy's furious red face looked over his shoulder.

"Keep out!" he shouted. "Come on, you slut, walk!"

It was only two steps. Merewether caught the man by the shoulder and spun him around, alert for the blow, stepping inside Conroy's vicious swing with the instinct cultivated during the years in the lower deck, then driving a left and right to the belly. The woman had fallen to her hands and knees beside them, and scuttled out of the way. The man was fit, a half head taller. Sober he might well have taken Merewether's measure. But the two trip-hammer blows to the midriff brought his hands and head down, and the third blow was flush on the jaw. Conroy collapsed on his face in the alley.

"Good on you!" said a voice behind him. The woman was on her feet now, bracing herself against the wall, fumbling at the tatters of her bodice dangling about her hips. Merewether looked around to see Harry Putnam, the proprietor of the grogshop, standing in the group.

"Can you get a carriage?" he inquired. The Cockney Putnam had been a sharp-faced little fellow when first he opened the establishment, but years of sampling his own wares had made him almost portly now.

" 'arf a mo', Captain." He spoke to a man in a white apron who turned and went down the street. "I'll lend you my tonga, all hitched and ready."

Merewether unbuttoned his coat and draped it about the woman's shoulders, shutting off from view her rather splendid display. "Come. Can you walk?" Conroy groaned and moved on the cobblestones, his hands flailing out to either side, as the barman led the horse up. Merewether handed her into the seat and took the reins.

"Where away, madam?" He had to repeat the question three times before it penetrated.

"Back the other way past five, no six, streets, and then left." The words were slurred, her jaw and eye were already puffed, and she swayed in the seat.

There was no conversation on the way, the combination of spirits and the blow had left her groggy. She roused up as they turned off the main street and indicated a substantial well-lighted bungalow with a drive leading to the door. Merewether handed Mrs. Hale down, and she pulled the bell knob. After a moment a sleepy Indian maid opened the door and gazed in astonishment at the spectacle of her mistress attired in a blue uniform coat and bearing all the evidences of violence. Mrs. Hale stepped through the door with dignity. Evidently her faculties had revived in the cool morning air.

"Get me a robe," she told the maid, and turned back to Merewether. "I owe you a reward, Captain, and ordinarily I'd pay it now, but you wouldn't care to bed a woman in my condition . . ." For a moment, Merewether did not grasp the import of her words, then the meaning penetrated and he stepped back in confusion.

"Why . . ."

"Never mind, Captain — Merewether? — I'll put it to your account. And now, I've made a complete fool of myself this night and deserve to be destroyed as I surely shall." Tears were running down the swollen cheeks, her left eye was almost closed. "That

Conroy! He seemed decent enough at the outset, and I'd have betrayed old Hale easily enough, but the man is a beast, his pleasure comes from inflicting pain . . ."

The maid reappeared with a robe. Mrs. Hale slipped out of the uniform jacket, handed it to Merewether and shrugged into the waiting robe.

"Good night, Captain," she said firmly, placing her hand on the knob of the door. He stepped back, and the door closed. It was ten minutes back to Putnam's where he found the proprietor waiting in the doorway, the lamps now extinguished.

"I'm really much obliged, Harry," Merewether told the little Cockney. There was no sign of Conroy.

"We sloshed a bucket of water on 'im, and he went back to 'is room to sleep it off. I blame meself for letting the pair 'ave the room, seeing as 'ow tipsy they was." Putnam shook his head. "I 'opes he don't make trouble for me, nor for you, Captain."

Merewether reached the ship as dawn appeared over the hills to eastward too tired to speculate on the night's events.

The saluting gun in the battery on the mole at Bombay Castle spat out its single sullen report at ten o'clock six days later to signal the convening of the Court of Inquiry to try the mutineers. While the reverberations were still echoing across the harbor, the master at arms and his mates marched in a doleful crew, chains clinking between their leg-irons, as the warder and prison governor held the doors open. The procession moved in a shuffle, the chains limited each man's step to no more than a foot. This was the same chamber where Merewether had stood his trial a year and a half ago, but now he was seated with the officers and witnesses from *Pitt* in two rows of chairs behind the recorder's table, occupied by a Lieutenant Mayfield. The master-at-arms pushed the men into two rows of five each before the court where they would stand thus during the course of the trial. Of the thirteen mutineers, Plunkett was separated as a prosecution witness, and two hands had died of gaol fever during this past week.

The convoy had arrived two days ago, and the Superintendent of the Marine immediately ordered the Court of Inquiry. Its composition was anomalous, five senior first-lieutenants from the Bombay Marine, with a post captain and commander of the Royal Navy completing the seven-member court. Such a combination was not without precedent, Tollett told him. When it had occurred in the past, it was because of a lack of disinterested Marine officers available to serve, and this was once again the case. Merewether stood with the rest as the master at arms intoned the call to order.

Captain Fontaine and Commander Bevan, Royal Navy, as senior officers on the court, briskly took charge. Merewether had met them formally less than an hour ago, and they appeared to be decent men, not particularly enthralled with their assignment to this duty. They were out of a frigate and sloop in the harbor, not part of the expedition to Ras ul Khymah.

"I have here orders from Sir James Campbell, Superintendent of the Honorable Company's Naval Service, to Commodore Evan Tollett, acting in the absence of Commodore Sir John Waldron as Commandant of the Marine, to convene a Court of Inquiry to try divers seamen and persons accused in specifications of charges appended thereto, of certain offences against the Company and its Naval Service, to-wit: a mutinous assemblage and overt acts of violence against the lawfully constituted commander and officers in HCS *Pitt* on or about February 22nd, 1808, while that ship was at sea in the Bay of Bengal. I read the orders." He paused, looked left and right, and then proceeded to do so.

"I might say in explanation of Commander Bevan and myself serving as members of this court that we were designated so to serve in orders from Sir Andrew Boyd, Rear-Admiral of the Blue commanding His Majesty's Naval Forces in the Arabian Sea, upon the request of Commodore Toilet, owing to the unavailability of disinterested officers of the Marine of the rank of captain. I read those orders." He read them, then looked at the double rank of prisoners. "Is there any objection or challenge of the convening authority or of any member of this court?"

"Yes, may it please the court." The plump young second lieutenant, Farris was his name, stood erect, his earnest face gleaming with sweat. Tollet had designated him with another young officer, Renfroe, to defend the men. "I submit, sirs, that the superintendent of the Marine lacks authority to delegate the appointment of any members of this court to Admiral Boyd, an officer not under his command." He paused, and then added hurriedly, "Nothing personal, of course . . ."

"Of course not, Mister . . . er," Fontaine looked down at his documents, ". . . Farris. Mister Recorder, do you desire to respond to the objection?" Mayfield, tall and stout, with a sardonic weathered face, stood up.

"Yes, may it please the court. The identical composition of this court was convened in 1804 to try Lieutenant Ambrose of the Marine. The same objection was made, denied, and the conviction was confirmed by the Governor-General in Council. It was then affirmed in an appeal to the Court of the Directors." He paused portentously, and picked up a paper. "I have here an exemplified copy of that decision which contains references to two other similar instances, one in '98 and the other in '82. I submit, sirs, that the objection is without merit." He sat down. Fontaine looked right and left along the table, receiving a series of nods.

"The objection and challenge to the convening authority and this court is denied," he said briskly. "Swear the court, Mister Recorder."

This was done.

"I now shall read the specifications of charges." He proceeded to do so, reeling off the list of names. "As to Williams and Sexton, I declare these charges abated by death since the event. And now, Mister Farris, how plead the accused?"

"Not guilty, may it please the court." There was a movement in the two ranks of prisoners and the clink of chains.

"So say you all?" demanded Fontaine. "Out with it. Let each man answer for himself!" There was a series of mumbled responses down the ranks, with Fontaine watching sharply to make sure each man had entered his plea. He then turned to Plunkett, the cooper's mate, who stood alone behind the recorder.

"And you?"

"Guilty, sir." Plunkett was pale, but otherwise composed.

Merewether felt a flash of sympathy for the young man, so desperately afraid for his life that he was willing to save it by the expedient of testifying against his shipmates. He had spoken in guarded tones to Mayfield yesterday of the willingness of Plunkett to give evidence of the conspiracy for the prosecution, and received an equally guarded assurance that the Recorder would recommend mercy in exchange.

"Call your first witness." Mayfield rose.

"I call Captain Merewether. Will the court swear all the witnesses now?"

Merewether took the chair set at right angles to the court and the ranks of prisoners opposite the recorder, so that all might see him and hear his testimony. There followed an interminable succession of questions to establish ownership of *Pitt,* his orders into her as master and commander, introduction of the Articles of Enlistment entered into by her hands, including the accused, the orders to proceed independently to Bombay, exemplified copies of her log, finally arriving at the early morning hours of February 22nd, *ult.* "And now, Captain, will you detail to the court the events which took place to your knowledge during the middle watch that date . . ."

Merewether made a bald recitation of fact, commencing with his awakening, the sounds had alerted him that something was amiss, the veer off course betrayed by the tell-tale compass, to the final round-up of the mutineers.

"Now, Captain, do you identify any persons now present before this court as participating in this mutiny?"

"I do. Batts, Sublett and Osborne are the men who entered my cabin armed with billy clubs." He pointed them out at the urging of Mayfield, seeing the yellow glare of Osborne's gaze. The others did not meet his eyes. "Reed was the man armed with a pistol posted as a sentry at the head of the ladder in the passage to the wardroom. Moser and Sexton, since deceased, had mounted guard over the officers in the wardroom. Turner was found armed in the warrant officers' quarters. The Marines took the others on deck outside my presence and I cannot identify them on personal observation." A number of questions followed, then the recorder turned him over to Lieutenant Farris for cross-examination.

The plump young officer approached his task with earnest enthusiasm, evidently beginning to enjoy his role in the trial. Hamlyn had reported that Farris had been articled as a solicitor in Manchester before he joined the Marines, and he put his questions in surprisingly professional tone.

"Now, Captain, you do not know the purpose with which these three men, Batts, Sublett and Osborne, entered your cabin, do you?"

"Why certainly," said Merewether. "I thought it obvious from my previous testimony . . ."

"But, Captain, isn't their action as consistent with the fact that they were coming to warn you and assist in suppressing the mutiny, as with their participation in it?"

Merewether was astounded at this sophistry, and looked narrowly at the young man, who flushed but stood his ground.

"Certainly not! They were armed with billy clubs and almost in my sleeping cabin before I confronted them. They offered no such explanation . . ."

"You have testified that you commanded them to keep quiet under threat of a blunderbuss, and then you gagged them . . ." Merewether stole a glance at the court and found all eyes fixed on him. With an effort, he contained his indignation at this petti fogging line of questioning, and forced himself to make a reasoned reply.

"Why, sir, I thought I made it plain. I had already heard the sounds of Mister Whaley being taken. The ship had veered far off course while the wheel was unattended, and then these armed men entered my cabin. Besides, I've heard Osborne was to be captain, and . . ."

"Objection!" interposed Farris. "Hearsay."

"Quite," said Captain Fontaine. "Let that part of the captain's answer be stricken."

And so it went, the forced admissions that he had not seen six of the defendants do any act in furtherance of the mutiny, and that he knew of no reason why responsible petty officers such as Batts, Sublett and Osborne should participate. Merewether finally escaped, resentfully conscious that the young man had made him look a proper fool in many respects, taking advantage of every loophole in his testimony, making evidence that had appeared incontrovertible seem ambiguous. But Mayfield soon demonstrated that he had other strings to his bow as he spun a tightening noose about the necks of these unhappy seamen. The trial ground on, a plodding succession of witnesses each describing in his own small segment in the affair, ultimately to weave the whole web of evidence, until the court adjourned at a half after four.

It appeared there would be three more witnesses for the prosecution, including Plunkett, before the defendants undertook their defense.

Merewether invited Dobbs and Buttram to go over to Harry Putnam's public house after the adjournment for a drink in the officer's bar. Whaley, Larkin, Hamlyn and Doctor Mefford went back to the ship; for Merewether still felt some unease for her safety, though she was anchored under the guns of the battery. The dispatch brig had come in this morning from the Red Sea bringing the overland mail, and the latest London papers were posted inside the door. Merewether felt a glow of satisfaction as he read that Bonaparte had invaded Spain last January. The mission to Persia must indeed have diverted the Corsican and his million soldiers from following Alexander's route to India.

Merewether and his party found an unoccupied table under a punkah and placed their orders.

"Ah, Captain, I hope you will forgive me," said a voice behind him. Merewether craned his neck to see young Farris, a glass in hand, at the bar. "You understand, sir, I'm only representing my clients . . ."

"Quite all right," said Merewether stiffly. The cross-examination of the morning still rankled, but there was no reason to be rude. "Come join us, Mister Farris," It proved to be an interesting hour of conversation. Merewether had consulted a solicitor only once in his life, last summer when he made his will, and the ways of all lawyers were mysterious.

"And how," demanded Buttram, "did a solicitor find his way into the Bombay Marine?"

Farris laughed. "I came into my chambers one morning and saw all those tin boxes stacked along the wall, each filled with deeds, wills, demises and contracts, all as dry as dust, and decided I needed a breath of air. My grandfather is a proprietor in the Company, so I had a bit of interest going for me to gain an appointment in the Marine." He laughed easily, and Merewether found his resentment melting. "But you know I think I have changed my mind again. I may lose these men to the hangman, but not for lack of a fair defense and the experience has been most exhilarating. I have concluded that I first chose the wrong branch of the law so I shall go back to

Lincoln's Inn to read more law and seek a call to the Bar as a barrister."

By the time he reached *Pitt,* Merewether was already hazy as to the mysterious distinction made between barristers who pleaded cases, and the solicitors who employed and briefed them, but he concluded that not all lawyers were bad.

There was a stack of official mail on the desk in the cabin. Merewether paid it little attention. Time enough for that once he had dined. Then he noticed another letter without the heavy red seals of the Marine. It was a single paragraph in a neat feminine hand.

> My dear Captain Merewether.
> A note of gratitude for your gallantry last week . . .

Merewether looked hastily for the signature. "Creusa Hale." Who? He turned back to the commencement.

> . . . in rescuing me from my folly. My life in Bombay is finished and I take ship later in the day for Macao where my mother's sister is the wife of the Commandant of Portuguese forces. I shall not forget my debt to you."

Of course! It was the woman he had conveyed to her home from outside the public house. He started to throw the note away, then slid it into the portfolio in the desk drawer where he kept his personal documents, and promptly forgot the matter.

The Court of Inquiry concluded the trial before noon the next day. Plunkett, cooper's mate, was the last witness called by the prosecution, and his testimony put the finishing touches on the nooses already spun about the necks of the mutineers. Farris rose to cross-examine.

"Now, Plunkett, what have you been promised . . ."

"Objection!" interposed Mayfield.

"I don't know what the question is yet," said Captain Fontaine pleasantly "Let him complete it."

"What have you been promised for your evidence against these men?"

"Objection! I have promised him nothing and neither has this court," said Mayfield.

"Let him answer," ruled the presiding officer.

"I haven't been promised anything," quavered the young man. "After I told the master at arms I wanted to confess, and did, Captain Merewether said he'd speak a good word for me . . ."

"Aha!" said Farris, leaning forward to fix the trembling man with a glittering eye "And you call that nothing? What will he say for these other men?"

"Dunno, sir."

"Well, I know. He'll say, 'Let justice take its course!' "

"Objection!" said Mayfield again. "The evidence shows this witness has been promised nothing, and that his confession came voluntarily out of conscience before ever he saw Captain Merewether."

"Yes, the court has the matter well in mind. Let us get on with the case, Mister Farris."

The remainder of the trial went quickly. Five men took the stand to swear fervently that they had had no part in the mutiny but Mayfield demolished each defense with his artful cross-examination. Batts, Osborne and Sublett did not testify. Apparently they had given up all hope. They stood sullenly staring at the floor.

"Let the record show that these defendants stand mute," said Captain Fontaine. "Now, do you gentlemen desire to sum up for the benefit of the court?"

"I don't believe it necessary," replied Mayfield.

"I do, may it please the court," said Farris.

"In that case, I shall make a short summation." Mayfield spoke for six minutes, driving his points home like nails in a coffin, then relinquished the floor to Farris.

"May it please the court, I submit that this case rests upon the testimony of a co-conspirator, without corroboration . . . The conduct of Batts, Osborne and Sublett is as consistent with their innocence as with their guilt . . . A reasonable doubt exists as to each and every of their defendants . . ." Farris made a damnably ingenious argument. Merewether looked sharply at the members of the court, but could read no reaction on their impassive faces.

"Clear the court, Master at Arms," said Fontaine at the conclusion of Farris's argument, and Merewether found himself in the hallway where he had awaited a verdict himself the year before last. He felt a curious anxiety. Farris had adroitly put him on trial with the mutineers, and he was relieved when the master at arms appeared to march the prisoners back in. The court had reached its verdict.

"This court will reconvene," said Captain Fontaine briskly. "Let the prisoners step forward." They did so, manacled hands clenched before them, and Fontaine delivered the judgment of the court.

"This court finds the specifications of charges proved, and the following prisoners to be guilty of mutiny; Batts, Osborne, Sublett . . ." He read through the list, all ten of the surviving mutineers. Merewether looked at the group. Batts and Sublett were as white as the others, but Osborne simply stared at the court, a derisive smirk on his face, eyes glittering. Merewether wondered for a moment if he could have presented so bold a front under such circumstances.

"And now, before this court passes sentence, has counsel for the prisoners anything to say by way of mitigation on their behalf?" Farris was a bit white himself, and his voice had a tremor in it as he spoke.

"I call to the attention of the court that the evidence against these men is not as strong as it might be, and request that this factor be considered in passing sentence."

"Very well. Now as to Plunkett, who entered a plea of guilty, does any person desire to say anything in his behalf before this court passes sentence?" Mayfield stood up, Plunkett's stricken gaze fixed upon him.

"In view of his repentance and honest confession, I would not object to tempering justice with mercy, sirs. I call on Captain Merewether for his recommendation." Merewether stood up self-consciously, feeling not only the imploring eyes of Plunkett fixed on him, but the ironic smile that Farris wore.

"I too have no objection to a reduced sentence for this man."

"Very well. Clear the court." It was only a few minutes before the court reconvened.

"This court has considered the evidence and law in this case. It is our unanimous judgment that in the cases of Batts, Osborne, Sublett . . ." He read down the list and continued, ". . . having been convicted of the most infamous crime of mutiny on the high seas, that they, and each of them, suffer death by hanging at a time and place to be fixed by the Superintendent of the Marine." He paused, and only a dry sob from one of the prisoners broke the silence. "As to the prisoner, Plunkett, in view of the recommendations of the Recorder and Captain Merewether we fix his punishment at ten years at hard labor, and to be transported for execution of the sentence to the custody of the Prison Governor in Australia."

Relief flooded over Plunkett's face. He could serve his time, and if he lived, be free by the time he was thirty.

"The findings and sentences of this court will be delivered to the Commandant of the Marine, to be by him transmitted to the Superintendent for his review, confirmation, commutation or reversal. This court is now adjourned without day. Remove the prisoners, Mister Marshal."

It was five days before a counterpart of the Superintendent's letter to the Commandant of the Marine came to Merewether:

> To the Commandant of the Marine:
>
> The undersigned has reviewed the findings made and sentences imposed by a Court of Inquiry convened to try divers seamen listed on the attachment hereto for the crime of mutiny on the high seas in HCS *Pitt,* Captain Percival Merewether commanding. This authority is of the opinion that these findings and sentences are fully justified in the cases of Batts, Osborne, Sublett and Plunkett, and they accordingly are in all respects confirmed. As to the other seven prisoners, this authority is of the opinion that the ends of justice will be satisfied by a commutation of sentence. Accordingly, the sentences imposed upon these seven men are now modified, and said prisoners are now sentenced to twenty years each at hard labor to be performed under the directive of the Prison Governor of Bombay.
>
> The sentences of Batts, Osborne and Sublets will be carried into execution seven days hence in the ship from which they came at eight, ante meridian. All ships present shall furnish as large a party of seamen as their boats will accommodate to witness punishment.
>
> Given under my hand and seal, this 30th day of March, 1808.
>
> Sir James Campbell, Bart.
> Superintendent

Consternation seized Merewether. The thought had never crossed his mind that the men would be delivered back to *Pitt* for execution. At the beginning of his career in the Marine as a boatswain's mate, he had been told off to serve in the hanging of a murderer, but the man had died of fever before the sentence could be carried out. He wondered at his squeamishness — he had killed other men in his time, albeit not in cold blood — but the thought of a party of seamen walking away at his command with the bitter end of a rope rove through a block at the yardarm to hang a man by the neck until he kicked his life away made his flesh crawl. Damnation! Why could the job not be done on the gallows at the prison by the Governor and Warder? Of course, he knew, these executions were designed to have the maximum effect on all hands in the expedition; that was the reason for the order to send witnesses to the punishment.

Merewether checked his morbid thoughts. He had no reason to fret himself into a blue funk. The die was cast and he must carry through the process of justice, unpleasant though the prospect might be. "Messenger!"

The lad appeared at the door.

"My compliments to Mister Whaley and Boatswain Caldwell, and will you ask them to see me at their convenience?" It was only a few minutes before they knocked and entered.

Merewether read the Superintendent's order to them, seeing Whaley's expression harden at the commutation of sentences for eight mutineers.

"It appears that we must carry out the executions in this ship. Do either of you have any experience in this sort of thing?"

Whaley shook his head. "I've witnessed several hangings, but never had the duty of turning off a man myself," he said in a tone of regret. "Simple enough, I would think."

"I've served in the hangman's party back when I was in the Royal Navy, but the master at arms always handled the details himself. I do know how to tie the knot . . ." Merewether knew that himself. It was a macabre accomplishment that every striker in the seaman branch learned early in his career.

"I don't want a botch job," Merewether told them. "None of this strangling for a quarter of an hour, and, by the same token, no jerking the man's head off his shoulders. I suggest you consult with the prison warder and the boatswains in other ships present for the details." The order had left a bad taste in his mouth and went ashore early to the public house to get the matter off his mind.

The day of execution dawned bright and clear, the sort of day to inspire a man to live. Merewether awoke at the first light and called Sangh for tea, then coffee when the tea failed to take hold, but took no solid food. The dreadful event was less than three hours away, and object depression possessed him. While he waited for the coffee to cool, he went through the packets of papers that imposed the duty upon him: the judgment and sentence of the Court of Inquiry, signed and sealed; the confirmation of the sentences by the Superintendent of the Marine; and the death warrants, signed, attested and countersigned. All appeared to be regular. He sighed, and drank the coffee.

Boatswain Caldwell, the chief master-at-arms, and the senior boatswain's mates comprising the hanging party had concluded only yesterday an intensive short course of instruction in how to hang a man efficiently, taught by the boatswain in HMS *Chiffone.* Merewether hoped there would be no bungling to embarrass him. *Pitt* had been warped in close to the mole where the military and naval forces in the garrison of Bombay Castle would be formed up to witness the executions. Other ships present had shifted their anchorages so as to give all hands a clear view of the proceedings. The other witnesses would be transported in boats to lie off *Pitt.* It was as though the event were a circus, a public entertainment designed for the amusement and edification of a vast audience. Of course, the purpose was clear: the certainty of swift vengeance for mutiny must be brought home to all.

A knock came on the door and Whaley entered. "All is in readiness, sir," he said with an air of satisfaction. "The scaffold is rigged, the nooses tied, and an extra platoon of Sepoy Marines from the Castle is aboard. The chaplain from HMS *Caroline* is with the prisoners."

Six bells sounded; the grisly event was only an hour away. "Very well, Mister Whaley."

It was time to shift into full dress with sword, Merewether decided, but he sat at the desk in a reverie until he heard seven bells.

The entire ship's company was formed up by divisions in the waist. The Sepoy Marines had formed a hollow square, facing outward, on the forecastle, bayonets fixed. Merewether with Purser Davis, now acting in his capacity as ship's clerk, to his left, made his way forward through the ranks as eight bells began to sound. *Pitt* was half encircled with boats, each crammed with silent men. On the mole there were solid ranks of scarlet coats standing at attention, and at one end a considerable assemblage of sightseers, civilians, dockyard clerks and artisans with a small contingent of Indians behind them. As the sound of the last stroke of the bell faded, Merewether could hear the solid clump of his heels striking the deck in the dead silence as he and Davis marched to the forecastle, the Marine ranks parting to allow them passage, then closing behind. As he reached the foremast, Whaley stepped forward. "Attention on deck!"

The Marines presented arms and there was a ruffle of drums as the officers and petty officers saluted.

"Carry on."

The mutineers were ranged in a row facing him just abaft the foremast, hands manacled behind them, leg-irons locked on. Batts and Sublett were pale but composed, eyes downcast, but Osborne's feral yellow gaze bored defiantly into his, almost with an expression of mockery. "I have here orders from Sir James Campbell, Superintendent of the Marine, by way of the Commandant . . ." He read the confirmation of the sentences. "The ship's clerk will read the death warrants." Davis did so in a high-pitched voice, one after another, identical but for the names.

"Have these men made their peace with God?"

"Yes, Captain," said Whaley. "The chaplain has been with them for nearly two hours."

Merewether took a deep breath. "Carry out your orders, Mister Caldwell," he told the boatswain.

Two boatswain's mates took each man by the arms and propelled the three prisoners towards the curious structure the carpenter had rigged last night. It was made of long planks battened together a yard wide, three-quarters of its length protruding beyond the bulwarks over the water, the inboard end lashed to a heavy ringbolt in the deck by hemp line. Three stanchions supported a rope along its forward edge to which the nooses at the ends of lines rove through blocks on the fore main yardarm were secured with loops of small stuff. It was the design of Benton, boatswain in HMS *Chiffone* , who claimed to have been in the hanging party at Sheerness after the Nore mutiny ten years ago. Its operation was simple enough. At the signal the line securing the inboard end of the scaffold would be cut with a hatchet, and the planks would simply fall out from under the prisoners leaving them suspended in the nooses after a drop calculated to break their necks. They would then be hoisted above the bulwarks and left hanging from the yardarm on display to the fleet for one hour. Merewether had approved the method proposed. It had appeared entirely humane as compared to the common practice of having a party simply walk away with the bitter end of the rope leaving the man suspended to die in the slow agonies of strangulation.

"Hoist the yellow flag," said Merewether as the party mounted the inboard end of the scaffold. "Stand by the gun!" The flag indicated the executions were in progress; the gun would signal the instant the mutineers were actually turned off. He looked past the party now shuffling along the platform to glimpse the half circle of boats off the starboard side holding a sea of upturned faces.

Batts reached the outboard end of the platform and one of the boatswains mates released the noose while the other pulled a black hood down over his head. Sublett followed, to stop in front of the second noose. Osborne moved out, taking the twelve-inch steps dictated by the chains between the leg-irons, and one of the boatswain's mates let go his arm to unfasten the twine securing the noose, while the other reached for the black hood tucked into his belt.

Osborne's knees bent suddenly, dislodging the one-handed grip of the boatswain's mate, then straightened, propelling his body backward in a lazy arc, to enter the water cleanly, head first.

Merewether's mouth opened in astonishment. He rushed to the bulwarks, a mass of bubbles was breaking the surface of the water in the centre of a widening circle of ripples. Osborne had cheated the hangman, but he wondered a moment if it were much easier to die of drowning, pinned to the bottom in the mud by the weight of leg-irons and handcuffs, than of a broken neck.

The thought passed through his mind that he would be the laughing stock of the fleet, but there was no help for it and he must get on with the grisly task, delaying only long enough to make sure Osborne did not surface in spite of the irons. The ripples had spread and vanished, there were no more bubbles, and he looked up to see the nooses in place, the bulky spiral knots positioned behind the left ears of Batts and Sublett. Merewether signaled the boatswain's mates in to the deck, and caught the eye of the gunner.

"Fire," he told him in a low tone. The blank charge in the forward port carronade belched out a hollow report, the hatchet blade flashed down, severing the line securing the inboard end of the scaffold, and both men were left dangling, their necks twisted sidewise at acute angles, their bodies twitching in brief involuntary spasms. At least this part of the affair had gone as planned.

Well," said Tollett an hour later. "He's just as dead as though he had been hanged, but the object lesson has failed, as least as to him. Osborne will be a hero in the lower deck for years to come for having cheated the hangman in the full view of a thousand witnesses."

"I know," said Merewether miserably. "But the thing appeared to be so much better than the usual method . . ."

"Spilt milk," said Tollett briskly. "Forget it, and let's get on with the expedition. The only thing holding up the sortie has been this affair. Can you sail on the morning tide?"

Merewether racked his brain. The water casks could be topped off this afternoon. There might be other small items. But he was sure Davis could manage them by morning. In any event it would be a relief to be underway after all the vexatious delays.

"Yes, sir."

"Very good. The sailing orders will be delivered during the day. Now, will you join Commodore Dunbar, Colonel Smith and Captain Seton with me for lunch. I haven't had the opportunity yet of talking to all of you together."

It was a pleasant affair in the flag officers' room of the Bombay Club. Tollett, an abstemious man, served only Madeira, and

Seton did not lose his self-control, as he had with the gin at Calcutta .Tollett came to the point quickly.

"I am informed that your expedition is in all respects ready for sea," he said to Dunbar. "The Sepoy Marines and Bombay Regiment will be embarked this afternoon, and the siege guns are already aboard ship."

"Yes," replied Dunbar with his hot glance. "But two of the four forty-two-pounders are in *Vesuvius,* an old bomb ketch that requires eight hours pumping a day, and the other two in a store ship that sails better sideways than ahead. I have doubts that either will reach the Gulf in time to be of any use."

We have to make do with what we have," said Tollett, reddening. "What with this operation and our other commitments, the Marine is stretched perilously thin." The meeting broke up after a few more remarks.

Merewether slept poorly again that night. No nightmares as he had experienced at Calcutta, but shadowy dreams that brought him awake with the conviction that he had overlooked some important detail, but he was unable to discover during his wakeful periods any omission. Only nerves, he decided, the reaction after that horrible morning added to the mounting tension in anticipation of the sortie. He finally dropped off to awaken in broad daylight with Sangh setting out the toast and pouring the tea in the day cabin.

Osborne felt the sting against the top of his head as it struck the water and jack-knifed his body as soon as it was fully submerged to sink with the weight of the shackles feet first to the mud bottom. His left hand was free of the handcuffs halfway down, and he took the bit of wire he had secreted in his cheek and bent over to get at the lock on the leg-irons, remembering to release a quarter lungful of air as he did so. The lock yielded, he left the irons sticking in the mud and struck out with a powerful kick and breast stroke angling upwards under the shadow of *Pitt* to emerge cautiously on the port side midships. He had been under water a little more than a minute and surfaced just in time to hear the gun fire above him signaling that Batts and Sublett had been turned off.

No one on deck could see him here. The nearest vessel anchored on this side was more than a cable's length away, and he paused long enough to inhale and exhale deeply several times before he sank beneath the surface again to swim to the stern. He came up beside the rudder post, shielded from above by the overhang of the transom, then found foot and finger holds on the gudgeons and pintles by which the rudder was hung.

"Fools!" he thought contemptuously, while he regained his breath. To think he would tamely submit to kick his life away at the end of a rope! He had been reared as an acrobat and performed his underwater escape trick at half the fairs in England before the press gang snaffled him. It had been a stroke of luck when they rigged that scaffold over the side, but he would have managed somehow to throw himself into the water no matter what. The bay was not uncomfortably cold and he endured the day, ducking his head under when an occasional boat passed, even hearing snatches of conversation that mentioned his name. He would be famous!

Osborne had little regret for the action that had brought him to this pass, though if he had to do it over his tactics would be different. He thought with cold hatred of Whaley, the hazing and continuous pressure, the niggling rules and heavy-handed vengeance visited upon the unlucky during the last cruise, though he had personally escaped the cat and disrating. The new man — Merewether? — appeared to be a decent sort, but he had not had time to make his character felt in the lower deck when the attempt was made. News of the impending operation in the fiery furnace of the Persian Gulf and the brutal floggings in which a man lost an eye had precipitated the mutiny prematurely while the ship was still in the Bay of Bengal, though the tales of the uncharted islands to the eastward peopled with beautiful women and food for the picking had had its influence.

Osborne regretted only his moment of indecision that night in the captain's cabin. If the three of them had jumped Merewether, he might have killed one of us with his blunderbuss, but the survivors (and he was sure he would have been one) would have subdued him. By now, he might very well have already been king of his own island with a harem of dark-eyed beauties to comfort him.

When darkness fell, before moonrise, Osborne swam underwater, surfacing at intervals to catch lungfuls of air, clear of the anchorage, then strongly on the surface westwardly towards a cluster of native huts on the mainland. There were fishing boats anchored in the shallows. He found a substantial one, pulled up the stone anchor and let it drift on the ebb towards the harbor entrance where he hoisted the simple sail. By dawn he was twenty miles south, and there was no pursuit. Certainly not for a dead man! He found a moldy loaf of native bread and some half-rotten fruit in the locker under the stern that staved off hunger, and two night later sighted the lights of Goa. He swam to the beach a mile or so north of the harbor, waited for daylight, and strolled nonchalantly by the day watch.

A Portuguese trader was shorthanded. Osborne found a berth with no questions asked, and sailed for Macao on the morning tide. At least the cruise was in the right direction. He had no intention of going back to India or England where there was a chance of recognition, dead though he was accounted.

Three months later when the ship reached Macao, he had grown a moustache in the Dago fashion, let his curly hair grow out in ringlets, and learned enough Portuguese to get along. What with the blood of his gypsy grandmother he could now pass without remark in this company. The constant attrition of disease and death out here made every colonial garrison shorthanded. Osborne had no difficulty enlisting as a master gunner in the provincial forces on duty in the colony. He felt reasonably safe; though there were agents of the Company here, they served its maritime and trading interests, not its Marine. He soon contracted a liaison with a half-caste Indonesian girl and adapted himself to a new way of life.

Two days northwest of Bombay came a gale, fomented by the change of season from the northeast to the southwest monsoon. The convoy had held together reasonably well to this point, under a steady succession of imperative signals hoisted by Commodore Dunbar to chivvy the stragglers back into formation. The blow, accompanied by four hours of blinding rain, forced the clumsy transports, most of them in ballast awaiting the Imam's troops at Muscat, to heave to under reefed storm sails, but they found themselves going to leeward more rapidly than the men-o'-war and in danger of colliding. *Pitt* was the leading vessel in the port column well clear of the unmanageable transports, and Merewether felt little concern for the blow.

In late afternoon the first casualty occurred. The messenger burst into the cabin leaving a visible trail of rainwater.

"Sir, Mister Dobbs says *Vesuvius* has sunk!"

Merewether ran up the ladder to the quarterdeck.

"Right there, sir," said Dobbs, pointing off the port quarter. "She was there one minute, and then all I could see was her masts sliding into the water!" In this sea, the huge weight of the siege guns must have taken the bottom right out of the old bomb ketch.

"Starboard your helm," Merewether shouted to the quartermaster, and *Pitt* played off, coming to the starboard tack under storm jib, stay sails and double-reefed spanker. The rain had slackened to a drizzle and the wind had moderated, but the seas were mountainous as the ship ran down the last bearing Dobbs had for *Vesuvius.*

There was a shout from forward as a dark object appeared on the crest of a wave a cable's length ahead.

"Heaving lines and grapnels!" shouted Dobbs. If the ship passed the floating object, it would never be able to beat back to it, and launching a boat was unthinkable in these seas.

Merewether saw the object again, almost dead ahead on the crest of the next wave but one. "Steady as you go!" He thought he had seen two white faces beside what now appeared to be a baulk of timber probably used as dunnage for the siege guns.

The object was on the crest of the wave ahead as *Pitt* slid down the slope into the trough. There were two men clinging to it as it passed to starboard thirty feet off. Lines arched out, at least three criss-crossing the timber, and the men took hold, abandoning their support.

"Port your helm!"

The ship came about, rolling horrendously in the trough for a moment, but easing the strain on the lines. Somehow, the pair managed to hold on as they were dragged through the water, then up the side of the ship where helping hands could pull them on deck. Doctors Mefford and Buttram ministered to the waterlogged, rope-burned young men. An hour later, exuding a powerful odor of medicinal brands, they were in the cabin making their report as Pitt pitched and rolled, hove to again.

"Marlowe, sir," said the elder, apparently about sixteen. The other lad was even younger. "Midshipman in *Vesuvius,* and this is

Cate, apprentice. We were hove to, sir, riding fairly easy, I thought, when she put her bow under, and it didn't come up."

"Were there any others got off that you saw?"

"I saw three swimming, but they couldn't have lasted long. We were lucky, the timber floated off right beside us."

It must have been a terrifying experience. Evidently, the rotten bottom had opened up under the tremendous concentrated weight of the forty-two-pounder guns, and the vessel had sunk like a stone, taking with her nearly fifty officers and men. Half the siege train was lost too, but Merewether refused to speculate on the effect this might have on the success of the expedition. With his luck running the way it had these past three months, he might have to stand a court of inquiry himself for failing to rescue the entire crew and cargo of the bomb ketch.

"There is only one midshipman aboard now, so there's no trouble to find you a berth. You will serve as junior watch officer with Lieutenant Dobbs, at least until we reach Muscat," he told Marlowe. "What were your duties in *Vesuvius,* Cate?"

"Why, sir, I was learning the cooper's trade."

As senior officer present in the Marine squadron, Merewether had full authority to deal with casual ratings such as this survivor. "Very well, report to the cooper, he has recently lost a mate. Both of you may see Mister Davis, the purser, and draw such clothing and supplies as you require from the slop chest against your pay accounts."

Merewether sat a few minutes more at the desk. Darkness descended outside, the wind subsided to no more than a fresh breeze. Even the drizzle had ceased, but the seas were still rolling relentlessly under *Pitt's* keel, lifting first bow, then stern in their passage as she lay hove to once more. His thoughts turned back to Calcutta, only two months before Caroline's confinement, and he wondered what the child might be. Girl or boy, the odds were even, though he realized he possessed a normal vanity in desiring to perpetuate his name. Unaccountably, his thoughts shifted to Osborne, wondering if the fish had picked his bones clean yet on the bottom of Bombay Harbor. Tomorrow would be a day to try his soul, he knew, the scattered convoy to be rounded up and herded again into formation. It behooved him to get a good night's rest.

Merewether heaved himself out of the chair and went on deck to deliver the night order book to MacCamy.

Five days later the convoy made its landfall at Ras Al Hadd, and course was changed to parallel the coast northwestwardly. The convoy was off Muscat by six bells in the morning watch next day. Merewether spent the morning in fuming impatience on deck, *Pitt,* hove to, as one flag hoist after another blossomed on the flagship giving the order of entry and place of anchorage in the cove. The first eighteen signals were addressed to the transports, and it was not until they were completed that the signal came to the cruisers to take anchorage in the open roadstead. It was safe enough in this season when the prevailing Shamal blew out of the northwest. If the Kaus out of the southeast, or the Nashi out of the northeast should come on to blow, the ships would have to put out to sea.

It took most of the day to get the transports into the harbor and anchored. Then the signal came for the warships to proceed to anchor, closely followed by the imperative addressed to *Pitt,* "Captain, come on board."

Captain Napier, commanding HMS *Caroline,* met Merewether at the gangway and escorted him to the cabin. Dunbar, Colonel Smith and Seton were seated at the long table, and Merewether took a chair opposite them.

"Well," said Dunbar in a hard accusing tone, his hot brown eyes flashing. "Already we have troubles! Tell him, Seton." Seton's thin face was impassive, but his voice was shrill with suppressed indignation.

"The Imam has failed me, Merewether. He professes to have only eight hundred troops equipped for the expedition, instead of the four thousand he had promised." The officer spread his hands to indicate his helplessness. "We had relied in our plans on the native forces to invest the town of Ras ul Khyrnah from the land side and prevent escape or reinforcement. It may be best to postpone the expedition . . ."

"Like hell!" interposed Smith "My force is ready, come what may! But I seem to get precious little assistance from my seafaring opposite numbers!" Seton's face was a pale mask of pure hatred, and Dunbar had turned almost purple.

The Colonel continued. "At the outset, Seton, I gave little enough credit to your bluster of the influence you possess with the Imam. It only means I'll have to detach two companies to stiffen your native rabble and prevent them from running away at the first shot." Seton started up from his chair, and Merewether reached across the table to place a restraining hand on his elbow. A duel at this point could only wreck the operation.

"Now, gentlemen," said Dunbar belatedly. "No need for personalities! It can't be helped." Evidently Colonel Smith had reached the same conclusion. He spoke now in a milder tone.

"Very well. I say, take what we have and get on with the enterprise!" He looked across at Merewether. "Of course, you've also lost half the siege train . . ."

Merewether understood instantly how Seton had felt. Blood pounded in his ears at the unfairness of the accusation. He had had no more to do with the decision to employ the rotten bomb ketch for the transport of the guns than Smith himself. He opened his mouth. But Dunbar was quicker this time.

"Gentlemen!" said Dunbar. "No more of these recriminations! There are enough other guns in the fleet to serve our purposes. Let us embark the troops that are ready and be on our way. Do you have a comment, Merewether?"

"I am in agreement."

"Oh, agreed," said Smith in a pleasant tone. "I intended no personal affront to anyone present. I just hate to see a mare's nest made of well-laid plans, and spoke from a full heart." Seton and Merewether declined the proffered refreshment and took their leave, while Smith remained behind in the cabin.

On deck, Seton was still trembling with fury, hectic spots now on his sallow cheeks.

"God damn him! God damn . . ."

"Now, control yourself, Seton. He knows as well as you that the Imam is at fault." Still, the gratuitous accusations rankled. Merewether came back on board *Pitt* feeling limp and exhausted in the blazing heat. It would obviously be the morrow before the Imam's forces could be embarked, and the next day before the transports would sortie from the cove. He felt a sudden overpowering desire for a drink in congenial company to erase the memory of the recent unpleasantness, and dispatched Sangh with invitations for Larkin, Dobbs, Buttram, Hamlyn and Marlowe to dine with him in the cabin.

It was like the old days in *Rapid.* Among the friendly and familiar faces, only Marlowe's was still strange. But Merewether desired a closer acquaintance with the boy he had snatched bodily from the sea. MacCamy was a loner, he would never notice the snub. Whaley had, indeed, looked narrowly at him as he passed; but Merewether could not bring himself to like the man and gave it no thought. The festivities lasted well into the first watch, and Merewether felt himself a little fuddled as he saw his guests out.

It was black dark, but Merewether was still conscious of the vaulted ceilings and rich tapestries on the walls. It must be a palace, but Caroline had met him in the garden and led him here, to blow out the candles in one graceful pirouette, and then draw him to her. Waves of passion were sweeping through both of them, her body was delightfully firm, skin smooth as silk, the unsightly bulge in her middle had vanished, and they mounted swiftly towards climax.

"Oh, Caroline, Caroline, I love you!" Her breath came in gasps as her lips sought his. No need to wonder how, she was with him!

There came a great burst, and he saw that the woman in his embrace had black, not red-gold hair. Who was she? The eyes were closed, the mouth twisted yet in the throes of passion, but the face was damnably familiar. Not Caroline, not his wife!

Merewether came awake in the sleeping cabin in *Pitt* feeling the hot discharge on his belly, looked automatically up for the tell-tale compass to see that the course was steady, then remembered that she was at anchor in the roadstead, off Muscat. God damn! He had not experienced such a dream since he was twenty. He rose, found the pitcher of fresh water, washed himself, then slipped into his robe to go on deck. All was well, it was a quarter hour to the end of the middle watch, and MacCamy had the deck.

He was ashamed of himself, though no one would ever know of it, the dream had been vivid, so real that he felt himself sated. He yet felt a lassitude; his weight these weeks past had remained below normal, though Buttram had found no objective symptoms of any disorder. The name swam unbidden into his consciousness. Creusa?

Yes. Creusa Hale. He almost laughed at the thought, and returned to sleep dreamlessly until reveille.

Pitt lay at anchor in four and a half fathoms a little more than two miles off Ras ul Khymah. Merewether had edged her in yesterday afternoon as close as he dared, the leadsmen in the cutter feeling the way. The town with the two stone towers of the fort rising on its northern edge, one with a staff flying the bloodred flag of the defiant Joasmis, was plainly visible through his glass. The town was built on a promontory some three miles long forming the western boundary of a lagoon in which the masts of upward of a hundred vessels could be seen, a major portion of the pirate fleet. A boat crew had discovered last night that there was no more than three feet of water over the bar at the entrance to the lagoon, which accounted for the presence of the vessels trapped inside, though the next nor' wester was likely enough to sweep the drifting sands again to a clear ten feet.

"It will be a hard nut to crack," volunteered Whaley, also sweeping the shore with a glass. "Not only the fort itself, but the houses in the town with their stone walls and flat roofs. Each one is a blockhouse." Merewether made no reply, intent on fixing in his mind as much of the terrain and defenses as he could in the cool of the morning with the sun rising behind the town. In two hours' time, the image would be shimmering in the fierce glare and dust devils dancing outside the walls.

Satisfied, he turned his attention inboard to the waist where Larkin, Hamlyn, Marlowe and Gunny were in the centre of a circle of seamen and marines. Dunbar had called on *Pitt* to supply the beachmaster and his party to oversee the landing and direct troops and material to their designated sectors in an orderly manner. Larkin was clearly the best qualified man for the responsibility, but Whaley had seemed a bit put out at the choice. Merewether had soothed his ruffled feelings with the explanation that he intended to be ashore during a portion of the operation and command of *Pitt* should devolve upon the first lieutenant. He wanted a man ashore not only possessing iron resolution, of which Whaley had enough, but one also capable of persuasion with something more than the threat of the cat. He watched Larkin now drive his points home, fist pounded into palm, pointing from time to time to the large sketch chart of the spit spread out for all to see. He anticipated no difficulty in the carrying out of this assignment. Gunny and his marines could provide security against any sortie by the pirates.

The landing was scheduled for daybreak the next day, though embarkation of the landing force would actually commence at four bells in the midwatch. The first elements to land would be the two companies of light infantry of the 47th Regiment who would serve as skirmishers and seize the low wall that ran across the spit some seven hundred yards north of the fort. The 65th would follow to take up positions five hundred yards farther north, entrenching themselves, and then the Bombay Artillery Battalion with its six twelve-pounder field guns would be positioned in sandbag emplacements in the centre. Merewether had small hope that the field guns would do more than pock the face of the fort — Seton's intelligence had reported the north walls were five and a half feet of stone — but with the remaining two forty-two-pounders, a breach might ultimately be made.

He turned his attention to seaward. The transports were engaged in launching the clumsy flat-bottomed troop lighters they had brought on their decks, and the four larger barges for the field guns that had been towed out here were alongside the Bombay Marine cargo vessels to take off the battery and its ammunition. This evolution appeared to be going well enough, though Merewether could imagine the sweating seamen and the profane exhortations of the boatswain's mates in each of the ships. He shifted the glass to the transport, *Ceylon,* with the two huge forty-two-pounders on her deck.

A barge with a pair of shearlegs protruding at an angle over her bow was being warped up against another barge moored alongside *Ceylon.* Her blunt bow slanted upward, exposing several feet of bottom, evidence of the pig-iron ballast she carried astern to balance the weight of the gun she would lift from the deck and deposit in the barge. Merewether watched with idle interest as the boatswain's mates spun their skein of blocks and tackles, preventers and stays, finally recruiting additional hands from the transport to double-bank the capstan bars and sway the gun up, then out, for deposit in the barge. An efficient evolution, he noted, as he racked the telescope and went below to look over the morning reports. It was an hour later when he heard the word passed.

"Away rescue natty! *Ceylon!*" The messenger came clattering down the ladder.

"Sir, they've dropped a gun and sunk the barge!" Merewether came on deck to see confusion on *Ceylon's* deck, heads bobbing in the water alongside, the men being pulled to safety, Other boats were closer to the disaster, and he checked the embarking rescue party in the quarterboat.

"They dropped the second gun clean through the bottom of the barge," Whaley told him with an air of satisfaction. Merewether put the glass to his eye.

The wrought-iron strongback joining the two timber legs of the shears at the top had broken right in half, releasing the heavy block through which the lifting cables led to the capstan, and letting the gun fall straight down into the barge, instantly sinking her. Both guns were four or five fathoms under, and although the second gun still had the lifting cables attached, there was no way to bring it up until the shearlegs were repaired. Divers would be required to attach lines to the other siege piece, if there were any available in the fleet possessing that skill. Merewether wondered sourly what more could go wrong with this commission as he awaited the inevitable summons to the flagship. He comforted himself in the meantime with the thought that the shearlegs had been manned by the Royal Navy.

By first light the next morning, the landing was well under way. Larkin with his party followed the two companies of light infantry which raced through the dawn to seize the low wall across the spit, then spread a line of skirmishers forward, taking shelter in the folds of the terrain southwardly towards the fort. With flags the beach party quickly marked the points of landing for the main force, while the marines under Gunny established an arc of rifle pits from the end of the wall to the water's edge as a second line of defense to secure the flank along the beach. Not a shot had been fired as yet, but Merewether heard the faint sounds of defiant trumpets and cymbals across the water from the fort, in the dead quiet of early morning. The Joasmi forces had sounded the alarm.

"Well," said Whaley unnecessarily. "It won't be long now." The flotilla of lighters, crammed with soldiers of the 47th and 65th Regiments, was crawling towards the beach under sweeps in an orderly array, and others filled with the Imam's troops were headed to a landing south of the town.

"Look there!" shouted Whaley.

From some concealed sallyport to the east a troop of mounted Joasmis had emerged at a canter in a loose column formation headed towards the point of landing a few hundred yards north of the light infantry positions. As they came westward towards the beach, the pickets and skirmishers began to fire shots at long range, then retreated, and paused to fire again. Merewether could see no results, and the Arabs pressed on. The first lighters loaded with the regulars were already in the shallows close to the beach, most vulnerable as they began to disgorge their cargoes in a stream of scarlet coats with bayonets flashing in the rising sun.

The cavalry troop changed course to aim at the beach at the point where the low wall ended in the sand, with the evident intention of flanking the light infantry along the wall and striking the disembarking force behind it before the regulars could form up. Their route took them squarely against the almost invisible semicircle of rifle pits occupied by the Sepoy Marines.

It appeared at this distance that the mounted Arabs had already overrun the pits. Then, Merewether saw puffs of smoke blossom all around the arc, and after an appreciable interval heard the faint sound of the volley. The troop split, men and horses were down, and the main body wheeled to its left and back up the beach out of range, while a smaller contingent veered to its right paralleling wall. The second group was instantly met by a volley from the light infantry company ensconced behind the wall, while the marines fired again into their backs. More men and horses went down, and the survivors galloped off in frantic retreat towards the fort.

"Well done!" shouted Merewether, waving his hat and dancing as though the marines could hear and see him. A well-disciplined and resolute infantry force had demonstrated once again its ability to deal with cavalry, particularly a troop as loosely organized as this one had been.

The landing proceeded without further incident, the regulars taking up positions some four hundred yards behind the low wall, digging trenches and fortifying them with sandbags. Other working parties began to pitch tents for the camp well towards the north end of the spit, and Merewether soon saw the twelve-pound field pieces with their limbers landed. A large party of Indian navvies were filling bags with sand and erecting a redoubt for the battery opposite the east tower of the fort where reconnaissance had disclosed chinks in the mortar and some stones fallen from the outer wall. His thoughts went back to the council of war yesterday afternoon following the loss of the siege guns, hearing again the bitter recriminations.

"Well, Dunbar, your blundering idiots have crippled me again!" Colonel Smith had said.

"It was a failure of material that no one could have foreseen," Dunbar replied. "I have already ordered the landing of four thirty-two-pounders from this ship to replace the siege guns."

"Too little and too late!" countered Smith. "If we had all the troops Seton promised, I would order a frontal attack with scaling ladders." He had paused and looked speculatively at the Marine captain. "In fact to get some use out of what we have, I think I'll order an immediate attack by the Imam's troops on the town from the south!"

"What?" cried Seton, leaping to his feet. "You have no right! I am in absolute control of the employment of the Imam's forces! I forbid it!"

"It was only a bad jest, Seton," the Colonel said. "I doubt you could induce them to move out of camp." Merewether decided to bring an end to this pointless bickering.

"Is there some further duty in which I can assist the operation, gentlemen?"

"Yes," said Smith unexpectedly. "Take *Pitt* up to the sea wall west of the town, and pound the backside of that fort!"

Merewether had asked one question too many. He opened his mouth to explain the impossibility of such action when he received unexpected aid from Dunbar.

"*Pitt,* as do all but the smallest cruisers present, has several feet too much draught to approach within gunshot of the shore, Colonel," Dunbar explained. "Now, Merewether, I think it only fair that *Pitt* furnish three gun crews for the thirty-two-pounders so that they may be manned around the clock. And I see no necessity for prolonging this council, gentlemen, though I desire a further word with Captain Merewether." Smith and Seton took their leave without delay, and Merewether resumed his seat with some trepidation as to Dunbar's motives.

"Well, Merewether," said the Commodore returning from the door to his place behind the desk. "You see what a dragon we have in that damned Smith! And with all due respect to your service, Seton is not my cup of tea either." He reached forward to ring the bell, and his servant emerged from the pantry. "What will you have, gin, rum or Scotch whisky? God knows, it's seldom enough I take a drink at sea, but this is purely medicinal." Merewether had not wanted a drink in the heat of the afternoon, but it would be rude to refuse.

"I leave the choice to you, sir." No need being finicky. Merewether could choke down the whisky and make his escape.

"Two gins and lemon, Akin." The servant departed, and Dunbar slid down in his chair, peering at Merewether from under his thick brows. "Of course, Smith is bracing for the brevet as major-general at Fort William during the leave of General Sir John Stanley next year. This operation will mean little enough in success, but disaster if it fails, since he possesses no interest beyond his own abilities."

The gin and lemon came in on two trays, and Dunbar paused while Akin served them. "Cheers, Captain!" He took a sip, and Merewether followed suit. The gin was exactly right, and the lemon complemented it perfectly even in the sticky heat.

"I have held post rank eleven years now. I did have a bit of interest going through my wife's family which is old in Devon, and has turfed out seven admirals in the last hundred years. But, from captain to flag is purely seniority, and I'm still a long way from the top of the list. I fear Bonaparte may be defeated before attrition brings me within striking distance, and peace time will be much slower." He shook his head dolefully, and took another sip. Merewether felt vaguely uncomfortable, but the drink tended to alleviate the tension.

"Well, you're still a young man to possess so much seniority, Commodore," he said in an effort to commiserate without giving the appearance of it.

"But if I could pull this operation off quick and sharp, I might get a command in an area where I could make some prize money. God, look at the fortune Pellew has made these past five years while he got fat sitting on his verandah!"

Merewether thought of the admiral, now so gross that he required assistance to enter his carriage, a caricature of the man who had made his reputation as the most dashing frigate captain of the decade, and wondered if money was sufficient compensation for such degeneration. He made a final effort to lend a word of cheer.

"This should not take long. We will have the siege battery set up by morning, and the Arabs are not noted for prolonged resistance to a siege." He hoped he could make his escape, the glass was almost empty, and he certainly did not desire another. Dunbar appeared to come to the same conclusion, he drank off his gin, rose and resumed his expression of goodwill.

"I suppose I'm in a blue funk, but I feel better after a bit of fellowship with another naval officer. Thank you, Merewether, and I expect to rely upon you implicitly. God knows, I have no one else." It was a left-handed compliment, but he could not doubt Dunbar's sincerity for the moment at least. He took his departure from a deck crowded with hands hoisting out the thirty-two-pounders to replace the lost forty-twos.

In the early morning light, Pitt's decks had little activity. Only the most inferior ratings were visible aside from the watch. With the Marine contingent and fifty-odd qualified gunners ashore, the ship served little useful purpose in the operation for the moment. It was merely a headquarters and supply depot, with the readiness to repel an unlikely attack from the sea. Merewether scanned the beach through the glass, examining the two batteries of light field guns the Joasmis had erected on the western beach outside the walls of the town. A single broadside from moderate range would knock down the sand and timber revetments that shielded them, and the back side of the fort was evidently much lighter construction than its northern face. He suddenly wondered exactly how much water there was off the town, and realized he had taken the estimates entirely on faith. There were not a half dozen soundings noted on the chart.

"Messenger! Would you ask Mister Dobbs to see me at his convenience?"

While Merewether waited, he examined the hands now appearing on deck after breakfast to turn to on ship's work. They no longer seemed to be the sullen crew who had witnessed the executions last month. The days at sea, the storm, and now the exhilaration of lying at anchor in the face of the enemy appeared to have swept away the unhappy mood. The old adage concerning idle hands was true enough, he decided. He saw Dobbs's head appear in the companionway.

"You see the batteries, Dobbs. I want a survey made of the bottom between this anchorage and a point some six hundred yards off the beach. Cast your lead at twenty-foot intervals on lines of bearings . . ." He saw that he had lost Dobbs, and started over. "What I mean is, I want the soundings recorded on the chart in the form of a grid, each on a bearing from an identifiable point ashore, so as to make a true profile of the bottom between here and the town. It is possible, what with the tidal range and the northwest gales that some channels could be discovered . . ."

Dobbs's face cleared. "Aye aye, sir. And since we may be in range of those batteries, I'll take the quarterboat to make as small a target as possible."

Merewether soon heard the coxswain pass the word for his boat crew. Half an hour later, it had commenced its monotonous task, Dobbs hunched over the chart, recording the leadsman's chant, while the oarsmen pulled on a succession of courses set by the boat compass's bearings on landmarks ashore. The enterprise might be wasted effort, but at least the Company would have, for whatever it was worth, first-hand information of the bottom profile of the sea west of Ras ul Khymah. And now, it was high time he went ashore to see for himself how his hands were faring. He called away the gig.

Merewether arrived ashore in time to witness the emplacement of the third thirty-two-pounder. It had been dragged a half mile across the spit by the sweating hands, on boards laid over the sand for the trucks of its carriage to roll on. The carpenters had knocked together a platform of heavy timbers to support it and its tackles within the sandbagged redoubt. The gun was inched into place under the supervision of a paunchy, self-important Royal Navy gunner, and the tackles secured. So far, aside from the abortive cavalry sortie yesterday morning, Ras ul Khymah remained ominously silent, with only an occasional figure silhouetted briefly on the parapet where the blood-red flag flew defiantly from its tall staff. The fourth gun was approaching, followed by a file of lascars bearing two thirty-two-pound round shot each slung over their shoulders in nets. The operation appeared to be progressing satisfactorily, and Merewether turned to go and find Larkin and his party.

The battery of twelve-pounders manned by the Bombay forces opened up, and he paused to watch. A few splinters flew from the wall, but there was no visible effect. The ragged salvo from the fort came as a surprise, missiles ploughed up the sand in a wide area about the gun emplacements, at least two striking solidly against the sandbagged emplacements. The file of lascars scattered like a covey of quail, leaving the shot in the sand. A dozen feet away, a seaman began to scream hoarsely; what had been his face now a featureless mass of blood. A shot had blasted up a great abrasive gout of sand as it ricocheted, to obliterate skin, nose, lips and eyes in an instant, leaving teeth and white bone gleaming through the torrents of blood. Fortunately, the man died in moments of the massive hemorrhage. He had been the only casualty.

"ere! Get on about yer business!" shouted the gunner in the accents of Cheapside. Petty officers were rounding up the lascars and chivvying them back to pick up their burdens of shot. "Sor, we'll be ready to open fire 'ere in arf a mo', and give those buggers sommat more to think on!" he continued in belated recognition of Merewether's rank.

He traced the trajectory of one of the projectiles to find it still smoking in the sand a hundred yards behind the battery. It was merely a round stone, the size of a thirty-two-pound shot, but probably no more than a third the weight. He found other stone missiles, some -shattered, together with nine- and twelve-pound iron shot, but no thirty-two-pounder iron balls. The pirates were evidently in short supply of effective munitions. He saw a powder monkey come trotting towards the battery, a covered copper bucket in either hand, bringing up the powder charge. It was only a few moments before two of the massive guns spoke, while the others were still being emplaced.

One shot was short, but it ricocheted to tear a gap in the light wall at the top of the parapet. The other hit squarely in the eroded target area of the wall, already pocked by the steady fire of the Bombay Artillery Battery. It knocked out a cloud of splinters, but it was a long way from penetrating; the stone under the mortar chinks was still sound. As Merewether came back to the battery, he saw that wet cloth pads had been draped over the barrels of the guns to cool them. Even so, after a half dozen shots, the metal was too hot to touch and it was hazardous to reload the weapons.

"ave to slack off, sor," explained the gunner. "Let them cool down a bit. These big guns 'olds the 'eat a deal longer than the smaller ones".

Looking towards the fort, Merewether saw a little cluster of men emerge in front of the wall from some concealed sallyport. They appeared to be searching for something on the ground, stooping, then rising in the posture of a man carrying a heavy weight to disappear into the fort again. He could not fathom their mission for the moment, and took shelter from the blistering sun in the shade of the sandbag parapet to watch the gunners again wet down the cloth pads on the guns with sea water. It evaporated almost instantly, leaving a rime of salt encrusting the barrels. The gunner put his hand gingerly on the breach. and opened his mouth to make some observation, but it was drowned out by the roar of the salvo from the fort.

Three tremendous shocks went through the redoubt. There were men down, and the gunner was looking incredulously at the blood gushing from the wrist where a moment before his hand had been. They had taken three direct hits, not by round stone balls, but by Navy issue thirty-two-pound shot. Merewether realized now what the stoopers had been doing: The pirates had come out to retrieve undamaged balls in the sand, and had now returned them with interest!

As senior officer present, he took command of the battery, saw a tourniquet applied to the half fainting gunner, and ordered him transported to the army surgeon's tent. The other wounds were slight, the guns intact, but the redoubt was damaged and there would be more to come.

"Stations!" he rallied the gun crews. "Load." The hands resumed their duties steadily enough.

Just as the gun captain was inserting the quill of priming powder in the touch-hole, the fort fired again and he felt the impact of the balls against the face of the redoubt. This was good shooting. A few more such hits and the emplacement would be demolished. Merewether shifted the point of aim of the gun, peering through the notches in breech and muzzle that served as crude sights, signaling the man with the hand spike as he levered the carriage around in train a fraction of an inch at a time.

"Mark!" The shots had come from three narrow embrasures halfway up the wall and fifty yards to the right of the former point of aim. Merewether moved clear of the gun.

"Fire!"

The gun roared out, but the smoke did not obscure the view from this vantage point, and a gaping hole appeared in the wall between two of the embrasures giving the face of the fortress a snaggle-toothed expression. The lack of lateral support in the wall occasioned by the openings on either side made this point of aim vulnerable to the heavy guns. He heard commands given to the Bombay Artillery Battery in its adjacent emplacement, and the twelve-pounders shifted their point of aim to the breach. If the fort's thirty-two pounders were not already out of service, this steady bombardment should make the position untenable, and prevent further fire from those formidable weapons, though the fortress mounted at least fifty smaller guns.

"Same point of aim," he told the gun captains. "And shift the guns a bit in train for each shot so as to enlarge the hole." The beginning breach was far too high on the wall to serve as a point of entry by infantry except with the dangerous expedient of scaling ladders. But at least it was a beginning. The third gun was in place, almost ready to open fire, and the fourth was on its way from the beach. He heard his name called and turned around.

"Sir, Colonel Smith sends his compliments and hopes you will join him at his headquarters at your convenience." The speaker was a beardless subaltern, wearing the aiguillettes of an aide-de-camp on his shoulder. He was standing at salute. Merewether returned the salute, and the officer brought his hand down smartly, but remained at rigid attention.

"Very well. Carry on."

The youth about faced, and marched out of the redoubt in the direction of the army camp. Smith was evidently a stickler in the formalities of military courtesy.

Oh, well, Merewether thought, might as well find out what that abrasive army commander wanted without undue delay. He left orders to continue the bombardment with the senior gunner's mate, and walked towards the army camp through the blistering sunlight, feeling the sweat trickling down the small of his back, to find the headquarters tent marked with the regimental colors. A soldier stood rigidly in red coat and full field equipment before the entrance, oblivious to the sun.

"Captain Merewether to see Colonel Smith." The sentry shifted his eyes to look him up and down without moving his head. Merewether realized that he did not cut a very impressive figure, powder grimed, jacketless, shirt open at the collar, wearing the broad plaited straw hat with the handkerchief, now dried, hanging out from under it to shield his neck. "Come, man," he said a bit sharply. "The Colonel wishes to see me!" At this, the soldier turned his head, made an unintelligible utterance, and resumed his stance. In a moment, a grizzled sergeant appeared beside the tent.

"And what is yer business with the Colonel, mister?"

"I am Captain Merewether of the Bombay Marine. Colonel Smith sent me a message by his aide."

"Oh," said the sergeant, saluting reluctantly. "That one. I'll send word." He disappeared into what must be the guard tent. In a few minutes, the subaltern appeared, held aside the flap, and Merewether entered.

Colonel Smith was sitting on a stool before his field desk, stripped to the waist. The side of the tent had been propped up to admit the mild northwest breeze, but the place was nevertheless stifling, and sweat rolled down the hairy torso.

"Well, you came promptly enough," Smith growled, looking up with cold grey eyes. "Pull up a stool." Merewether seated himself gingerly on one of the folding wood and leather contraptions, and looked about. The tent was furnished with spartan simplicity: only two brass-bound campaign chests set at either end of a cot along one side, and the unfolded desk in the centre with two more stools before it. "Dunbar and Seton should be here before long," the Colonel added.

"I was already ashore at the battery," Merewether explained.

The Colonel picked up a cup and drank. "Only cold tea," he said. "Spirits in this climate don't agree with me." He turned his attention back to his desk, picking up a quill as though to write then pausing to re-read what appeared to be from upside down a report of several sheets. Merewether sat in discomfort, sweat oozing down his spine and belly, a premonition of prickly heat beginning to creep down under his arms and belt. He hoped Dunbar and Seton would soon appear, then heard their voices outside.

"Well, gentlemen," said Smith, once they were seated. "I'm plain spoken, and I'll get to the point at once. I don't like the situation. I don't like the progress you have made in establishing a siege. My men are camped here with nothing to occupy them. There have been three bloody brawls since we landed. We have had twenty cases of what the surgeon called heat stroke. Can you give me an unvarnished report of where we stand?" His eyes glinted under heavy brows as he looked first at, Dunbar, then Seton. Dunbar colored a bit at the tone, and looked at Seton, then at Merewether, before making a careful reply.

"A breach has been started by the thirty-two-pounders, and they are enlarging it with every shot, but it must be twenty feet above the bottom of the dry moat at the present. With scaling ladders . . ."

"No! " exploded Smith. "No, and no again! I'll not have my men slaughtered in any such asinine venture. I was promised a respectable breach would be blasted through the wall by bombardment or your sappers, and the guns silenced before the attack. Lord knows, it will be hard enough fighting from house to house once we gain entry to the town!" He glared from one to the other a moment, his bare torso heaving.

"The full heavy battery has only just commenced its bombardment," said Dunbar. "We've lost one man killed, and a warrant gunner wounded so far. Give the battery a chance, Smith." His square ruddy face still wore its expression of good humor, but it appeared nearly ready to crack. Seton sat quiet, looking from colonel to captain, a curious expression of triumph on his narrow face, as though he knew a secret not shared by the others.

"Very well, Dunbar," said Smith in a milder tone. "All the artillery is under your control. But I warn you, give me a respectable breach at ground level, or nearly so, within forty-eight hours, or I re-embark my force and leave you to the tender mercies of Seton here and the Imam's troops!" Seton bounded to his feet. Just as suddenly he resumed his seat without uttering a word.

Merewether had watched the curious tableau with foreboding; the three-headed monster of command was snapping and growling, a bit more and each set of jaws would be ripping and tearing at the other's throats. Dunbar obviously was near to losing control of his temper. But Seton had resumed his cryptic expression of self-satisfaction.

"Colonel, I shall set out the details of this remarkable interview, and your stipulation — more accurately, your unreasonable ultimatum — in my reports to the Governor-General," said Dunbar in a tight voice.

"Quite all right," Smith said. "My complaints are already in writing here on my desk, lacking only signature and seal!" He pointed his finger at the sheets. "And you say, 'remarkable'? I've cited chapter and verse for each of your remarkable failures and blunders!"

Merewether realized Dunbar's self-control had reached the breaking point. At the risk of involving himself, he decided to intervene before the irretrievable challenge was thrown.

"Gentlemen, I suggest we adjourn this council of war. The Colonel had made himself plain enough, and duty calls all of us."

There was a moment of silence, punctuated only by the heavy thuds of the siege guns in the background. By common consent, Dunbar and Seton stood up, wheeled and marched rigidly out of the tent without a word or backward glance. Merewether rose to follow them. Smith caught his eye and crooked his finger, then looked past him out the entrance. After a moment, he threw back his head and laughed.

"Well, Captain, did I throw it in hot enough for them?" he inquired, a sardonic grin now creasing the hard face. "I intended to blast them both off their backsides! I fully expected to be called out by one or both, but it is just as well that you spoke when you did. Such affairs of honor in the field tend to become messy."

Merewether hesitated. He was in a ticklish position. Being technically under the command of Commodore Dunbar it was impossible for him to agree with Colonel Smith, but he could not offend him either. He despised himself for the equivocation, but felt compelled to adopt it.

"Then I would say you accomplished your purpose, colonel," he said.

"You know, Merewether, this is no major campaign, important mainly to the Company, but bungled, it may wreck a man's career. General Sir John Stanley goes back to England on leave in October, and he has promised me a brevet as major-general to command Fort William during his absence." He paused, looking keenly at Merewether. "I'm almost forty, nothing spectacular in my record, and I don't descend even from a county family, but I've made my own way in the Army and with the brevet in my record I'll be in line for the permanent commission."

Merewether could sympathize with the man, appreciate his anxiety to get the operation over quickly and effectively without a bloody butcher's bill to stain his record. "I wish you luck, Colonel," he said. "Of course, the batteries are making every effort to enlarge the breach."

He made his escape in the twilight to go back to Pitt, hearing the measured reports of the siege guns from across the water. He could not make out the effect on the breach he had started high up, but if the bombardment persisted, the wall eventually must fall. He sponged the salt rime from his body with a pint of fresh water, consumed a light meal and dropped off to sleep immediately.

Merewether surfaced to consciousness as though rising from a great depth. Midshipman Marlowe was tugging anxiously at his shoulder.

"Sir, oh sir, Mister MacCamy says the magazine must have exploded over on the beach!" He repeated himself as Merewether tried to grasp the import of what the boy was saying.

"All right, lad, I'll come!" He struggled into the fresh uniform Sangh had hung out, then into the heavy landing force boots, still soggy with the sweat of yesterday's shore excursions. By the clock, it was almost six bells in the middle watch. On deck he found MacCamy and Whaley peering through glasses at the shore two miles away. He could see lights there dancing like fireflies, evidently torches and lanterns.

"What is it?" he demanded.

"I'm not sure," replied Whaley. "A heavy explosion, followed by a series of smaller ones . . ."

"It appeared to come from the gun emplacements," interposed MacCamy. "And then there was a bit of musket fire."

"Gall away the rescue party, and send for Buttram and Mefford. Pistols and cutlasses for the boat crew." The launch and cutter were already in the water, riding to the boat boom rigged on the port side, but it was a quarter of an hour before they moved towards the shore.

As they approached the landing area, there was a brisk challenge out of the darkness, evidently from a Sepoy Marine outpost. Merewether stood up in the boat and opened the slide of his dark lantern to focus its ray of light upon himself.

"Pitt!" shouted the coxswain. The sentry apparently was satisfied, and the keel grated on the beach.

Once ashore a small party was left to guard the boats while the rest pressed forward in a rough formation across the spit, stumbling in the soft sand, burdened with their gear. Doctors Buttram and Mefford panted along beside Merewether, their medical kits borne by four loblolly attendants. It was no more than a quarter of an hour before they reached the site of the battery.

The sandbagged revetments had vanished, the heavy timber platforms which had supported the thirty-two-pounders were in splinters. The guns themselves, including the lighter field pieces, were scattered over a wide area, dismounted, half-buried in the sand. There was a crater, forty feet across and more than a fathom deep, where the sand was blackened and the acrid odor of sulfur hung in the air. There were dead and wounded men scattered about in the flickering light of the torches, with three army surgeons and their orderlies trying to minister to the living. Buttram and Mefford took off their jackets and pitched in with the rescue party to lend assistance. Merewether heard footsteps in the sand, and recognized Colonel Smith a dozen yards away, formally attired, scarlet coat and all.

"You've certainly played hell now!"

The injustice of the accusation set Merewether's blood to boiling. He opened his mouth to reply in kind, to hurl or accept the inevitable challenge, then caught the glint of gold lace on blue cloth to his left, and realized that he was not the target of the remark.

“Me!” shouted Dunbar, coming into view, in outraged tones. “It was your light companies that let the buggers in, and never a shot or word of warning!” Merewether saw an expression of doubt across Smith’s face, and the balance of the conversation between the colonel and commodore became inaudible. He looked about to see Jemadar Gunny approaching.

“Sah, we were posted to guard the right flank where the cavalry made its attack. I think the Joasmis sent a party crawling along the beach to the east along the lagoon behind the light infantry pickets and struck the men off watch first. My men heard pistol shots after the attack had commenced and sent a platoon to investigate. The enemy used scimitars on the sleeping men first, then overwhelmed the gun crews. They moved the powder barrels from the magazine into the redoubt and exploded it to destroy the guns.”

“How much of a breach has been made in the wall?”

“It has been widened, but it is still a good ten feet above the bottom of the ditch.”

“Were any of your men injured?”

“Only slight wounds, sah. They were more than a hundred yards away when the explosion came.”

It had been a daring and incredibly successful sally with only the lightest of casualties, and Merewether felt reluctant admiration for the enterprise and courage of the beleaguered Arabs. They had effectively destroyed the siege train of the expedition for the present, and if Smith held to his forty-eight-hour ultimatum, had saved their town as a base of operations.

“Thank you, Gunny.” He moved back to the nightmarish scene.

Each heavy gun had had three crews of sixteen men to man it around the clock, two hours on duty, and four off. Most of the men on duty had escaped the massacre by scattering in all directions from the redoubts when the enemy appeared, but of the one hundred and twenty-eight men off watch under their tarpaulin shelters, thirty-three had been killed outright in their sleep, Buttram reported, and another twenty-nine wounded, some mortally. *Pitt* had lost seven killed and three wounded out of the three crews she had supplied.

Merewether heard his name called, and joined the cluster of officers to find that Seton was now present.

"No need to wash our dirty linen in public," said Smith. "And Seton here says he has momentous news to impart. We'll adjourn to my quarters."

The conference in the flickering light of two lanterns in the tent resembled that of yesterday only superficially. The chill in the pre-dawn air made it comfortable enough to keep coats and jackets on. Smith pulled out a drawer of one of his campaign chests to produce a dark bottle, brandy by the looks of it, and four silver cups from a leather case.

"Purely medicinal, gentlemen," he said, pouring them full in a row. It was an excellent Spanish vintage.

"Now, Seton, what is your news?" demanded Dunbar. Seton leaned forward to sniff the aroma from his cup, then raised his head to display a triumphant expression.

"You have seen fit to belittle and disparage me and the Imam's troops," he said slowly. "But now I alone possess the means to take Ras ul Khymah without the firing of another shot or the loss of a single man!" He looked about the circle, a benign smile on his thin face, then raised the cup to sniff again.

"Get on with it, man!" snapped Dunbar impatiently. Seton ignored the interjection as he enjoyed the aroma again, then finished off the brandy in a gulp, and held the cup out for more. Merewether watched the scene as though it were a play; what solution Seton fancied he possessed, he could not fathom. Certainly his force had neither the numbers nor inclination to mount a successful attack on the town.

"You gentlemen who follow merely the profession of arms do not understand that there are stratagems and expedients in many instances mightier than the sword," he continued pedantically. Dunbar opened his mouth, then resigned himself to wait and hear Seton out. "I confess I was disappointed," continued Seton, "at the force the Imam made available for this expedition, but among its numbers there are several quite accomplished men with acquaintances, even kinsmen, who are with the Joasmis in Ras ul Khymah." He looked around the group again with a slight smile. Merewether felt a flush of exasperation, wishing that the officer would come to the point. Smith poured another tot of brandy for himself, his hard face perfectly impassive.

"Take your time, Seton," said the colonel. "You have nearly forty hours before I order my force to re-embark." The remark seemed to amuse Seton. He threw back his head, laughed, then sobered. After three tots of brandy his face was flushed, but he appeared to be in complete control of himself.

"Within an hour of our landing, I had my intelligence within the fortress, and by nightfall had a complete report of the situation there." He shook his head as Smith offered more brandy. "As for small arms, the Joasmis are well supplied. They have some four thousand troops in the town, and are prepared to make a building-to-building resistance if the fortress is breached. They have a great store of powder, captured in the Company store ship *Princess Caroline* last year. As for missiles, they have an ample store, but for thirty-two-pound shot — and they expect to recover enough of our spent balls to supply their largest guns. They have a three-month supply of grain, and their wells flow freely. Their spirits are high, as witness the attack just made and the destruction of our siege train . . ."

"Are you saying we should abandon this operation?" Dunbar demanded in a hard tone.

"I should be, but for one factor," replied Seton. "And this I shall come to in my own time." He sat on the stool staring a moment at Dunbar over his laced fingers. "I only wonder whether you possess the courage to act when I disclose it!"

"What!" shouted Dunbar, leaping to his feet.

"Wait him out," said Smith. "It had better be good."

"Back in '64," continued Seton. "Major Hector Munro of the 89th Native Infantry under Clive suppressed a mutiny among the Moslem Sepoys. He executed twenty-five of the mutineers by blowing them from the mouths of his guns." Merewether had heard of the savage mode of execution employed in more unsettled days as an example to strike terror into the hearts of the Indians in a manner that a simple hanging or firing squad somehow failed to do. The Moslems had always reckoned it an ignominious and shameful death, to be bound spreadeagled over the muzzle of a field gun, and then blasted to bloody rags, but he wondered at the relevance of the anecdote. Seton continued, "I've heard that even Arthur Wellesley used it on occasion."

"Interesting," said Smith. Seton went on as though he had not heard the comment.

"Yesterday afternoon my intelligence reported that a considerable number of women and children had been evacuated upon the appearance of our fleet, including the wives and children of Sheikh Hussein Bin Ali and his brother, Saood Bin Suggur, the rulers of the Joasmis." Seton looked about the assemblage, eyes glittering. "They were sojourning in a house some twelve miles south of here under guard. I knew immediately my course of action! A mounted party, led by myself, surprised their guard last night, and seized the four wives of Hussein Bin Ali and three of his brother's, together with nine children, including the eldest son of Bin Ali."

"Well, I'm damned!" said Smith with evident admiration. "Should be able to make the Sheikh jump through hoops holding those hostages!" Dunbar's face had lighted up too.

"Where are they?"

"I delivered them within the hour on board *Pitt* with a detachment of my troops to serve as guards. They are occupying the flag cabin . . ." It was Merewether's turn to be angry.

"By what authority —" he commenced.

"It is the most secure place to hold our hostages, and I can conceive of no valid objection on your part." said Seton evenly. "But you had already come ashore, and I could not inform you."

Merewether resumed his seat. Better wait the man out, he decided, though he knew in his bones what was coming.

"Will those buggers over there honor a flag of truce?" inquired Smith.

"I think so," said Seton. "Provided one of my native officers carries it. Besides, I have here a talisman the Sheikh cannot doubt!" He held out a glittering gold amulet set with a single large ruby. It appeared to be made for a child. "This is the device worn by his eldest son as a token that he is heir apparent to the sheikdom."

"Now," said Dunbar. "How best can we couch our ultimatum?"

"I have it already written out." Seton pulled a folded paper from his pocket. "I will read it for you: 'To Sheik Hussein Bin Ali, Most Revered Leader of the Joasmis, Greetings: Be it known that we have as our honored guests, your wives and those of your princely brother, Saood Bin Suggur, together with nine of your children, including Salim Ahmed, your firstborn son and heir apparent. We are desolated to inform you that unless within twenty-four hours hence you lay down your arms and march out of Ras ul Khymah in unconditional surrender, we shall be compelled at intervals of one hour to blow your wives and children from the mouths of guns until your line is extinct. Should you deem it prudent to accept our terms, you and your brother, Saood Bin Suggur, shall signify the fact by an approach to our lines under a white flag to surrender your persons to us as further sureties for the behavior of your forces. Herein fail not!' " Seton looked up, his thin face alight with pride. "Of course, I shall dress up the language a bit when I translate it into Arabic."

"Twenty-four hours," said Dunbar. "Why not make it twelve?"

"Or six," said Smith. "We hold all the cards now!"

"No," said Seton. "I know the nature of these men. Too short a time and they would defy us in bravado. Give them time for their imaginations to work a bit."

"Bye the bye," asked Dunbar. "How old is this heir apparent?"

"Oh, four, possibly five. The Sheikh only came to power last year. He is still quite a young man."

Merewether felt outrage boil up and course through his body as he looked at these three callous men sitting around the desk in the yellow lantern light in their cold-blooded moment of triumph. That they would even consider the slaughter of women and small children seemed incredible, no matter how important the end to be gained might be to them. He decided instantly that he would have no part of this monstrous scheme of blackmail, and if it came to be accounted mutiny, let them make the most of it. When he spoke, his voice cracked as it had that day at Bombay when he ordered the mutineers turned off.

"Gentlemen . . ." All three officers looked at him. "I cannot agree with this course of action. It violates every law of war and humanity . . ."

"What of that, sir?" snapped Smith "We are not dealing with Europeans, but with blood-thirsty pirates, and we must meet them at their own game, fight fire with fire! You saw what they just did out there to our siege train . . ."

"The conventions of war, as Europeans observe them, do not obtain in this operation," said Dunbar pompously.

"Entirely a legitimate stratagem of war in these parts," said Seton. "Even Cornwallis took the sons of Tipu Sultan as hostages for his good behavior. Besides, under the operation order you have no authority over its conduct, and if you did, you have been out-voted, sir!"

Merewether considered for a moment simply washing his hands of the affair. He could easily enough disavow any responsibility for the atrocity in his reports of the operation, and let these men justify their own action. And then, it was entirely possible that Seton's estimate of the reaction of the Arab Sheikhs was accurate, that with twenty-four hours to consider their situation, they would capitulate. Success in the capture of Ras ul Khymah would not invite close examination of the means employed, while failure or even delay would almost certainly be fatal to the ambitions of these men. He was, he realized, perilously close to wrecking his own career. A report of insubordination, or even a simple failure to co-operate, would surely deprive him of any further command in the Marine. He had no present solution for the dilemma in which the expedition found itself other than the obvious one of ferrying more heavy guns ashore to blast a breach in the wall, and the time was far too short for that. He temporized, despising himself for his sudden irresolution.

"Are you certain that Sheikh Hussein Bin All will capitulate? Could it only make him resist all the more?"

"I am certain," snapped Seton. "This boy is the apple of his father's eye, the living image of the Sheikh." Seton held up the glittering amulet to the light again.

"We would prefer, Captain, to make this decision unanimously, though you exercise no authority over the operation," Dunbar said.

The sudden realization came to Merewether that two of these three officers were by no means as certain either of the success or the morality of their gambit as they wished to appear. If the blackmail failed and the Sheikh defied them, their hands would be forced and they would be compelled to commence the executions. There was grave doubt that British seamen with their traditional sentimental regard for women and children of whatever race would carry out an order to blast such innocent beings from the muzzle of a gun. He decided to see if he might shake the resolution of one or more of the officers and divide the triumvirate.

"Of course, George Barlow, my wife's uncle, might well agree with your plan, but Gibby Elliott is a somewhat different kettle of fish," he said offhandedly. He saw Smith and Dunbar look up sharply at his use of the familiar diminutive in referring to the Governor-General. Undoubtedly, they were recalling that he had been closeted with Minto in chambers last January when they were ushered in for the conference, and suddenly were uncertain as to how close and cordial his acquaintance with the Governor-General might be. And Barlow as Governor of Madras was still a factor to be reckoned with in India, and Merewether had reminded them that he was related to him by marriage. He allowed the doubts to take root, realizing the fragility of the bluff he was attempting. He was particularly conscious of Seton's anger.

"I fear that once your ultimatum is delivered, you are irrevocably committed, and upon continued resistance would be compelled to carry out your threat . . ."

"Balderdash!" shouted Seton. "In my judgment the mere delivery of the ultimatum will result in immediate surrender —"

"But if it does not, do you conceive that British seamen will carry out your order to execute helpless women and children? And think of the stir in the Ladies' Literary Circle, not to mention the cries of 'shame' in the *Calcutta Gazette* . . ." He saw Smith look at Dunbar a moment as though seeking a signal. "I suggest you defer any ultimatum for the present. The hostages will keep, and the Sheikh will soon enough learn of their unexplained absence from their place of refuge. Uncertainty may very well bring him out under a flag of truce without our having to commit ourselves." Merewether saw glances exchanged again between Smith and Dunbar, and suddenly was certain that his bluff had succeeded, at least with those two officers.

"I think your suggestion has some logic and merit," said Colonel Smith slowly, as Dunbar nodded. "And I particularly like the idea of not immediately exposing our trumps to those buggers. I am inclined to extend by twenty-four hours the re-embarkation of my troops in the expectation that the matter will be resolved within that time either by surrender, or by you and Dunbar completing the breach you have started."

"Yes," said Dunbar. "And in recognition of your eloquent plea to conclude the operation by conventional means, I direct that you proceed to do so."

"Possibly you may prevail on Gibby and George to bear a hand," said Seton. "In the meantime, guard well our hostages!"

The implications took a minute to sink in. For Merewether had won his plea to refrain for the time being from the monstrous use of Joasmi women and children to compel surrender of the fortress of Ras ul Khymah, only to have the entire responsibility for the success of the operation devolve upon him. *Pitt* was the only ship in the Marine squadron which mounted thirty-two-pounders. While he could require working parties from other ships present, it would still be a back-breaking evolution to hoist the guns out and into lighters, then to drag them through the sand to the site of the battery. Merewether experienced sudden doubt that even the twenty-four-hour extension would suffice to accomplish the mission. He struggled to conceal the dismay he felt.

"Do I have full authority and discretion?" he demanded.

"Anything your heart desires," replied Dunbar airily. "And now, I think we may well adjourn this council since the matter rests in capable hands."

In the broad daylight, the sun outlined the masts of the pirate vessels trapped in the landlocked lagoon across the spit. The site of the battery with its blackened crater and debris was deserted but for a party of Sepoy Marines sojourning in shallow pits nearby, the dead and wounded removed, with only brown stains in the sand to mark where they had lain. Merewether had time to reflect as the launch made its way back to *Pitt,* the sleepy landing force huddled together in the bottom still, though the pre-dawn chill had melted away.

He did not regret the stand he had taken as to the hostages; his conscience would permit no other course. But he resented the sudden turn of events by which the commanders of the operation had foisted off their responsibilities upon him. In his preoccupation, he brushed aside Dobb's attempt to speak to him as he came on board.

"Early breakfast, Mister Dobbs, and I want all hands on deck as soon as possible. Send the boatswain, gunner and carpenter to see me at their earliest convenience . . ." And seeing Whaley approaching. "You, too, Mister Whaley, in the cabin in ten minutes . . ." He hurried on; aft, already feeling the precious minutes ticking by, to pull up short as he glimpsed the strange spectacle in his ship.

There was a party of Arab soldiers squatting in a semi-circle on the port side outside the entrance to the flag quarters, Brown Bess muskets furnished by a generous King George to his ally, the Imam of Oman, laid carelessly aside. These were dark, hawk-nosed men, robed in white, wearing the silver badges of the Imam's service, a part of his scanty force contributed to the expedition. The scene bore little resemblance to a disciplined performance of military duty. Half a dozen children tumbled and played among the soldiers. There was one sturdy olive-skinned boy, evidently the oldest of them, with dark liquid brown eyes and a ready smile, who clambered on to the shoulders of the squatting men to slide head first down their backs to the deck with squeals of joy. Hands had paused nearby in their work to watch the sport with weak sentimental smiles on their faces, and Merewether shuddered at the thought of being called upon to destroy this attractive, happy child, evidently the Sheikh's first born, along with the others. A fat young woman, veiled to her eyes, called out sharply, and the children disengaged themselves from their play to run to her in the cabin doorway. The gaze of a frightened doe met Merewether's over the veil for an instant before she turned to herd the brood back into the cabin. He saw Dobbs coming aft and remembered his brusque interruption of the young man earlier.

"Oh, Mister Dobbs. I believe you had something to say to me at the gangway."

"Yes, sir. I have finished the chart of the soundings between the ship and the beach. It is in your cabin." Merewether tried to remember how long ago he had assigned this task to Dobbs. Two days? Three? He had lost track of the calendar during this period of labor, alarums and midnight conferences.

"Indeed, Mr. Dobbs. I have a meeting just now. Come in afterwards and show me what you found." He went into the cabin calling for Sangh to pour the tea. There was a packet on his desk, endorsed in Dobb's small precise hand, "Soundings off western shore of Ras ul Khymah." But he took no time to examine it for the present. His officers were at the door.

The council of war was brief and the warrant officers departed, shouting for their leading petty officers. The first lieutenant would co-ordinate the complicated task of loading four ponderous monsters into lighters, together with powder, shot and tools. Whaley soon left in the launch and cutter to press enough boatswain's mates and able seamen out of other ships into service to provide the skilled manpower, while the boatswain and his mates began to lay out the lines, blocks, tackles, spars and gear that would be woven together to lift out the guns. Dobbs had apparently been lurking just outside the companion, and the chart with its grid of tiny figures was soon spread on the desk.

"I can't see a sounding of more than two fathoms, and most of them are a half or quarter less," Merewether complained.

"Yes, sir, but I noticed a curious phenomenon. Here is *Pitt's* present position just off the bank," he said, pointing a finger. "On the west edge you see a sounding that is some three-quarters of a fathom more than the others. Now watch!" He began to trace a faint pencil line on the chart, first northwardly, then in an arc through east to almost due south, thence in another arc almost north again. The line formed a sprawling reversed letter "S" on the chart some two miles across the bank, its base nearly parallel to, and some six hundred yards distant from, the western edge of the town of Ras ul Khymah.

"Well?" inquired Merewether, leaning forward to look more closely at the chart.

"This line passes through a series of the deeper soundings, all at least three and a half fathoms," explained Dobbs. "It indicates that there is what amounts to a stream bed cut in the bottom of the sea. I've read about such things during my studies in navigation." He looked up at Merewether, his plain blunt face alight "I've adjusted the soundings for mean low tide as well, sir, and following this old channel there's at least two feet more water than *Pitt* draws all the way in!"

Merewether knew he could trust the accuracy of Dobb's observations. To be sure, there was always the chance of a rock or shallow spot protruding towards the surface between soundings, but it would take relatively little time for the quarter boat to follow out of the channel confirming its depth at every point and placing unobtrusive buoys to mark it. Why the thing was perfect! He could take *Pitt* right up to the beach and demolish the citadel from its backside! He looked up to meet Dobb's eves, opening his mouth to issue the order, then saw the altered expression.

"There's only one difficulty, sir. The entrance is blocked from the sea by a wreck . . ." Merewether stared at Dobbs. He might have known it was too good to be true. He wished Dobbs had never called the matter to his attention.

"But I have a scheme that may let us enter in spite of it . . ."

"Well?"

"Over the south end of the wreck, the water lacks only a little more than two feet of being deep enough to allow the ship to pass over it. By using those four lighters as camels, two to a side, we should be able to lift her at least three feet . . ."

The idea was by no means novel. He had seen camels or pontoons often enough employed to lift a stranded ship from a bar or mud bank, or to enable a deep draft vessel to cross the sill of a shallow graving dock. But the idea of taking *Pitt* into a channel whose only exit was solidly blocked did not appeal to Merewether. He would be willing enough to take his chances on traversing the underwater stream bed if the maneuver promised an early accomplishment of the destruction of Ras ul Khymah, but he had no intention of sticking his head into a blind hole with no assurance of getting back out.

There were too many uncertain contingencies. The lighters were the property of the Royal Navy, and he had the uncomfortable feeling that if his approach to the fort were successful, he might very well find them unavailable to lift his ship back out. Then there would be the very real technical problem of positioning the cables that would pass under *Pitt's* keel, attached at either end to a lighter, so that the lift would be uniform. It would be necessary to flood the barges almost to the gunwales, probably by the expedient of boring holes in their bottoms, with the risk of miscalculation and sinking them. It would be a tremendous all hands evolution to rig the thing, pump out the lighters, move the ship across the barrier, and reverse the process on the other side. He did not for a moment consider attempting to take *Pitt,* supported by the camels through the winding channel on the chart. The lash-up would be completely unmanageable; the partially exposed rudder unable to get enough bite to control the unwieldy mass.

"No!" said Merewether. "And again, no!" He saw the expectant expression fade and disappointment replace it. It had been an ingenious idea Dobbs had conceived, and it was difficult to back away from using the channel he had discovered. With two hours of uninterrupted broadsides thundering into the soft underbelly of the fortress, he would stake his life upon the surrender. Too bad, too damn bad! Then to temper his refusal, he made an idle inquiry. "And this wreck. Can you determine its size, age, condition?"

"Only generally, sir. I had the carpenter make me a water glass after my soundings found it, and when the light is just right you can see the outlines quite clearly. Of course, it is all covered with weed and barnacles, lying about half on its side, and sand drifted against it to seaward."

"I want to see it for myself."

It was little more than half a mile to the point where a piece of timber protruded from the water anchored to the bottom with a stone to serve as a buoy.

"She lies roughly north and south," explained Dobbs. "I would guess her to be about two-thirds the size of *Pitt.*" He looked up at the morning sun. "With this light, I think you can follow her outline as we row slowly." He handed over the water glass.

The contraption was a truncated four-sided pyramid, a pane of glass caulked and sealed with pitch forming its base. Merewether looked in the small end, his head blocking off the light, to see through the greenish water right to the bottom, glare and reflection eliminated. There was a dark mass just to his left, shimmering with weed, that he judged to be the stern of the hulk. Dobbs conned the quarter boat slowly the length of the object, then retraced his course. The wreck had been a substantial ship, and so the hull was evidently largely intact; it had probably been constructed of teak. He could see the outline of a large hatch almost amidships, but the masts and any superstructures had vanished.

"Hand me the sounding rod." Merewether plunged the long rod into the water, finally to strike solidly against the hull. He jogged the rod several times, moving it back and forward. The wreck was damnably solid, still holding together in spite of the movement of the sea and the teredo worm.

He looked back towards *Pitt.* The hands were still in the rigging weaving the tackles that would lift out the guns. He had nothing to lose. It would be hours before they were actually lowered into the lighters.

"Return to the ship, Mister Dobbs."

* * *

A flush of frustration surged through Merewether. Was the gunner being deliberately obtuse, or simply avoiding a display of ignorance? He had laid out a problem to be solved by this expert in the field of ordnance, and was met by a blank stare.

"Yessir, Captain," said Mister Vance. "I can cut a piece of slow match to burn most any time you fix, give or take a mo'. But not under water . . ." Merewether considered restating the problem in simpler terms, wishing desperately that he had MacLellan with his vast technical knowledge and inventive turn of mind at hand. A knock came before he could recommence.

"Captain," said Whaley, sticking only his head through the door. "We will be ready to hoist out the first gun within the half hour.

"Very good," said Merewether, irritated at the interruption to convey a trifling bit of information. It was almost noon and his precious time was slipping away. "Come in a moment. Mister Whaley," he said on second thoughts. "I want you to listen to a problem I shall pose for Mister Vance. I wish to demolish the hull of a sunken ship, Mister Whaley. Obviously I cannot use fire or the sledges and crowbars of the ship-breakers. The question I put to Mr. Vance is, how I can place and ignite a sufficient quantity of powder to accomplish my purpose."

He saw a flash of comprehension cross the sullen face with its broad cleft chin and rigid mouth. Vance still appeared baffled. "During a previous commission," Merewether went on, "my first lieutenant accomplished an underwater explosion at a distance of several leagues by means of a mechanical timing device, but such refinements are not necessary in the present instance, in my opinion."

"How deep is the hull?" At least he had Whaley's attention.

"Roughly three and a half fathoms."

"And how large?"

"Two-thirds the size of *Pitt.*"

Whaley shifted his gaze to focus on the left upper corner of the day cabin, lips moving soundlessly. Merewether sat back, hearing the tick of the clock on the bulkhead as time moved remorselessly towards the day after tomorrow when he would have to admit his failure.

"In water that shallow, a deal of the force would go up," said Whaley in a musing tone. Merewether could remember MacLellan saying almost the same thing when confronted with a similar problem at Calcutta almost three years ago. Possibly this fellow knew something. He could only hope.

"The hulk is half on its side, and there's an open hatch amidships, if that will help any."

"Might serve to confine the explosion more effectively if we can place the charge inside the hull." He seemed to reach a decision and turned his gaze back to Merewether. "Two hundred pounds of powder might do the job, so I'll use four to make sure. Quick match still burns at five seconds and slow match at five minutes to the foot, doesn't it, Vance?"

"Er . . . Yesser. Least it did the last I timed a length . . ."

"You know, Captain, in '96, the first full year I was in the Marine, I served a tour as aide to old Captain Folger, the Wreck and Salvage Master for the Company at Surat. The *Gem of India,* first voyage out, capsized and sunk crossways of the fairway into the anchorage. We had to demolish her to get the homeward bound convoy out. Three separate times we exploded a barrel of powder in her before she broke open . . ." Whaley paused, then said briskly, "I'll need Vance here, the cooper and carpenter . . ." He went out in his short brisk gait with Vance at his heels.

You never know until you ask, Merewether decided, as he watched the pair go out. If the obstacle barring entry to the channel Dobbs had discovered could be removed, he was prepared to risk the ship in an effort to end this affair in short order. He remembered Seton's grisly proposal again with horror after seeing on his own deck the children who would suffer the fate he advocated. Even if the way should be cleared by demolition of the wreck, there was the very real hazard of stranding at a point where it might be impossible to kedge off the frigate, and it might be overwhelmed by an attack in the helpless interval from the shore in small craft, a favorite method of the Joasmis. To compound the problem, there were still the light batteries commanding the westward approaches to the beach within easy range. These factors had to be weighed against the enormous advantage to be gained by bringing eighteen thirty-two-pounders, plus the two long nines, within carronade reach of the town, shooting through flimsy walls into the backside of the citadel. If he could bring his broadsides to bear, he could make the town and fortress untenable in a fraction of the time required to transport his siege battery ashore, let alone enlarging the breach to practical proportions. He temporized, unwilling yet to make a decision on this rash venture. But on the chance that the passage would prove practicable, he sent for Dobbs.

"Mister Dobbs, will you sound out the channel and mark it with buoys? I think a length of timber anchored with a stone will be sufficient. No need to go beyond the final turn. Too close to the battery."

The young man brightened. At least his discovery was not forgotten.

It was almost mid-afternoon before the first thirty-two pounder was finally loaded and secured in its barge. Merewether was on deck to see the completion of the operation, but not to supervise. The boatswain knew his trade and had rigged the elaborate skein of spars, stays, preventers and tackles, first to lift, then to swing out and finally to lower the ponderous weapon to its platform in the barge. This was child's play compared to the effort that would be required to move the piece nearly half a mile through the sand to its emplacement. He turned away, shaking his head in frustration; at this rate, he would be hard put even to have the siege battery in action before his deadline. He saw Whaley coming aft, threading through the maze of gear on deck.

"Captain, you might take a look at the lash-up we have put together before we put the lid on." They walked forward to where a large water cask rested on the deck.

"Since gunpowder has great bulk for its weight, I had to put enough shot in the bottom to make sure it sinks. Then there's a partition, and the rest of the cask almost to the top lined with tarred canvas to make sure she stays dry. Then another partition, and this small space below the head filled with sand . . ." Merewether could see the length of slow match pressed into the sand just within the circumference of the barrel. "Six feet of slow, and a foot of quick into the powder, and it should give us half an hour to place the charge and retreat . . ."

Whaley was fairly beaming with pride of creation. He addressed the cooper. "All right, lead the end of the slow match into this hole, and button her up. Be sure you have a bung that's a tight enough fit. And bring your tinder box, Mister Vance."

A sudden complication occurred to Merewether. Dobbs still had the water glass away in the quarterdeck placing his buoys. Yet the four hundredweight of powder would have to be lowered through the hatch where it would have its maximum effect. He called Marlowe over and directed him to hoist the recall for the quarterboat.

By the time the launch reached the wreck, the quarterboat had joined it. The cask was lifted over the bow of the launch, the bottom just touching the water, supported by a line running through the fairlead, and snubbed to the bitts.

"Let's get as close to the spot as possible before you light off that fuse, Mister Whaley," Merewether commanded, seeing the gunner beginning to strike flint and steel into his tinder box. He transferred to the quarterboat and hung over the gunwales to peer into the water glass. "Give way. Handsomely! Port a point. Steady. Stop!" With the light now coming from the west, he could see the hatch's outline much more clearly than this morning. "All right, light her off."

The gunner had ignited his tinder and now transferred the fire to a piece of slow match When it was burning cleanly, he handed it to Whaley, who applied it to the end of the match protruding through the bung hole. It took fire, shooting off smoke and a shower of sparks, as the first lieutenant observed it critically, then blew on it. Satisfied, he turned to the cooper.

"Drive home your bung!" It was the work of a moment to hammer it in, then smear a handful of tar over it. "Now, Captain, are you ready to guide it down? The sooner we get it placed, the better, because that match is generating a deal of heat in that small space in spite of the sand, and the fire might jump!

"Lower the cask. Handsomely!"

Through the water glass, Merewether watched it sink as the boatswain's mate played out the line, leaving a trail of bubbles in the clear water. He hoped this was not evidence of air escaping from the cask to be replaced by water.

"Belay!"

The barrel was about halfway to the canted deck, but the line was beginning to slant to the west. There must be an appreciable current running across the hulk.

"Come ahead slow!" The oars dipped. "Lower away." The cask was approaching the hatch, streaming more noticeably to the westward. The current along the bottom accounted for the existence of the channel; it had been dug and scoured out as though with a spade. "Now, let her down easy!" The bottom hung for just an instant on the coaming, then slid out of sight into the hold. A moment later the line went slack.

"She's touched bottom, sor!"

"Very good. Now tie a buoy to that line. If it doesn't explode, we might want to bring it up again."

Not me!" said Whaley fervently. "That damn fuse might smolder half a day in a spot the saltpeter didn't penetrate, then burn again."

"Give way!" The hands required no urging. The launch was drawing near *Pitt,* and the faster quarterboat a half mile into the channel to complete its marking when the thing exploded.

Four hundred pounds of powder under twenty feet of water inside a waterlogged wooden hull generates fearsome forces when it explodes. Confined by the incompressible water, much of the force is upward, but expanding in the shape of a cone as it rises. And, of course, the timbers against which the cask rested transmitted the shock to still other beams and planks to which they were fastened. A great column of water rose from the sea, flecked with darker objects which must be wood fragments, and they heard the muffled explosion an appreciable interval after the boat danced from the shock transmitted through the sea.

"Twenty-nine minutes!" said Whaley with satisfaction, looking up from his watch. "Shall we go back? The water may stay murky for a bit." The launch encountered the expanding concentric circles of waves halfway back to the site, and pitched as it pulled through them.

There was a wide area of discolored water to mark the point of the explosion. Merewether found the water glass quite useless, and put a seaman in the bow with a lead line. There were very few fragments of timber floating, but this would be natural enough since the hulk must have been thoroughly waterlogged. There was a steady chant of three and a half fathoms as they rowed through the centre of the discoloration towards Dobbs's first buoy.

Now come about," Merewether told the coxswain. The soundings soon disclosed that the bow and stern of the wreck were still in place, but the waist had vanished. There appeared to be a good twenty-five yards blasted out the hulk to provide a passage for *Pitt.* With careful handling and a calm sea, she might slip through! Satisfied, he gave the order to return to the ship. He had one more task to complete before dark.

"That was a magnificent accomplishment, Mister Whaley! My heartiest congratulations." The officer actually looked embarrassed at the words of praise.

Merewether realized that he had committed himself. He was determined to take the risk, barring some other obstacle located by Dobbs. As the boat approached the ship, the second lighter burdened by its siege gun was just pulling away towards the beach. Well, let it go, there were enough others in *Pitt* to do the job if he could bring them within range. He sought out the carpenter.

"No rest for the weary, Mister Svensen. I want a Danube rudder rigged . . ."

"Vhat, sur?"

"An extension fished on to the rudder so as to increase its area by at least half again. I need more control of the ship . . ."

"Oh, you mean what we call in Sweden," he paused, evidently searching for the correct word in English, then continued, "I think, a salmon tail."

"Whatever its name, you understand what I want."

"Oh, yessir."

Such an extension would be much easier to control than the half-submerged hogshead streamed astern that that old master's mate at Calcutta — Jenkins? — had described to him two years ago, and he would have to steer small to negotiate that winding channel. He called a sweating Boatswain Caldwell over.

"Knock off hoisting out the third gun. Tomorrow is soon enough." He might regret the act, but moving more guns ashore was useless at this late hour, he would sink or swim on his ability to take *Pitt* through the winding channel tomorrow. He saw Dobbs come back on board, dripping with sweat.

"Did you find any more obstacles?"

"No, sir. I think we will have at least two feet under the keel all the way." Merewether was beginning to feel the reckless exhilaration he had experienced the year before last when he led his party of marines ashore to march through the streets of Canton to the sound of drums and bugles in violation of the laws of China, but it was entirely possible that this action could lead to another Court of Inquiry in view of the temper of the tripartite command of the combined operation. "It is too near dark to move tonight. We will go in on the morning tide."

He saw the purser emerge from the galley. There had been snacks for the hands at intervals during the long arduous day, but no regular meal served, and they deserved a treat. "Mister Davis, you may serve out a double ration of spirits before mess." The cheers were deafening, but a sudden disquieting thought struck him.

The women and children! He cursed himself for his preoccupation during the day. Seton should have been notified long since to remove them to another place of safety. He plunged below to dash off the urgent request, and sent Hamlyn off in the gig to deliver it in the Imam's camp.

An hour later, Merewether was relaxing in the cabin after a comfortable dinner when he heard the boatswain's pipe, and a moment later the messenger knocked and entered.

"Sir, Mister MacCamy reports Captain Seton of the Marine is coming on board."

"Very well, I'll come." Courtesy demanded that he meet the officer on deck, though he had no desire to see the man again after the bitter session before dawn this morning.

Seton came up the ladder nimbly enough as Merewether stepped forward, opening his mouth to utter the hackneyed platitudes of welcome, difficult though it might be.

"Aha!" cried Seton. "There you are, Merewether, God damn your eyes!" His eyes were blazing with fury in the lantern light, and there were hectic red spots on either cheek. MacCamy and the deck watch were in easy earshot, staring with astonishment at the confrontation.

"Come below, Seton! No need to entertain the hands on deck!"

He stood aside, gesturing aft. The smell of brandy on Seton's breath was unmistakable.

"Tea?" Merewether inquired politely, on reaching his cabin. Seton shook his head, and stood facing Merewether across the desk. There was an appreciable interval, as though the man were gathering his forces. Then Seton spoke.

"I do not know your motives, Mister, but of the senior officers in this expedition, I thought I could rely at least upon a fellow Marine officer! You have failed me, Merewether, failed me most miserably, a fact that I feel compelled to bring to the attention of Bombay at the earliest practicable moment. But for your sea-lawyer arguments this morning, we should be in possession of Ras ul Khymah by now." He paused to catch his breath, and Merewether seized the moment.

"Captain, your scheme violates all the laws of war and of humanity! It degrades the British forces to the level of barbarians —"

"I intend," Seton shrilled on, "to see that you are cashiered and broken, not only for insubordination to an officer years your senior in the Marine, but for incompetence as well! I am informed that you have not yet set the siege battery ashore. And then you have the impertinence to send me orders by an impudent midshipman to remove my hostages from this ship, for what reason I cannot conceive."

"Because I am taking this ship into action against the fortress within the next twelve hours," Merewether said. "I think your hostages would be of little value to you dead from enemy fire. For that reason, whether you concur or not, I shall see them removed to another ship tonight. I recommend one of the empty transports, and I have the launch alongside to take you and the hostages to her."

"You are a madman!" said Seton flatly. "You have lost your mind! There is no possible way you can bring this frigate within range of the fort . . ."

"Let me be the judge of that. And now, I must insist that you embark your party."

Merewether felt exhaustion flood through his body. It had been a strenuous period — he could not call it a day — not so much from physical exertion, but from the stress generated by the destruction of the siege battery, the bitter council following . . . He rang the bell, and Sangh soon brought a pot of coffee, while Merewether began to write his report. An hour later he seemed to have revived a bit, and, the report finished, began a letter to Caroline. It must be almost her time, he computed, wondering whether she still was thriving, and what the child might be, son or daughter, vigorous or feeble, or even born dead. He scratched off a few lines, and the quill snapped in the middle of a word. There were other pens sharpened in the shot bowl, but he threw the useless nib away and collapsed fully clothed on the cot.

By four bells in the morning watch the hands had been fed, the launch and cutter manned, and special sea details were stationed fore and aft to stand by bower and stern anchors. The tide had been making for almost two hours, the high was predicted by Dobbs's calculations to be at close to two bells in the forenoon watch, and the wind was light but steady out of the west-north-west. Merewether sniffed the morning air, and looked out at the massive structure of Ras ul Khyrnah now outlined against the rising sun, wondering if he could indeed navigate *Pitt* across those two miles of shallows. Whaley came up to make his report.

"All stations manned and ready, sir. Both anchors are at short stay. Hands are standing by to set the jib, main and mizzen staysails and spanker." These four sails comprised only a fraction of Pitt's canvas, but they had the advantage of converting her into a fore-and-aft rigged vessel with the ease and speed of handling sheets rather than the slower bracing about of her yards in these narrow waters.

"Very well, Mister Whaley. You may weigh the bower anchor."

As Whaley hurried forward, Merewether felt a thrill of anticipation as the desperate venture began.

"Pass the word to the boats to take a strain."

The launch and cutter, with their oars double-banked, were linked in tandem to the light cable leading through the eyes of the ship, Dobbs with a compass in the quarterdeck to show the way.

"Stand by to set sail. Weigh the stern anchor." The leading boatswain's mate delivered a volley of reports as the windlass clanked around.

“She’s straight up and down. Breaking ground. Anchor’s aweigh!” The die was cast, the ship was under way. He climbed to a point of vantage in the starboard mizzen ratlines a dozen feet above the deck

“Sheet home!” roared Merewether. “Port your helm. Course northeast. Launch and cutter, give way.” The pulling boats took a strain, the four sails filled, and *Pitt* came sluggishly around to the point of entry into the channel. God grant that no rib or timber still protruded from the sand in the narrow gap blasted in the wreck to plunge like a stiletto into the ship’s bottom! She passed through, but he could see from this height the dark shadow of the remaining bow structure of the hulk slide by a dozen feet to starboard. “Change course, steer north-northeast.” The ship inched along the channel to the first turn east in the sprawling reversed “S” of the approach to Ras ul Khyrnah, and then began to pick up speed as she came almost before the wind. The launch and cutter were hard pressed to stay ahead of her. “Take in both stays’ls!”

Under jib and spanker, *Pitt* crept almost south towards the final bend in the channel that would take her to a position just off the town. If she grounded, he wanted it to be as gently as possible, with the tide still rising. Coming out of the bend, he would have to jibe.

“Mister Caldwell, extra hands to the jib and spanker sheets.” It might be better to manhandle the sails to the opposite tack than have them go over with a rush as the ship came out of the bend. “Haul over!” With the sheets snubbed, the sails were hauled back against the wind, held there as *Pitt* straightened out, then the sheets payed out again as she settled closehauled on the port tack.

Dobbs was still ahead in the quarterboat, two leadsmen sounding the way to the ship’s final berth. Another hundred yards, and the light battery on the beach opened fire from its revetments with a salvo.

“Mister Larkin, see what you can do for that battery.” The gun crew hauled the forward pivot around. The first shot was in line, but high, dashing up a gout of sand behind the battery. The second had the range but with the ship changing course was right of the target The third struck in the centre of the revetment, overturning a gun, and there was a general exodus of white-clad artillerymen from the battery, and across the beach into the city. A cheer went from *Pitt’s* hands. Men had appeared on the rooftops of the houses along the sea, shaking long guns in the air in defiance and firing, but the range was far too great for their firelocks. Merewether looked at his timepiece; just past one bell in the forenoon watch. The interval of high tide should endure almost another hour, and he felt compelled to try to turn the ship now, so as to be in a position to stand out the way he had come before going into action. The channel was far too narrow for a conventional turn, but here at slack tide he should be able to wind her about her stern anchor dropped underfoot as a pivot with the pulling boats.

In the middle of the manoeuvre, his heart came up into his throat as he felt the stern touch bottom with the ship squarely across the channel. She paused, scraped, paused again, then broke loose from the clutching sands, and came on about to anchor bow and stern headed south. Thank God she was lighter by two guns and their ammunition!

Merewether found himself drenched with sweat, and quite drained of vitality. He turned to see Whaley in like condition, wearing a wan grin as he mopped his streaming face.

Now their efforts would be put to the final test. "You may commence firing when ready, Mister Larkin."

It was almost an anticlimax when the first broadside thundered out just as two bells in the forenoon watch sounded. Five hundred and ninety-four pounds of iron delivered at near point-blank range from eighteen thirty-two-pounders and two nine-pounders was devastating.

By the time the fourth broadside had been fired the buildings forming the seaward wall of Ras ul Khymah were a shambles. The soldiers on the rooftops had vanished, masonry walls had collapsed, and the place had become a hellhole with thirty-two-pounder balls ricocheting through the narrow streets. Merewether remained perched in the ratlines to observe the effect of the bombardment, watching between shots the activity on deck as the guns were served. The concentrated power of efficiency worked guns mounted in a ship was an awesome thing, far more deadly than any siege battery that might be transported ashore. He remarked the smooth teamwork of the gun crews, the darting movements of the powder monkeys as they delivered fresh charges, and remembered that no man had been brought to the mast since their arrival here. In spite of the heat and the hard labors on board and ashore, spirits appeared high. He decided that this crew would do.

He heard a hail from the lookout at the crosstrees of the mainmast, but could not understand him, and beckoned the man down just as the fifth broadside fired.

"Sir, the Arabs are abandoning the fort!"

"Where are they going?"

"Why, across the lagoon in boats, some of them, and others around the beach to the south. I could see them streaming over the hills to the east by the hundreds."

"Women and children?"

"Yes and soldiers too!"

Merewether considered the situation. The guns after half a dozen broadsides in rapid succession were getting too hot for safety. He must reduce the rate of fire, keeping up just enough to discourage any stragglers in the town or citadel, and the hands must be fed. He signaled to Larkin and Whaley, then sent the messenger for the purser.

"Reduce the rate of fire to one section every five minutes, Mister Larkin." It was near enough noon, and he turned to the purser. "Feed the starboard watch, Mister Davis, and then have it relieve the port." And to Whaley, "When the hands are fed, I'll want a landing force of twenty-five steady men told off. Muskets and bayonets for fifteen, pistols and cutlasses for the rest. Oh, yes, and a large size Marine ensign." He saw Midshipman Marlowe standing by, round hat in hand. "Mister Marlowe find Mister Hamlyn, and both of you equip yourselves for duty with the landing force."

Merewether went below to eat a light lunch, for it would not be wise to dine at length before the expedition in the blazing midday sun. Sangh had laid out his pistols, freshly loaded and primed, his sword and landing force boots, still ripe with the sweat of two days ago. He chose the broad-brimmed straw hat with its wetted neck flap, and decided to leave off the sword. The guns still shook the ship at five-minute intervals, methodically working across the back side of the fort, now exposed by the demolition of most of the dwellings screening it. The masthead reported that the stream of refugees had diminished to a trickle. They must be heading for the smaller town of Ram, several miles to the northeast, but also heavily fortified. He waited until two bells in the afternoon watch to permit the town to be fully evacuated before ordering a ceasefire, then called away the landing force to row to the beach just south of the citadel where the first broadsides had been concentrated.

"Form up in two sections," he told the midshipmen. "Have the men load their weapons." Here close at hand he saw why the seaward walls had crumbled so quickly under the gunfire. What had appeared from a distance to be stone was in actuality sun-dried bricks made of a white clay in many instances, and whole walls had simply disintegrated at the passage of a thirty-two-pound shot.

The party made its cautious way across the rubble, through what had been a substantial dwelling in which clothing, smashed furniture, dried fruits and splintered roof beams mingled with sharded tiles, to emerge in a narrow street. Merewether was alert for the slightest movement. It was one thing for these pirates to flee the deadly impersonal round iron balls howling through the town in horrendous showers of shattered stone and splinters, and quite another to find a lightly armed party of infidels within arm's reach. He saw the flicker of a movement in the doorway of an almost intact house a hundred feet down the alley, and held up his hand to check his force, motioning his men to take shelter in doorways and alcoves. He drew one double pistol, cocked it, and with two musketeers edged along the ruined walls until he was only a few feet away. There was another flicker of movement a querulous cry, and he saw a gnarled claw of a hand scrabbling at the edge of the door. He leaped forward, aiming the pistol through the door.

They were pitiful specimens, two old cronies, wrinkled, almost blind, and so feeble they could no longer stand or walk. They held up their hands imploringly, making unintelligible sounds, then pointed to what appeared to be a cistern.

"Draw them a jug of water," Merewether told Marlowe. "And see if there is any food in that cupboard."

The party pressed on, heading for the main entrance to the northern citadel. They passed a dozen bodies in the wreckage, already covered with flies, and rescued a man still alive, pinned down by a beam across his legs.

The red flag of the Joasmis still flew defiantly from the west tower, but inside the place was a ruin, guns dismounted and bodies of soldiers, numbering in the hundreds, strewn through the debris. The outer walls to the north were quarried stone, five feet thick, but the walls on the town side had been economically constructed of sun-dried brick in the secure belief that no enemy could approach from that quarter.

"I want that flag struck, Mister Hamlyn." And then a thought came to him. The arrogance and high-handed conduct of Dunbar, Smith and Seton still rankled, and Merewether decided to offer them an affront to which they could take no official exception.

The flagstaff was substantial, almost of topgallant mast proportions, round and smooth. Merewether saw Ames, the top-man he had transferred out of Osborne's mizzen top into the master at arms force.

"Ames can you nail this ensign to the mast above the pirate rag?"

"Yes, sor," he said, almost contemptuously at the implied doubt of his abilities.

They found iron nails in the debris as Ames removed his shoes and rolled his trousers above his knees. Another thought struck Merewether.

"Wait a moment." He looked among the shattered lockers that had held supplies for the guns, and soon found what he was looking for, a pot of grease, still half full, used by the Joasmi gunners to lubricate the axles and trunnion gudgeons on the carriages. "Hang this on your belt, and once you've nailed both flags to the mast, make sure that you smear a liberal dose on it as you come down!" The man's face creased into a delighted grin as the import of the order sunk in.

Ames shinnied up the flagstaff nimbly as a monkey, the folded ensign tucked inside his shirt, the pot of grease hung on his belt, nails in his mouth, the protruding points giving him the expression of a grinning cat. He hammered them home, first through the ensign, then the pirate flag, into the seasoned wood with the butt of his pistol, to leave the Bombay Marine's thirteen red and white stripes, quartered by a red cross, St. George's cross in the canton, sparkling above the red Joasmi flag.

Merewether looked up feeling exhilaration at the brave display, the conqueror's badge of triumph, then out over the parapet to see the Army troops advancing, skirmishers in the van, toward the fort. The force stopped in the shelter of the low wall across the spit, and a single officer under a flag of truce advanced towards the fort. When he reached a point about a hundred yards away, he recognized the young subaltern aide de camp who had brought Colonel Smith's summons a few days ago. He stepped to the parapet and shouted through cupped hands.

"Tell Colonel Smith we hold the town!" The officer shook his head, and advanced another forty paces where Merewether repeated his message, Evidently it was understood, for the aide saluted, about faced and marched back to the main body of troops.

It was more than a quarter of an hour before Smith and Dunbar appeared at the sallyport in the eastern wall of the fortress at the head of three companies of the 65th. The colonel wore a scarlet coat in spite of the heat, and had his sword buckled on, evidently in anticipation of a formal surrender ceremony.

"Welcome, gentlemen, to the Citadel of Ras ul Khymah!" said Merewether in ringing tones. Smith looked at the carnage among the batteries and the devastation in the fort with an expression of disbelief.

"You did this in a matter of two hours?" he demanded.

"Yes, Colonel." Merewether realized that he had just demonstrated to Smith a classic example of sea power, the ability of a man-o'-war to transport to a strategic point a concentration of guns of far greater caliber and destructive power than any invading land force could hope to manage.

"I wouldn't believe it if I had not seen it!" Smith shook his head, and an expression of determination crossed his face. He turned to speak inaudibly to his aide de camp.

"Well done, Merewether," said Dunbar, offering his hand. "I had no expectation that you could ever bring that frigate in so close." He looked at Smith with an expression of puzzlement as his aide departed at a canter, gave a start, and turned hastily to speak inaudibly to his own midshipman.

Merewether had a clear premonition of the import of each order that had been issued, and decided that he should be absent when the time for execution arrived. He gave a covert hand signal to Hamlyn to move out with the landing force.

"Gentlemen, I believe this concludes my mission in this operation, and I shall return to my ship to make preparation for moving her out to a safer anchorage on the ebb tomorrow." He saluted smartly, and hastened out across the rubble to overtake his party.

Halfway back to *Pitt,* Merewether could still see the two knots of contestants on the top of the tower, face to face, arms waving, one attired in the blue and gold of the Royal Navy, the other in the scarlet and white of His Majesty's 65th Foot. The Navy had a blue ensign, and the Army its regimental standard in hand. Just before the launch came alongside the ship, he saw the blue and gold cluster about the base of the mast, while the scarlet and white withdrew to stand at one side. Evidently Dunbar with his temporary appointment as a commodore had prevailed over a stubborn Colonel Lionel Smith.

As he came on deck, he snatched the glass from its bracket to focus again on the scene. One seaman was standing on the shoulders of another, arms about the flagstaff, scrabbling hopelessly as he made the effort to climb the greased pole. He remained so for a long moment, then slid down. The Bombay Marine colors still shimmered triumphantly in the breeze above the blood-red Joasmi banner on the Citadel of Ras ul Khymah.

Merewether went below.

PART II

Action at Aden

Merewether could not imagine what Buttram was talking about.

"I haven't the foggiest notion of your meaning, Doctor."

"Why, it is Caroline's time by my computations. Surely this week. Mayhap this very day! " Realization only then had flooded into Merewether, Caroline had not entered his mind since that night he had commenced the letter, to be abandoned in his exhaustion. She could even now be experiencing the agonies of childbirth.

"Well, Doctor, there is little enough I could do if I were in Calcutta." He comforted himself with the recollection that Caroline had spoken for the services of the most competent midwife in the British community, with a physician standing by should his services be required. The messenger of the watch knocked and entered, to hand over a sealed missive.

> Please be advised that I intend to explode the magazines under Ras ul Khymah at precisely six post meridian this date. s/Smith, commanding His Majesty's Land Forces.

The event was only a half hour away, by Merewether's timepiece and it should be a sight to see from the safety of two miles away.

"Tell Mister Marlowe to pass the word for all hands, and I'll come on deck when they have assembled" He passed the message to Buttram. "I don't believe anyone will want to miss this."

There had been nearly forty tons of powder found stored in the magazines beneath the fortress. The town itself had held almost nothing of value; its treasures evidently had been removed at first sight of the invasion fleet, though a sergeant of the 65th was rumored to have found a cache of jewels under a flagstone in the courtyard of the house of Sheikh Hussein Bin Ali. It had been an unprofitable expedition. The Company paid prize money only for vessels brought in and sold, not those sunk or burned. Now Smith evidently was ready to carry out the final direction in the operation order: Raze Ras ul Khymah to the ground. The messenger knocked again.

"Hands are formed up, sir."

The fire in the slow match must even now be creeping towards the powder trains leading into the magazine. High time to get on deck himself.

It was a spectacular event. One moment the tower was visible, the Bombay Marine ensign still flying proudly above the red Joasmi flag, then it blurred, seemed to hang a moment in the air, and disintegrated as a huge orange pillar of fire and smoke shot a thousand feet into the air. Seconds later the shock wave set *Pitt* to rocking and the sound of the explosion deafened them. Every dwelling, stone or brick, within a quarter of a mile of the citadel appeared to have collapsed as though made of cards. Merewether took his fingers from his ears and picked up the glass. There was still fire in the enormous crater, but there was little left to burn. A cheer went up from the hands to see the hated stronghold of the enemy totally destroyed, and Merewether dismissed them from quarters. He had led his below, and soon was able to propose a toast.

"Gentlemen, the successful completion of our mission is occasion enough for this celebration. However, first I give you the officer who discovered the path by which we were able to succeed: Lieutenant Dobbs!" Dobbs's face was red before Merewether had half completed the toast, but he was modest enough as he accepted congratulations. "And now, to Lieutenant Whaley who unlocked the gate that barred our way to the fortress!" The officers drank again with enthusiasm. All present were relieved that a period of strenuous and exacting duty had ended and indulged themselves accordingly. Whaley came across the cabin just before Sangh announced that dinner was served.

"The dispatch brig, *Courier,* came to anchor just before I left the deck."

"Very well. And now, gentlemen, shall we dine?" It had been a long uproariously happy evening.

Now on deck, with the heat already growing oppressive, Merewether massaged the back of his head as though that would heal the ache, still thankful that the disagreeable operation with its cold-bloodedly ambitious commanders was for practical purposes concluded. He went below to drink the coffee he had poured out to cool, and filled the cup again.

The ache had diminished and he had taken breakfast when Davis came in with the official pouch and a slender packet of letters in his hand.

"With your leave, sir, I'll open this now." He unlocked the pouch and laid out an assortment of communications bearing the seal of the Marine. "And here is your personal mail, sir." Merewether saw the round hand of Caroline in the superscription on three letters, and hastened to break the seal. The first was dated February 22nd.

> My dearest husband.
>
> I find myself quite unable to sleep this night. I am possessed with terror that you are in great danger, and pray for your safety. . .

Merewether looked back at the date. February 22nd? Then he recalled, and it was the early morning of the mutiny! Was Caroline clairvoyant? He read on.

"Our child is becoming more active . . ."

There was more, gossip of Calcutta, the imminent removal of Mary Wilkins and MacLellan to his new post at Bombay. He picked up the second letter: more of the same, lacking the foreboding. The third letter was only a month old. Caroline was again despondent. "I think the day shall never come . . ." Well, little enough in the way of news. He had of course written her from Bombay and again from Muscat, but he could salve his conscience a bit with the thought that nothing momentous had occurred during his absence.

He sighed, and turned his attention to the stack of Marine correspondence, slitting open the dispatches in reverse order of the dates inscribed on the wrappers. The first communication was terse to the point of rudeness:

> Percival Merewether, Master and Commandant The Honorable Company's Ship, *Pitt:* When directed by the Commander, Naval Forces, Combined Expedition to Ras ul Khymah, and when in all respects ready for sea, you are required and requested to proceed in consort with the Honorable Company's sloops, *Comet* and *Vigilant* to the Red Sea and the port of Jeddah. There you will report your arrival to the senior officer present representing the Commodore acting as the Deputy of the Company in executing its duties as Admiral of the Mughul . . .

Merewether came to a halt. Admiral of the Mughul? Deputy of the Company? Then he realized that these were only the stilted formal terminology for the post of Commodore at Surat, the most lucrative single office in the Company hierarchy. Fifty years ago, Commodore Watson had led the Marine forces against the Seedee, hereditary Lord High Admiral of the Mughul fleet, suppressed his revolt against the Mughul and his Nawad, and taken his seat at Surat Castle. By the terms of the treaty with the Great Mughul, the Seedee was forever stripped of the dignity and emoluments of his high office, and the post with its revenues was conferred upon the Company. A senior Commodore of the Bombay Marine was assigned annually to administer the office as deputy for the Company. The appointment was for only the one year, but the perquisites and fees accruing to him for enforcement of customs, convoy, and other naval services often exceeded 100,000 rupees, enabling the fortunate incumbent to retire to England a wealthy man. It was the ambition of every officer entering the Marine to cap his career with the appointment, since it carried with it luxurious quarters in Surat Castle, and the Commodore's own flagship flying the Marine's colors at the peak and the Mughul's banner at the main. He read on.

> . . . and the Company's agent ashore. When the convoy shall have assembled and embarked its passengers, you are further required and requested to assume command of the naval escort and without fail to bring said ships safely to Surat.
>
> This 23rd day of March, 1808

> By direction of the Superintendent of the Marine. s/Tollett, Acting."

Merewether was puzzled. The annual pilgrimage to Mecca with the substantial convoy escort fees exacted by the Commodore at Surat, was one of the most profitable sources of his revenues. He employed a number of well-armed, handy vessels to furnish the escort, and he could recall no previous instance in which Bombay Castle had been required to supply three of its cruisers for this duty. And the tone of the order was out of character for Tollett; it was what Commodore Land had often termed a "Do or be damned" order in the days of Governor-General Sir George Barlow at Calcutta, requiring an officer to succeed at his peril in a mission. Well, he thought, he had had such a mission once before, and would have failed to bring back the pirate, Abercrombie, but for the marksmanship of Larkin and MacLellan. He shook his head, wondering what might lie behind the harsh order, then turned his attention to the enclosures. The first was in a neat clerkly hand entitled, "Situation Estimate: Central and Western India; Spring 1808."

He looked for the signature: "A. Napier, Colonel Aide de Camp to His Excellency, The Governor-General." Who? Then Merewether placed the man. He had met Napier at one of Barlow's receptions, a small ginger-haired man with the face of a fox, and eyes that roved constantly, scanning his surroundings with an intensity that was disquieting. Napier had been a left-over from the Wellesley regime, a man of such accomplishments and understanding of the tangled native political situation as to make him valuable enough to survive three changes of administration. He turned back to read the text:

> Jasvant Rao Holkar of Rajputana remains the single most influential prince among the Maratha Confederation since the treaty of 1805. The policy of concession and forbearance conceived by Lord Cornwallis and continued by Barlow has influenced Holkar to keep the Marathas in check, and he has become a valuable ally of the Company. Pierre Perron and Louis Bourquin have left his service, but a cadre of near a score of French officers continue to train Maratha troops

including strong elements of Pindari and Pathan mercenaries who bear no loyalty to him. His lieutenants, Chitu, Wasil Muhammad and Karim Khan, lead forays into neighboring states for massacre and plunder, but they do not molest the Company's interests. The ports in the Gulf of Cambay give easy access to Rajputana from the Arabian Sea. The Nawab of Surat continues to be the firm ally of the Company, but our forces in the other ports of the Gulf are greatly diminished since Wellesley's departure . . .

Merewether paused to consider the baffling information contained in the simple didactic sentences. He had no real understanding of the matters the staff officer discussed. The Company's military operations in the interior of India were so varied and complex — so many strange names of persons and places to remember, the bewildering unstable alliances that made a native prince an ally today, and a blood enemy tomorrow — that he had never concerned himself with keeping abreast of such affairs far from the sea. Arthur Wellesley had made his reputation as a soldier in the brilliant succession of campaigns against these princely states under the patronage of his brother, Richard, and had brought the Company to the threshold of empire. He wondered briefly how Bonaparte might be faring with his Spanish adventure, and whether there was yet a possibility of an attack on India from a quarter other than through Persia.

He turned his attention back to the monograph.

Since Holkar poisoned his brother, Kashi Rao and his nephew, Khande Rao, in 1806, there was no dissident element at his court until his former concubine, Tulsi Bai, and his illegitimate son by her, Malhar Rao, returned from exile last summer. Holkar welcomed his son, now eighteen, since his legitimate son is simple, but not Tulsi, and she returned to Surat where she solicited the support of the Nawab in a venture to overthrow Holkar and place her son on the throne . . .

Gad, thought Merewether, this was blood and thunder intrigue fit for a penny dreadful presented as sober fact by a responsible senior officer! He read on:

> Madame Bai is reputed to be the product of a liaison between a Maratha woman of noble birth and a French officer, and she has strong allegiances to France. After her exile from Rajputana, she was the mistress of General Lamont, Commandant of the garrison on Mauritius until his recall to France in 1806. She is a woman not only of beauty, but of iron resolution who is determined to put her son on the throne of Rajputana. Last year, Holkar sent his son, Malhar Rao, on the pilgrimage to Mecca. Tulsi Bai joined him at Surat, and they will return in the convoy departing Jeddah in June.

A bit of light began to glimmer as Merewether read on:

> Our man in Port Louis reports that three frigates of thirty-six guns have been fitted out, together with four transports capable of carrying two battalions of French regulars for departure in May. Their initial destination is reputed to be the Gulf of Aden. The Company must take the most stringent measures to prevent Tulsi Bai and Malhar Rao from making contact with this force.

Merewether laughed bitterly as he tossed the sheet on his desk. The response of the Superintendent of the Marine to the "most stringent measures" was to dispatch a thirty-six-gun frigate and two fourteen-gun sloops to oppose a force of nearly twice their firepower! But he could now comprehend the concern of the Governor-General: Holkar was a villain, but for the time he was the Company's villain, and it had no desire that he be supplanted by a puppet controlled by a half-French adventuress. And *Pitt* had no charts of the Red Sea or the Gulf of Aden in its allowance, but it might be possible to borrow some from the Royal Navy.

Merewether picked up the next dispatch and slit the oilskin wrapper. It was a counterpart of orders to Lieutenant Joseph Whaley.

> When a relief as first lieutenant in HCS *Pitt* is in all respects qualified, and when directed by its commanding officer, you will proceed to HCS *Vigilant* and assume command of that vessel. . .

It was a mixed blessing, Whaley would no longer be his hair shirt in *Pitt,* but he would be in command of one of the ships of his squadron. He wondered for a moment whether the man had adjusted his philosophy of the enforcement of discipline. True, there had been far fewer cases brought to the mast and no use of the cat since the abortive mutiny; or had he merely conformed for the time to Merewether's methods? He hoped it was the former, he must be able to rely upon *Vigilant* in the coming operation. He sent Sangh to find Whaley.

"Congratulations, Captain! " he greeted the officer, extending his hand. He saw the china-blue eyes light up as he handed him the order, then the face fall slightly as he read it.

"Well, I'm pleased enough, Captain, though I had hoped for the substantive rank, not just a courtesy title . . ."

"I'm sure it will come soon enough with this command in your record," said Merewether, despising himself for his casuistry. "And your first duty will be to sail in company with *Pitt* and *Comet* to the Red Sea. I understand that Corcoran in *Vigilant* is going back to England for three years' leave."

"When may I be detached?" Evidently Whaley had no more desire to remain in *Pitt* than Merewether had for him to stay.

"As of now," said Merewether, dipping his quill in the ink well. "Larkin was my first lieutenant for more than a year in *Rapid,* and is in all respects qualified for the post." But for the teredo worms, the American would be commanding his own vessel now. Bad luck!

"Very good, sir. I'll get my kit together and be ready in an hour to read myself in."

Merewether turned his attention to the remaining dispatches. All routine; except some enterprising clerk at Bombay Castle had sent three charts of the Red Sea and Gulf of Aden. Merewether had the gig called away, donned full dress and sword, and departed, orders in hand, to wait on Commodore Dunbar.

He was back on board within the hour, just in time to offer Whaley the dignity of being transported to his new command in the gig. He shook the man's hand at the gangway as the watch rendered the honors to which his new status entitled him. Corcoran and *Vigilant* were well regarded in the Marine, and he hoped again that Whaley had moderated his opinions enough so that he would not turn her into a hell ship.

Larkin knocked and came in, and Merewether welcomed him warmly.

"Thank you, Captain. It has been a bit of a strain when you've been a first yourself to have to conform to some of Whaley's pet notions, but I never let myself have a cross word with him. And now, since we'll be short on officers, I consider Hamlyn entirely qualified to stand a top watch under way. I shall undertake Midshipman Marlowe's further education in seamanship as junior in my watch, if this is acceptable with you."

"Entirely. Now we have orders to the Red Sea and Jeddah, and I want you to acquaint yourself with our mission." He handed over the order and situation estimate to Larkin, and sat back to think of Caroline a moment while he read them. Corcoran had been commissioned in the Marine only four months earlier than Merewether, and he wondered if this coming September he would actually request the leave and expend the vast sums necessary to transport himself, Caroline and their child halfway around the world to England for the three years that was his due. Oh well, he would make the decision when the time came. He might be dead before this month was out if he encountered those French frigates.

Larkin looked up. "I haven't the foggiest notion of who these people are, or where, but I gather we stop off this woman and her son from meeting with the Frogs, or be damned."

"Exactly. Now pass the word to make all preparations for getting underway, and signal *Comet* and *Vigilant,* 'Captains, come on board'."

With the prevailing wind steady out of the southwest at this season, the squadron had to make a long reach south by east almost to the Equator once it had cleared Cape Ras el Had and the Gulf of Oman, there to go about and set a course close hauled for Cape

Guardafui, the eastern tip of Africa. It was a pleasant voyage, the weather fine, only an occasional rain squall to mar the days and cool the decks with fresh water. They passed huge rays basking on the surface that disappeared with a report like a cannon shot when disturbed. Shoals of flying fish burst from the water to skim the wave tops ahead and beside the ship, iridescent bodies glittering in the sunlight, only to plunge again into the sea. An occasional straggler misjudged his landing and came to rest flapping on deck, there instantly to become the prey of one or another of the ship's cats. Merewether stood at the break of the poop in the shade cast by the spanker to watch the sport. Apparently every cat on board had come on deck from their usual haunts in the storerooms and holds in anticipation of a tasty morsel. Another fish skimmed over the bulwarks and skittered across the deck. There was a concerted rush for the prey, but one huge tom brusquely shouldered the others aside to seize the fish in his jaws, then crouched back and tail up, one clawed fore-paw cocked, hissing around his prize, daring the others to dispute his title.

Merewether laughed at the little drama. The big cat was almost red in color, arrogant and truculent in bearing, and insatiably ravenous. Some months ago he had come out of the hold to adopt Sangh, and soon made his quarters in the pantry, though he often could be found lounging on the transom in the cabin, or even lapping up the dregs of tea from a cup forgotten on the desk. From his size, bearing and color of hair, the resemblance was unmistakable, and Merewether to Sangh's eyerolling dismay at being reminded of his old master, had christened him "Abercrombie" after the red-bearded pirate he had fought to the death two years before.

The cat treated him as an absolute equal occupant of the cabin, courteous but aloof and dignified, never deigning to rub against his ankles to wheedle a morsel, while Sangh as custodian of the keys to the panty and victual locker commanded his daily homage. Merewether had never owned a pet of any kind; cats had been forbidden at Bellflower House and dogs kept only at the country seat of Sir Jeffrey Meigs during his childhood. He had rather enjoyed the association with the doughty, self-sufficient tomcat these past months.

While he remained on deck, he kept an unobtrusive eye on Midshipman Hamlyn, now standing a top watch underway in regular rotation. The young officer had stationed himself on the weather side, just abaft the helm where he had an unobstructed view forward. The boatswain's mate and messenger of the watch crouched a few feet forward with the relief quartermaster. There came the suggestion of a tremor in the main topsail, and Hamlyn issued a quick command. The boatswain's mate loped forward, calling the watch to man the braces, and in a trice the sail was perfectly trimmed. Merewether decided that Larkin had been entirely correct in his appraisal; this officer would do. He must remember to recommend him for the examination for second lieutenant at Bombay Castle next September.

He looked out to see *Comet* on the starboard beam two cable's length distant, then to port where *Vigilant* was equally on station, and went down to the cubby where Dobbs was plotting the morning-star sights.

"Almost there, Captain. If my computations are correct, we should make a landfall on Guardafui by tomorrow morning."

"Good." Merewether examined the chart again. He had never actually entered the Red Sea, though he had been to the port of Aden a time or so in his younger days in the Marine. Navigation in the narrow waters could be hazardous. The Port of Jeddah, in particular, lay behind three parallel reefs with only a narrow channel for entry. He hoped a pilot would be available to conn the ship in with local knowledge. But he felt no need to worry yet. Even with Cape Guardafui in sight the port would still be a good thousand miles away.

Morale in *Pitt* appeared to be high. The backbreaking labors at Ras ul Khymah had been taken in stride, and if there were still dissident hands in the ship, they concealed well their discontent. The frigate had been in commission near three years now, but never had been in action other than the few broadsides it had taken to overcome the fortress, with only a single salvo in return. It would be quite different to lie muzzle to muzzle with another ship of equal force, shot crashing through the planking in showers of splinters, dead and wounded men underfoot, and still have the will to serve the guns and work the ship. He saw Doctors Mefford and Buttram emerge from the companion.

"Good morning, Captain," said Mefford. "We still have a dozen cases of the dysentery some of the hands brought back from

Ras ul Khymah, but this fresh sea air has done wonders, and we are marking them to return to light duty this morning."

"Very good, Doctor." Merewether considered his own physical condition. The lassitude he had experienced during the winter and early spring had vanished since the departure from Ras ul Khymah, he had regained the weight lost on the Persian Road last autumn. No nightmares came to haunt him. He felt entirely fit once more.

He wondered if his escape from the domination of the tripartite command of the combined operation, or the fresh sea air, had wrought his cure. In any event, it was good to be his own master again, though under the most imperative of orders. He was ready to go below when Larkin came up.

"By the bye, Captain, young Marlowe has been after me to establish a drill he calls, "Form Lion's Mouth". I never heard of the thing, but he says all of the smaller Marine ships practice it." Merewether searched his memory. He had served briefly as a boatswain's mate in a ten-gun snow years ago, and recollection slowly came to him.

"I think I know what it is, but it has been a long time since I've seen it done. As I recall, small vessels in danger of being overwhelmed by boarding had parties stationed fore or aft, with a boat gun, four- or six-pounder, loaded with loose musket balls. If the enemy got a foothold on deck, they fired the gun into them, then made a concerted charge with cutlasses on the survivors. None of the larger sloops or frigates use it any more, to my knowledge, and I had almost forgotten the maneuver. Of course, he came out of a bomb ketch where it must still be in fashion." Merewether saw that the midshipman was bright and eager, evidently anxious to make an impression. It was unlikely that such a drill ever would be required in a frigate of *Pitt's* force, but it could do little harm to practice the thing. "All right, I have no objection. Let him use the seaman after-guard and quarterdeck gunners for his party — no Marines, they already have definite duties assigned in case of boardings."

Larkin went forward, and Merewether gave the matter no more thought until a morning or so later he saw a perspiring party of seamen dragging the little boat gun to the break of the poop, where priming powder flashed in the vent, and then charging down among the startled hands in the waist with bloodthirsty shouts, brandishing cutlasses.

"Oh, Mister Marlowe." The midshipman came over, his face shining with sweaty enthusiasm. "Your drill was quite realistic. Tell me, have you ever seen it used in earnest?"

"No, sir, but the captain of *Vesuvius* said he had back in 1805 against the Joasmis in the Gulf." If *Pitt* reached such dire straits, there would be little enough hope anyway. Merewether decided, but he would not discourage the lad.

"Very good. Carry on." He went below to bring his journal up to date, thinking again of Caroline and their putative child.

Pitt, Comet and *Vigilant* lay at anchor a cable's length off Customs Island in the harbor of Jeddah close to the four ten-gun snows that flew the burgee of the Commodore at Surat under the colors of the Bombay Marine. They had been the escort for the score of ships at anchor off the quay across the harbor which had brought upward of three thousand pilgrims to this port serving the Holy City of Mecca. They made a motley fleet, ranging from a towering spick and span Indiaman, to shabby country barques with patched sails. The visit to Mecca was easily the most important event in the lives of these devout Moslems, an end to justify a lifetime of scrimping and sacrifice to accumulate the substantial passage money exacted. The gig took Merewether through the anchorage to a landing on the quay, passing close aboard the vessels, seeing the idling hands, mostly lascars, lounging about the decks awaiting the return of their passengers. He stepped ashore, and looked about to get his bearings.

The senior officer of the escort force had made his official call on Merewether late yesterday afternoon almost as soon as the pilot had left *Pitt.* Lieutenant MacCracken was a plump jovial man a few years his elder with an easy flow of gossip and small talk. He had put the officer at ease with a glass of Scotch whisky at his elbow to encourage the stream of information.

"No, Captain, there's little enough of trade here for the Company, mostly hides, skins and tallow, and the people are too poor to buy many of our wares. We do have an agent ashore, an Anglo-Indian named Fitzgerald. His father was an Irish writer for the Company, made his pile in private trade in gems, then legitimatized the boy to take him back to England to be educated. He had influence enough to get him an appointment at Calcutta, but, of course, the English community would not accept a half-caste there, and he took this post where it didn't matter."

MacCracken laughed, and sipped the whisky appreciatively. It was MacLellan's favorite brand. Merewether was entirely familiar with the rigid color line drawn in India; it was impossible for an Anglo-Indian to cross it. But this man had fared better than most half-castes who were accounted Indians out here, in that he had been acknowledged and given an education.

MacCracken continued, "He's married to a good woman, has a child or so, and lives quite comfortably over in the town."

Now Merewether recognized the place some two hundred yards inland from the quay, a substantial white stone house of two stories, surrounded by a whitewashed wall of sun-dried brick. The Company's grid-iron flag flew from a staff above the door, and there was a heavy door with a small barred grill set in the wall. He rang the bell that hung beside it and an Arab boy responded.

"Mister Fitzgerald, please. I am Captain Merewether of the Bombay Marine."

Fitzgerald proved to be a tall man with ruddy regular features, fair hair and side whiskers, possibly thirty years of age, who would have passed without remark on any street in London. The Irish blood had overwhelmed the Indian in him, and no trace of his maternal ancestry was apparent.

"Ah, yes, Captain," he said in measured tones. "I had word that the convoy escort would be reinforced. Bombay must have got the wind up we had a report of a French privateer cruising off Socotra a month or so ago." Fitzgerald put him at ease in a comfortable chair. There were elaborate draperies on the walls, a punkah swaying overhead, and thick Persian rugs on the tiled floor. MacCracken had been correct. The man indeed lived well.

"Yes, Mister Fitzgerald, and is there any other intelligence I should have before departure?" It was on the tip of Merewether's tongue to amplify the question by volunteering the Governor-General's true concern in the premises, the man appeared safe enough, but some innate caution stopped him.

"No, I believe not. The last of the Pilgrims are expected to return momentarily from Mecca. Of course, there usually are some festivals and entertainments before they embark. We have several Indians of high rank, and their retainers, who chartered the Indiaman, *Countess of Surrey,* and the local nobility has plans to honor them." Merewether wondered if young Malhar Rao and his mother, Tulsi Bai, might be among the guests, then decided it made no difference. He had already written off the courtesy call — the man obviously had no information of value — and he intended to depart after only the politest of intervals. He heard a feminine voice behind him, and saw Fitzgerald look past him.

"I'm sorry we intruded, Harry, I did not realize you had a visitor." Fitzgerald stood up, and Merewether followed suit, turning towards the door.

Two women in European dress were standing one behind the other in the entrance. One was a conventional housewifely type, round face, fair hair, moderately obese, thirtyish, entirely unremarkable in appearance. The second, a bit taller and older was beautiful, a face molded in classic planes, white skin with an undertone of ivory tint, large sparkling brown eyes, dark hair parted in the centre and drawn to a knot at the back of her head. Merewether saw her appraising gaze, bold, wise and penetrating, scan him from foot to head before a polite smile appeared. He had an uneasy sensation that he had somehow seen that face before.

"Not at all, my dear. Come in," said Fitzgerald easily "May I present Captain Percival Merewether of the Honorable Company's Marine, my wife Claudia and my sister, Madame Bai."

"Enchanted, ladies" he managed. "And now I am in the way. . ."

"Not at all, Captain," said Mrs. Fitzgerald cheerfully. "It is time for our elevenses, and I do so hope you will join us." Merewether's first impulse had been to cut and run as soon as courtesy permitted but he decided that while it might serve no useful purpose, it could do little harm, either, to stay. "We see only the same tired old faces here from one month to the next among the Marine officers in the escort force, and they never seem to have any news," continued Mrs. Fitzgerald, showing animation in her round face. "Perhaps you can describe the fashions in Bombay or Calcutta for Tulsi and me."

"Well," said Merewether, yet a bit wary at encountering face to face the woman who was the subject of Colonel Napier's monograph. “I have no conflicting duties, and am delighted to accept your kind invitation.” He realized that Madame Bai had said nothing beyond the polite murmur acknowledging the introduction. She spoke now in a strong contralto.

“I too am weary of your officers who can converse only of their little world, Surat to Jeddah, and back, with never a word of what is taking place elsewhere.” She moved gracefully to take the chair he offered and Merewether resumed his seat. “I’ve enjoyed my visit with Harry — my half-brother — actually, we had different fathers. I had not seen him since he was ten, and took the opportunity to visit while my son made his pilgrimage.” She made a sort of moue, “But I am hungry for news of India — the Overland Mail brings us the London papers, but little from eastward . . .” The words were commonplace enough, but he thought he detected the restless spirit behind the beautiful face.

“My news will be stale enough,” he told her. “I am more than three months out of Bombay.”

“And I am dull,” broke in Mrs. Fitzgerald over her shoulder, She was superintending two Arab girls at the sideboard. “Fashion is my passion, and I pay little attention to political or military affairs. But it is hard on Tulsi to have to find her news in the digest of dispatches to the India or Foreign Offices printed in a London paper. Halfway around the world, then almost as far back again!” Two children, a girl about six and a boy possibly four, had come in to stand unobtrusively on either side of their mother, faces raised expectantly below the sideboard.

“Ah there, chaps,” said Fitzgerald, holding out his arms. “A kiss first!” The children ran to him and he bussed each in turn. “Emily and young Harry,” he told Merewether proudly. “Say good morning to the Captain.” The children responded gracefully, and then went back to their mother to keep an anxious eye on the preparations in progress. Merewether wondered if he might be the centre of such a familial scene in the not too distant future.

The homely little byplay had diverted his attention from Madame Bai. He now looked back to discover her studying him intently. In repose, her face assumed an expression of calculation, eyes now hooded and speculative, quite at variance with the mood it had expressed a moment ago. Her face altered at his glance, smiling again, as the maids began to serve the refreshments. He wondered again at the familiarity of the face. He was certain he had never encountered the woman before, and decided that she must resemble some portrait he had seen.

The elevenses proved to be a delicious repast, tasty kickshaws, relishes, tidbits of choice fish, fowl and beast, even a plate of crumpets with the tea. It certainly would serve as his noon meal, Merewether decided, regretfully declining a second serving. The conversation had dealt mostly with the children during the interval, but surfeited, they now took their leave for siesta. As she turned away from the farewell, Madame Bai spoke again with an expression of ingenuous curiosity.

"The name — Merewether? — somehow strikes a chord of skimmed through the obstetrical details, to come to the last year to Bombay but I seem to associate it with Persia . . ."

"I am just returned from the south Coast of the Gulf, and have several times visited the Empire in years past," he said a little brusquely. "Not recently". She continued to look at him with a slight smile of speculation.

"And how does Lord Minto fare? I departed India when Wellesley was still called the new Governor-General. There have been Cornwallis, and Barlow too, since then."

"Why, very well" he replied. "Of course I only met Minto the one time some months ago . . ."

"Will he renew Wellesley's policy of conquest and tribute, or continue conciliation with the princely states as Cornwallis and Barlow have done?" Merewether was flustered at the question; it revealed a profounder knowledge of high political considerations than he would normally expect of a woman.

He tried to remember some of the glib dinner table assertions Percy had made to MacRae and him last summer during the voyage in *Comet* to Bushire. "I think Lord Minto is compelled to follow the policies fixed by the India Board." A glimmer of recollection came. "The Company may very well have almost run its course out here as the governing power of a sub-continent. Government is taking a much stronger part in its affairs; the India Board has strengthened its hand, as witness Minto's appointment in preference to Barlow. He was president of the Board, you know . . ." He paused, seeing her rapt expression, and realized that he was telling her what she wanted to hear, not that it mattered.

He hurried on, parroting Percy's exposition. ". . . and there is no logical reason why a nation of more than a hundred million persons should be governed by a private company. The Company has managed to survive these two hundred years mainly by playing one native ruler off against another, keeping India fragmented, and employing mercenaries and bribes to hold its pet princes in place . . ."

He did not quote her Percy's further quip, "Why, if all the people of India could agree to piss at one time, they would sluice our few thousand British residents right into the sea!" but rather concluded "Carried to its logical conclusion, this policy might well at some point substitute a British Emperor for the Company's governmental functions, and leave the princely states to rule their own internal affairs . . ." He saw again that he had said the words Madame Bai wanted to hear, and suddenly knew why she appeared familiar to him. She wore the face of the deadly spider in his nightmare of last December!

There were hoofbeats outside, the peal of the bell at the gate, and Merewether welcomed the interruption.

Malhar Rao was a slender languid youth, resembling his mother, but several shades darker, witness of his double dose of Indian blood. His eyes were insolent, likewise his mouth. His mother embraced and kissed him at the gate while his retinue sat their horses outside. He entered to remain only briefly, saluting his Uncle Harry with a casual wave of the hand, impatient to be away again. Fitzgerald made the introduction. Merewether prepared to take his leave.

"I hope to have the pleasure of foregathering with you again during one of the fine days at sea, Madame," Merewether told Tulsi, hoping that no such opportunity would present itself. Recognizing her from his dream, he fancied that he could see the cruel, scheming nature of the woman that lay behind the classic beauty of her face. He knew that he was being melodramatic. Still, Colonel Napier's estimate credited her with iron resolution and the determination to put her son on the throne of Rajputana to the extent that his squadron had been dispatched to this port in anticipation of her attempt to rendezvous with a French force strong enough to accomplish her purpose. He hurried his departure, anxious to escape this pleasant room.

"Pull for the Indiaman," he told the coxswain of his gig.

Captain Cosby of the *Countess of Surrey* was a bald fat man, with the belly and jowls that went with twenty years of rich provender and little need to exercise. He sat ready for his siesta, barefoot, shirt open to his navel, under a vent in the great cabin where a windsail diverted the desultory noontime breeze into a pleasant draught. His manner was courteous but condescending, as befitted a master in the Company's Maritime Service who took precedence over a captain in its naval service.

"No, Merewether, your Bombay Buccaneers have not seen fit to confide their secrets in me. I have no estimate of the situation beyond the report of a French privateer cruising north of Socotra. I would prefer to sail without the convoy, make the return trip in half the time these lard tubs will take, and earn half again as much on the charter." Cosby paused to mop his bald head with a sodden linen handkerchief. He looked shrewdly at Merewether. "Even so, it will be the most profitable haul I ever made. Some up-country potentate — does Holkar ring a bell? — paid the first price I asked in gold, sent his son and about forty of his dog robbers, even a cabin full of birds for his pleasure, over there. The whole sum is net, too. I would have had to lie at Surat and Bombay four months waiting for cargo anyway, and these sons of the prophet provide their own victuals as well."

"I just met the young man ashore, and his mother."

Cosby looked up with interest. "Good! We should be able to get out of this hole before too long, though I'm told the local sheikh plans an entertainment for the feller." He shook his head. "I can't imagine a party without spirits."

"And how did Madame Bai impress you?" Merewether inquired idly. To his surprise, the man colored, looked uncomfortable, and then stammered a bit in his reply.

"Why, a most attractive and intelligent woman. A pity she's of mixed blood . . ." Crosby then tossed out in an elaborately offhanded manner, a question that brought Merewether up short "And how much would make it worth your while to allow *Countess* to proceed independently?"

What in hell? Was it nothing more than the bit of hanky-panky he had suspected at Crosby's reaction to his idle question of a moment ago, or had Madame Bai seduced the captain into doing her bidding, even though it might constitute treason? He managed to reply in what he hoped was a negligent tone to match the captain's inquiry. ". . . I am afraid it would be quite impossible. My orders are most explicit, I am required to take the convoy intact to Surat."

Well," said Cosby, "never hurts to ask, and I'd be willing to divide some of the extra profit . . ."

Merewether went back to *Pitt,* found all well, and prepared to take a siesta himself on the cot under the new vent cut in the overhead in the crowded sleeping cabin for the windsail. The man's reaction puzzled him. Captains of Indiamen were often enough reputed to have taken advantage of women travelling with them, though the offence was punishable, by instant dismissal. But from his brief encounter with Tulsi Bai, Merewether was certain that no man could take advantage of her without her willing it. Rather, he began to suspect that Madame Bai had taken advantage of a fat, middle-aged master to bend him to her will. It was a vexing thought. He would make certain that the *Countess of Surrey* was in company when the convoy departed.

Merewether slept until the first dog watch was called away.

It was an orderly sortie, the Marine cruisers going out first to take stations in accordance with Merewether's orders. Attack was unlikely from northeast around to northwest with the prevailing wind out of the southwest. He formed the convoy up in two columns, one of the regular escort vessels leading each, then stationed *Comet* with her superior weatherly qualities on the port flank to counter any attack from that unlikely quarter. *Vigilant* guarded the starboard flank, and he took position in *Pitt* on the starboard quarter, dead to windward. From this vantage point he could interpose the frigate against an attack on any part of the convoy from downwind, or run down on an interloper approaching to leeward. The other two small escorts were stationed astern of each column.

Merewether congratulated himself on the smartness with which the convoy had formed up with a minimum of signals required. He had held his briefing of the escort commanders and the merchant ship masters yesterday afternoon in *Pitt,* passing out counterparts of his diagram of the formation, issuing instructions, and then answering their questions as to the intervals between ships, and the shielded lights to be displayed astern during the hours of darkness. Only one thing had disturbed him.

"And, Captain," said MacCracken just as the meeting was about to conclude "Remind these officers that once we pass through the straight, Bab el Mandeb, they call it, we lay our course for Cape Guardafui so as to pass south of Socotra . . ." This was news to Merewether.

"By what authority?" he demanded. It took the convoy away from the direct route to Surat.

"Why it was in the revised Convoy Instructions we received a week or so from the Commodore at Surat. I thought you had been furnished a copy . . ."

"No," Merewether said sharply "Do you know the purpose of prolonging the voyage?"

"I can only presume it's because of the French privateer cruising north of Socotra. He made a pass at the convoy coming out, but sheered off when he sighted the Indiaman. Must have mistook her for a seventy-four . . ."

The instruction obviously had been written before Bombay Castle had acted to reinforce the escort at the direction of the Governor-General, and there certainly was no need to avoid a single privateer with the forces now under his command. But Merewether doubted his authority to countermand the order; if he did and some casualty befell the convoy, he would be in peril under his own "do or be damned" orders. It really did not make that much difference, and he reluctantly acquiesced in the order as the briefing adjourned.

In the endless inventory of naval duties, escort of a merchant convoy was easily the dullest and most frustrating. Its speed was dictated by the sailing qualities of the slowest ship. There were interminable delays when cordage parted, spars sprung, seams opened, rotten canvas blew away or even a halt for the brief service before a shrouded corpse slid into the water. For no accountable reason vessels sheered out of line, or fouled one another, or a stern guide light failed, and there was a collision in the darkness. The regular escort commanders were old hands at this sort of thing and dealt with each impossible casualty with speed and decision. After an anxious first day in which imperative signals were two-blocked in *Pitt* most of the time, Merewether washed his hands of the matter and left MacCracken and his captains to deal with the internal discipline in their own fashion.

The convoy crawled sluggishly down the latitudes from-twenty-one degrees north to thirteen, finally to emerge from the Red Sea into the Gulf of Aden. Merewether took his departure from a bearing on the reddish volcanic peak that rose above Ras Siyan on the African shore, and two-blocked his flag hoist to signal the course change to due east. He had felt no particular apprehension during the voyage through the narrow waters of the Red Sea. There were no reports of the enemy passing Bab el Mandeb — only ten miles wide, and literally translated as the "Gate of Tears" — but in the widening approaches to the Arabian Sea, he established extra lookouts at the masthead, and spent the night watches mostly in his canvas chair at the weather rail of the quarterdeck.

It was a suffocating day. The calm had descended before daybreak, and by noon the ships were as motionless as though painted on a sea of glass. There were many boats in the water passing between ships on social missions, and Merewether was not surprised when Hamlyn sent the messenger below with the private dispatch from *Countess of Surrey:* "Request your presence for dinner. Bai." Merewether regretted his passing remark that day ashore in Jeddah, now that it had been acted upon. Still, there was no reason to be rude. No enemy could approach the convoy in this situation, and Dobbs predicted the calm might well endure until nightfall. He scribbled his acceptance and told the messenger to call away the gig.

Countess of Surrey piped the side for him, navy fashion, and Cosby, dressed formally now, shook his hand at the gangway.

"Welcome aboard, Captain, delighted you could come. My fifth mate fancies himself somewhat of a diviner, and prophesies this calm will last the night."

Merewether was escorted aft, passing pens of sheep, two bullocks, and hen coops in the waist. Cosby must have replenished his live provisions at Jeddah, he thought, with a twinge of envy. Madame Bai was holding court in the great cabin with the first through sixth mates, the purser and two relief mates dancing attendance on her. There was a sideboard bearing a selection of wines and spirits, and another groaning under its burden of rich provender. The woman disengaged herself from her circle of admirers, and came to greet him with a dazzling smile.

"Ah, Captain, how delightful that you were able to come. Captain Cosby tells me that we may remain becalmed for another day. Now, may I present these officers to you?" She did so in order of rank, Merewether bobbing at each introduction, wondering what it would be like to have eight watch standers in *Pitt.* "And now, will you refresh yourself? Here are spirits, wines . . ."

Merewether poured a glass of gin, cut a lemon into quarters, and joined the group. He nodded in passing to Malhar Rao, lounging by himself in a corner, a glass of wine in hand, reminded momentarily of that other charming, ruthless would-be Moslem emperor, Tipu Sultan, who was no teetotaler either.

It proved to be a pleasant interval of small talk, gossip and speculation. Merewether found that he had later news of Bombay than the Indiaman's officers, and was happy to impart it. Madame Bai had seated herself in an easy chair, pillow under her feet, joining easily in the chitchat, and he forgot for the time the revulsion he had felt for her that day in Jeddah. She possessed a keen intellect, and remarkable directness of expression. He found himself coming to admire the manner in which she managed to keep all the officers, Cosby included, engaged, and saw that they all were her devoted servants. After another glass of gin he allowed Captain Cosby to persuade him to take a plate loaded with roast beef, thin slices of chicken and savories. (He declined the leg of lamb because he fancied the fleece would stick in his teeth as though it were mutton; it was a silly prejudice that he held against the sheep family, but he could not help it.) The food was delicious, the first fresh meat he had eaten since Bombay. A servant filled his glass with another gin, more than he really desired, but he found a chair near Madame Bai and Cosby, giving first attention to the food, but following the conversation.

"May I have your plate replenished?" inquired the captain solicitously.

"No, thank you," Merewether replied. He was sure the dinner and gin would make him drowsy, and he hoped to call by *Comet* on his way back to the ship if the calm held. He glanced out of the port to assure himself that no breeze yet stirred. Cosby cleared his throat and looked at him speculatively.

"Captain, might I see you a moment in private?" He indicated his sleeping cabin with an inclination of the head.

What now? Another proposition? Merewether could not refuse to talk to the man in his own ship, he decided, as he rose and followed Cosby. Madame Bai appeared hardly to notice their withdrawal, as the door was closed and a chair indicated.

"Now, Merewether, I spoke to you once before when the matter meant more to me than the extra profit I might make by a faster passage, and I think I made you a very fair offer then. You declined, and I can't blame you if your orders so dictate, but I have passengers who claim the most pressing of business at Surat . . ." He paused and indicated the main cabin with his head. ". . . and as a matter of fact they have offered to make it worth my while to conclude a faster passage than the convoy will . . ." Merewether wondered if there would be an offer to divide the bonus ". . . a thousand pounds, five hundred for each of us . . ." The captain smiled winningly at him "Just like finding the money . . . A ship straggles off in the night . . . Happens all the time in the best regulated of convoys . . ."

This was a bald enough proposition. The man had disclosed his principal and made a specific offer. Merewether wondered what additional rewards in kind the captain might be enjoying from Madame Bai, and decided to be obtuse.

"Captain, I do not see how we can speed up this convoy . . ."

"Oh, I agree, no way to do that. *Countess* will just sheer off after dark . . ."

"But what of the Frog privateer?"

"I carry thirty-six guns, as you do, sir."

"But less than a hundred hands to serve eighteen-pounders and also work the ship, while I have four hundred and carry thirty-twos."

"Hell, Merewether, I'm under no orders to stay with the convoy!" Cosby's face had turned mottled red. "And I have precedence of a captain in the Marine as well!"

"Quite so, Captain. But I am under the most explicit orders to take this convoy intact to Surat . . ."

"No affair of mine!"

"I think it is. They are the Governor-General's own orders."

"Now look here, Merewether! I can just sail away and you couldn't stop me!"

"I think I should be compelled to," Merewether replied, striving for a light tone of reason. "The matter is moot for the nonce in any case with this calm." Cosby subsided then spoke again with restraint.

"How about the whole thousand?"

"I do not follow you," said Merewether.

"Well," said Cosby rising. "Let me discuss the matter with my principals. I shall be back in a moment." Actually it was nearer ten before the door opened again.

"Now Captain, you'll not obstruct me, will you?" The contralto voice was a tone above its normal timbre. Madame Bai still wore her dazzling smile, but her eyes had darkened and the set of her jaw was firm. "My son and I have the most urgent affairs in Surat . . ."

"My orders, Madame, are by direction of the Governor-General. I have no discretion. The convoy must stay together."

"If it's money . . ."

"It is not." The smile vanished for a moment, tiny crowsfeet about his eyes and lips were visible in the harsh afternoon light, then it reappeared in the guise of a calculated expression of sensual enticement, and the woman spoke in an almost diffident tone as she moved forward.

"Or better yet, a reward in kind in addition to the money . . ."

She was pressing her body against his in the most explicit manner, a hand slipped over his shoulder to the back of his head as her lips touched his. Merewether responded in surprise, the fiery embrace and kiss arousing him in spite of his resolution. Her lips released his, and she tilted her head back to look directly up into his eyes.

"Now! Latch the door . . ."

He wavered, then regained his self-control and stepped back just as the door burst open. Merewether half expected the woman to rend her clothing and cry "Rape!"

Cosby's expression was one of simple anger, but his face faded to disappointment as he saw Merewether standing aloof from Madame Bai. She only looked at him a moment longer, then gathered her dignity about her, turned and hurried out as the master stepped aside to let her pass.

"And have you reached a decision, Captain?" he asked lamely.

"I see no reason to change the one already made for us. *Countess of Surrey* continues in company with the convoy."

As the gig pulled away from the Indiaman there was a bare hint of air stirring, not enough to ripple the water yet, but clouds were building in the southwest promising a breeze before nightfall. Merewether decided to take the time to visit *Comet* and alert MacRae to the possibility that *Countess* might make an attempt to escape. The small Scots officer met him at the gangway.

"An unexpected pleasure, Captain!"

"A pleasure, certainly, but line of duty also." MacRae led him below where he refused more refreshment and came quickly to the point, explaining the situation and the efforts already made to obtain permission to sail singly, but omitting any mention of the bonus offered by Madame Bai.

"So you see the temper of the people. Stay close but use no unnecessary force. After all, Cosby outranks us in the Company."

"I'll not let him escape, Captain."

It had been a curious interlude, Merewether reflected, as they rowed back through the idle ships now lying as askew as jackstraws in the calm. Other boats were moving between ships, and Merewether made a mental note to signal the convoy to hoist them in, anticipating the coming breeze. The stroke oar had piped up with an interminable rollicking ballad that detailed the salacious adventures of a young man from Bath on his way to see the Queen, with the other hands joining in a roaring chorus after each quatrain. The ditty attracted the grinning attention of the hands in each ship they passed. The monotonous repetition was euphoric, and he relaxed to turn the situation over in his mind, staring blindly ahead.

The opening gambit at Jeddah had been forthright enough, a simple inquiry as to Merewether's price for permitting *Countess of Surrey* to proceed independently. There were many legitimate reasons for this request. The Indiaman could make twice the speed of the convoy; lacking the intelligence summary from Calcutta and the explicit orders, Merewether would have granted the request as routine without thought of any reward. The second approach by Cosby had been much more urgent, specific sums mentioned with the hint that more might be forthcoming, then anger and a bit of bluster, and the withdrawal to consult with his principal.

At this point, Madame Bai had decided to intervene herself. Either she or Cosby must have considered him incredibly naive, a man to yield instantly to physical temptation. Or perhaps the woman fancied her charms to be irresistible. On second thought, he decided that the maneuver was the stratagem alone of Madame Bai. It was unlikely that the captain could have conceived a variation of the ancient badger game wherein the pimp surprised his whore *in flagrante delicto* with a man who could not afford a scandal. His reaction on entering the cabin had been more plausibly that of a man motivated by simple jealousy, that Tulsi might invite another to share her favors. He reached a conclusion: the pair had exposed their hands, and he intended to keep a tight leash on *Countess* lest she slid away into the night. He felt the coxswain's movement beside him as he held up four fingers and answered the hail, *"Pitt!"*

The breeze freshened after dark, and there was a night-long mêlée as the escorts strove to sort the scattered convoy into some sort of order. If the Indiaman intended to make a run for it, now was the time. Merewether hoped that MacRae's psychic powers were functioning as well as they had last year in the Bay of Bengal when he predicted the movement of the French privateers.

At dawn, Merewether's heart leaped into his mouth as he swept the horizon to find *Countess of Surrey* missing. He was comforted only slightly to see that *Comet* also was gone. The convoy was still scattered over miles of sea, but with daylight, the escort snows were snapping at the heels of the stragglers, signals flying, with an occasional gunshot to underscore their orders, and by noon the convoy had converged again into a reasonably compact formation. By Dobbs's calculations, they should raise Cape Guardafui tomorrow and take departure for their eastward course south of Socotra, there to bear up east-northeast across the Arabian Sea for Surat. Just after noon, they sighted *Countess,* lying hove to, *Comet* to leeward of her. Merewether breathed a sigh of relief as the pair joined the formation but within the hour, the wind had failed again.

Merewether was staring out the sternlights in the day cabin, fidgeting from one foot to the other in irritation at the delay as *Pitt* lay almost motionless in the calm, when the messenger knocked and entered.

"Sir, there's a lady on deck to see you." Hellfire and damnation! Had Tulsi come to beard him again in his own ship?

"I'll come."

Madame Bai was standing in aloof dignity near the gangway, Dobbs hovering nearby. Technically, the ship was still underway, but he had left his station on the quarterdeck, evidently to oversee the rigging of the landing stage and ladder over the side to accommodate the gig from *Countess.* It now lay too, some fifty yards off the starboard beam, its crew tricked out in crimson jumpers, white trousers and hats.

"Good afternoon, Madame," he greeted her formally.

"May I see you privately a moment, Captain? The boat has strict orders to return within an hour."

"Certainly. This way." He led her aft and seated her in the cabin, leaving the door open, then took his place formally behind the desk. She kept her head averted, appearing to stare at her clasped hands, shoulders shaking, finally to look up, eyes brimming with tears. Gad the woman was a consummate actress!

"Captain, I have come to offer my abject apologies for my inexcusable conduct of yesterday, and that of Captain Cosby last night in attempting to proceed to our destination independently . . ." Her eyes filled again, and Merewether was instantly more uncomfortable. He had hoped the incident would expire without further remark, let alone tears.

"Why . . ." he began uncertainly, and she raised her face to look directly at him, to speak in a faltering voice

"May I have a cup of tea, please? I feel quite faint . . ." Possibly the social amenities incident to the formal service would calm the woman, Merewether thought, and rang the pantry bell.

Sangh poured the cups with his practiced grace, looking a bit disapproving at finding his captain *tête à tête* with a woman in the cabin at sea, then withdrew. Madame Bai balanced the saucer against the faint movement of the ship, then took a cautious sip of the hot brew. Her tears had dried and her eyes sparkled.

"Oh, Captain, I should have asked your servant, but would you be kind enough to see if my boat is still waiting? Captain Cosby was most explicit . . ." Merewether was sure it was, it had not been a quarter of an hour since she came on board, but he was glad to humor her, to escape a moment from her overpowering presence. He stepped out on deck to see for himself. The gig was, as he knew it would be, still lying off in the motionless sea, its brightly clad crew asprawl on the thwarts. He took an additional moment to comment on the weather and the possibility of a breeze later in the afternoon with Dobbs and Larkin, and made his way leisurely below again.

"All is well," he reported as he took his seat and stirred a spoonful of sugar into the cup. The woman now wore almost an expression of expectancy, evidently recovered from her faintness of a few moments ago.

"Good . . ." began Madame Bai, then shrieked and sprang to her feet, the cup and saucer shattering on the deck in a splatter of amber fluid. What now? Another badger game in his own ship? She had retreated to a corner of the cabin, hands covering her eyes, shaking uncontrollably. The thing did not make sense, but now she was pointing towards the pantry door.

"Get it away! Oh, God, get it out!"

Merewether whirled to see Abercrombie, tail erect, frozen in astonishment, standing in the doorway to the pantry. The cat was the only living thing visible in the cabin, and he looked back at Madame Bai for some explanation of her remarkable conduct.

"The cat! Take him away! He makes me ill!" Understanding came to Merewether as he moved to shoo the tom back into the pantry and close the door. This woman must be one of those persons who cannot abide cats and become physically ill in their presence. He had heard of the phenomenon, but never before witnessed its effect, and the very real reaction of Madame Bai was startling.

"I must leave at once. Even out of sight, I feel his presence!" The woman was in real distress, face pale, brow wet still shaking.

Merewether was glad enough to see her go, and escorted Madame Bai to the gangway to signal in the gig. "Delighted to have seen you again," he told her, bowing formally. It was difficult to rationalize the antipathy he felt for the woman in spite of her beauty. She appeared still to be distraught as she was handed over the slide, and only murmured indistinctly in response.

It had been a puzzling and unpleasant visit, Merewether decided as he made his leisurely way aft. He was certain that she had intended more than a mere apology, but the entrance of the cat had apparently driven all thought of anything else out of her mind. He must inquire of Buttram as to the validity of the phobia the woman suffered, but it had appeared real enough, and there was no other explanation for her reaction. He swept the horizon with his eye at the companion, seeing clouds building up in the southwest with the promise of a breeze, and entered the day cabin to see Abercrombie crouched on his desk lapping at the cup of tea, stone cold by now. The open pantry serving window showed his means of entry.

As Merewether came in, the cat looked up at him, then froze, jaws opening wide, lips drawn back in a snarl; the body arched, appearing to fold in upon itself, and the animal fell off the desk heavily on its back. A half dozen violent convulsions accompanied by a high keening sound followed and the contorted body lay still, jaws still locked open in a macabre grin.

"Sangh!" The little Hindu came out of the pantry to stop, eyes wide at the sight of the cat. "Ask Doctor Buttram to come at once." The doctor, accompanied by Doctor Mefford, was in the cabin within the minute. "He was on my desk drinking cold tea from my cup, then fell off and was dead in a moment. What do you make of it, gentlemen?"

Both medical men knelt to examine the furry corpse.

Mefford rose and dusted his knees. "He died quickly but not easily!"

"He was drinking your tea?" inquired Buttram in a tone of disbelief.

"Oh, yes. Quite often he lapped the dregs, but this is the first time I remember that he had a full cup available." Buttram bent over and sniffed the cup.

"Cold tea is all I can smell," he reported. "However, I do not propose to sample it in view of the cat's fate." He looked in the sugar bowl, then picked up the cup, placed the saucer over it, and continued, "I am willing to wager my medical degree that it contains an extract of the seeds of *strychnos nux-vomica,* and that the sugar does as well. I will consult my Pharmacopeia and see if I can make a definite identification." He and Mefford departed with the cup of cold tea and sugar bowl. Merewether rang the bell.

"I think you had better remove the late Abercrombie," he told Sangh. "Poor fellow. I think he met the fate that was intended for me!" Eyes wide, Sangh picked up the cat and withdrew.

Buttram was back within the hour, a vial containing a spoon-full of white crystals in hand.

"This is what I managed to extract from the cup of tea alone, Captain," he said, holding it up to see. "It is strychnine, derived from the seeds of the fruit of *strychnos nux-vomica,* a tree native to India. It has been employed for centuries as a favorite tool of the poisoner, and as little as two grains' weight may be fatal within minutes. There was enough in your tea to kill a dozen men, but it also serves as a valuable medical drug when administered in minute doses." He paused and looked quizzically at Merewether. "Now I know about the lady's visit to the ship, but not why, and her murderous motive escapes me."

Merewether looked at the doctor, his face no longer so fresh and young as it had been two years ago. The fair complexion had coarsened, sun lines formed crowsfeet about his eyes, and his middle had thickened. He knew that Buttram was considering submitting his resignation as surgeon in the Marine by the end of the year to return to England with his young wife and daughter, and for a moment he envied him his independence of a lifetime career in the Company's Navy. Still, the doctor was very nearly his closest friend, outranked only by MacLellan. He decided he could certainly use a second opinion, and detailed his orders, the situation estimate, the original tentative overtures made at Jeddah, the propositions made to him yesterday, explicit as to money and sexual favors, the attempt of the *Countess of Surrey* to escape last night, and finally, the curious call of an hour ago ostensibly to offer an apology.

"I can only conclude in light of your identification of the poison, Doctor, that a brazen attempt has been made to assassinate me in the expectation that discipline in the escort force would suffer. It is fortunate that the woman has this curious fear of cats. I suspect that Madame Bai and her son have a rendezvous with the French squadron and military forces from Mauritius, and intend to overthrow Holkar with their aid to place Malhar on the throne." Buttram had followed the account with rapt attention, and now sat back, one forefinger laid alongside his nose, thumb under his chin, scrutinizing Merewether as though he were his patient seeking a diagnosis of a baffling malady.

“I agree with your analysis, Captain,” said Buttram judicially, dropping his hand and leaning forward. “She must be entirely desperate at this point to conclude the rendezvous, having failed in friendly persuasion, bribery, seduction, simple escape, and now murder.” He paused a moment, staring past Merewether’s head through the stern lights at the motionless sea. “I would give serious consideration to the obvious measure: put a party of Marines aboard the Indiaman . . .” The thought had occurred to Merewether, but it would be a grievous affront to a captain, certainly with powerful friends in the courts of proprietors and directors in London, and he had reluctantly discarded the remedy.

“No,” Merewether said finally. “I believe we must hold a short leash on *Countess* and Madame, but nothing so drastic as putting a prize crew in a Company Maritime Service vessel.” Buttram soon departed, and Merewether went on deck to survey the second afternoon of glassy calm. He was turning to go below when he saw Sangh approach the stern carrying a pitifully small packet held in both hands. He paused, head bowed, holding his arms straight out, then slowly lowered them until the bundle fell into the sea. Sangh remained bowed for a long moment then straightened, and marched below.

Abercrombie had been given his last rites as ship’s cat in accordance with naval tradition.

Dawn brought a repetition of the previous day’s confusion. The wind for several hours the night before had blown erratically, fair for some ships in the convoy, even as it left others becalmed. *Countess of Surrey* was on station, *Comet* hovering to leeward, MacRae evidently taking no chances after the abortive escape attempt two nights ago. Merewether signaled a reduction in speed while the escort vessels chivvied the stragglers over miles of sea into a reasonable formation. At this rate the convoy would be a long time yet taking departure on Cape Guardafui, if the pattern of afternoon calms persisted. To his relief, the wind held, light but steady, and a little after dawn the next day they sighted the precipitous grey mass of the cape on the starboard bow. An hour later, Dobbs recommended that the convoy change course to east by north so as to pass just south of the island of Abd Al Kuri, and north of the islets called "The Brothers", thence to take a new departure from the eastern tip of Socotra.

"So signal the convoy, Mister Dobbs." Once clear of these hazards, it was a clear run across the Arabian Sea to the Gulf of Cambay and Surat, with the likelihood of favorable winds at this season. Merewether felt a sense of relief to regain the relatively open sea again after the narrow confines of the Red Sea and enter the Gulf of Aden.

A little after noon, Merewether was relaxing with his chair set under the vent for the windsail, enjoying the steady flow of air, when he heard the maintop hail the deck.

"Deck there! Sail ho!"

"Where away?" responded Larkin.

"Near two points on the starboard bow." Well, on that bearing it might very well be the westernmost islet of The Brothers rather than a ship, Merewether thought, relaxing again. Two minutes later, the messenger knocked and entered.

"Sir, Mister Larkin reports two sail, frigates by the cut of them, bearing two points on the starboard bow."

"They're sails, not islands?"

"Sir, Mister Larkin took the glass to the crosstrees before he sent me below."

"I'll come."

Larkin had excellent eyesight, Merewether did not doubt his identification since the upper works of the newer French frigates were distinctive in design.

"Made certain myself from the crosstrees," Larkin told him on deck.

"Very well. Signal the convoy, "Enemy in sight bearing east by south". Can you estimate their course?"

"About north-northwest on the port tack. Dobbs says they should intercept the convoy about fifteen miles ahead if we maintain course and speed." The island of Abd Al Kuri was a dark smudge on the northern horizon. There was no longer any necessity for the convoy to maintain a course so as to pass south of Socotra in view of the appearance of the French squadron.

"We'll make it a stern chase then to upset their calculations. Signal, 'Change course to northeast'."

Flags blossomed on the signal halyards, and Marlowe acting as signal officer waited impatiently, sweeping the convoy with his glass, for the response of each vessel to the signal. Finally, all ships had the flag hoist two-blocked to indicate, "Understood". Merewether nodded to Marlowe to execute the hoist.

With the threat of an enemy just over the horizon, the convoy began to close up as masters of country ships cracked on canvas and squared away before the wind. It was only a few minutes after the change of course became effective that the lookout reported the French ships had also altered course, and that he could now see a third ship. There was little doubt now of their intentions, and Merewether found himself examining the hands on deck with an eye of anxious appraisal, wondering how they might react in the heat of battle, if they had finally melded into a cohesive crew of old hands and new. Time alone would prove the fact, and he called a council of war of all officers and warrant officers immediately in the day cabin.

"Gentlemen," he began, feeling almost as self-conscious as he had a year and a half ago when he addressed the officers of his squadron in the Bay of Bengal, but thankful that he had no Wolfe present now to dispute him. "In view of the intelligence provided us from Calcutta, and its apparent corroboration by certain recent events, I think it certain that a French squadron is in pursuit of the convoy. I am also of the opinion that its principal objective is the Indiaman, *Countess of Surrey,* although it likely would not pass up other prizes of value. As most of you know, we are under the most explicit orders to bring the convoy safely to Surat. I think it, therefore, prudent to clear for action and lay out firefighting equipment now, though there is no need yet to send the hands to quarters or put out the galley fires and smoking lamp. Any question?"

"Yes, sir," spoke up Hamlyn. "Of what force are these frigates?"

"Thirty-sixes, I'm told, if these are the same ships."

"Good! It should be an interesting action." The fires of youth, thought Merewether indulgently.

"Bear in mind we are not here to seek the bubble reputation in the cannon's mouth," Merewether told him lightly, proud of his literary paraphrase. The meeting adjourned and the hands soon began to knock down partitions and remove encumbrances from the gun decks, set out buckets of sand and water, lay canvas hose to the pumps, and rig boarding nets of hammocks. Spirits appeared high, he was encouraged to note, and Larkin reported *Pitt* cleared for action in a good six minutes less time than the previous drill.

Half an hour later, the maintop reported that the frigates had altered course to the west. They had just sighted The Brothers, Merewether decided, and must give them a wide berth, putting them farther behind the convoy. The longer he could spin out the chase, the better chance he had to escape. Last year, a lightly escorted convoy in the Bay of Bengal had played the game of blind man's buff and artful dodger with a pair of French privateers in the Bay of Bengal for five days, to come up fortuitously with two of Pellew's frigates, which promptly made prizes of the hounds. He had no hope of such good fortune, but a gale, a change of course in the night, or some casualty to the pursuers might achieve the same result.

By dusk, the frigates were still only three specks to the naked eye on the southern horizon. The alteration of course had conformed to the best sailing qualities of the ships in the convoy and reduced the rate of gain, proving once more the old adage that a stern chase is a long chase. Before nightfall, Merewether signaled the convoy to darken ships. It was worth the risk if they could slip away into the night. He toyed a moment with the idea of ordering a change of course at an arbitrary time, then decided it was too dangerous an evolution with the probability of collision and stragglers. Play the string out as long as possible, leave something to chance, and let the Frogs commit themselves. He dined lightly in the cabin, then settled himself for the night in his chair rigged on the weather side of the quarterdeck.

The stars glittered bright in the night sky, moonrise would come close to three bells in the first watch and in spite of the anxieties of the moment, he fell into a reverie. By now his child must be more than two months old, assuming he or she had survived the hazards of birth and the first days of infancy. Of course, Caroline had survived childbirth before, but it was no guaranty that she would again. He tried to visualize how the child might look, then abandoned the effort; he had no close acquaintance with infants. He felt no different, no wiser, no more mature, by the fact of fatherhood, and wondered if he were capable of cherishing and guiding a child in its development of moral character, wisdom and learning in the ways of the world. His own short childhood before his mother's death had left him ill prepared, and most of his learning had been accumulated through the bitter years and hard knocks of experience. The guidance and education of a child became suddenly a vast and frightening responsibility. He was thankful that Caroline with her firm moral convictions and love of learning would share the task with him, but he felt that it was yet his own responsibility, and he doubted his qualifications. The reverie ended in the tramp and bustle of the mid-watch relieving the first watch. Merewether dozed off for an hour.

At dawn, Merewether looked first for *Countess* and found her in place under the close surveillance of *Comet.* Then he searched out the enemy squadron. It appeared no closer than at dusk last night. The westward detour it had been compelled to make to avoid The Brothers had cancelled out its superiority in speed for the time being and left it almost dead astern. With no navigational impediments now, it stood a chance of coming up with the convoy by noon. He decided to reorient the escort, leaving *Comet* in her present position, but signaling *Vigilant* to a station astern, moving the starboard leading snow around to the starboard quarter, then positioning *Pitt* in the centre of the escort force astern where it might dash off in either direction to counter an attack. He waited on deck until he saw the order accomplished, then went below for breakfast. As he came into the cabin, he saw a flicker of movement on the transom out of the corner of his eye.

"Sangh!" The little Indian came out of the pantry and bent in his first meeting of the day salaam. "What is this?"

"Sah," replied Sangh, looking up with his most melting gaze. "It is a son of our late cat . . ." Sangh could not bring himself to say, "Abercrombie"; the name evidently recalled too many painful recollections of his days of bondage under the heavy-handed pirate. "I thought, sah, you might call him after another of your late enemies . . ." He looked expectantly at Merewether.

"Well, who?" he demanded, unable to fathom what Sangh had in mind.

"Why, sah," looking now self-conscious. "Why, Tipu Sultan."

"Done!" laughed Merewether. "And now, let's have a look at young Tipu!" The kitten cuddled in his hands, emitting a coarse purr as his ears were scratched. "You're sure it's a tom? Otherwise, we might have to change the name to Madame Bai!" It was almost as red as Abercrombie, but with more pronounced stripes in its fur. Merewether had no objection to Sangh keeping the pet; it would deter rats and mice in the pantry. He handed the kitten back to Sangh and called for breakfast.

Before two bells in the forenoon watch, the wind began to play an exasperating game with the convoy. It died away completely, leaving the ships becalmed, while it continued to serve the French squadron, bringing it hull up before failing there too. Then it blew again, but drew around out of the south-south-east, taking several of the less alert ships aback. At least the convoy could still hold its course, and it then made amends of a sort by leaving the frigates still becalmed, so that they receded again to mere specks on the horizon. But there were thunderheads building up in the southwest, and Merewether kept a wary eye on them lest a sudden squall catch the ships with too much sail set.

The squall struck halfway through the first dog-watch, a grey line of torrential rain blotting out the squadron and sweeping through the convoy. He had had signals flying to shorten sail, but even so the force of the wind preceding the rain made *Pitt* stagger through some anxious moments before squaring away before it. It swept past them in the space of a quarter of an hour, and Merewether found the frigates nearer, but not quite full up, in line abreast. Darkness found the situation unchanged, and near the end of the second dogwatch, Merewether resumed his vigil in the canvas chair on the quarterdeck, dozing in intermittent catnaps.

Half an hour before the end of the first watch, Merewether came wide awake. Everything appeared in order, the ship ghosting along at an easy four knots or so, Dobbs standing at ease on the weather side of the quarterdeck just abaft the helm. The sails were drawing well and the quartermaster could hold his course with little effort. There was little to be gained by remaining on deck any longer. Better to get a good night's rest against the possibility of a strenuous day tomorrow. Suddenly Merewether felt a desire for conversation in the fashion of the long entertaining discussions in the night with young Harris, the Yankee shipowner, on the voyage back from Ile de France last year. Dobbs had never displayed any gift of small talk, most of his utterances being limited to terse line of duty subjects, and on impulse he cleared his throat, then spoke.

"Mister Dobbs." The young officer came over to the chair, his face barely visible in the light of the gibbous moon. Merewether was suddenly uncertain and self-conscious, and continued lamely, "And how do you find your service in the Marine?"

"Why . . . Very well, sir."

Merewether regretted for a moment commencing the conversation, Dobbs was still tongue-tied, and he might as well terminate the effort. He opened his mouth to utter some platitude in dismissal when Dobbs continued, "Of course, there is enough to keep me busy, what with the navigation, though I find it much easier now that I use the new American method. . . ."

"American method?" Merewether had learned Moore's method by rote in preparation for his examination for a commission as second lieutenant ten years ago, and still could toil through the tedious equations to a solution when the necessity arose. He was no mathematician, and had not heard of a new method, American or otherwise.

"Yes, sir, a theory of navigation published five or six years ago by a man named Nathaniel Bowditch. The work is called *The New American Practical Navigator,* and it presents a method that is shorter and more accurate than Moore's. I found a copy at Fort William last winter, and then showed it to Captain Wilkerson, the fleet surveyor and navigator, at Bombay. He proved out the equations, and suggested that I use both methods until I was sure the new one worked. And it does! He asked me to write a report of my experiences with my comments and recommendations. Possibly, he said, the entire Marine should adopt the theory, if I found it superior to the Moore method. I have all the results, and a rough draft of my report to submit when we reach Bombay." There was genuine enthusiasm in Dobbs's voice. There were more depths to this young man than he had previously discerned, Merewether concluded.

"How did you learn so much about mathematics?"

"Mostly since I came into the Marine. Of course, I had some education, but Lieutenant Massey in my first ship taught me the theory, and MacRae helped me too, so I've studied ever since."

"How did you chance to enter the Marine?"

"Sir, my parents died of smallpox when I was fifteen. My father had a greengrocer's shop in Manchester, but of course I was not able to carry on the business, and my uncle sold it as my guardian. I wanted a warrant as midshipman in the Royal Navy, but we didn't have the connections. My grandfather had sailed as mate in an Indiaman, and one of his old shipmates had the influence to get me a place as a volunteer in the Marine. I took the examination for lieutenant two years ago, became a passed midshipman, and then you got me the commission as second lieutenant last year."

"You have made very good progress in the Marine, and earned every step of it. You know I made special mention of your services at Ras ul Khymah?"

"Yes, sir. You showed it to me. Thank you."

"No thanks are necessary. It was your due. Will you make the Marine your career?"

"I hope to. I enjoy navigation and seamanship, though I don't have the flair for gunnery that Larkin has. By the way, sir, did you see the report in the London papers at Bombay of a steam-propelled vessel?"

"No. Is there such a thing?"

"Yes, sir. An American named Robert Fulton built such a ship last year at New York. It has boilers and a steam engine that turns paddle wheels on either side, and it can sail right against the wind and tide . . ."

Merewether thought instantly of the problem of finding and storing enough galley firewood even for a three-month voyage.

"Would there be room for a crew and cargo after stowing enough wood for a voyage? And wouldn't the vessel be likely to catch on fire?"

"I don't know, sir. Perhaps you could use Newcastle coals, they burn hotter and longer than wood."

"A long way to Newcastle," Merewether replied dryly. Something in the idea of a ship with its white wings of sail being corrupted by a smoking, stinking, clanking engine like the ponderous Puffing Billy that pumped the graving docks dry at Bombay offended him. And, too, he had spent the major portion of his life learning the art that enabled him to take a vessel from port to port regardless of wind direction. Should this hard-earned mastery be superseded by a mere machine that any dolt could manage? "It will be a long time, I think, before such a contraption becomes practicable."

"I have hopes I may serve in one before my career in the Marine is finished," said Dobbs in a far-away tone. Merewether could dimly distinguish the blunt features in the moonlight as Dobbs looked up to check the trim of the sails, then drifted over to look in the binnacle. When he returned, he spoke in a different voice, but with a studied air of offhandedness. "Sir, do you have any intimation of where our next commission may be?"

Merewether responded with complete candor.

"None whatever."

Merewether had a sudden conviction that the young officer was blushing, though it was impossible to see in the darkness.

"Well, you know *Rapid* was in the scouting squadron with Commodore Waldron last year east of Malacca. We called at Penang going out, and again returning . . ." Dobbs paused as the messenger approached. "Yes, you may call the watch." He turned back to Merewether and continued, "Anyway, when we were there the first time last year I met a girl at the ball Mister Raffles gave and I saw her several times again last year . . ." He went on in a small diffident voice. "She said she would wait for me, but there are others, particularly a lieutenant in the Royal Navy . . ."

"Have you heard from her?"

"Yes, in the mail we got at Ras ul Khymah. She sounded a bit impatient."

"I cannot predict our next operation, provided we survive this one, but if we come back to Bombay, and the requirements of the service permit, I would entertain a request for a reasonable amount of leave." There was an appreciable pause while Dobbs assimilated the statement.

There was a tramp and bustle as the midwatch began to come on deck and relieve. Dobbs withdrew to impart the situation and night orders to MacCamy preparatory to his taking the deck.

You never know, Merewether mused. He had not pictured square, inarticulate Dobbs as "the lover sighing like a furnace" or suffering the pangs of unrequited passion. The thought of the quotation recalled that delicious, spontaneous interlude of his own with Caroline last summer just before he left for Persia with Rob Percy. He racked his brain to recall the sequence of events leading up to his carrying her off bodily to bed, but the words would not come. Was it "soldier"? He remembered quoting "the justice", and certainly "the lover" had triggered the climax, but as a result of that brief idyll, he had fathered a child. He felt uncomfortable for a moment at the present uncertainty, the lack of news, then consoled himself with the thought that he could have been no more than a moral bulwark to Caroline had he been present. He was suddenly weary, arose, found the glass and swept the horizon, now distinct in the moonlight. He could not discern the frigates and went below, leaving word with MacCamy for a call at daybreak. Just before he dropped off, he determined to inquire of Dobbs which of the young ladies at Penang had caught his fancy.

Dobbs came awake slowly, conscious of the messenger's rough hand on his shoulder. Good God! Was it time again? He had only just closed his eyes, it seemed, after coming off the first watch at midnight.

"Mister Hamlyn says sky and horizon are clear, half an hour to sunrise."

"All right. I'll come." The messenger went out, the horny soles of his bare feet whispering along the teak deck. Dobbs did not dare to let his eyes close again. He needed a star fix to verify Pitt's position after the change of course and squall yesterday. There had been too much cloud cover to observe even a single star last night, and the captain was most particular about his day's work in navigation, though the dead reckoning position was never far from that established by celestial observation.

The thought of Merewether produced a warm sensation in his heart as he remembered the report of the operation last spring at Ras ul Khymah. He could recite from memory the paragraph dealing with himself:

"I wish to call particular attention to the services of Lieutenant John Dobbs whose survey of the bottom disclosed the shallow winding channel leading to a point just off the town, allowing *Pitt* to approach the fortress within pointblank range. His energy, resource and attention to duty are in accordance with the highest traditions of the Company's Marine, and largely responsible for the success of the operation."

Dobbs put his feet on the deck and groped for his trousers, then found his boots and clumped into the wardroom to pour a cup of tea. On deck, Hamlyn and Gaffner, the duty quartermaster, had the sextants laid out and the hack watch already compared with the chronometer. The motion of the ship was easy, the sea calm, the sky almost cloudless. The stars were still brilliant and the horizon just becoming distinct, as he gulped down his tea and picked up the sextant. The captain's canvas chair at the weather rail was empty, he noted, before he looked up at the heavens.

"Betelgeuse," he told Hamlyn, sighting through the reversed sextant on the star, then moving the arm on the arc until the horizon became visible in the mirror. He turned the instrument right side up and made the fine adjustments to bring the star down precisely on the line of the horizon. "Mark. Mark. Mark." Hamlyn echoed him and Gaffner made a note of the time, then the altitude each officer read off from the ivory scale inletted in the ebony instrument. Only a slight difference, Dobbs was pleased to note. They repeated the observations on four more stars, then Dobbs and Gaffner went into the cubby to commence solving the intricate equations conceived by Nathaniel Bowditch in his New American Method that eventually would result in a position he could plot on a chart. Hamlyn would work out his observations for comparison when he came off watch, but for the present the diminutive Gaffner would also work out the sights according to Moore's older formulas as a continuing check on the new method.

Finished, Dobbs painstakingly plotted the indicated position on the chart, marking it with a faint dot, surrounded by a circle, then added the date and time, and looked over at Gaffner, hunched on a stool, his sharp face intent on his figures. In the yellow light of the lamp, the quarter-master resembled a gnome in a drawing out of a story book. He set down the final figures, slid off the stool, and rapidly manipulated the parallel rules on the chart, then placed an almost invisible dot.

"Less'n a mile of difference, sor," he reported in a high Cockney voice. "Oi wuz 'opin' to catch yer off this toime." He grinned, showing yellow teeth. Dobbs grinned back at him.

"And so you might, but I threw out the star I mistook for Capella," he said over his shoulder as he went out on deck into the light of the rising sun.

“I make it twelve degrees, thirty-one minutes north, fifty-two fifty east,” he reported to Hamlyn, who entered the position in the deck log, then sent the messenger to the cabin with the slip showing the date, time, latitude and longitude, initialed by Dobbs.

Dobbs looked about the deck, then astern, yawning mightily. The topsails of the frigates reflected gleaming white in the oblique rays of the sun. They were measurably closer than at dusk last night, but not dangerously so, he decided. By noon, assuming the wind held and no squalls, *Pitt* might well be in action. A spot of breakfast would help now.

The wardroom mess steward had actually found two swine in Moslem Jeddah, and there was still bacon for breakfast. Larkin was alone at the table finishing a cup of coffee before he took the deck for the forenoon watch. Dobbs would succeed him in regular rotation at noon, and they grunted amiable good mornings at one another before Larkin picked up his hat and went out.

While the tea cooled, Dobbs thought of his conversation with Captain Merewether last night, and felt again the inner sense of warmth. The man was essentially kind, he decided again, though he brooked no nonsense and demanded efficient performance of every duty assigned. There had been no obligation on his part to offer a leave, even if the exigencies of the service permitted, and Dobbs would not have asked for such indulgence on his own initiative. Even if granted, it would take a mighty and fortuitous combination of luck and circumstances to transport him to Penang and back. Possibly it would be more realistic to ask for transfer to a ship serving in the Straits area, though it would mean leaving Merewether for some unknown quantity as a commanding officer.

But Judith was worth it! Her vision swam before his eyes as he stared blindly at the sideboard across the room. She had been a pert slip of a girl, the youngest of the group, when he met her at the Governor’s Ball at George Town more than a year ago, and he had monopolized her evening. She had put him at ease instantly, he had found no need to talk as she bubbled along in a stream of inconsequential gossip, identification and judgments on others present, punctuated with indirect inquiries about himself. And yet, when he spoke, she had listened. By the end of the evening, he knew she had been born in Bombay, daughter of a sailing master in the Marine who now served as Port Captain for Penang since he had lost an arm, married to the sister of a writer in the Company's Bombay establishment. Dobbs had found himself for the first time in his life in the close company of a girl, albeit one some five years his junior. He had asked to see her again, and she had consented. On *Rapid's* last call at Penang last fall, he had summoned the courage to ask her to marry him, and she had made a conditional acceptance: that the marriage take place within the year.

Cold hatred welled up in Dobbs as he thought of Lieutenant Garner, serving in HMS *Argus,* based on Penang, who persisted in pursuing Judith during his absence. He had been within an ace of calling the obnoxious rival out last fall, but Judith had dissuaded him. Still, the danger persisted, absence might not make her heart grow fonder and he felt the most urgent compulsion to make her his own. Life would not be worth living if he could not have Judith Johnson.

He pushed back the chair and hurried to his room to take pen in hand and compose a letter to be posted in Bombay, hopefully as specific as he could make it. He was working on the third draft when he heard the drums and bugles summoning the hands to quarters. He laid the writing kit aside, inserted a brace of pistols in his belt, clapped on his hat, and mounted the ladder to assume his post as officer of the watch.

The situation had changed dramatically in the last hour. For no apparent reason, the frigates had in one quick burst of speed closed the gap that had held them off the past forty-eight hours. Merewether watched the approach, trying to forecast the tactics they might employ. If that Frenchman played his cards astutely now, he could cut out the *Countess of Surrey* with one frigate while holding the escort force immobilized with the other two. Even as he visualized the tactical situation and its alternatives in his mind, Merewether saw the outboard frigate alter course to port, while the other two pressed ahead in the chase. He looked back and saw the silhouette of *Countess* changing in shape. The Indiaman was wearing about on the port tack making a run for it almost due west, hoping to gain refuge under the frigate's guns.

"Signals! To *Comet* and *Ariel:* "Board the Indiaman". Send the hands to quarters, Mister Larkin."

It was one thing for Cosby to try to slip away from the convoy in the night for a quicker passage to Surat, but quite another to defect in the face of the enemy with the evident intention of joining them. Still, even now he acted at his peril in taking such action against a Company Maritime Service ship whose master took precedence over a captain in the Marine. The burden would be on him to prove his charges, with the presumption in favor of Cosby, if the matter should reach the courts.

The bugles shrilled their urgent summons, drums rolled in the staccato beat to quarters, and boatswain's mates passed the word down every companionway and hatch. Merewether took his eyes off the Frenchmen long enough to observe the disciplined speed with which the seamen manned their battle stations, a far cry from the sullen crew of four months ago. He looked back at the diverging frigate, attempting in his mind to solve an equation containing an infinite number of variables.

The decision he made now was vital. *Comet* with fourteen guns could not oppose a thirty-six-gun ship with any expectation of success. And yet if he took *Pitt* in pursuit of *Countess* and the single frigate, the remaining escort force mounted four less guns than the two frigates. It was the classic example of the old tactic of divide and conquer, though he guessed that if the Indiaman made its escape, the squadron would break off the action, mission accomplished.

The silhouettes of *Comet* and *Ariel* had also altered as they wore about in pursuit of *Countess.* But *Countess* was almost the equal of a frigate in speed if handled properly, and she was setting studding sails and skysails, cracking on canvas in an effort to run away from the big Salem-built schooner. His first move must be to prevent the Frenchman from joining forces with the Indiaman, even though it meant abandoning the rest of the convoy. He turned to issue his orders and was surprised to find Dobbs only just in the act of relieving Larkin, so little time had elapsed.

"Hands to the braces. Starboard helm. Your course is north by west!" The commands echoed forward. "Set stuns'ls, driver, flying jib, and skys'ls." This was far more sail than he wanted to carry into action, but the first order of business was to intercept the frigate. He checked the binnacle, then looked out to gauge the bearing of the target as *Pitt* settled on the new course. The Frenchman was drawing ever so slightly forward. "Come a half point to starboard," he told the quartermaster, and heard Dobbs pass the word forward to perfect the trim. Larkin materialized before him.

"All stations manned and ready, sir."

"Very well." The tall man made his way forward to his station by the pivot gun on the forecastle, stopping for a word-of encouragement to each gun crew in the port battery. Merewether looked back to starboard for *Comet* and *Countess,* interrupted for a moment as Sangh delivered his pistols and sword to him.

MacRae, from his position to leeward, had cut across the wake of the Indiaman to seize the weather gauge. *Comet* was flying the arbitrary imperative, "Heave to!" but *Countess* pressed on. It was another moment or so before he saw the smoke of the gun, and seconds later heard the distant report. MacRae had reinforced his signal with a shot across the bow, but to no avail: the Indiaman persisted in holding its course. Merewether wondered if he had issued an impossible order. *Countess* was at least three times the tonnage of the schooner and would survive any collision.

He looked astern to see the two frigates coming up on the escort with bones in their teeth. MacCracken had signals flying, too. The three snows, *Vestal, Psyche* and *Thetis,* were formed in a close order line ahead with *Vigilant* in the last position as the heaviest armed of the four, to windward of the predicted course of the French cruisers. It was clearly the best formation to concentrate the puny firepower of the small vessels, but how long it would hold together in the face of a few well-aimed broadsides was problematical. Nothing he could do now. MacCracken had taken prompt and proper action.

The bearing of the intercepting frigate had drawn almost imperceptibly aft. Merewether let *Pitt* run another two minutes, then altered course a half point back to port to regain a collision course. The Frenchman was less than two miles away now, broad on the port bow. Merewether beckoned to Dobbs.

"Send the messenger forward to Mister Larkin and tell him he has permission to open fire when he sees fit." In a moment, he saw Larkin wave his hat in acknowledgment, and the stir on deck as the powder monkeys dashed down to the magazine for cartridges. On second thoughts he gave the same order to Hamlyn at the after pivot, though it could not yet bear on the target.

The minutes ticked off at a snail's pace, a dreamlike atmosphere seemed to settle over the ship, the crews standing quiet beside the guns, only the sound of wind and water breaking the silence. Larkin's hail came with startling clarity, even against the wind.

"I shall open fire, with your permission!"

"You have it!" There was an expectant stir among the hands, a mutter of comment all along the deck. But the tall American officer did not immediately open fire, though the piece was now loaded and primed. He remained stooped, hands on knees behind the gun, the sight set at maximum range on its tang, the piece at its full elevation. It seemed an age while Larkin adjusted the sight for deflection, then signaled the minute alteration in train to match the correction.

"Stand by!" he said, stepping smartly aside. "Fire!" He twitched the lanyard as he cleared the path of the recoil.

The high-pitched spiteful report cracked out, the smoke blown instantly off to starboard. Merewether had the glass to his eye, but he failed to find the splash.

"Not observed," he shouted forward, and Larkin waved negligently as the hands sponged out, then rammed home cartridge, wad, shot and wad again, and the gun captain inserted his quill of priming powder, all in the stylized economical movements of a well-rehearsed cotillion.

The bearing of the frigate remained steady, about a point forward of the port beam. If each ship held its course and speed the two would collide at an angle of about forty degrees some two miles ahead, but they would be in easy range long before that time.

The crack of the long nine interrupted Merewether's calculations by seaman's eye of relative speed and movement. He put the glass to his eye in time to see the cloud of splinters rise just forward of the break of the poop on the Frenchman. It was a hit, but caused no significant damage. He judged that the two ships were already within what he would term long gunshot of each other, and was opening his mouth to order the main battery to be run out when he saw the six after ports on the frigate's gun deck open. The French captain must be nettled by the hit at long range, he thought, as he braced himself for the salvo. It was woefully short, the nearest splash a cable's length off the port quarter. That was poor shooting, if, as was usually the case with French ships, she carried long guns on her gun deck. He heard Larkin fire again.

"Good shot!" The hit was almost midships, the bulwark showed a ragged gap beside a deck carronade, and there were men down. Ports opened on the frigate, the Frenchman was showing his teeth, but no broadside followed immediately, and Merewether looked back for *Comet* and *Countess.*

Far off the starboard bow the silhouette of the Indiaman had altered; she was almost bows on with *Comet* still alongside.

Even with the glass he could not distinguish any activity on her decks, but MacRae was at least staying with her. *Ariel* was a half mile beyond, and closing in on the pair. He turned back to see MacCracken leading his doughty little line of battle across the bow of the nearer frigate. Smoke erupted from the escorts one after another as they fired their puny broadsides, and the shape of the Frenchman altered as it yawed to port to permit its own broadside to bear. He waited a moment, hearing the distant rumble of the guns, and saw that *Vigilant* and the three snows had survived the first salvo. Merewether turned his attention back to his own problem, feeling as though he were a juggler with three balls in the air. The full broadside came from the frigate. Though fired at a moderate long range, there were solid hits on Pitt, one forward, the other crashing just about the flag cabin, and the main topmast staysail halyard was severed so that the sail thrashed about the deck. He saw Boatswain Caldwell leading his party on the double to deal with the casualty.

"Port batteries, stand by! " The ports opened and he put the glass to his eye watching for the instant the enemy guns would be run out again, hoping that the French captain had not yet granted authority for independent fire to his gun captains. A solid broadside pumped in just before the command might disturb their aim. Muzzles began to appear in the ports, he waited an instant longer, and gave the command. "Fire!"

It was a good broadside, though delivered at almost the maximum effective range of the carronades. Hits were visible all along the side of the Frenchman, and when its broadside followed, seconds later, it was ragged, evidence of casualties to guns or crews; and Merewether felt no hits on *Pitt.*

The frigate was altering course to port, coming almost squarely before the wind, but Merewether held on long enough to fire the second broadside. He was baffled a moment by the maneuver, an edging away, until he looked back to see *Countess* some four miles distant under a full press of sail, *Comet* still dogging her. MacRae must have failed in his attempt to board her, and the Frenchman had computed a new point of interception. The guns roared out, and a moment later Dobbs gave a cry. "Got her!" he shouted, waving his hat in the air. "You're a dead duck now, Mister Crapaud!"

The main topmast, topgallant and royal masts were folding in upon themselves in a welter of thrashing canvas and snarled hemp. Even as he looked, the fore royal and fore topgallant masts bent slowly backward, and with gathering speed, crashed on top the wreckage of the main. Merewether could appreciate the disaster; he had lost his main topmast in *Rapid* last year. The Frenchman had been carrying staysails and studding sails to compound the confusion. It was high time to get his own extra sail in, but there was no stopping now. Strike while the iron is hot!

"Hands to the braces! Wear ship! Starboard helm!" His voice cracked with excitement as he delivered the volley of orders. Closehauled on the port tack, he set his course to cross the stern of the helpless frigate. "Starboard battery! Stand by!"

Most of the wreckage was dragging over the frigate's port side; she was unmanageable, and she was slowly coming about to port. He could see with the naked eye the frantic activity on her decks, axes flashing in the sun as the commander strove to cut loose the dragging mass of canvas in the water and restore control. Only a slight alteration of course now would permit the battery to bear.

"Come left two points." He measured the angle with his eye as the gun crews inched their pieces around in train. "Fire as your gun bears!"

The guns and carronades began to explode one or two at a time down the side, fore to aft, and then again in a ragged broadside as *Pitt* crossed the stern. Most of the shots were solid hits. A third salvo blasted out as she began to draw clear. The frigate had responded with only two or three wild shots from her gun deck. Merewether estimated that there was room to wear about and cross the stern again on the reciprocal of his present course, and the advance and transfer would bring her back across the stern at point-blank range.

"Hands to the braces," he told Dobbs. "Wear ship. Your course is due east." As the ship swung round, Merewether had time to survey the situation. The position of *Countess* and *Comet* appeared unchanged, and he turned to see what had happened to his escort force and convoy, not to mention the other two frigates.

What he saw startled him. The Frenchmen were much closer than they had any right to be, target angles almost zero, and bearing down upon him! He had more pressing business right here, however, to finish off the crippled frigate without interference. The turn was almost completed, the quartermaster eased the rudder, then met the swing of the ship as Dobbs conned her on her new course.

"Port battery, stand by!" *Pitt* would pass the helpless frigate less than half a cable's length off her port side, still fouled with wreckage, her batteries unable to fire. Merewether saw French seamen running for shelter on her deck as his gun ports opened, then heard a wordless shout from Hamlyn at the after pivot gun.

"She's struck!" shouted Dobbs, his face alight. The tricolor was coming down and a white flag ascending. The French commander could not face the prospect of another series of broadsides ripping through his helpless ship.

"Belay!" Gun crews all along the port battery looked around in disappointment, then saw the surrender, and raised a cheer.

Merewether turned his attention back to the other frigates, less than a mile distant. Far beyond them he could see the escort vessels in their line ahead still barring the way to the convoy. They appeared to be intact. The Frenchmen must have broken off their action with the small vessels after a single broadside, and headed for *Pitt* to give succor to their consort. Too late now, but he had no time to put a prize crew aboard her, and the crippled ship might very well retract her surrender, given time to make repairs. It was a chance he was compelled to take. The Indiaman, *Comet* and *Ariel* all appeared to have drawn closer together, still about four miles distant. It was a good omen, MacRae might be able to bring *Countess* to bay at last. But Merewether had more pressing matters to think about here. He tried desperately to decide his next maneuver at this critical juncture.

"Take in all light sail!" Best strip to fighting trim while he had the chance.

Pitt was still on the starboard tack, closehauled, course almost due east, now dead ahead of the crippled frigate where all activity appeared to have ceased. The approaching Frenchmen were on the port tack, wind on their quarters, abreast of one another, and about a quarter of a mile apart. He tried to assimilate the various factors of the situation into one solid picture in his brain, and from it to distil some resolution of the problem. They held the weather gauge on *Pitt,* with all its tactical advantages, but he was yet uncertain of their intentions. Were they coming to the rescue of their consort, or was their objective still the *Countess of Surrey?* In either event, it was plainly his duty to engage them, but his strategy in one event might not serve so well in the other. He hesitated, unwilling to commit himself, then temporized by ordering Larkin and Hamlyn to try ranging shots at the frigates with the long nines.

He missed the fall of shot in his preoccupation with the next move, then temporized further by ordering the starboard battery to stand by. The frigates were within long cannon shot, but beyond the range of the carronades. Merewether gave the order almost absently.

"Divide your battery, Mister Hamlyn. After section aim for the starboard frigate. Fire when you are on target." The commands went yelping forward, relayed by each gun captain in turn. In a moment the cries of "Mark! Mark! Mark!" came echoing back along the battery. In that brief interval before the broadside roared out. Merewether came to a tentative conclusion: *Pitt* was only an irritant to be dealt with if it became an active nuisance. *Countess* was still the objective, and somehow he must divert the enemy.

He took the time to observe the fall of shot. Most were short, but there were two apparent hits on the starboard frigate, and at least one on the port. Not bad shooting for the range. He saw smoke blossom from the bow of first one, then the other as their bow chasers fired, but he could not see the fall of shot.

It would be suicide to throw himself in the way of the two ships; with the weather gauge, they had freedom of maneuver and could choose their point of attack, sliding by, fore or aft, punishing him as they passed, or even leaving one to deal with him while the other hurried on after *Countess.* He thought he saw a chance to reduce the odds by assuming the role of artful dodger.

"Hands to the braces! Stand by to wear ship. Starboard helm." *Pitt* began to swing. 'Course north.' The frigates were almost dead astern now and Merewether watched them closely for any reaction, then saw their bowchasers fire again. There was one splash a cable's length to starboard, but they held their course, towards the predicted position of *Countess.* This was confirmation of his earlier conclusion.

The crippled frigate was almost abeam, two cable's lengths distant to port. Merewether looked astern, measuring the rate of gain by the frigates. He held on another moment or so as the bearing of the crippled ship drew aft to the beam.

"Hands to the braces! Wear ship. Starboard helm. Your new course is west by north." *Pitt* came around to settle on the new course, thrashing along as closehauled as she would lie, aiming to pass as near under the stern of the dismasted frigate as possible.

Merewether stood on the port side of the quarter-deck, hands clenched together behind his back, head pivoting right to see his course, then left to judge the relative movement of the Frenchmen. A dead silence had descended on the decks. The weathered faces of the gun crews all turned to watch him as he appeared to be sailing away from an engagement with the frigates. He caught a glimpse of Dobbs, a curious expression of anticipation on his homely face as though he had already deduced the stratagem, standing tense, ready to execute the next maneuver. The breeze had freshened, snoring through the taut lines of *Pitt's* standing rigging as she plunged across the stern of the frigate only fifty yards distant. Men were running for cover on her decks, fearful that he had returned to pour in another broadside. Now!

"Stand by to go about!" Dobbs relayed the orders forward. There was always the very real danger when sailing as near the wind as *Pitt* was now that her way would be insufficient to carry her around to settle on the opposite tack, leaving her in irons, unable to move. "Starboard helm!"

The rudder bit, *Pitt* began to swing. She did not lose her way, and her advance and transfer were enough to carry her ahead of the Frenchman. There was a long moment of indecision as the yards were braced around, the heart-stopping instant before the sails cracked full of wind again on the starboard tack, and then the ship began to pick up speed again as she passed the bow of the motionless vessel and settled on an eastward course that would intercept the nearer frigate within moments.

But there was a vast difference in strategic situation now. Pitt held the weather gauge on the frigates, only a quarter mile to the nearest, and Merewether could dictate the exact moment of engagement. His first objective was simple: a few moments of uninterrupted broadsides against the nearer frigate while screened against intervention by her consort. He estimated her speed, and solved without conscious calculation the course that would put him in that position.

"Come to port! Course northwest. Starboard battery, stand by!" Locks clicked as they were cocked along the deck. *Pitt* had almost squared before the wind. The guns would bear now.

"Fire!"

Twenty guns spoke almost at once, and it appeared that every shot struck home. The frigate returned the fire, but its broadside had gaps in it, evidence of casualties to guns or crews. The battery was run out again and the second broadside erupted. If the drill ran true to form, he could count on getting off three shots from his shorter guns to two from the Frenchmen.

"Fire at will!"

There was no need to control the gunfire any longer. Let the faster crews set their own pace. The firing assumed a galloping tempo as the ships edged together, and clusters of grape were now being rammed down on top the round shot. The frigate had lost its bowsprit and headsails, the mainyard was shot in two, and the spanker boom splintered, in addition to major hull damage. In a single ship action she would strike within a few more such broadsides, but he saw the second ship coming across her wake. In a moment it would be in position to repay *Pitt* with interest.

"Starboard helm! Port battery, stand by." If she would just come around fast enough, he could avoid her broadside and be in position to rake the consort. The last shots from the starboard battery were fired even as the ship swung, the first frigate was wavering, out of control. Only a few yards more, and he would be across the bow of the second frigate.

There came a last despairing shot from the main battery of the first Frenchman, and disaster struck. *Pitt's* fore topmast bent forward, then crashed across the starboard bow in a thrashing welter of canvas and tangled cordage. With the loss of the foresails, she would not answer her helm, and sagged off before the wind as the second Frenchman swept across her stern. There must have been at least a dozen hits. The main yard fell, as did the spanker gaff, fouling the helm. Two quarterdeck carronades were dismounted in the port battery, and men were down along the deck. Even so, the port battery roared out as the frigate came into range, making solid hits all along the side of the ship.

The second ship put her helm up and spilled the wind from her sails. Evidently she intended to tarry a bit and punish *Pitt* before resuming her dash for *Countess.* Merewether heard firing from starboard again, and looked around. The first frigate had managed to rig a foresail and was creeping up to starboard. His guns were firing steadily now from both batteries, but somehow the enemy's masts remained intact, and the starboard frigate obviously intended to board. There was nowhere to go. He was caught fast in a trap. There was nothing he could do but try to fight off the attack.

"Canister!" he shouted in desperation as the starboard frigate crashed into the bow, driving *Pitt's* head around and causing her bowsprit to tangle with the standing rigging of the port frigate.

There was a frenzied activity in the ship to port as her hands tried to cut loose the tangle and free themselves, but she had lost her way and the wind inexorably pushed her against *Pitt.* The guns were almost muzzle to muzzle now, and those that could still fire threw flaming wadding into both ships. Smoke was boiling up through the forward companion, and a party was dragging a length of hose from the pumps, while powder monkeys doused a dozen smaller fires with pails of sea water.

He saw the carpenter standing before him shouting. "Near four feet of water in the hold!"

The words came through with startling clarity. He saw Dobbs look around. Hell, they might sink before they burned!

"Stop it as best you can," Merewether told the carpenter, and turned to see a party forming up with cutlasses, pikes and pistols in the waist of the port frigate. "Repel boarders! Repel boarders!" he shouted, and saw the Marine detachment on the forecastle drawn up in two rigid ranks, muskets already aimed. The smoke from the volley obscured them, and he looked back to starboard.

The batteries of all three ships still fired, not in measured broadsides, but in an irregular tempo as the serviceable pieces managed to reload. There was activity on the deck of the starboard frigate, blue and gold clad officers rallying a party of French marines while seamen swung out over the bulwarks to slash at the boarding nets. *Pitt* would be engulfed from either side, Merewether thought, as he saw the Marines advancing at the double, bayonets extended, to meet the first elements of the portside party as they leaped down to the waist. He looked for Dobbs, but could not find him in the smoke, then took the double pistols from his belt and discharged them despairingly, one barrel after another, aiming into the milling mass of boarders striving to break through the thin line of Sepoy Marines. He could distinguish no effect, but the four shots must have struck something. The din had become almost rhythmic, as though two smiths were alternately striking a gigantic anvil with their sledges. The ships on either hand continued to fire with only an occasional shot from *Pitt* now to punctuate the horrid tempo.

The scene was a nightmare, worse than the one he had dreamed at Calcutta last year. The situation was hopeless. He would die here in the approaches to the Gulf of Aden, uselessly, without a glimpse of his own child. A cold tide of terror flooded through him without warning.

"I shall die!" he said, not realizing that he spoke aloud. "I do not want to die! I must not die now!" He felt his mouth work and saliva run from the corners.

Merewether wiped his chin with the back of his hand as he moved towards the flag halyards, unreasoning panic hastening his steps. He must survive at any cost, and only a single avenue was left: he must strike his colors, surrender the ship and thereby live!

He came hard against a sturdy blue-jacketed figure in the murk just forward of the helm. One quartermaster lay already dead, and the other writhed weakly in a puddle of blood. The wheel was unattended, but the ship was going nowhere. He tried to shove past the figure, feeling momentary anger at the unexpected obstacle, then recognized the plain blunt features through the swirling smoke.

"Captain!" shouted Dobbs, his high voice penetrating above the clamor, as the smoke of another discharge again engulfed them.

"Move!" shouted Merewether in desperation, using his hands to try to push the officer to one side and reach the halyards. "Stand aside! I must strike! Surrender!" His voice cracked.

Dobb's face became visible as a slant of wind dispersed the smoke again. His expression was of disbelief; then incredulous dismay, mouth opening, eyes staring, before his face began to work, crumpling in upon itself as tears started and he wept. God damn the man! Did he possess no imagination, have no desire to live? Merewether's body tensed to exert the force to shoulder him aside and press past. He shouted again, almost in his ear.

"I must surrender!"

There was a shattering blow, incandescence exploded behind Merewether's eyes, and he felt himself fly through the air, observing with a sense of detachment the curious phenomenon of the mizzen upper works rotating lazily above him. He crashed to the deck on his back and lay stunned, fighting to regain his breath.

Was this it? Was this death? The end of his mortal existence? He began to breathe again, and consciousness flowed back through his body. With an effort, he managed to roll over, get to his knees, then shakily on his feet. There was a bloody heap of blue and white rags pitched against the port bulwark beside a dismounted carronade.

Dobbs? Merewether could not bring himself to look. He turned to face forward again. The scene was as though frozen in time, boarders still pressing against the Marine detachment to port, guns thundering from both sides. There was yet time to reach the halyard, haul down the Marine ensign, end this horror. He drew his sword, then staggered towards the pin rail to slash the halyard. He saw movement in the waist of the starboard frigate, men brandishing pikes, cutlasses and pistols as they poured shouting across the narrow gap between ships into *Pitt.* Good God! Was there time even to surrender?

"Form Lion's Mouth! Form Lion's Mouth!" The high pitched command behind him was audible over the din of the battle. What? The command made no sense to him as he whirled around to look.

That child, Marlowe, was running forward, cutlass in one hand, a glowing length of slow match, dripping sparks in the other. The hands from the starboard quarterdeck carronades were snatching cutlasses and pikes from the racks. Even as he wondered the boy reached the three-pound boat howitzer set just forward of the mizzen and jammed the slow match into the touch-hole.

A hat full of musket balls fired at point-blank range was a fearsome thing. It cut an expanding swathe through the boarding party from starboard, and Merewether joined Midshipman Marlowe in leading the screeching, shouting Lion's Mouth charge to fall upon the shaken survivors, driving them willynillv across the deck. Some managed to scramble back into the Frenchman, but the majority were cut down, or dropped their weapons in surrender. He came to a halt, seeing blood on his sword and a trickle blinding his left eye. He had not felt the blow, but his fingers found the slash across his forehead into his hair.

No time to stop. Hamlyn was now leading the Lion's Mouth force to fall on the flank of the port boarding party, as Marlowe crouched on the deck, shoe off, blood oozing through the toe of his stocking.

There came the crash of a broadside of many guns from somewhere forward. Good God! What now? Had the crippled frigate somehow revived and joined the action? He ran towards the forecastle, leaping up the ladder to peer forward through the smoke as the breeze rolled it back to reveal *Countess of Surrey* for a moment before her eighteen-pounders roared out again. She was lying less than a hundred yards dead ahead of the port side frigate, sails brailed up, every raking shot crashing through the length of the Frenchman.

Merewether looked about as though in a dream, wondering when he would awake with a start to find himself back in the lodgings at Calcutta with Caroline beside him. It was only a moment ago that he was ready to betray himself, his men and the Marine by hauling down, striking his colors, intent only on preserving his own life. And Dobbs was gone, dead, struck down by a cannon ball even as he tried to push the young officer out of the way in his craven attempt to surrender. But it was no nightmare, he knew, seeing the long pivot gun on the forecastle smashed and dismounted. The mutilated bodies strewn about it were real enough, and he was thankful that he did not recognize Larkin's among them. He stood, sword dangling from his nerveless hand, as the breeze pushed the smoke back again to reveal *Comet* and *Ariel* lying just ahead of the starboard frigate pumping broadside after broadside into the Frenchman.

Five minutes later the port frigate hauled down her colors, quickly followed by her consort, and silence descended on the scene.

* * *

The chaos was deadly serious. It was touch and go whether *Pitt* would sink under them before they could get the sail fothered under her bottom to check the torrent of water that poured through the gaping wound on her starboard side at every roll in the long swell. Boats from *Comet, Ariel, Vigilant* and *Countess* disgorged parties of artisans armed with the tools of their trades, and the men joined the frenzied activity, rigging pumps, moving the carronades across the deck to give the ship a port list, plugging shot holes. The surgeon assigned to the escort force came on board with his mates and loblolly boys and dived below to the sickbay. Merewether made no conscious decisions: the instinct of a lifetime at sea served him. MacRae out of *Comet* ensured execution of his orders. The crews of the escort vessels were decimated to furnish the prize crews for the frigates, and soon the flag of the Bombay Marine was flying over three French tri-colors. The lines to the sail now stretched over the side and bottom of the ship were just being secured when the thought struck Merewether.

"MacRae! The transports!" Somewhere over the horizon to the south were ships filled with French soldiers bound for some point in the Gulf of Cambay to assist the uprising against Holkar in Rajputana. The small Scots officer looked at him, the cast in his eye evident.

"Dinna wurra a muckle about them, Captain," said MacRae in the thick accent that he affected in moments of stress. "They wull go nowhere now. We have the she-tiger and her cub battened down below decks, and Cosby's dead."

"Dead?"

"He met my marines on deck with pistols and was hit on the head with a musket butt — just a wee bit too hard." Just as well, it would have been a sticky affair to bring a Company Maritime Service captain to trial for treason. "His officers claimed they did not know his motives or intentions, they only obeyed orders. I left my marines aboard to make sure they continue to do so, and brought her here as fast as she would sail. Her gun crews made an excellent practice, I thought, considering that they are merchant seamen."

"Yes, you saved *Pitt* — and me." A wave of nausea flowed through him, and he felt an almost overwhelming compulsion to blurt out the nearness of his surrender and his blind panic, but he managed to control himself. He saw MacRae looking at him with concern.

"Do ye feel all right, Captain? That cut . . ."

"Only a fleabite. And now, if you will be kind enough to send off your press gang to pick up lascars from the convoy to man the pumps, I'll be much obliged." It was after midnight when he came into the flag cabin to throw himself fully clothed on the cot that had survived the bombardment and sleep until dawn.

MacRae sat wearily in the sternsheets of *Comet's* gig as it pulled away from *Pitt.* It had been touch and go as to whether they would save the frigate, but with a sail now fothered under her starboard side, the flooding had been checked to the point where the pumps could just barely contain it, and the lascars impressed from the country ships in the convoy provided a fresh reservoir of manpower to serve them. By moving guns and water casks to port to induce a list, the shattered planking might be exposed sufficiently to permit more permanent repairs. He had left all of the carpenters out of the escort force aboard to lend assistance, and they would work through the night plugging holes and caulking the lower gunports in preparation for the ship to be heeled over.

It had been a long yesterday. Now it was halfway through the midwatch in a new day, and MacRae felt his body slumping. He realized now that he had been on edge ever since Merewether assigned him to the duty of holding *Countess* on a short tether. If the decision had been left to him, he would have landed a detachment of marines on her deck, put the master in irons, and hang the consequences. Still, he could appreciate the considerations that had dictated otherwise.

As for Merewether, he had appeared to be in a daze, though he had given every proper order to save *Pitt.* When MacRae arrived on board at the head of his rescue and salvage party, it was as though he was a stranger, silent, withdrawn, looking past him as though he were unable to focus, even a perceptible hesitation in his usual brisk gait. Intent on collaring *Countess,* MacRae had missed much of the tactical maneuvers by which the deadly frigate action had been played out, but he had observed the last few minutes as he conned the Indiaman into position, and had seen the inferno Merewether had survived with the three ships locked together, and many of the enemy guns still in action. As for his own role in the action, he characteristically minimized the part he had played. He had done no more than the duty enjoined upon every officer in the Marine: engage the enemy with all the force he could bring to bear.

He thought with deep regret of young Dobbs, destined to be committed to the deep this day. The boy had developed into a first-rate navigator and ship handler, and his single-handed attention to duty made him a most desirable junior officer. Hard lines! And Hamlyn had confided that Dobbs was betrothed to a young lady down at George Town. MacRae was sure he remembered the girl from the ball there last year. Hard lines!

And Larkin, that confident, sanguine, proud American, lying even now in a drugged sleep amid the horrors of the loblolly, his left arm amputated above the elbow. His philosophy and way of life were at variance with MacRae's tidy cautious Calvinistic Scots nature, always pessimistically expecting the worst, but he respected the man's courage, abilities and plainspoken common sense. Of course, Nelson had gone on to glory after losing an arm, but in a service such as the Bombay Marine it could be a well nigh insurmountable handicap, and he could not see Larkin accepting some safe shore billet to wait out the years until retirement. He heard the hail, and the coxswain's reply, *"Comet"*, and came back to the present as he mounted the ladder.

His steward had laid out tea, with biscuit and a pot of jam, and MacRae was suddenly ravenous. He had done all he could for the present to aid *Pitt* and he felt the necessity for a medicinal dram for himself before he began the repast. He felt the whisky expand through his body, dissipating some of the fatigue, and he ate the biscuit, heaped with preserves, with relish. Finished, he felt a craving for the pipe he occasionally took. Tobacco was shaved off the plug and tamped into the clay bowl, then lighted with a spill from the lamp. When it was drawing well, he sat back, blue smoke eddying over his head, and thought again of Merewether.

He recalled his first meeting with the man almost three years ago in the chamber of Commodore Welchance in Downing Street. Only the fortuitous presence of a newly promoted captain in London had deprived MacLellan of the command of *Rapid* on her dash to rescue the Governor-Designate of Madras from that pirate, Abercrombie, but MacLellan had never resented the fact. MacRae could confess some initial reservations; he had not known Merewether before that day. But the manner in which he had unmoored a strange ship in close quarters in the Thames had won his seaman's heart. The captain normally possessed an optimistic, outgoing nature and the bleak disconsolation he had exhibited since the action was at variance with any mood MacRae had previously observed. Something was seriously wrong. Had the man lost his nerve in that horrendous battle yesterday? MacRae was instantly ashamed of the thought, though he had seen such instances in the past. He recalled Hamlyn's first-handed account of the action.

"Three fourths of our guns were out of action, Gunny was barely holding off the boarders to port, when they came pouring over from starboard l" Hamlyn had said, rolling his eyes for dramatic effect.

"I thought it was too late even to surrender, that we would just sink with colors flying. And then that cub Marlowe fired the boat gun full of musket balls into them, and he and the Captain, with me following like a fool, went dashing down the deck shouting and waving our hangers just as you appeared off the bow. . ."

That account did not square with MacRae's half-formed theory that Merewether had lost his nerve. There was something missing, overlooked, but he could not fathom what it was. Ah weel, no need to trouble himself further at this hour of the morning. He was almost asleep when his father's old comment upon the village eccentric came unbidden into his mind.

"Just like my old razor: Honed too fine, and it cracked!" MacRae chuckled, and drifted off.

It was midmorning when Merewether picked up the quartermaster's notebook and rough deck log from Gaffner, the gnomish little quartermaster, in the navigator's tubby and read them to refresh his recollection. A short length of plank balanced across his knees had to serve as a desk, the list of the ship made the one that had survived in the flag cabin temporarily unusable. He braced himself and wrote his report on deck as the sound of hammers and saws pervaded the ship. The carpenter and his mates were over the side fitting new planking to replace the splintered section at the waterline. Once that was accomplished, the ship could be righted and the other leaks dealt with. Both his sleeping and day cabins were a shambles, desk and cot smashed, and a carronade dismounted and hurled bodily through the bulkhead that separated his quarters from the flag cabin. But repairs to living areas held a low priority as compared to hull damage. He drank the cup of tea that Sangh had just refilled for him, and looked again with horror at the summary of the casualty list that Buttram and Mefford had compiled for him: "Killed in action, thirty-nine; wounded, forty-two, of whom eight are accounted mortal." Almost a fifth of his crew dead or disabled!

It was still hard to believe that the steady, earnest, reliable Dobbs was gone, struck down by a round shot. What was left of his sturdy body had been found pitched against the port bulwarks between two of the quarterdeck carronades. And Larkin, that American free spirit, able to take any event in his stride, left with only one arm. Boatswain Caldwell had lost a foot, and there had been another ten amputations. It was cold comfort that the three French frigates had also suffered severely. Two of them lay hove to a cable's length on either side of *Pitt,* water pouring from their scuppers, and the third frigate was a mile south, a stumpy jury rig now replacing her mainmast. Dillon, first in *Comet,* had come over to act as first in *Pitt;* Hamlyn now held the new dignity of acting third lieutenant, and Bowman the leading boatswain's mate, an acting warrant as boatswain.

Shouts came from over the side, and the carpenter with his mates were hoisted on deck. The ship was no longer in imminent danger of sinking, though the pumps, manned by the sixty lascars recruited from the convoy, clanked steadily as they sucked out the water in the lower holds. Now the Herculean task of moving the guns and water casks back to starboard would commence. As each gun was moved, the list would diminish, making the job progressively easier. With the working parties out of the escort force to provide the manpower, he might expect an even keel by midafternoon. Merewether dipped the pen into the inkwell, and continued his report:

> ... Having shot away bowsprit, foresails and spanker, as well as inflicting severe hull damage to *Glorieuse,* her consort,

Thetis, wore across *Pitt's* stern to engage her to port. As *Pitt* was wearing to port to counter this maneuver, her fore topmast and headsails were shot away, making the ship unmanageable, and causing her to collide with *Thetis. Glorieuse* managed to come along the starboard side, and heavy cannonading by all three ships continued. *Thetis* organized a boarding party and managed to reach *Pitt's* deck, where it was contained and then repulsed by the Sepoy Marine detachment under the able command of Jemadar Gunny. A second boarding party from *Glorieuse* also reached the deck to starboard where it was met and destroyed by a Lion's Mouth charge, most gallantly organized and led by Midshipman Paul Marlowe, formerly of the Honorable Company's Bomb Ketch, *Vesuvius.* At this point, Captain Ian MacRae of HCS *Comet,* having seized control of *Countess of Surrey* from her master, brought her in company with *Ariel* and *Comet* across the bows of the French ships, from which point heavy cannonading persuaded them to strike within the quarter hour . . .

Merewether went back to read the bald report. Words could not express the inferno that had engulfed *Pitt* during that last interval, but some of the men who would read it had experience that would enable them to understand. He wondered if any of them had been beset by blind unreasoning panic to the point that they would have hauled down their colors. Then he re-read the account to see if the terror showed through the words of the account. Not Waldron, certainly, nor Tollett; they were men of iron nerves, devoid of fear. He was bitterly ashamed of his moment of weakness, the sudden overwhelming compulsion to save his own life at whatever cost. But for Marlowe, he would be a prisoner of that French captain over there, broken, dishonored, his career at an end.

Merewether stared blindly at the sheet of foolscap. He had made no overt move to betray his cowardice, his intent to surrender *Pitt;* no living man could accuse him, but he would carry to his grave the memory of the expression on poor Dobbs's face just before he was struck down. He shook his head as though to erase the recollection, and resumed the report:

> The gallantry, enterprise and resource of Captain MacRae of *Comet* and Captain Pegram of *Ariel* in coming to the succor of *Pitt* is entitled to great praise, and is in accordance with the highest traditions of the Marine . . . The escort force under the command of Captain Robert MacCracken, joined by HCS *Vigilant,* Captain Joseph Whaley, interposed itself resolutely between the enemy and the convoy and prevented loss . . .

The report was finally finished as *Pitt* came almost on an even keel again, Larkin, Dobbs and Caldwell praised in their mutilation and death, and Hamlyn mentioned for his leadership of the last charge on the flank of the port boarding party. The ink had dried in the breeze almost as fast as the words were written, and there was no need to sand the sheet. He was preparing to rise when Sangh came up before him to stand silently, head bowed, until he should be noticed.

"Yes?"

"Sah, I have cleaned the flag cabin and moved your gear into it. The desk and cot are usable."

"Good, I'll come down." He stoppered the inkwell, gathered the sheets of his report and followed Sangh.

The cabin was habitable, though marred, the dismounted carronade still jammed against the port side with a huge hole in the bulkhead through which it had come allowing him to see his own ruined quarters. He had a long way yet to go in his report since he had omitted all mention of Madame Bai and Captain Cosby from his report of the action, which was strictly Marine business. Now he must prepare a separate account of the curious train of events involving the pair that had culminated in yesterday's bitter engagement, which should be of interest to Company and Government.

Napier's intelligence had been uncannily accurate. There could be no doubt now that Madame Bai had conspired with the French to mount a venture designed to unseat Holkar and place his son, Malhar, on the throne of Rajputana. Once accomplished, she would be the effective ruler of the most powerful state in the Maratha Confederation, and with her ties by blood and affinity with the French, would also be in a position to do incalculable harm to the Company's interests in Central India.

Tulsi Bai had easily enough subverted the gullible Captain Cosby and bent him to her will with her feminine wiles. Merewether recalled MacRae's laconic report in the flickering lantern light last night as all hands fought to save the ship from floundering.

"A hell-cat, she were, Captain!" The small Scots officer had told him, gingerly touching the three glistening red furrows across his right cheek. "Screeching, biting and kicking, four men could hardly hold her. We finally got irons on her, and locked her in the cabin . . ." Cosby had died ignominiously, his head broken with a musket butt, as he still sought to serve the woman in his infatuation.

The officers of the Indiaman had disclaimed all knowledge or responsibility for Cosby's actions; they had merely followed orders, they said, which was reasonable enough, though they had confessed themselves puzzled by *Comet's* strenuous efforts to stop their ship. Having met Cosby, Merewether was inclined to give them full faith and credit for their testimony. MacRae had finally risked collision to come close enough to grapple *Countess of Surrey,* and though suffering some damage in the process, to get a boarding party on deck.

Once informed of the true situation, the officers and hands in *Countess* had been delighted to join in the dash to succor *Pitt,* and under MacRae's command had fired the half-dozen raking broadsides that induced the Frenchman to surrender.

Where to begin? Merewether felt the sweat begin to run under his arms as the sun rose towards meridian. The flag cabin had no vent or windsail fitted, and he had been more comfortable on deck. Before he could decide his point of beginning, Sangh announced Lieutenant Dillon.

"Come."

Dillon was a tall, broad, pleasant man, *Comet's* first, and a man of many accomplishments.

"Sir, your purser says he will pipe the hands to mess in half an hour. I thought it might be as good a time as any for the burial services. In this heat . . ." The officer was right of course. Get it over with.

"Right, pipe all hands, Mister Dillon."

He wondered if he could extemporize the Service For the Burial of the Dead at Sea. The shelf of books that Caroline had painstakingly assembled for him last winter had been hurled across his cabin, scattered, some of them with their backs broken, and the Book of Common Prayer had been among them. "And make a signal to the convoy and escorts."

A moment later Sangh laid the book on his desk, and he sought out the place. The volume fell open to the page.

The convoy had its flags at half mast as Merewether came on deck to read the service for forty-one canvas-shrouded corpses. Two more had died since Buttram's report. Indeed, there were so many that they had to be slid over the side in relays from half a dozen planks, covered only briefly by the Bombay Marine ensign before they would make sullen splashes alongside. The hands were formed up by divisions in sober-faced ranks.

"Attention on deck! Off hats!" sang out Dillon.

Merewether's finger marked the place in the Prayer Book, and he read the Twenty-third Psalm, paused, then began the sonorous phrases of the ritual for the Burial of the Dead at Sea, culminating in the Sentence of Committal:

"And the corruptible bodies of those who sleep in Him shall be changed and made like unto His glorious body; according to the mighty workings whereby He is able to subdue all things unto Himself."

Merewether nodded to the hands manning the planks and in unison they were tilted as the sea received its first installment of the heroic dead. Among them, he knew, was what was left of poor John Dobbs.

The hands lifted another corpse on to each plank, and Merewether again intoned the Committal. By the third repetition he knew it by rote and no longer needed to read from the page. When the last five had made their plunge, he spoke out to the hands.

"Let us pray: "Our Father who art . . ." The hands joined in, heads bowed, earnest voices rumbling along in unison to the "Amen". Dillon looked at him for the signal to dismiss.

Merewether had never attempted to deliver a eulogy on such occasions in the past, but in his present state of conscience he felt compelled to make some expression of his gratitude to the departed and to those who survived for their magnificent performance of duty yesterday. With his inner sense of shame, he might well make a botch of it, expose himself to ridicule, but he must make the effort. He tried to shape the words in his mind.

"Men! My thanks to you is a puny reward for your courage and devotion to duty during the late action with the enemy, and even that I am unable to express . . ." No, it would never do, far too stilted and insincere. He tried to think, conscious of the ranks of brown faces, every eye fixed on him, thinking how he would have failed these men, let their valor go to waste. He cleared his throat, still raw from the powder fumes, and plunged ahead. His voice felt thin and shrill when he spoke, but the words came from his heart.

"Men! My thanks and God bless you!" He turned to the purser. "You may serve out a double ration of spirits, Mister Davis."

"On hats," commanded Dillon. "Dismiss."

The formation dissolved, the hands solemn in demeanor. There was no skylarking or cheers at the announcement. The ceremony would have to be repeated an unknown number of times in the days to come, Merewether knew, as gangrene and other complications took their grim toll of the mortally wounded. It was a gloomy prospect, but he would face each day as it came. For the present, with the flooding stopped, he would get the spare main yard fished to the stump of the foremast and carry enough sail to permit *Pitt* to steer a course across the Arabian Sea to Bombay where the Parsee shipbuilder, Jamsetjee, would make her whole again. As he turned to go below, he saw the wizened quartermaster, Dobbs's special favorite, Gaffner, squeeze into the line of hands drawing their issue of spirits, pannikin in hand.

When the burial ceremonies had been completed and the hands lined up for the issue of spirits, Gaffner left his refuge in the navigator's cubby beside the after companion. When a man is over forty, barely five feet tall and a scant seven stone in weight, he has learned to avoid jostling deck hands as much as possible. His stature, or lack of it, had made him the butt of many pranks at the hands of callous seamen these past thirty years. Only last week that ape, Bowman, now promoted to acting boatswain, had picked him up by the scruff of the neck, and held him out at arm's length to the vast entertainment of a score of mirthful idlers. Well, he told himself viciously, Bowman's new rank and dignity as a warrant officer would not avail to shield him; he would repay the insult with interest at a suitable time and place, but in such manner that there could be no retribution. He slipped past the line of men drawing their ration to insert himself ahead of a friendly face, pannikin in hand, pretending not to see the captain pass as he went aft, then withdrew to sip the liquor in the privacy of the cubby.

The only person for whose death he had felt something resembling grief since his mother died had just been given the deep six. Mister Dobbs had treated him with dignity and consideration, had selected him from all the other quartermasters to be his assistant at celestial observations, and trusted him to have the sextants laid out, initial error noted, hack watch compared with the chronometer, notebook and lead pencils in hand. Gaffner wondered who would succeed him as navigator — not MacCamy surely, he would be a fortnight just completing the computations, and then they would be dead wrong. Hamlyn just might do, but he tended to be erratic in mood and a little too highhanded for his taste. He sipped the spirits, savoring every drop, sorrowful when the pannikin was drained, but enjoying the sense of well-being they engendered.

Gaffner had neither the strength nor weight to stand a trick at the wheel, but he could measure the altitude of sun, moon or stars as accurately as Mister Dobbs, and work out the equations almost as rapidly. It was an unlikely enough accomplishment for a Cockney waif, orphaned at six, living on the verge of starvation during his childhood, but he had managed it. He thought of the unfrocked schoolmaster who eked out a livelihood as a scrivener in the Cheapside row where he had lived who had befriended him. The man had lost his position at a private school because he liked little boys too well, but Gaffner had been willing to accommodate him in exchange for food, shelter and being taught to read and write and cipher. He had early concluded that he could never make his way by manual strength, but he might live by his wits if he possessed an education, and he had obtained enough to suffice.

He thought again of Lieutenant Dobbs, the broad sturdy torso and powerful legs. He had admired his physique, that was the body he would have chosen rather than this frail, scrawny one. Only one other man had he actually envied both for his physical endowments and native cunning, and that was Osborne, the gypsy acrobat who had cheated the hangman at Bombay last spring. He shuddered at the thought of the man; with him dead Gaffner's secret was safe enough, but for a period of weeks before the date of execution, Gaffner had been petrified with fear lest Osborne inform on him. He had known of the conspiracy among some of the old hands in *Pitt,* and had explicitly agreed with the topman to navigate the ship to the South Seas where the mutineers proposed to commence a new life in the fashion of *Bounty.* But Osborne had not peached, and no one else in the plot knew of his commitment. He had taken no part in the attempt, had in fact been tied up along with Dobbs and the others in the quarterdeck middle watch. He put the pannikin away regretfully, and sat on his stool, leaning back against the bulkhead, wondering once again that he was serving in the Bombay Marine at all, and what might have been his lot had the mutiny succeeded.

The anomaly of a London urchin who wrote a fair hand and could spell had attracted the attention of a Thames shipping agent. When Gaffner discovered that he was doing the work of men three times his age in drafting bills of lading for starvation wages, he had helped himself to the money in the till one night, and stowed away in an Indiaman berthed at Blackwall. He was discovered after the ship had cleared Land's End, and spent the balance of the voyage to Bombay at hard labor in the scullery. With the perennial shortage of European seamen, particularly one who could read and write, he had found a berth as ship's boy and powder monkey in the Marine, eventually to rise to quartermaster. Gaffner, in his time, had served a score of competent navigators, and soon knew as much of the theory as most of them, but he was content with his billet and the perquisites that went with it.

One other accomplishment he possessed that he never mentioned was the ability to read lips. The schoolmaster of his childhood had instructed him in the art, and with his prying secretive nature, Gaffner enjoyed eavesdropping on conversations quite beyond ordinary earshot. He had become privy to many otherwise well-kept secrets, as well as scandals and assignations, but he merely stored the memorable episodes in the dark recesses of his mind, to be extracted and savored again from time to time. A shadow darkened the door, and he looked around to see Merewether.

"Good afternoon," said the Captain. Gaffner noted for the second time this day the frown and stern set of the brown face in contrast with the startling white expanse of scar tissue across his right cheek. He had never exchanged much more than a score of words with Merewether, a few aye aye, sirs, and perhaps a brief response to an inquiry as to wind, weather or position. "I return the notebook and deck log, with my thanks." Gaffner took them and placed them in the locker without comment.

It had been Gaffner's duty to keep the quartermaster's notebook at general quarters under the supervision of Dobbs as officer of the watch. It recorded in exact chronological order every command, change of course, alteration in sail, or other event affecting the operation of the ship. Gaffner had turned the half-hour glass as regulations prescribed, but had also consulted the navigational watch to fix the precise times. He already knew that yesterday's action had consumed two hours and eleven minutes from the first broadside into the French frigate, to the time the last enemy ship hauled down her colors. Now, in this second encounter with the captain in a matter of hours, Gaffner did not meet his eyes lest he somehow betray his secret knowledge.

Gaffner resumed his perch on the stool and leaned back comfortably against the bulkhead, closing his eyes. This should be a delicious interlude of total recall, he told himself, as he extracted his latest secret for its first examination since the event itself.

Yesterday during the final moments of the action, he had been crouched on hands and knees, sheltering the half-hour glass and notebook with his body, scuttling back and forward to stay within reach of the captain and Mister Dobbs and be sure of catching and recording each order and event. It had been a soul-searing experience, the worst of his life, but he had performed his duty. Now he experienced a thrill of expectation as the drama began.

"I shall die! I don't want to die! I must not die now!" The recollection of the saliva dripping from the corners of the captain's mouth added titillation to the utterance, and he hugged himself with ecstasy at the recollection.

Dobbs had faced the captain, and he had heard, not read on his lips, the greeting above the din of battle.

"Captain!" Gaffner treasured the moment, visualizing again the scene in his mind. It was the last utterance of a man he had admired. He anticipated the climax of the scene, and hugged himself again.

"Move! Stand aside!" Merewether had said, trying to press past Dobbs. "I must strike! Surrender!"

He recalled the sequence of expression that crossed Dobbs's face, feeling a lump rise in his throat at the memory. Disbelief at first; incredulous dismay, mouth opening, eyes staring; then how his face began to work as tears started. And the captain's final words as Mister Dobbs was struck down.

"I must surrender! "

Gaffner contemplated the scene for a long moment more, then put the secret back into its compartment in his mind until such time as he should again desire to extract and re-examine it. Gaffner opened his eyes.

The word was being passed on deck to make all preparations for getting underway. Gaffner gathered up the accoutrements of his trade and went aft to stand in his customary position just abaft the helm.

It was stifling hot below decks in officer's country, no breeze penetrated here, as Hamlyn and Marlowe made an inventory of the personal effects of Lieutenant (late) John Dobbs of the Bombay Marine. There were garments, shoes and boots, and a sword to be stowed in the sea chest, along with the small library of books, all treating of navigation, seamanship, astronomy and geography. A leather pouch with a drawstring contained a dozen gold guineas, assorted rupee pieces, and a worn gold band, possibly his mother's wedding ring, along with a horn handled clasp knife, badly nicked, the homely accumulations of twenty-one years of a young man's life. Merewether sat in the one chair in the cramped room, sweat trickling under his arms as Hamlyn called off each item and Marlowe entered it on the inventory to be signed, sealed and witnessed.

"One writing kit, poor order," said Hamlyn. "One sheaf of notes entitled, "Notes and Observations On the New American Method of Navigation, by Lieutenant John Dobbs, Hon. Co's Marine" . . ."

"I'll take those," said Merewether. "They go to Captain Wilkerson, the Fleet Navigator."

"So noted," said Hamlyn. "Here is a packet of letters, and some unfinished ones as well, though two are pretty well crumpled. Johnny was in correspondence with Judith Johnson down at Penang, you know, and you might want to forward them, though they seem to be more drafts than finished letters . . ." The gloomy task was finished, and all three officers signed the inventory.

Back in the ruined flag cabin, he laid the packet and the two crumpled balls of foolscap in the basket on the desk. He was in no mood to write the letter of regret and condolence to the next of kin, whoever that might be. There would be time enough on the voyage to Bombay. Each thought of Dobbs revived the specter of his panic at the crux of the battle, the unreasoning desire to live at any cost, and his shameful determination to surrender the ship to achieve survival. The memory of the expression on Dobb's face haunted him. Merewether wished for a moment that Dobbs had not been so stubborn. Had he stepped aside, the ball would have struck Merewether instead. Oh, hell! This train of thought could lead to madness. But his mind would not leave off the morbid train of thought as he stared blindly out the shattered stern lights.

There was no doubt, he told himself: *Pitt* had been *in extremis,* a frigate of equal force locked to either side battering away with their heavy guns as musket balls rained from their fighting tops to decimate the topside hands. And then, when the portside boarding party had been just barely contained by Gunny's Marines, the second attack had come leaping across the gap from the starboard frigate to race aft. At that point, even as he drew his sword to cut the flag halyard, who could have predicted that Marlowe would leap into the breach? No, he tried to tell himself. As the situation appeared at the moment he formed his resolve to surrender, it was the only prudent decision; to resist further would have been only a vainglorious sacrifice of lives to salve a foolhardy pride.

But his logic failed even to convince himself. The very fact that *Pitt* had survived the action, by whatever chance, proved the fallacy of his arguments. Naval history was replete with instances where resolute men had snatched victory from the jaws of defeat. Hopeless as a situation might seem, it could appear quite different through the eyes of the enemy captain. No, he had intended with all his craven heart to surrender, and he would never trust his courage and resolution again. Better to resign from the Marine and find a less demanding calling. Something touched his ankle, and he came back to the present with a start.

It was the tiger-striped kitten, Tipu Sultan, Sangh had adopted, but his appearance was materially altered from the last time Merewether had seen him. He now had only a raw stump to mark the place where his saucy little spike of a tail had waved. God, even the cat had been maimed in the action!

"Hulloa, little fellow!" He picked him up and examined the wound. It appeared to be healing cleanly, and the kitten began to purr, then escaped from his hands to the desk top, there to bat the crumpled balls of foolscap about in the basket. Evidently the cat was in no present pain and had accepted his loss philosophically. Merewether nudged one of the playthings and the kitten sprang on it, then seized his hand with forepaws, rolling on his back to kick clawlessly with his hind feet, alternately gnawing at his knuckles and then licking them with his rough tongue. The cat had spirit. He did not permit his wounds to daunt him.

"Sangh! I think young Tipu requires some refreshment." Sangh took the kitten back to the pantry. The antics of the animal had been a pleasant diversion for his gloomy thoughts.

One of the crumpled sheets had been knocked out of the basket by the cat and lay in the centre of the desk, half unfolded. There was writing visible in Dobb's small precise hand. Without willing it, Merewether could read the salutation, "My Dearest Judy," and part of the first line, "Wonderful news . . ." Curiosity overcame him. He flattened the sheet and read the balance of the unfinished paragraph. "I may be able to get leave enough to come to Penang this autumn, and if I do, will you marry . . ." The writing stopped, but there followed several irregular repetitions of names.

"Judith Johnson"; then, "Mistress John Dobbs", in much embellished script "Judith Johnson Dobbs", and in shaded block letters, "Lieutenant and Mrs. John Dobbs". There followed a series of geometric abstractions, then a stylized heart with the initials, "J.J." and "J.D." entwined on the spoiled sheet. Obviously the young man had been indulging a pleasant fantasy, visualizing a not too distant day in which Judith Johnson would be Mrs. John Dobbs.

Merewether felt a sudden sense of shame at thus peering unbidden into the soul and secret heart of a young man, but it was too late to recall his impulse. Seeing this pitiful memoir of an idyll shattered by a cannon ball, Merewether was sick at heart. He felt worse, even guiltier than before his spirits had momentarily been revived by the playful kitten. There was no remedy. A mere resignation was not enough; death by his own hand was the only expiation for his failure. But lest he compound his sins, he must first bring the convoy safely to Surat in accordance with his orders. There was a knock on the door, and the carpenter and Bowman, the leading boatswain's mate, wearing the new dignity of an acting warrant as boatswain, came in.

"Sir," said Mister Svensen, "if we hit no full gales. I tink de ship floats until ve reach port."

Bowman agreed, showing his broken teeth, souvenirs of his long fight from the lower deck up to boatswain, the king of warrant officers. "And the mainyard is fished and stayed and the sails bent on ready to set forrard."

"Very good. Ask Mister Dillon to see me at his convenience, and you may pass the word to make all preparations for getting underway." Merewether resolutely refused to let his mind return to the morbid thoughts of a moment ago. He concentrated upon the signals necessary to get the convoy moving again, and the course he must set to raise Surat.

Wearing the twin dignities of acting third lieutenant and navigator of a thirty-six-gun frigate at age eighteen had not changed the outward appearance or manner of Midshipman Hamlyn. Always inclined to be cocksure and a bit impatient with those who possessed slower wits that his, the young officer was already looking past the examining board for lieutenant at Bombay in September as a mere formality. Once commissioned, he was certain that his rise in the Marine would be nothing less than meteoric. However, he did not let his thoughts dwell on the future, bright as it appeared, but concentrated on keeping *Pitt* on course under her clumsy jury rig. Unbalanced as it was, with a spare mainyard serving as a stumpy foremast, he had soon discovered the tendency of the bow to wander. The helmsman seemed incapable of assimilating this simple fact, and for the third time in this afternoon watch he saw the luff of the spanker beginning to tremble, evidence that the ship had gone off course again.

"Mind your helm!" he told the quartermaster sharply.

The man was sulky and resentful in manner, and for a moment Hamlyn was tempted "to skin him alive", in Larkin's idiom. Then he restrained himself. The hands had had a hard enough time during and since the battle day before yesterday, and this man was a striker endeavoring to replace one of the two quartermasters killed in action. The thought immediately revived memories of poor Johnny Dobbs.

As the two junior officers in *Rapid,* Dobbs and Hamlyn had naturally gravitated towards one another, though there was marked contrast in their characters. Dobbs had been slow, methodical, tenacious, single-minded in his performance of duty, and lacking in small talk. Hamlyn was quick, mercurial in temperament ready to believe the worst of his fellow man, inclined to gloss over routine housekeeping chores, and articulate in the civilized prattle taught by the public schools of England. While he had been Larkin's junior watch officer, he had preferred to call on Dobbs to explain a knotty problem in seamanship or navigation, and had found him willing to stand even an occasional watch in the rare instances when the ship had been in port and he had a pressing social engagement ashore.

He though now of Judith Johnson down at George Town, not a particularly pretty little girl, and he had sheared away from her when he discovered that her flow of conversation was not only constant, but unsophisticated. He preferred women a bit older than himself at this point; they were usually more approachable by a fluent, polished younger man with keen Norman good looks. Yet Johnny and Judith had hit it off, and Dobbs had confided only last month that she had accepted his proposal of marriage within the year. He wondered as he watched the compass card come back to the base course what those crumpled balls of foolscap on the desk had contained. Under the stern eye of the captain, he had dared not look.

With the innate snobbery of a scion of the gentry (albeit a third son and compelled by the entail to make his own way) Hamlyn had never made an effort to ingratiate himself beyond the necessities of the service with Captain Merewether. The man had risen from the lower deck, and while Hamlyn maintained correct professional relations, he considered Merewether his social inferior by several degrees since he had not entered the Marine by the genteel route of midshipman, or even volunteer. Still Merewether had been entirely fair to him and had promised his recommendation as qualified to take the examination for lieutenant at Bombay.

"Mind your helm!" he said for the fourth time, and the watch barely half over. *Pitt's* motion had grown a bit sluggish, he decided, and time to pump again. "Turn those lascars out. Man the pumps," he told the boatswain's mate of the watch. "And mind you have the carpenter sound the well before they start." It was important, Dillon had insisted, that they established the rate of leakage, but for the last twenty-four hours, one hour of pumping out of each four had sufficed to clear the bilges, and the carpenter was still finding and plugging holes.

The thought recalled the holocaust he had survived. He remembered with contempt his bright observation that an engagement with three frigates of equal force should be an interesting affair. Even the action with those privateers in the Straits last year had not prepared him for the reality of an all-out naval battle. And the captain had hung on beyond reason to the point where it became a foolhardy slaughter. Hang the glory and prize money. Life was more precious than either!

Hamlyn wondered suddenly if regret for the men killed and wounded was the cause for the captain's gloomy preoccupation since the battle. In his year and a half of service under Merewether, he had never seen the man in so bleak and melancholy a mood. He wondered what secret guilt might be concealed behind the taciturn scarred face. Hamlyn's father was fond of saying that he could read peculation in the mien and manner of an embezzling estate agent long before the rent books revealed the fact, that no man was capable of entirely concealing a guilty conscience.

That woman! Suddenly he was sure she was the cause of Merewether's dejection. Of course! The time was almost exactly right since her mysterious visit last week. The saintly Merewether had bedded her in his cabin, and she had peppered him! He almost chuckled at the thought, though it was enough to give concern to any man returning to a wife after long absence. He would make a discreet inquiry of Mefford or Buttram to confirm his theory, but he was convinced in his own mind of the reason for the captain's remorse. Hamlyn finished his watch in high spirits, elated at having divined Merewether's guilty secret.

* * *

The third day there was enough of a blow to cause the convoy to shorten sail, and Merewether and the carpenter concern. Merewether, Dillon, Mister Svensen and the acting boatswain were down in the middle hold where a mare's nest of timbers braced the shattered frames on the starboard side. The ship was working enough in the sea that the seams in the outer planking alternately opened and closed, spewing oakum, and admitting jets of sea water at every roll. Four carpenter's mates were fitting yet another brace designed to stop the movement, and two others were hammering home spikes and wedges in the existing braces to take up the slack. Bowman had a party of seamen standing by with pots of molten tar and bundles of oakum, but it was useless to try to caulk the seams until the planking had been immobilized.

"It vill four new rib take to make her whole," grumbled the carpenter. "Easy in the graving dock. But ve only make patchwork here."

"Well," said Merewether. "We are only pumping twelve out of twenty-four hours so far, even with this blow. If the sea moderates, we should still make Bombay. He and Dillon came back on deck, passing the off-watch lascars sprawled in the shade of the mainsail, while their mates swayed at the brakes of the pumps; he could never have kept the ship afloat except for these dark muscular men. "I'll pay my call on the wounded now," he told Dillon.

The gundeck was serving as a hospital, windsails rigged at two hatches diverting a cooling breeze along it. Pallets and a few cots covered the deck, each occupied by a wounded man. There were fewer sounds of misery today than yesterday; there had been three more corpses to bury in the sea this morning, but now the race was against gangrene. All those men who had been accounted mortally wounded on Buttram's initial report had died, and Buttram would account himself a failure for each that succumbed hereafter from the complications of infection. Loblolly attendants passed along the rows, doling out water and easing the positions of the casualties, while Buttram and Mefford were bent in consultation over a cot forward. Some of the men spoke to greet him; others lifted a shaky hand in salute, and some merely acknowledged him with their eyes.

The doctors looked up. “Good morning, Captain,” they said almost in unison.

“Don’t let me interfere — carry on.”

“We’ve completed morning rounds, sir, dressings all changed,” said Buttram. “All these slugabeds have to do now is wait for the next issue of medicinal brandy, and then have dinner while they’re deciding how to spend their prize money!” There was an appreciative titter down the deck as Merewether thought grimly that these men would go through hell itself if they could see a few shillings of prize money on the other side, and the share they received would be squandered without a thought of the blood and sweat that had bought it. He saw the doctor eyeing him intently, and wondered who had attracted his attention, then looked down at the man on the cot. It was Larkin, still pale and drawn under his tan.

“How do you feel, Mister Larkin?” he asked stiffly. The bright blue eyes under the disordered yellow hair met his for a moment, then shifted away.

“Oh, tol'able, Captain, tol'able. I was just trying to find out from these two sawbones why a hand that ain’t there any more should itch!”

“A common enough phenomenon,” broke in Mefford. “Such sensations will gradually decrease, then disappear.”

Merewether felt a cold chill run up his spine at the thought of an amputated arm, already food for fishes, still sending sensations to the brain of a man, real enough to judge by Larkin’s expression. He was no malingerer inventing imaginary symptoms, but a man of raw courage and common sense. And Merewether had brought him to this pass. He could no longer meet his gaze, the man would read the secret of his guilt in his eyes if he met it. He turned away and continued down the rows of wounded. But he did not deceive his conscience. Then he escaped to the rainswept weather deck and took refuge in the flag cabin to await Svenson’s report.

A man keeps few secrets from his valet and in two years of serving him, Sangh had developed an almost clairvoyant ability to gauge Captain Merewether’s temper. He sat now on his stool in the pantry, head bowed, staring at the tailless kitten stretched out asleep on the deck at his feet.

He had brought such order to the cabin as he could out of the wreckage, and was able to carry on his duties until the carpenters accomplished their pressing repairs and could turn to lower priority items. In the meantime, the captain was occupying the flag cabin since most of its furnishings were intact.

The little Indian was deeply troubled. He had never seen Merewether in such a state of dejection; though he dealt promptly and effectively with day-by-day decisions, he sat even now at his desk simply staring into space with an expression that Sangh could only read as bitter sorrow — this man who only three days ago had won a great victory. Sangh reached back through recent events seeking some clue that might explain the mood. Aside from the battle, he could recall nothing out of the ordinary that had taken place since the ship departed from Jeddah. One day had been much like another, periods of progress, then interludes in which the convoy had been becalmed. Becalmed? Light dawned in Sangh's mind. That half-caste woman!

The cold hatred he had felt for Madame Bai since she had poisoned his cat flared suddenly hot. The whole matter became crystal clear in his mind: She was one of the *yoginis,* a sorceress! Walking the earth in the guise of a mortal woman! In her rage and frustration at being thwarted in her scheme to kill the captain, she had cast a spell upon him.

The solution was so simple and logical that Sangh was angry at himself for not divining it earlier. He had often enough heard of such cases, though this was the first he had encountered in person. He opened his eyes and slid down from the stool, disturbing the kitten, which rose and stretched. Through the serving window he saw that Merewether was still seated in the same position, oblivious to his surroundings. A perfect example of the sorceress's art: she had planted a demon in his soul to devour it and thereby destroy him!

What was the remedy? He came back to the stool and strove to recall the days of his childhood when he had received instruction in the theology and canons of Buddha at the knee of the village guru. The master had been a good man, and Sangh had conscientiously followed his precepts, though the exigencies of the life he had been forced into had also forced many compromises upon him. Bhimu had been an adherent of the new Buddhism called *Mahayana,* the Great Vehicle, which taught that a man by the spiritual merit which he gained might assist other men on their way to perfection. The older sects, following what was sometimes called The Lesser Vehicle, had rejected this theory of the transference of merit from one individual to another, and held that a man might only help another on his way by example and advice. Sangh recited to himself the Vow of the Bodhisattva:

> I take upon myself . . . the deeds of all beings, even of those in the hells, the other worlds, in the realms of punishment . . . I take their suffering upon me, . . . I bear it, I do not draw back from it, I do not tremble at it, . . . I have no fear of it, . . . I do not lose heart . . . I must bear the burden of all beings, for I have vowed to save all things living, to bring them safe through the forest of birth, age, disease, death and rebirth. I think not of my own salvation, but strive to bestow on all beings the royalty of supreme wisdom. So I take upon myself all the sorrows of all beings. I resolve to bear every torment in every purgatory of the universe. For it is better that I alone suffer from the multitude of living beings. I give myself in exchange. I redeem the universe from the forest of purgatory, from the womb of flesh, from the realm of death. I agree to suffer as a ransom for all beings, for the sake of all beings. Truly I will not abandon them. For I have resolved to gain supreme wisdom for the sake of all that lives, to save the world.

The doctrine was good. Sangh felt a warm glow of satisfaction spread through his small body with the conviction that it was within his power to make Captain Merewether whole again, rid him of the demon that possessed him. But how? Bhimu had taught that these she-demons must be compelled, coerced, rather than persuaded. He must pronounce the right formula, the *mantra,* in the correct manner. He racked his brain, trying to remember some of these magic phrases. But try as he might he could recall only the most common, having never before had the need to use such an incantation. He repeated to himself the Six Syllables: *"Óm mani palme húm."* It could not hurt to try it, he decided, though "Ah! The jewel is indeed in the lotus!" did not sound promising as a *mantra* to exorcise a demon implanted in a man by a sorceress. He heard a knock on the cabin door and Merewether's greeting.

It was the carpenter and boatswain, to announce that the caulking still held.

When the warrant officers departed, Sangh peeped through the crack of the serving window. Merewether had changed position, unstoppered the ink well, and was beginning to write.

Marshalling all the force and concentration he could muster, eyes fixed upon Merewether's face, Sangh repeated the magical Six Syllables, once, twice, thrice. He remained staring at the captain, seeking by force of will to drive the demon out of him, then repeated the incantation three times more. Merewether looked up suddenly, meeting Sangh's gaze, and started slightly.

"I had forgotten you were in the pantry. A cup of coffee, please." The spell was broken. All Sangh could do was hope and say a silent prayer.

When he served the coffee a few minutes later, Sangh could discern no alteration in the stern set of the captain's face. By midafternoon, he was sure that he had failed in his effort to exorcise the demon, obviously because he did not possess the correct *mantra.* He cast about for some solution to his dilemma, but he was the only Indian in the ship's company, and there was no one to consult. He decided to go on deck for a breath of air and a look about. Mister Hamlyn had the deck, but was in the process of being relieved by Lieutenant MacCamy. He heard him call to the new boatswain's mate.

"Turn those lascars to at the pumps, Mac." The thought of the lascars brought on board had not crossed Sangh's mind. He went forward. They were all of impossibly low caste and ignorant, but he would see if he could communicate with them. He found a group squatting or sitting about the deck forward, dark muscular men, who looked at him curiously, then spoke to one another. Sangh caught a scrap of the conversation which commented humorously on his lack of stature. It was in a dialect that he could understand, and he addressed his inquiry generally to the group.

"Is there one among you who is learned in the Precepts of Buddha?" It was a forlorn hope. He saw the blank stares from two dozen pairs of dark eyes. Then one slender man stretched at full length on the deck with his eyes closed spoke lazily without opening them.

"Ghandi professes that once he was a monk, but he works at the pumps now."

"Thank you." Sangh squatted down in a scrap of shade to wait for the man to be relieved. When he came, he was a heavily built man with sweat pouring down his face and torso. One of his fellows nudged him and pointed, and Sangh beckoned him to one side.

"Yes," said Ghandi when the question was put to him. "For ten years I was a monk of the Buddhist Order, and begged my food through the village, but I tired of the life, put aside the saffron robes, and left it. Now, what is it you want?"

"It is a spell, a demon planted in the soul of my master," Sangh explained earnestly. "And I cannot pronounce the *mantra* to expel it . . ." He explained the captain's mood and his deduction that one of the yoginis walking the earth in the guise of a beautiful woman had cast the spell, while the man stared unblinkingly at him with eyes as hard as obsidian.

"Ah, yes," Ghandi broke in. "And the *mantra* for one thus possessed is most difficult. Such demons are very strong, and it is not without danger that one opposes them. Perhaps some silver will help me gain courage . . ."

"How much?" demanded Sangh, conscious of the small hoard he had accumulated during his two years in the Marine.

"Well," said Ghandi, looking away for a moment, then back with an appraising glance at the small man. "I shall have to repeat the *mantra* four successive days just as the sun touches the sea, and I demand ten rupees for each pronouncement . . ."

"Done!" agreed Sangh, pulling his small bag of coins from his loin cloth and counting them out into the avaricious hand of the former monk. "And you can begin tonight?"

"Yes, but expect no result until the fourth pronouncement!" Sangh hurried back to his pantry, feeling that a great burden had been lifted from his own small shoulders.

The depressing task was done. Merewether had often enough in the past written such letters to the next of kin expressing his regret and extending condolences for the death of a kinsman by blood or marriage, but the one for Dobbs was the hardest of his career. He remembered writing for young Burcham who had died so uselessly at the hands of Tipu Sultan near Vellore two years ago, but he had not been present at that death, and it had been something fortuitous, unpredictable, the angry whim of a madman in frustration. He had not then felt the crushing burden of guilt. The first letter was to an uncle and former guardian of the young officer, and, he thought cynically, the man would be comforted by the revelation that a substantial share of prize money might be forthcoming. Nothing like a legacy to cheer up a grieving kinsman!

The second letter to Miss Judith Johnson at Penang had been a bit easier. He had an insight into Dobbs's sentiments, but none to hers, and he kept the message as impersonal as he could, while expressing his deep regret. In any event, the thing was done, and he even felt a sense of relief as he sealed the missives up, then called Sangh to take the letters down to Davis to be deposited in the private mail bags.

Merewether was conscious of a sharp scrutiny. The small man was looking at him in a manner that he had never noticed before, and he wondered briefly what prompted it. On this, the fourth day after the battle, the convoy was measurably closer to its destination, and there had been no burials this morning. Buttram had asked permission to move some of his more advanced convalescents to cots under an awning on deck to take advantage of the fresh healing breeze. He had granted the request, but their presence on deck would be a constant reminder of his betrayal of them.

The sea had subsided since yesterday, and the necessity to pump had diminished to one hour in four again. Merewether came out on deck for a last look around before darkness fell. Dillon had the watch with Marlowe as his junior. The wind was over the starboard quarter, and the ship was sailing easily in spite of her much reduced sail area forward, but she presented a continuous problem to the helmsmen to keep her bow from wandering. He saw Dillon look sharply at Marlowe, who started, then spoke to the quartermaster.

"Mind your helm!" *Pitt* was back on course as he stepped forward to the break of the poop to look into the waist.

Sangh had apparently found a friend among the lascars manning the pumps. He squatted beside a short, heavily muscled fellow on the deck a dozen feet away conversing in whispers. The man looked up, unwinking black eyes boring into his for a moment, and he saw his lips move, but heard no sound. They remained so for a moment more, and Merewether turned away, conscious somehow that the gaze still was fixed on the back of his head as he entered the companionway.

Dillon, first lieutenant in *Comet,* and now acting in the same capacity in *Pitt,* was a tall, broad pleasant man with a stock of droll stories off duty but he was a martinet when he held the deck, as Midshipman Marlowe soon came to know. Marlowe's attention had been called three times this watch to sloppy steering on the part of the duty helmsman, and in injured silence he now stationed himself beside the binnacle where he could issue a *sotto voce* warning before the stem sagged off noticeably to leeward. The jury rig just did not balance, and what normally would be an easy point of sailing had become difficult. His left foot still ached where the boat gun had recoiled across his toes, and his right hand was bandaged with goosegrease smeared on the powder burn he had suffered when he touched off the piece four days ago. But the recollection was pleasant, and he savored Captain Merewether's brief words of praise a few hours after the action had concluded.

"Mister Marlowe," he had said in a low voice. "That was a magnificent Lion's Mouth you formed, and I am most obliged to you." And yet the captain had seemed unable to meet his eyes, and was most unhappy in expression but he had continued, "I shall mention your services in my report."

Marlowe had been on board a relatively short time after being snatched bodily out of the sea when *Vesuvius* sank, and certainly he did not know the captain as well as the other officers did, but he had heard Mister MacCamy remark this morning to the purser that the captain still seemed "shaken". In his carefree adolescent spirits, the battle at its outset had seemed more of a lark, a game of high adventure, than the almost fatal affair it had turned into.

"Watch it!" he told the quartermaster in a loud whisper, and the man rotated the wheel four spokes to the right, held it a moment peering into the binnacle, added two more, then came back hastily four to the left. The ship had sagged off less than a point before he caught it, and was now back on course, though Dillon was staring hard at him.

Marlowe thought again of his moment of glory. His station at quarters was the starboard battery of quarterdeck carronades, though he bore small responsibility once the order to commence fire was given, and the gun crews settled into their rigid ritual of loading and firing. His pieces and most of his crews had somehow miraculously survived the holocaust, which accounted for his ability to form the Lion's Mouth from them. In the early stages of the action he had moved from one gun to another, shouting encouragement. By the time all three ships were locked together, his voice could no longer be heard, and he had felt desperately alone on the deck exposed to the torrent of enemy fire. He saw the boarding party forming up in the waist of the frigate to starboard, but his guns could not train enough forward to bear on it. The three-pounder boat gun, crammed almost full of musket balls, was already secured pointing forward at the break of the poop. He had had presence of mind enough to cut off a length of slow match smoldering in its tub before his resolve somehow failed and he froze to the spot in cold terror. The memory was uncomfortable. He had been thoroughly indoctrinated during his brief career in the belief that an officer of the Marine never experienced fear.

He came back to the present as Captain Merewether had come on deck, and he looked hastily into the binnacle.

"Mind your helm!" Marlowe snapped, although *Pitt* was exactly on course. He watched Merewether go forward to the break of the poop and then resumed the examination of his recent performance of duty.

Merewether, he remembered, had been just then saying something to Lieutenant Dobbs, and then was hurled across the deck as Dobbs seemed to disappear into thin air. He had remained frozen to the spot, unable to move, horrified by the phenomenon, expecting death at any instant, only to see the captain rise, draw his sword and rush forward as the boarding party poured over the starboard side. That action had somehow unlocked the irons of terror, by example galvanized him to utter the command and run forward to fire the boat gun into the invading mass. He had found himself beside Merewether, shrieking like a banshee, swinging a cutlass as they rushed the survivors of the boarding party, and only moments later, *Countess, Comet* and *Ariel* had commenced the bombardment that had induced the surrender of the frigates. He tucked his guilty secret out of sight in his mind, certain it would never emerge again. The fearless example of Captain Merewether had rescued him from disgrace, and he was thankful.

From his station on the starboard flank of the convoy, Whaley could see only the main and mizzen upper works of *Pitt* outlined against the setting sun. The sea was calm, the breeze steady, and *Vigilant* under plain sail was beginning to forereach again on the slower ships. He cocked his ear, expecting the order to change course so as to lose enough ground to regain position. No order was forthcoming from Pelfrey, the officer of the watch, and with difficulty, Whaley restrained the stinging rebuke that was on the tip of his tongue. Pelfrey had no natural bent for seamanship and had learned his duties by rote but he finally noticed that the bearing of the guide had drawn noticeably aft, and gave the belated order.

"Hands to the braces! Wear ship. Your new course is east by north." Better later than never, thought Whaley feeling a flush of irritation, but he managed to hold his tongue as he had resolved to do at the outset of his command.

It was difficult to alter the mental processes and prejudices acquired in the years as a junior officer charged with enforcing the will and whims of a commanding officer. He had often enough had to compromise his own principles to conform with the idiotic orders issued by a captain. In Whaley's mind, there were no shades of grey; things were black or white, dead wrong or unequivocally right. But now he was a commanding officer himself and must rely upon his subordinates to execute his orders. It was easy enough to compel, even coerce his officers, demand that every duty be performed in the exact manner that he directed, but there were not enough hours in the day to follow up and ensure compliance with the letter of his orders. He had begun to realize in the last months under Merewether, seeing the quiet efficient performance of duty by Larkin and Dobbs, that it was the result that counted. He recalled Merewether's parting words at the gangway as he embarked in *Pitt's* gig to read himself in.

"Captain, you stand now in a lonely and slippery place, supported only by the loyalty and efficiency of your officers and crew, and this is won more often by persuasion than compulsion. I wish you every good fortune in your new command . . ."

It was the philosophy of those that Whaley had always categorized as "nambypambies" in bitter contempt. But the statement had somehow hung in his mind and made a profound impression. It was a concept that had not occurred to him, and he found himself unaccountably making no sweeping changes in the custom and mode of performance of duty in Vigilant. He managed to repress many of the criticisms that he was accustomed to utter, and to look the other way on minor infractions that had formerly infuriated him. He soon discovered that Murray, his first lieutenant, was crackerjack at getting things done if left alone, and the boatswain had the crew in the palm of his hand. The performance of duty by all hands in the brief flurry of action with the two French frigates five days ago had been entirely creditable. He wished he had had a more active duty assignment than merely barring the way to the convoy, but *Vigilant* would receive a full share of any prize money realized.

Whaley thought back to his first impressions of Merewether. He had, of course, known that Merewether had been jumped over the heads of a score of more senior and deserving lieutenants in the Marine, that he owed his promotion to captain to political influence in the Court of Directors of the Company, and he was married to the niece of the former Governor-General, now Governor of Madras. Whaley, in his disappointment at being passed over himself for promotion to captain, had been entirely prepared to dislike the man and to discover him to be weak and incompetent. The apparent reluctance to inflict punishment had confirmed his initial opinion but he had gained respect for the man after he had thwarted the abortive mutiny. Merewether had told the assembled officers in the grey light of that early morning that every officer in the ship, from himself down, bore a share of the responsibility for the event, that each must examine his own conscience and mend his ways to insure that such would never again occur.

Perhaps it was the example of the executions at Bombay, the removal of the dissidents from the ship, or the efforts of the officers to improve their performance of duty, or the firm competence and fair play of Captain Merewether. Whatever, the hands in *Pitt* had welded into a crew that had fought to the last gasp. It was difficult to fault such an achievement.

It was almost dark, Whaley could still see the guide in the convoy, now almost exactly on bearing. He did not look around, gave Pelfrey no cue, but he heard the order given only ten seconds late this time.

"Hands to the braces! Wear ship. Your new course is northeast."

Whaley turned and went below in his short brisk gait, confident for the moment that though he stood in a lonely and slippery place, he was adequately supported, and that the precepts of Captain Merewether held merit.

Seven days after the amputation, Larkin still felt shaky and he could not seem to bring his thoughts into focus. He was content to relax in a canvas chair rigged beside his cot under the awning Buttram had ordered spread forward, appreciative of the steady breeze from the southwest that found its way under the canvas, and sip the thrice daily ration of port the surgeons had prescribed. It was intended to stimulate replacement of the blood he had lost from his wound, but he considered the prescription mere superstition. He had no taste for wine. Red meat was the best remedy.

There was little pain in his stump now. It appeared to be healing well, though a twinge would come when he involuntarily reached for something with the non-existent hand. He had suffered no sickness or serious injury since childhood, his recuperative powers were excellent, and he anticipated no complications.

Larkin's thoughts turned to his own future. While he might be permitted to stay on in the Marine, the prospects for a crippled junior officer were not bright. And he had grown weary this past year of the constant pressures of service at sea. The last time he had really enjoyed his duties was a year ago on the voyage to Mauritius. The scouting expedition to Java last fall had been hard, serving as first to an ambitious and demanding officer such as Tollett. Then he had been denied his own command in *Rapid* due to her unseaworthy condition, had become second lieutenant to Whaley's first with all its complications of the unsuccessful mutiny. He would have resigned after Ras ul Khymah, but for Whaley's transfer.

He thought of Dobbs, that quiet earnest young man, and felt a pang of regret at his death. He had never been close to Dobbs — their interests were too disparate — but as first lieutenant of a man-o'-war, he had learned that he could rely implicitly on the officer to carry out his orders. He had been happy to see Dobbs receive his due for the success of the operation at Ras ul Khymah, and happy for him again when he confided that he intended to marry that talkative little girl at Penang he had met last year. Bad luck!

The thought of the girl made Larkin consider his own situation. He had had no more than a passing interest in any woman since Jane Wisdom encouraged his attentions at Bombay two years ago, and then married another. He had seen her again at Bombay last winter, one child in arms and another imminent, now fat and blowsy.

His thoughts turned once more to his own career. He had no desire to wait out the years in the Marine in some backwater station. He had saved most of his pay, all of his prize money, and the occasional gain from a bit of private trade. He had the capital to take him back to Kentucky, if he so decided, and establish himself in some appropriate venture, but he was uncertain of conditions there since it had become a state thirteen years ago. Possibly there were greater opportunities south or west since the United States had purchased Louisiana from Bonaparte. He was not sanguine as to his chances of making his way on the frontier with only one arm, but he had always had a bent for trade, he could drive a shrewd bargain, and had an instinctive feeling for what the traffic would bear. But the trade of merchants was too confining. Possibly he could pick up some land grants in the new territories and resell them at a profit. Though he had no moral scruples, he did not consider the slave trade; he had had enough of that, and it had no future. He could reach no conclusion, of course, until he returned to the United States and saw for himself the conditions there, but he realized that he had not even considered India or England. They were too crowded for his free spirit.

Buttram and Mefford appeared with loblolly attendants carrying their medical kits. Larkin permitted the bandages to be unwrapped, and forced himself to look at the raw stump with the black loops of the sutures tying off the blood vessels protruding.

Buttram bent to sniff delicately at the surface, then looked up with a smile.

"Healing cleanly, Mister Larkin." He tested the sutures, pulling gently with thumb and forefinger. There was a stab of pain and Larkin winced. "It will not be long before these will come out. If you feel equal to it, I suggest you take a turn or two about the deck twice a day to build up your strength."

"Yes, Doctor. I'll commence tomorrow." Buttram coated a wad of lint with a medication, pressed it against the stump, and began to replace the bandage.

"Have you talked with the captain lately?" he inquired.

"Oh, yes, he's stopped by each morning to inquire as to my health."

"Have you noticed a change in him since the battle?"

Had there been a change? Merewether had always been quiet and courteous, no bluster or bombast in his manner. But — yes, he had appeared much more subdued. Now that Larkin thought about the matter, Merewether gave the impression that he was bearing a secret burden and was embarrassed or self-conscious. Possibly it was the butcher's bill. (The old hands in *Pitt* insisted she had suffered the heaviest casualties in a single ship in the history of the Marine.) Perhaps Merewether felt guilt at having called upon his officers and men to face such overwhelming odds last week. He decided on his reply to Buttram.

"No, Doctor. He appears entirely his normal self to me." It might be only blind loyalty, Larkin thought, but he would not corroborate any suspicions Buttram harbored. The doctor made no reply for a moment as he tied the split ends of the bandage, but then he stepped back and looked shrewdly at Larkin.

"Well, I have!" he said in a positive tone with a frown. "I think he has a problem — a monkey on his back as the hands would say — but I wondered if a man who has known him as long as I had noticed anything. Oh, well — now remember, a turn about the deck . . ." Buttram turned to the next patient.

Larkin turned the matter over in his mind. Merewether had never evaded responsibility, nor had it appeared to weigh heavily upon him. He thought back to the day of the action with the French. When the frigates made their move, the captain had acted properly by Larkin's lights. The only chance with three vessels, each of a force equal to his own, was to divide them, seek successive encounters with single ships where the speed of *Pitt's* broadsides could cripple the enemy. The scheme had worked to perfection with the interception of the first frigate. The French commander had made a serious tactical error there in detaching one frigate. Undoubtedly he had anticipated snapping up a few prizes before breaking off to escort *Countess* in her escape from the convoy.

The second phase of the action had commenced as a thing of beauty to Larkin's professional eye. With one frigate crippled and her colors struck, the other two were compelled to come back to the serious business of their mission to detach *Countess.* Merewether had not made the obvious move of throwing *Pitt* in their path. With the weather gauge, they could choose the moment and method of joining or avoiding action. Instead, he had used the crippled frigate to mask his intentions, circling her, then coming to the wind to shift to the opposite tack, gain the weather gauge, and emerge within easy gunshot of the nearer vessel while screened by her from the fire of her consort.

The nearer frigate had been crippled, within minutes of striking, when the second sheared across her wake expecting to get in a raking broadside or two before Merewether could respond, but he was already coming to port to counter the maneuver and place himself in position himself to rake the enemy when misfortune struck. *Pitt* had been within one cannon ball of victory, Larkin thought softly, when that last despairing shot from the crippled Frenchman took down the foremast, throwing the ship out of control and causing her to collide with the frigate to port. There had been only two alternatives then: hold fast, serve the guns as long as there were men to load and fire them; or surrender.

Larkin remembered almost with disbelief the hell that had ensued, the crippled frigate able to close again to starboard and grapple, while the undamaged one pumped in her broadsides. from the other hand. He had seen the boarding party assembling in the waist of the ship to port and was training the long nine around to dose it with canister,. when the blast of grapeshot wiped out his crew and took his arm. He could not remember anything more until he awakened from his drugged sleep sometime in the midwatch next morning and asked for water to wet his parched throat. His first question to the loblolly attendant after he gulped down the cooling cup had been whether they were prisoners.

"Naw, sor. Them Frenchies struck right after you come below!"

It was hard to believe. *Pitt* had been *in extremis,* two-thirds of her guns out of action, the deck littered with dead and wounded. He could remember looking aft just before he was hit to see the Bombay Marine ensign still flying, and wonder at Merewether's tenacity. In his judgment, the surrender should already have been made, but events had proved him wrong.

He thought again of Buttram's question and his reply. Of course, the doctor was a trained observer. Possibly he read into Merewether's manner something more than regret that so many of his men had been killed or maimed as a result of his stubbornness. The concept did not trouble Larkin, his own philosophy was simple: if a man hired out, signed articles of enlistment in a naval service, he assumed the risk, took the bitter with the sweet. Larkin's train of thought was interrupted by the appearance of mess attendants with the evening meal. Somehow there was fresh roast beef and — great balls of fire! — it was a bit rare, just the way he liked it.

The word swept through the sickbay that Flint, acting as master of *Countess,* had slaughtered his last bullock, and sent over a side of beef for the wounded with his compliments. That should replace the lost blood quickly enough, but Larkin took his glass of port afterward in accordance with Buttram's prescription as reinforcement for the red meat.

The sense of wellbeing engendered by the delicious meal encouraged Larkin to rise and take a turn about the deck a day earlier than he had planned. Dusk was not far away, the sun just beginning to touch the horizon here halfway through the second dogwatch. Some hands on the forecastle had brought out fiddles, flutes and other instruments, and they launched into a sprightly tune. He made his way slowly through the waist aft, past where the party of lascars squatted twittering like a flock of birds, and saw Merewether leaning against the bulwark on the weather side of the quarterdeck. He would have raised his good hand in salute, but the scarred face was set in an expression of such despondency, dull eyes staring blindly forward, that Larkin chose not to intrude. He saw that Dillon had the watch with Marlowe as his junior, and decided to pass the time of day with him in the hope of entertainment by way of one or another of his stories. As he approached the ladder he saw Sangh and a thick-set lascar squatting on the deck looking up towards the captain. The lascar's lips were moving. Larkin wondered idly what the pair were up to.

In spite of keeping a sharp eye on young Marlowe and the ship, Dillon was in rare form, and when the watch ended, Larkin started forward still chuckling over the last of his yarns. Dusk was falling, the concert on the forecastle had ended some minutes ago, and the new watch was making the ship secure for the night. Halfway to the ladder, he came face to face with Captain Merewether.

The metamorphosis was astounding. The stern gloomy countenance of a few minutes ago had been transfigured. Somehow, Merewether had resumed his normal expression of cheerful resolution and his eyes had regained their sparkle. A smile of genuine pleasure blossomed on the captain's face.

"Why, Larkin, I am delighted to see you up and about!"

"Pleased myself, Captain. Buttram says the exercise will hasten my recovery." Something beyond his comprehension had occurred had wrought this transformation in the man, restored his normal spirit. It was, Larkin thought, as though a condemned man had been delivered by the King's pardon at the foot of the gallows.

"And you will join me for a tot of brandy in the cabin? I seem to recall the medical men prescribe it for patients on the mend."

Larkin hesitated. He was happy that the mood of the past week had been somehow dispelled, but he was a bit apprehensive that something he might say or do could bring it back. Let well alone, he decided.

"Thank you, Captain, but I should return to my cot. I have already taken my dram for tonight, and should not overdo myself."

"Very well Larkin. Again, I am delighted with your progress. You can make your way? And, good night!"

Forward, Larkin encountered Buttram coming from the wash-deck pump, evening rounds completed, but he only lifted his hand in passing. He was afraid of saying anything at this point as to the captain's transformation lest he jinx the man. The duty attendant came over to assist him to his cot, but was waved away. Time enough he became accustomed to undressing with one hand, Larkin decided, feeling drowsiness possess him, anticipating a night of untroubled sleep.

Buttram rinsed his hands for the third time under the gush of salt water from the wash-deck pump, finally removing the scum of harsh soap. He put his fingers one by one under his nose and sniffed. The smell of corruption from dealing with the gangrene during the evening rounds was gone, he decided, reaching for the towel the loblolly attendant held out for him. He moved over, drying his hands, to look in the fragment of mirror fastened to the bulkhead, noting again with disapproval his coarsened complexion and the yellowish tint under the tan, wondering yet again what had possessed him to take service in the Bombay Marine. It had been good to him in its fashion, he admitted and otherwise he would never have met Jennifer. But India was still the Englishmen's grave, and three years out here was enough for him. He thought with nostalgia of the Kentish countryside and the comfortable old house where he had grown up before Cambridge. Well, he had determined to submit his resignation as surgeon to the Commandant of the Marine by New Year. It was high time his daughter made the acquaintance of her grandparents!

The sounds of musical instruments and voices raised in song came to an end as the first watch was called, but it was a good sign. The age-old axiom held that losses of one in ten destroyed a military force's effectiveness, but morale among the hands appeared to have survived since they sang with such spirit. Buttram thought with distaste of the evening rounds just completed. There was gangrene in at least five of the wounded, and the prognosis was poor for three of them. He had just finished trimming proudflesh from the foot of Boatswain Caldwell for the second time in the forlorn hope of saving half of it, but when a grapeshot had sheared off the toes, there were usually complications in the rest of the foot, and he might yet have to amputate.

Larkin was taking the loss of his arm philosophically, already planning how he might swivel a staff to the forearms of his long rifles to serve as a rest when he fired them. The tall American had little formal education, but possessed a quick intelligence and was perceptive in his judgment of persons. Buttram had tried a while ago to draw out his opinion of the state of mind of Captain Merewether, but Larkin had dissembled — had not been frank with him. Merewether had visited the first lieutenant each day and his despondency must have been apparent. Loyalty was an admirable trait, but it should not be permitted to interfere with honest diagnosis.

His mind turned again to Merewether. He had come to know him these past thirty months in the close confines of shipboard life, and he felt he understood him as well as one man might another. The first year he thought he had detected an undercurrent of insecurity, a consciousness, perhaps, of humble origins, with a tendency to overcompensate by assuming an air of gentility often not practiced by those to the manner born. That personality had altered just about the time *Rapid* departed on its voyage to Mauritius. The captain in the six-month interval before Buttram saw him again seemed to have acquired a new confidence. Possibly it was his successful mission to Persia in the company of that blue-blooded diplomat — Percy? — that had wrought the change.

But this past week the gloomy preoccupation of the man had been a facet of his character never before displayed. Merewether had faced adversity often enough in the past, but he had never permitted it to obsess him for any great period of time. Buttram recalled many cases of men whose spirit had cracked and broken under great stress and strain, or were haunted by events into madness. He was reluctant even to contemplate this hypothesis in the case of Merewether, but the symptoms he had observed thus far pointed in that direction. If there were some method by which he could discover the man's problem, he might be able to exorcise it. Such things that loom large in the confines of one man's mind often evaporated when exposed to the light of reason.

He came out on deck and saw Larkin walking towards his cot. The man raised his hand in salutation as he passed but did not speak. Buttram was glad that he was taking the exercise he had prescribed; it should aid him to regain his strength. He looked about the deck. It was a pleasant evening beginning now to cool, but it would still be hot in the wardroom, and without conscious logic the doctor decided to pay a call on Merewether. He had the excuse of updating his medical report after all.

The greeting that responded to his knock was in a stronger voice that Buttram had heard Merewether use the past few days. The captain was leaning back in his chair, shirt unbuttoned, pen in hand and a sheet of foolscap on the deck. Buttram was instantly conscious that the captain had altered materially in the past few hours. His expression of dejection had lifted and been replaced by the normal air of resolution he had worn since the doctor had known him. In his surprise, Buttram almost forgot his opening gambit as Merewether waved him to a chair.

"Sir," he began lamely, trying to remember some development in the sickbay that was important enough to justify his visit. "I think . . ." and then decided to abandon the stratagem. "I came by on no particular mission, Captain, just to talk a bit, and if you are otherwise engaged, I shall depart . . ."

"Not at all, Doctor," said Merewether, sticking the pen in the shot bowl. "Delighted to see you any time." His gaze met Buttram's squarely for the first time in a week, clear-eyed and serene. Of course, Buttram had seen persons who could rise from the depths of despondency to ecstasy in the drawing of two breaths, but instability had never appeared to be a part of Merewether's temperament. "And I was about to violate one of my own rules at sea by having a glass of gin. Will you join me? Claret? Brandy?"

"Brandy."

Buttram was recovering from his astonishment, and he took advantage of the interval while Merewether rang the bell and gave Sangh the order to make a closer study of the man. He was thinner — the high cheekbones stood out more than they had a week ago — but otherwise he was to all intents and purposes in body and manner the same Merewether that Buttram had known before the battle. He shifted his gaze to Sangh as he turned to go back to the pantry.

The little Indian steward had worn an expression of perpetual sadness since Buttram had first known him, but now he too was transfigured. His face was alight, eyes glowing, radiating happiness as he disappeared into the pantry. The doctor could not fathom the change in Sangh any more than he could that in Merewether. There must be more here than met the eye, but he could devise no means to unearth the secret. The brandy was set before him.

Half an hour later, Buttram made his way to his room, still baffled. He took the time before he retired to write in the journal he kept of unusual medical problems an account of Merewether's case, the sudden descent into acute melancholia, its duration and outward symptoms, then the almost instantaneous arrest and reversal of the affliction. Completed, as he usually did, he added the word, "Comment:" then sat back in contemplation trying to distil some helpful present from the case. Try as he would, he could reach no satisfactory or logical conclusion. His eyes were growing heavy as he picked up the pen and added two words: "God knows!"

Halfway through the second dogwatch, Merewether came on deck to stand on the weather side of the quarterdeck at the break of the poop. The sun was almost touching the horizon, the breeze was steady out of the southwest and the columns of the convoy stretched out ahead in reasonably good order. The quiet scene on deck was a far cry from this same time a week ago today. Then every able-bodied hand in the ship had been pumping, plugging shot holes, or fothering sail, as Pitt sank under them. Only the quick assistance of artisans out of the other ships present had saved her. Now, thanks to Mister Svensen, his mates, and the carpenters out of the other vessels of the escort force, the lascars need pump only one hour out of four. The view of the cots and pallets ranged along the waist forward under the awning reminded him of the visit he had made to the loblolly an hour after the action ceased. It had been horrifying beyond his experience. The cacophony of screams, groans and sobs caused physical pain to his ears. Buttram and Mefford had been too busy to talk as they cut, sawed and stitched, assisted by the surgeon's mates out of *Vigilant, Countess, Cornet* and *Ariel* in the stifling heat, amidst the acrid stink of urine and vomit and flickering light of the battle lanterns. Larkin had lain comatose to one side, arm already amputated, snoring stentoriously from the effects of the laudanum he had been dosed with by the surgeons. A blast of grape from a French gun had wiped out all but two of the forward pivot's crew, taking Larkin's arm as well. Merewether had given such comfort and encouragement as he could to those men able to comprehend, and escaped to the fresh night breeze on deck where sailmakers were working their way down the long row of pitiful remains laid out in the waist to swathe each corpse in canvas with a thirty-two-pound shot at the feet.

Now, seven days later, the ships routine had shaken down to near normal, and some of the hands off watch and the walking wounded were skylarking on the forecastle as though there had never been a battle. They had brought out a brace of fiddles, three flutes, a drum, trumpet, and even a small harp. There were tentative trills and notes sounded; then at a signal from a portly storekeeper the ensemble struck up a tune that in a moment had the younger seamen setting to partners in a sprightly dance. The tempo changed and two of the ship's boys engaged in a competitive hornpipe, faces flushed with exertion, as the hands clapped in steady rhythm, punctuated with an occasional wordless cheer. The tune shifted again into a slower melody, and the hornpipers collapsed, wiping the sweat from their face as the assemblage burst into song, led by a red-haired Irish gunner's mate with a fine tenor voice.

Leaning against the bulwark, Merewether stared forward at the hands, listening to the roaring choruses of the shanty. He looked down to see Sangh and his lascar friend squatting on the deck below him, their eyes fixed upon him, lips of the lascar moving, and then looked back to the hands on the forecastle. If there were still undiscovered mutineers from last winter among them, they had concealed it well during the arduous exertions of the combined operation at Ras ul Khymah, and the crew's performance against overwhelming odds last week had been magnificent. The old hands in *Pitt* and the men from *Rapid* in the space of half a year had welded into an able and courageous crew undeserving of a captain who would have betrayed them.

He could only now fully admit to himself the extent of his terror, his mindless unreasoning panic, the frantic desire to live at any cost that had possessed him, but he could yet find no rational explanation within himself. He had managed to put such fears out of his mind in the past, but he had never before been so literally *in extremis* as in the last few minutes of the engagement. His courage and resolution would forever be suspect in his own eyes, though there was no other living mortal to accuse him.

Merewether was not fit or qualified to hold a commission, let alone exercise command in the Marine. Once back at Bombay he would submit his resignation, gather up Caroline and their child, and slink back to England. He might even-make a passable greengrocer if he put his mind into it. He had, he realized, reached the nadir of shame and despondency. There was nowhere to go. No way to make amends.

The tempo of the music shifted again, something now slow and sonorous, the hands singing along earnestly. It was out of the Hymnal of the Church of England, provided along with the Book of Common Prayer and the Bible from the earliest days by a God-fearing Court of Directors to the Company's ships, maritime or naval. Regulation also required observance of the Sabbath with services, but this was more honored in its breach in the Marine. Merewether had spent his youth in an Indiaman commanded by a devout captain, had been compelled to learn his catechism and be confirmed in the Church of England. He had given the matter of religion little enough thought since those days, and nurtured few strong convictions on the subject. He was entirely unable to comprehend the bitter differences that continually arose between followers of competing sects, and delegated the duty of presiding at services to Davis, the purser, an accomplished lay reader.

Now, as daylight faded, Merewether heard the hands pause before they began the second stanza of the hymn, the magnificent tenor voice rising above the baritone rumble of the rest:

> Forgive me, Lord, for thy dear son,
> The ill which I this day have done,
> That with the world, myself and Thee,
> I, ere I sleep, at peace may be.

The couplets he had heard a hundred times before suddenly took on a meaning. He had done ill, forgotten his duty in panic, sought to save his own life at any cost, and a man had died in the interval. It was often impossible to undo the ill a man had done, but the cumulative burden of guilt would become intolerable unless there were some means of casting it out. There was common sense expressed in the philosophy behind the words of the verse: If a man could not make literal amends, he might yet do so in spirit.

He began to rationalize his conduct of seven days ago. The cold terror and panic he had suffered, the blind unreasoning instinct for survival that had compelled him toward a surrender of the ship, had not of themselves caused the death of Dobbs; that was simply an incident of the service. The Lord must have willed *Pitt's* survival by providing Marlowe's Lion's Mouth, and MacRae's race to bring the heavy batteries in *Countess* to bear upon the enemy. For no apparent reason, the same arguments and logic that he had rejected all this past week now made sense. Possibly it was more than time dulling the edge of his conscience, but the weight of guilt he had borne again to lift from his soul as he heard the hands sing:

> Teach me to live that I may dread
> The grave as little as my bed;
> Teach me to die, that so I may
> Rise glorious at the judgment day.

There were two more stanzas, but Merewether did not hear them. The world would not end, life would continue; he would remember, regret, but no longer permit the episode to haunt him. More wisdom had been distilled out of human experience into religion than he had given it credit for. He realized that he had somehow exorcised his guilt. The Evening Hymn ended the impromptu concert as the first watch came on deck and he saw Larkin coming towards him.

He bespoke the officer with an easier conscience.

PART III

The Wrath of China

The boat stank of fish, and the hoop-supported canvas shelter amidships confined the stifling heat while excluding most of the breeze. Tulsi Bai sat quietly against the starboard gunwale, her veil now cast aside and the sari loosened for comfort. Even so, sweat beaded her forehead and gathered in her armpits. But surely it was worth a little discomfort to escape the Bombay Government? She listened to the slow regular thump and creak of the sweeps against the thole pins as the two fishermen propelled their craft through the shallows west of Bombay Island. The wind was dead foul until they should clear the harbor entrance; then by keeping well inshore they might take advantage of the land breeze to beat down to Goa.

Tulsi thought with cold fury of the ruin of what had appeared to be a well-conceived and executed plan for the overthrow of Holkar. It was difficult to believe that the scar-faced captain had proved to be incorruptible — was it possible she was losing her beauty, showing her age? She ran fingertips over her cheeks; still firm and smooth, and her body, she knew, was that of a girl in spite of her thirty-three years. The man was a fool. He had been offered money and even her charms as a bonus, simply to look the other way. Of course, Cosby, that jealous nincompoop, had guessed her intention and intruded just as she had felt Merewether waver. Served the bumbler right to be knocked on the head, she thought. And then her assassination attempt had failed due to her own weakness. God damn the cat and that scar-faced captain!

There had been time during these past few weeks of sailing to Bombay to talk to Malhar, time to convince him that power was more desirable than mere wealth. But she was not sure that she had succeeded. Her scheme to place her son on the throne of Rajputana had only been postponed, not ended. Holkar would welcome his son back, she was sure, and it was incumbent upon the boy to ingratiate himself with his father while currying favor with the French mercenaries who trained his army, and enlisting support from the Pindari leaders, Amir Khan and Wasil Muhammed. But Tulsi was by no means certain Malhar possessed the resolution to follow through without her presence. He was not stupid, merely indolent and easily diverted by the pleasures of the flesh. The risk was simply too great for her to chance entering the country at this time, and she must go away to a place secure even from Holkar's thugs. God damn the cat and that scar-faced captain!

She thought briefly of her twin brother, Rene, a man of force and guile, far different from her half-brother, Harry Fitzgerald, who looked British and had wholeheartedly adopted their ways. Rene had acted instantly once the bum-boat man delivered her note last night. He dealt in jewels and contraband opium, and his sources of information penetrated even the Governor's establishment. The delivery had been easy: that stupid captain of the guard was so complacent, so sure a woman was incapable of escape, that he had not even bothered to arm his soldiers while he transported her from the ship to a place of confinement. Lucky for him he had not resisted the rescue, or he would be a headless corpse this moment!

But Rene had disquieting news once she reached one of his hiding places on the outskirts of Bombay. Holkar had been furious when he learned that Tulsi had accompanied Malhar on his pilgrimage to Mecca and his agents were even now sojourning at Surat in the expectation of her arrival there in the *Countess of Surrey.* So be it. They would be as disappointed as the Bombay Government at her absence, but Rene insisted there was no safety for her even here from the assassins once the news of her escape reached Surat. Madame Bai was devoid of fear, but it would be folly to risk death when a little time might solve the matter and enable her to achieve her ends. She reluctantly agreed to travel to Goa where she would be under the protection of the flag of Portugal. She had lived there for a time in the beginning of her first exile from Rajputana and understood enough of the language to get along.

The creak of sweeps ceased, there was a clatter on deck as they were laid aside, and she parted the curtain to look back at distant Bombay. Blocks squealed as sails were hoisted and the small vessel picked up way south. It was safe enough now to come out on deck and luxuriate in the fresh breeze as it dried her soggy garments.

Rene had provided a basket of provisions, and she sat in the stern to consume a noon-time ration, washed down with a half bottle of wine.

Her thoughts returned to Merewether. Somehow he had avoided the poison potion she had designed for him. With the captain out of the way, she was sure the Indiaman could have sailed away in the confusion during the change of command, concluded the rendezvous with the French squadron, and by now Malhar might well have been on the throne. That God damned cat! The mere thought of the animal caused a shudder of revulsion to course through her body. She had been compelled by her phobia to leave the cabin before she saw the strychnine ingested and Merewether had survived to capture the French force. Madame Bai compelled herself to put the rankling memories out of her mind, and tried to think of her childhood instead.

The man painted in the ivory miniature had been boldly handsome, dark hair in ringlets, blue eyes and prominent nose. Tulsi had no other recollection of her father, who had died of fever before she and Rene were a year and a half old. He had been the Comte Hilaire de la Houssaye from Normandy, her mother said, serving as a mercenary officer in the Maratha forces. After his death, her mother had moved to Surat and soon contracted a liaison with the Irishman, Fitzgerald. She remembered him well; she had been fourteen when he went back to England, a wealthy man, taking Harry with him to be educated as an Englishman. Her mother had come back to her native Rajputana, and within a month Tulsi had caught the eye and fancy of Holkar, to become his concubine and bear his child. She had lost his favor ten years ago, but with the proceeds of her jewels had sojourned in exile, first in Goa, then during the Peace made her way to Port Louis. Her beauty had attracted the commandant of the Ile de France, and she had lived as his mistress until his recall to France two years ago. But before she departed the island, she had conceived the plot and laid the foundation of her scheme to supplant Holkar with Malhar. Her thoughts came full circle. God damn the cat and that scar-faced captain!

Three days later she landed at Goa and found the house of her brother's correspondent in the opium cartel, a swarthy Portuguese by the name of Rancisco Coutinho. Upon Tulsi's recital of the recent misfortunes which had beset her, he took instant alarm. Goa, he insisted, was not beyond the reach of Holkar, and he had no desire to be implicated. His wife was present during the interview, and Madame Bai had no opportunity to employ her other wiles. She reluctantly took ship two days later, bound for Macao with munitions and supplies for the garrison, cheered only slightly by a rumor that the city would soon be occupied by French forces with a view to denying the British trade with Canton. God damn the cat and that scar-faced captain!

Just before she boarded the vessel, a furtive man who said he was from Rene in Bombay pressed an oilskin packet into her hands with the injunction to deliver it to one Don Miguel de Silveira at the Governor's Palace in Macao. Tulsi would have declined the commission, but it was accompanied by a small but weighty bag of escudos to ease her sojourn.

The warm glow of happiness and pride still pervaded his body as Merewether took his second cup of tea in the tiny cubicle assigned to him in the transient officer's quarters adjacent to Bombay Castle. The news was second hand, but authentic, in Caroline's own hand. The mail pouch for *Pitt* had gone to Surat in anticipation of her arrival there, but *Pitt* had entered the graving dock here yesterday morning for the urgent repairs necessitated by her recent action in the Gulf of Aden. It had been a strenuous twelve hours to warp the frigate through the gates, centre her exactly over the blocks that would support her keel, and then wait the interminable interval that it took Puffing Billy, spewing sparks and smoke, to pump out the dock. The hands had been shifted to barracks ashore and the officers assigned to these dingy quarters. *Pitt* was a dead ship, out of commission for at least four months while her whole starboard midships section was removed and replaced.

He had called on Tollett, still acting in the absence of Sir John Waldron as Commandant of the Marine, late yesterday afternoon. The officer had leaped to his feet, grasped the extended hand with both of his, his face wreathed in smiles.

"Glorious, Merewether! Simply glorious!" There was no doubt of his sincerity: he glowed with admiration. Merewether felt a twinge of conscience, a residue of his shame and guilt still lurked in the recesses of his soul, though he had come to terms with himself.

MacRae and *Comet* had preceded *Pitt* into the harbor the day before yesterday to alert the Castle to the necessity of having the dry dock in readiness to receive the damaged ship, and undoubtedly had given the commodore a full account of the action.

"Have a chair while I finish signing these dispatches, and we'll go to the club where I shall propose a toast or three while listening to some amplification of MacRae's report."

Merewether turned to the window and looked out over the harbor where the three French frigates rode at anchor, Marine ensigns sparkling above their tricolors. They were excellent ships, of recent construction, and once the battle damage was repaired they should bring a pretty price. It was entirely likely that the Royal Navy would purchase them into the fleet, what with its shortage of fast cruisers out here.

"Bye the bye," said Tollett, looking up from his papers. "Your old friend, MacLellan, reported for duty at the Castle last month."

"Good. Where is he?"

"He and his bride are staying for the nonce in lodgings in Harry's public house outside the gate until their bungalow is ready. And now, I think that takes care of the drudgery for another day. Are you ready?" Tollett put on his hat, and they went out to cross the yard to the club.

The first drink was cool and delicious, the lemon exactly right in flavor. "This glass must have had a hole in it," said Merewether apologetically, signaling the waiter. Tollett laughed and tossed off his whisky and water, then leaned back.

"God, I would have given a year's pay and my right arm to have been with you at Aden!" the commodore said ruefully. "You know, in over twenty years of service in the Marine I have never been in a major engagement, and now I guess I never will . . ." The man was entirely sincere, Merewether saw, expressing genuine regret at what he considered a misfortune.

"I can't exactly recommend the experience," Merewether replied. "It was touch and go there for a while before MacRae brought up the heavy batteries in *Countess* and *Comet.* I confess I was beginning to give serious consideration to striking . . ." Pure sophistry, he told himself, he had done all in his power to surrender, and had only been thwarted by a combination of unlikely events. But he had made peace with himself on that score and must needs present an unruffled face to the world.

Tollett drew him out skillfully, leading him through the initial tactics of the engagement, putting in a shrewd question from time to time to amplify a point. ". . . and then, with boarders on deck to port, French marines made an attack from starboard, and Midshipman Marlowe formed a "Lion's Mouth" to repulse them just as *Comet* and *Countess* commenced their bombardment from ahead . . ."

" 'Lion's Mouth'?" ejaculated Tollett incredulously. "Why, I haven't heard the term since I was midshipman in a six-gun snow!"

"Seems still to work," said Merewether. "I made special mention of the young man's services in my report" The rest of the account was soon over, just as he finished the third gin, and Tollett rose regretfully.

"I must go. We have a dinner engagement. But tomorrow we shall call on Governor Duncan to discuss with him the political implications that Madame Bai's plot presents."

Merewether was at a loose end. He had drunk all the gin he desired for the time, and it was yet a bit early to dine. Then he remembered that MacLellan was close at hand, and he felt he knew the big Scots officer well enough to call on him unannounced.

"Why, Captain!" shouted MacLellan. "And congratulations!"

"For what?" demanded Merewether. He saw little Mary Wilkins hovering in the background.

"First and foremost, for your son . . ."

"Son?" asked Merewether. Then realization flooded over him. "When? And is Caroline . . ." There must be a letter for him somewhere.

"Here is Caroline's letter we received last week, interposed Mary. "He was born the twentieth of May, seven pounds, seven ounces, and both are fine . . ."

"Thank God!" said Merewether, feeling the sudden emptiness in his stomach subside. He took the proffered letter and skimmed through the obstetrical details, to come to the last paragraph:

. . . and with Percival absent, it has fallen to me to name our son who will be christened this Sunday at St. John's. Accordingly, with great trepidation, I settled on George, for my uncle; Robert, for that Percy my husband so admired, and Percival, naturally. It is quite a name for a very small boy to carry! Commodore Land and Jennifer Buttram have graciously consented to stand sponsor for him as god parents . . .

"George Robert Percival!" repeated Merewether wonderingly.

"I believe this is an occasion for a toast, sir," MacLellan said. "Your pleasure."

The toasts to the new son were drunk in gin, whisky and Madeira according to individual taste. The happy mother and the proud father were toasted, then almost as an afterthought, the victory at Aden. It was a happy hour before Merewether took his leave and came back to the club pleasantly fuddled, but relieved that he had a vigorous heir and a healthy wife. There he encountered MacRae, Whaley, Dillon, Larkin, MacCamy, the junior officers from three ships, and the celebration commenced all over again as he made his announcement.

Now having breakfasted on melon, fresh eggs, crisp bacon and toast. Merewether felt the malaise engendered by last night's celebration subside as Sangh stacked the plates on the tray and went out. He turned his thoughts to what this day might hold for him. Tollett's note had been delivered before he was awake. They would wait on the Governor at eleven, ante meridian. Time to bathe, shave and dress. Perhaps after these formalities were completed, he might have a few days for himself.

The tonga was waved past the sentry at the gate and they dismounted at the door to the Governor's Mansion. "Commodore Tollett and Captain Merewether of the Marine. We have an appointment to see Governor Duncan," Tollett told the secretary. They were admitted almost immediately.

The Governor's usual calm manner was somewhat ruffled this morning. He rose to greet the officers with quiet courtesy, seated them, and resumed his place behind the desk only to speak in a tone of chagrin.

"That woman, Madame Bai, she's gone! Got clean away this morning as the guard was transporting her to a place of confinement . . ." Merewether was instantly alarmed, she had been in his custody, technically under the guard of Jemadar Gunny and his Marines in *Countess,* and he wondered if he could be held accountable for the escape. "No," continued Duncan as though he read his mind. "Your Jemadar holds the Officer of the Day's receipt for Madame Bai, and her loss is chargeable to him alone, not that he had much choice from what I can discover."

"When did this happen?"

"A bit after sunrise, I am informed. The *Countess of Surrey* was to sail on the morning tide for Surat. I had concluded that Madame Bai's crime was against the princely state of Rajputana, and not Government or Company. I intended to hold her in custody pending advices from Holkar as to her disposition. Captain Reagan left the ship a little after seven, and the rescue was perhaps half an hour later, within a square of their destination. He had a sergeant and three private soldiers to handle her baggage, and Mrs. Hobbs, one of my housekeepers, to preserve propriety, all unarmed and riding in a barouche. A native sprang into the street, seized the bridles of the team, and four others armed with Ghurkha knives held the guards at bay while the woman entered a tonga. Once her luggage was loaded, one of the men cut the traces, hit the team with the reins, and it ran away. They all vanished in an instant, leaving the guards sitting there with their mouths open!" Duncan gave a mirthless laugh. "Thus so much of the subject of Madame Bai as you wished to discuss, Commodore, in this audience has become moot."

"You're searching for her, of course?" inquired Tollett.

"Oh, yes, the guard and the Bombay Watch. But in that rabbit warren north of us, it is nearly hopeless, and she was wearing native dress." Duncan abruptly changed the subject. "Now, Merewether, had Tollett not asked for this audience, I would have sent for you anyway. You stay, Tollett, this is both Government and Marine business." He turned to pick up a packet of papers and leafed through them, separating them into two piles.

Merewether took instant alarm. He had anticipated an easy four months here while *Pitt* was repaired, a matter of a morning visit to the graving dock to ascertain progress, and slight administrative duties. And with so much time, there was the very real chance that he might find a ship bound for Calcutta, wangle enough leave, and see Caroline and his child. He sat back in resignation.

"You are generally familiar with this matter, Tollett, but I shall make a brief summary for the benefit of the Captain here. For some months, intelligence has insisted that the French have a scheme to take Macao at the approaches to Canton, and thereby deny the Company's trade with China. Portugal, of course, has long been the ally of England, though neutral in its war with Bonaparte. With his invasion of Spain, however, the situation has become so critical that the Royal Family has found it necessary to take refuge for the time in their colony of Brazil, and they find it impossible to reinforce the garrison at Macao. In this situation, the Governor-General took up the matter with the Viceroy of Goa, who exercises supervision of Macao, with a view to reaching an agreement that substantial land and naval forces to supplement the Portuguese troops be dispatched and landed. The Viceroy indicated complete agreement with this offer, and promised to draft an order to the commander at Macao so directing. For some reason, known only to the Viceroy, it has not been forthcoming as of this time . . ."

"Your Excellency, I beg your pardon, but Macao is the property of the Emperor of China, and the Portuguese hold it only at his sufferance." Merewether hurried on, seeing two lines form between the Governor's brows. "I mean to say, sir, the Viceroy is on dangerous ground unless the Emperor consents . . ."

"Precisely what Minto intends, but consent certainly will not be forthcoming unless the Viceroy first acts on his order." He looked speculatively at Merewether. "Pellew was here in Bombay only last month, and while he approved the plan for the reinforcement of Macao, he thought the danger was slight. Now it appears to be imminent. There are two French ships with a number of auxiliaries carrying troops at Manila, only six hundred miles distant, and last month two frigates were reported by an American ship to have touched at Mauritius en route to the Eastern Seas. In the opinion of the Governor-General and his staff, the danger has become quite real. Accordingly, Minto has ordered the forces to be assembled for the occupation of Macao under the command of Rear-Admiral O'Brien Drury, Royal Navy."

He paused and looked again at Merewether. "I know your connection with Barlow, but are you also well acquainted with Gibby Elliott?"

"Why, no, sir. I only met him the one time when the combined operation against Ras ul Khymah was being formed . . ." Merewether wondered what had provoked the question.

"Your credit seems to be quite high with him. I have here orders for you to proceed in *Pitt* to the rendezvous with Drury's squadron and the transports at Penang. Thence to proceed in company to Macao, and be attached to Drury's staff as the personal representative of the Governor-General. Of course, there are two alternates named should you not be available, and you have rather thoroughly eliminated *Pitt* as a means of conveyance as a result of your recent action, but you have *Comet* available, Tollett. I am constrained to ask for her services . . ."

"Certainly, your Excellency. She will require victualing, water and some maintenance, but she can be ready for sea in forty-eight hours, I am sure."

No rest for the weary, Merewether thought with resignation. He had anticipated a restful period while *Pitt* was in the dock, and now he had been bilked of it. He became conscious that Duncan was speaking again.

"I also have here an assessment of the situation prepared by Colonel Napier for the Governor-General, to which are appended some rather explicit instructions, as to your duties as his representative. You may receipt for these items now." The Governor pushed one stack of the papers across his desk, and handed Merewether a freshly dipped pen. "And now, a much more pleasant duty: by proclamation I have designated the usual monthly levée tomorrow night to be in the honor of the victors in the Action at Aden . . ."

Back in his quarters, Merewether subsided over a cup of tea to sort through the packet, still feeling a bit put upon at the recall to duty so soon after two strenuous operations in the past six months. Duncan had done a magnificent summary of the intelligence estimate, and he soon cast this aside, to concentrate upon the memorandum of advice and admonition as to his authority in the premises. It quickly became clear that the "personal representative" of the Governor-General must depend largely upon moral suasion insofar as the military decisions were concerned, since this authority was vested in Admiral Drury. The admiral had been granted a very broad discretion as to the action he should take, dependent upon the local situation and the advice he should receive from the Select Committee of Supra Cargoes at Canton. At the mention of these arrogant men, Merewether wrinkled his nose in distaste, wondering if the obnoxious Elphingham was yet President of the Select Committee. That individual more than two years ago had preferred charges against him for violation of the laws of China, though he had been most honorably acquitted by a Court of Inquiry at Bombay Castle. Oh well, time for a drink and then dinner.

He found every officer out of *Pitt, Comet* and *Vigilant,* plus MacLellan, at the club already having drinks set before them. In a port as secure as Bombay, it was considered safe enough to leave a warrant officer as duty commander aboard ship, with responsible petty officers to stand the gangway and anchor watches. Before he reached a vacant seat at the long table, there was a babble of voices in greeting. He soon learned the reason for this extraordinary turnout.

"Slyboots here," explained MacRae, indicating Larkin, "was going to take French leave with never a word to his old shipmates . . ."

"Now, Mac," protested the tall American. "I was going to call around and say goodbye to everyone . . ."

"Likely story!" There was good-natured chaffing up and down the table as the servants finished serving the drinks, then Buttram stood to propose a toast.

"To Lieutenant Alexander Larkin, who has seen the error of his ways, and proposes to mend them by departing the Marine for the greener fields of Kentucky and Louisiana, may his fortunes proper!" Glasses were downed as cries of "Speech! Speech!" echoed along the board. Larkin arose slowly, a bit red in the face.

"Gentlemen, I'm most appreciative of this farewell. To save repetition, I'll say my piece this one time. I had concluded some months ago I had had enough of India and the Marine. When I lost this flipper, I decided the time had arrived. A fortunate combination of circumstances makes it now. The Indiaman, *West Riding,* sails on the morning tide. She was short two mates, and her master very kindly offered me passage to London and a hundred pounds in return for standing a regular watch home-ward bound. Thence, I shall go back to America, where the United States has bought half a continent from Bonaparte. I can only believe that there are great opportunities there. And now, to each of you I wish all good fortune, plenty of prizes and plenty of duff!" He sat down as the table rose spontaneously to toast his health again.

The affair only broke up after midnight when a group of the younger officers departed for the European brothel over in Bombay. Larkin was in no condition to be trusted alone to make his way out to the Indiaman, and MacRae volunteered to see him aboard.

"And have you received your orders?" Merewether inquired.

"Yes, Captain, and I indented on the victualing yard this afternoon. You had best see to any cabin stores you desire for yourself as well, for I travel light. Are you taking a servant?"

"Yes, Sangh, of course." Quarters would be cramped enough in the schooner, but he really should have an aide along, someone he could trust to carry a message, or serve as his eyes and ears when he was absent. Hamlyn was bright and quick, with considerable force of character and the assurance of one to the manor born, but somehow Merewether doubted that he would wear well on a long voyage in close company. Then, too, there were the examinations for lieutenant here at the Castle in September, and Hamlyn was already recommended for them. Marlowe was a relatively unknown quantity, but he admired the boy's spirit and was indebted to him for his providential Lion's Mouth last month. He reached a decision. "And I shall take Marlowe as my personal aide, if you can accommodate him."

Two days later, Merewether stood at ease on the quarterdeck as *Comet* weighed anchor to be towed out of the harbor against the wind by the pulling oars of two dockyard launches. He had no difficulty this time keeping hands off as MacRae and Dillon conned the vessel in the weary beat south to Goa. He could watch Bombay slide below the horizon with little regret. There was nothing to hold him there. They must put in at Goa and wait on the Viceroy in the unlikely event that he had decided to issue his order to the Governor of Macao to permit the British to reinforce his garrison. If no such order was immediately forthcoming, he must proceed without further delay to the rendezvous at Penang. Admiral Drury was an unknown quantity, only recently arrived on the Indian Station, and it behooved Merewether to get off on the right foot with the commander of the force.

He thought of the social affair last night. Much sound and fury, signifying nothing, he decided, a mere repetition of the dozens he had attended. He had enjoyed foregathering with MacLellan and Mary, and Mrs. Tollett had been pleasant enough in her shy way. But he had for the second consecutive night drunk far too much, and a period of abstention in the fresh sea air would be therapeutic. He watched Marlowe unobtrusively, serving on the voyage as Dillon's junior, and thought he discerned a new confidence in the lad as he gave his orders to the helm.

When he had summoned the midshipman to his quarters to acquaint him with his new assignment, Marlowe appeared ecstatic, and Merewether had allowed him to read through the packet of orders, assessments and instructions to impress him with the gravity of the mission. There would be no time for skylarking, he told the boy, this was serious business, and much of his future in the Marine might depend upon how well he performed his duty. Cock and bull, possibly, but he might well have to rely on the wits of this sixteen-year-old officer.

Comet anchored off the bar at Goa, and Merewether accompanied by Marlowe dressed to the nines, boots gleaming, made a sprayswept passage in to the port. He did not penetrate beyond the single English-speaking secretary to the Viceroy.

"No Captain," the haughty Don said as he returned to the anteroom. "His Excellency is not prepared to issue such orders at the present time . . ."

"Please express my profoundest thanks and the compliments of the Governor-General to His Excellency," said Merewether with a sweeping bow. "And now, I bid you good day!" He had expected nothing more. The Dons, Spanish or Portuguese, were famous for their ability to procrastinate. Still, it would have been pleasant to walk out of the palace with the order and surprise Drury with his enterprise.

Once clear of Ceylon, the big schooner fairly flew across the Bay of Bengal to raise Pulo Rondo, north of Sumatra, four days later. Merewether came on deck to survey the island where he had destroyed Abercrombie's lair nearly three years before.

Two hours later, they overhauled three transports under escort of *Phaeton,* 38, *Greyhound,* 32, *Diana,* 12 and *Jaseur* (brig), 12. According to the operation order, this was the European contingent of troops from Madras. MacRae pressed on by, flying the current recognition signal, having no desire to be dragooned into forming a part of the escort force. At least, they would not be late for the rendezvous. They came to anchor off Fort Cornwallis in early morning.

Rear Admiral Drury had his flag in *Russel,* 74, with *Dedaigneus,* 36, present, and the Company's ships, *David Scott* and *Alnick Castle,* carrying the six hundred sepoys from Calcutta moored close by. Merewether saw that the absentee pennant was not hoisted. He bundled up his orders and made an immediate call upon the admiral.

Drury was a man who wore his dignity like a cloak, reserved and precise in speech, and yet neither cold nor aloof. The innate kindliness of his nature showed through his formal manner, though he was clearly a man of force and resolution. Merewether remembered the anecdote of the Royal Navy captain at the levée that last night in Bombay. He had made discreet inquiry of the officer who had come out with the admiral on his staff with orders to relieve Pellew early in the new year.

"I've known Obie since we were midshipmen together, and he has a most unusual philosophy as to the mission and social rank of a naval officer. In his mind it is the highest and most honorable calling to which man may aspire. Why, on the voyage out here we were strolling on quarterdeck one fine evening, wondering a bit what service in the Eastern Seas might be like — neither of us had been here before — when he asked my opinion in all seriousness whether he should claim precedence of the Governor-General by virtue of his rank! "Clayton," he said, "the Governor-General is merely the servant of the East India Company, while I am a King's Officer!"

The captain had laughed, and Merewether took alarm. Was he to be afflicted with another George Barlow, a man jealous of the last perquisite, ruffle and flourish due his office? Something of his dismay must have shown in his face, for the captain laughed again, and continued, “But he is not all that bad. He is essentially a kindly man, though a stickler for performance of duty, and so long as you show due respect for the lofty nature of the office he holds, you will receive fair and considerate treatment from the man himself. And he will not call upon you to do anything he would not do himself . . .”

Now, seated across the desk in the flag cabin of HMS *Russel,* face to face with Admiral Drury, Merewether could see for himself something of the complicated nature of the man. He was entirely courteous, yet encouraged others to keep their distance; solicitous of the comfort of an officer of a fellow naval service, but compelling consciousness of the great gulf that separated them.

“I see that you did not come in the frigate as your orders directed, Captain. Is there an explanation?”

“Yes, sir. *Pitt* is docked for major rebuilding at Bombay.”

“Damaged in a recent action, Captain?”

“Yes, sir, at Aden.”

“And the result of that action?”

“Three French thirty-sixes taken, sir.”

“I have seen no report of that engagement, and we left Madras after Pellew arrived from Bombay.” What the hell, did the man doubt his word?

“The admiral departed Bombay almost a fortnight before we came in sir.” He looked at the bland face, and added, *“Comet* brought a pouch of mail for you, sir.”

“Good. Is the consent of the Viceroy included?”

“No, sir. I called at Goa last week, but no such order had been signed.”

“It is by no means essential, but I would prefer to have such a direction in hand when we call on the Governor at Macao. And now, Captain, I am informed that you are entirely familiar with the situation at Canton, and that I may call upon you for such information as I require. In fact, Lord Minto was most complimentary of the services you have rendered to Sir George Barlow, and more recently to him in a mission to Persia and the destruction of Ras ul Khymah.”

“My knowledge of Canton is somewhat stale, sir. I was last there two years ago.”

"No matter. Little change in the Orientals, they tell me. And Captain, are your quarters in *Comet* adequate? We are somewhat crowded here in *Russel . . ."*

"Entirely, sir." Merewether had no desire to be crammed into the quarters of some resentful evicted lieutenant in the flagship for the long voyage to Macao.

"Very well. The balance of our force should be here by tomorrow, and I intend to sail the next day. Not many facilities here for a place planned to be the major operating base for the Eastern Seas. Are you acquainted ashore? There seems to be no more than an acting first secretary here in charge since Governor Dundas died last year."

"Yes, sir. Tom Raffles, I presume." He paused a moment to see if the admiral had another comment. "He was most helpful to me last year, when I commanded the Bengal squadron." Once he escaped from this interview, he intended to call on Tom and Livie. The thought of that charming enigmatic woman gave him a thrill of anticipation, though he was now a married man and a father.

"I think we understand one another, Captain. Possibly, some fine day on the voyage we may be able to foregather for a more extended discussion of the situation and tactics. I am anxious to see if there is any later intelligence in that pouch." Drury rose and inclined his head in formal dismissal.

On his way back to *Comet* Merewether tried to sort out his impressions of Rear Admiral O'Brien Drury, Royal Navy. Without the shrewd observations of Captain Clayton that night at Bombay, he would have been at a loss to explain the man, and he might yet be dead wrong, but he felt he had at least a glimmer of what made the admiral go. The man beneath the mantle of rank and authority was able, modest and unassuming, even a bit surprised that he found himself cloaked with such power and dignity, but under compulsion to exact full respect and deference to the office he filled for the time.

It was only in the last fifty years that the naval officer had come to be accounted a gentleman in the ordinary sense of the term, though ashore even now he was likely to be looked down upon as a parvenu by those who felt themselves born to the title, and many officers still possessed little enough confidence in their social standing. But the day of the gruff, horny-handed old sea dog was largely past, the entering midshipmen likely to be from the landed gentry or minor nobility of England, particularly the southern counties, and accounting themselves gentlemen by birth rather than by virtue of the King's Commission. The distinction had caused Merewether concern in years past, but he had been accepted at face value in the British community in India as an officer of the Marine, and since his tacit acknowledgement last year by Percy the fact of his bastardy had ceased to trouble him.

Drury had first made it plain that Merewether was present only to supply him such information as to the situation as he might require, but on parting there had been almost an intimation of a hand in the development of strategy and tactics in the affair. Possibly it was no more than a matter of semantics, Merewether concluded, and resolved to govern himself with the utmost restraint in his dealings with the admiral.

Somehow the almost magical spell that Livie Raffles had cast over Merewether a year and a half ago had dissolved. Not that she had changed. She was as vivacious, charming and witty as before, and he wondered if marriage and fatherhood had somehow made him less susceptible to the allure of this woman of the world. He now sat in the familiar room in their hillside bungalow, listening to the witty crisscross of statement and comment that flew back and forth between Tom and Livie, with an occasional tangent darting out to include him in their conversation. But the exhilaration that had bubbled in his veins last year when he was in her presence was lacking. He could discern no visible difference in her appearance or manner, and her welcome had been warm enough, an embrace and kiss on the lips, but it had not ignited the fire that had consumed him on the other occasion. He became conscious that Tom had addressed him.

"Captain, we plan a reception in honor of Admiral Drury for tomorrow night, and have invited several of the residents for refreshment and a buffet beforehand, since supper will be quite late." The young man had removed his formal coat and the waistcoat with its magnificent chain and jingling seals that he affected, and sat now in his shirt, collar open. "We would be delighted if you will join us."

It should be a pleasant affair, Merewether decided, and accepted the invitation gladly. "And now, I must go back to the ship.

You know I am entertaining the officers in *Comet* at Mister Moulton's public house tonight." He rose and bowed to Livie. "It has been as delightful to see you both as I remembered . . . No, Tom, it is an easy walk to the landing and I need the exercise . . ."

Merewether made his escape, wondering at the sense of uneasiness that had possessed him in the company of this charming pair, then dismissed the thought as he made his way briskly down the hill to the boat landing, stopping off at the public house for another gin while he renewed acquaintance with Mister Moulton, the proprietor, and bespoke the private dining room for the entertainment he planned for the officers of *Comet* that evening.

Two days down the Strait of Malacca, Merewether took the glass to the crosstrees to try to make out for himself what young Mister Thomas Stamford Raffles professed to see as the site for the eastern capital of the British Empire. There was an island off the mainland that appeared to shelter a considerable expanse of water for a snug anchorage, but at this distance he could tell little about the terrain. There were several trails of blue smoke rising into the sky, but he could not see the village of Singapore itself. He thought for a moment of the handsome, energetic man, risen almost from obscurity to be the *de facto* governor of the Presidency of Penang, and the vibrant woman almost ten years his senior whom he had married. He wondered again at the rumor that Raffles owed his appointment and meteoric rise in the Company to the fact that he had removed an embarrassment to a senior Company official by marriage to Livie. The man was facile, alert for the main chance, ambitious, and entirely capable of making such a bargain, but he also appeared to be devoted to his wife and she to him.

Last year during his days of glory as Commodore of the Bengal Squadron, Merewether had lusted after the woman, felt her spell possess him, envied Raffles his enjoyment of her charms. He had had the provocation and opportunity the day he delivered his gift of the Chinese desk to cuckold the young man, but had stepped back, and in retrospect had often regretted his sudden surge of principle. Now, he concluded, he had been entirely right.

He thought of the reception for Admiral Drury two nights ago. It had been a glittering, Raffles-managed affair, with Livie sparkling at his side as he introduced the British residents to the officer, then dancing and liquid refreshments, and finally a sumptuous supper served. Merewether had retrieved the letter he had written to Miss Judith Johnson from the mail pouch, and had it in his pocket for personal delivery with his condolences to the young lady at some appropriate time. It was a duty he dreaded — the probable hysterics and tears, the blasting of an idyll — and almost he determined to leave it with Raffles for delivery after he departed, then concluded that he owed it to Dobbs to impart the sad news in person.

He had remembered her as a slip of a girl, but she had bloomed in the year and a half since he had seen her. She came in on the arm of a junior lieutenant he remembered vaguely as out of HMS *Argus* to take their place in the line approaching the guest of honor. Once through the introductions, he followed them to the room where punch was being served, to come close alongside. He saw recognition in her eyes.

"Why Commodore . . ." Her escort looked sharply at him, then bobbed in a bow.

"Miss Judith Johnson! am delighted to see you again." Not really, and this was certainly no time to give the grisly news.

"No longer, Commodore, Mistress Judith Sargent since last March! And this is my husband, Lieutenant Hilary Sargent, Royal Navy . . ." Merewether bowed in response feeling all of Dobb's dreams turn to ashes. He was suddenly thankful that the young officer had not survived to face this heartbreak. A few platitudes, and then an escape without an inquiry as to Johnny Dobbs, to go outside and shred the letter.

Now, he turned his attention to the activities in the various ships of the expedition, observing a fire drill in *Russel,* man overboard in *Greyhound,* and gunnery exercises in *Comet* below him. He could appreciate Drury's concern, he had often enough experienced it himself to make sure of the state of readiness of the ships he would have to depend upon in the forthcoming operation. It might be drudgery, but it was essential, and he made his way down to the deck passing the sweating hands as they hauled the eighteen-pounders up to battery once more.

Almost before they sighted the islets called The Ladrones, Merewether could smell China. On the ebb tide, the excrement of millions of persons living ashore and afloat was carried out to sea from the network of streams that converged to become the Pearl and Canton Rivers. Drury had ordered an anchorage in the roadstead off Macao since warships were not permitted to go above Boca Tigre in any event, and this was the point from which a landing could most easily be made in the Portuguese colony. To reach the Company's compound at Canton, it would be necessary to travel by boat, a wearisome journey of many hours in the oppressive heat of the day. A boat from *Russel* soon made its way in to a landing to report the squadron to the Captain of the Port and request *pratique,* a legal nicety considering the admiral's intentions, and after a short interval the salutes began to bang out.

"Your best bib and tucker, Mister Marlowe!" The midshipman was dressed in the usual informal fashion affected by junior officers in the tropics, wide plaited straw hat, sleeveless shirt, loose pantaloons and sandals of braided coir. Only a few minutes after the boat returned to *Russel,* the coxswain of the admiral's barge had passed up a note from Drury's flag lieutenant. "Admiral requests your presence eleven ante meridian this date." Evidently there had been some news ashore, and he might as well initiate Marlowe into his new duties, at least to carry the portfolio of orders, situation estimate and instructions from the Governor-General. "A quarter of eleven at the gangway." The young officer departed at a canter.

There were two Company Army officers in the flag cabin when Merewether and Marlowe were ushered in, a short obese lieutenant colonel with a florid complexion and a thin hard-faced major. The admiral was not present, but his flag lieutenant made the introductions.

"Colonel Patrick Kelley, commanding the occupation forces, and Major Silas French, commanding the Calcutta Sepoy Battalion, Captain Merewether of the Company's Marine, and his aide, Midshipman Marlowe." It was only a moment or so before Drury entered from his sleeping cabin and took his place behind the desk.

"Gentlemen, I have an urgent communication from Mister Roberts, President of the Select Committee of Supra Cargoes at Canton, requesting an audience at noon today. I thought it well that we foregather and discuss the situation and any impediments that might delay an immediate landing, if that is to be our course of action."

"None that I know of, sir," said Kelley, after a glance at Major French. "Of course, my orders put the force at the disposition of the Company's Select Committee . . ."

"Quite," replied the admiral. "But under my orders, I choose the time, place and necessity of making the landing, and I certainly shall not order it until I have communicated with the Governor of Macao, and if at all possible, obtained his consent, as well as that of the Viceroy of Canton and the Emperor, to an occupation of the town until peace shall be secured. I wish you gentlemen to be fully advised of my resolve in this respect." Kelley and French looked at one another again.

"Sir, that is a matter between you and the Select Committee. If it orders us to jump, we jump!"

"Very well, gentlemen, I think we understand one another. I shall permit no hasty or ill-considered action by the Committee." There was desultory conversation between the Company officers until the messenger announced the arrival of Messrs. J. W. Roberts and T. C. Pattie, the president and second member of the Select Committee.

Roberts was a tall fair man of possibly forty, but his hooded eyes belied the politely languid manner he affected. Pattle was short, dark haired, ten years younger, and gave the impression of passion barely contained. Drury unbent enough to offer his hand to each in turn, and they were seated at the opposite end of the desk from Merewether and the army officers. He wondered what had been the fate of the old arrogant John Elphingham who had been the president two years ago when he had influenced the Hoppo to withhold Grand Chop to certain Indiaman in the hope of private gain — Sir George Barlow had promised that he would be sacked — but this was no time to inquire.

"Now, Admiral," Roberts drawled, "I think it imperative to make a landing and take possession of the Portuguese defense works at the earliest possible moment . . ." Drury wore the bland expression of complete self-confidence in his rank and position that Merewether had seen last month. He listened to an amplification of the demand, and the numerous reasons advanced in its support. Roberts finished his exposition, then spread his hands, "So . . ."

"Has the Governor been apprised of your intentions?"

"Only in general ,sir . . ."

"And his reply?"

"He wants to await an order from the Viceroy of Goa. Did you bring it?"

"No. Captain Merewether made a renewed request in person, and it was not forthcoming. I think it not essential, but I do consider it no more than common courtesy to call upon the Governor and formally acquaint him with our demands in order that he may in turn inform the Viceroy of Canton and the Emperor of China . . ."

Pattie appeared on the verge of erupting, but Robert's expression did not change as he leaned forward in his chair.

"I have no objection to informing the Governor prior to the actual landing so that he may restrain his troops, but I am of the opinion it would be productive of great mischief if the Chinese are informed in advance . . ."

Will you elaborate?"

"Why . . ." Apparently Roberts had thought that his opinion would be accepted without justification. "Why, principally the distance to the Emperor and the delay in getting the troops ashore. I am sure they do not thrive penned up in transports . . ."

Merewether saw that this was a reason that appealed to the two Company officers. "Then, too, the Emperor takes little interest in the affairs or trade at Canton — this is a perquisite of the Viceroy — and I can stop it with a word, depriving him of the customs duties which account for a major portion of his income . . ."

"Doesn't that cut both ways, Mister Roberts?" inquired Drury. "If the Chinese decided not to trade, it would be the ruin of your Company."

"I think the Viceroy needs us far more than we need the Chinese." Roberts looked down at his hands. "I agree with your opinion that the Governor should be informed, but not the Viceroy. There is little enough he can do once he does learn of the action . . ."

"And the Emperor?"

"I doubt the Viceroy will see fit to communicate with him even when he discovers the occupation."

"Is the Viceroy the only eyes or ears the Emperor possesses in Canton?" It was a rhetorical question only as Drury continued, "But first things first. I shall call upon the Governor at his earliest convenience to broach the subject in person. Will you be kind enough to ascertain when it would be convenient to see him?"

"No need," said Pattie, reaching into his pocket. "I have here an invitation from His Excellency, Senhor Bernado Alexe de Lemos e Faria, requesting the pleasure of your company at a reception in your honor this evening beginning at nine — which means ten — o'clock at his mansion. While this will be entirely a social occasion, I have no doubt but you can make a formal appointment with him . . ." He handed over a vellum sheet handsomely lettered in black ink, and bearing an imposing seal. He looked over at Roberts, received a nod, and continued, "And now, we must conclude this interview, sir, leaving our course of action somewhat unsettled, but with the hope that we can reach an early conclusion." The Supra Cargoes rose, bowed and went out.

The admiral sat at his desk a moment, bemused. "Arrogant bastards!" he said almost as though to himself, then picked up the invitation. "It is in English, gentlemen, and includes my staff, you officers, the captain and one officer from each ship present . . . Flags, will you see this communicated without delay to all ships present. Full dress, but no swords — can't risk an incident — and stay in their boats until I step ashore . . ." He paused and looked at the four officers a moment. "I shall see you later. Oh, Merewether, remain, if you please." Once they were out, Drury leaned back and faced him.

"I gather you did not know those gentlemen?"

"No, sir. A man by the name of Elphingham was president when I was here two years ago, but these appear to be worthy successors to him."

"What do you mean by that, Captain?"

Merewether related the train of events that had culminated in the issuance of Grand Chop by the Hoppo and the frustration of Elphingham's plan to delay the sailing of certain "New Indiamen" for his private gain. ". . . then he sent a member of the Select Committee to Bombay to prefer charges of violating the laws of China against me. I was tried and acquitted by a Court of Inquiry, and Sir George Barlow recommended to the Court of Directors that the entire committee be replaced I can only assume that it has been, but by men of like stripes . . ."

"Do you still have contact with those Chinese in Canton?"

"I am sure I could find them. Their grandfather, if he is still alive, is a Mandarin of Canton, the old Chinese Dynasty, not Manchu. And I am acquainted with the resident agent of British Intelligence in the city . . ."

"Well, perhaps you will be of assistance to me. I really had no knowledge of what qualified you to be sent on this assignment. Now, I am bound to pay attention to the desires of those gentlemen, they control the use of the troops, but I am by no means satisfied with the course of action they urge. Once I talk to the Governor, I should have a better idea of which way to go. I shall see you later."

Comet's gig lay fifty yards off the landing as the admiral's barge proceeded in. Seniority among the commanders of the ships present made MacRae with his recent promotion second from last, and the admiral was already being greeted by Roberts and Pattie, together with a thin anxious appearing civilian, by the time Merewether and his party caught up. There were flaring torches set in iron sconces along the mole, and a few yards inland a cluster of brightly uniformed officers in front of two rigid files of troops, evidently the honor guard. He fell in hastily behind Drury as the party moved off. There were elaborate introductions, sweeping bows, the guard to be inspected by the admiral, and then the guests were loaded into a succession of barouches which moved off towards the Governor's mansion.

There was a fugleman standing at attention a pace forward of the first rank, his face clearly visible in the torchlight, darkly handsome with curly side whiskers and a bold moustache. His yellow eyes swept across Merewether's face without the slightest flicker of recognition as the barouche passed, but Merewether felt a hand of ice seize his heart. Osborne? Was it possible? *Osborne?* Could a man rise from death in the mud at the bottom of Bombay Harbor? He almost turned in his seat to look back, and then decided he was being ridiculous, the man was long since food for fish. The type was common enough; it had been said that Osborne had gypsy blood to account for his swarthy complexion. But the resemblance was uncanny! The barouche was coming to a stop at the door of the mansion, and he put the matter out of his mind as the elaborate formalities of the Governor's welcome commenced.

The thin anxious man turned out to be Mister Wickham, the British consul at Macao, fluent in Portuguese, and ready to serve as interpreter. This was an old colony, albeit a small one, and protocol was rigidly observed. The Governor and his lady were flanked by close to a dozen couples, several of the men in uniform glittering with gold lace, and the others in civilian formal dress.

Senhor Bernado Alexe de Lemos e Faria was an erect, dignified man of middle years with a full head of iron-grey hair, clean shaven, with a bold nose and penetrating black eyes. His lady was considerably younger, a raven-haired beauty of much fairer complexion than most of the other women present. Merewether watched proceedings as he waited in the line and the British consul made the presentations. The Governor apparently had at least some command of English, and he and Drury had their heads together for a moment before the admiral moved on. The introductions were soon over and the party adjourned to another area of the ballroom where wine was served and formal toasts proposed. With so many candles blazing within the room, and the press of people, the air soon became stifling and Merewether felt sweat begin to trickle under his arms.

There were double doors open at the end of the room and a patio beyond looking out over the roadstead. Candles were shielded in colored paper globes to shed a mellow light over numerous small tables set about, many of them already occupied by chattering groups of officers and ladies, while servants moved along them setting out wine and dainty morsels of food. The sea breeze was pleasant, and Merewether found an unoccupied table at the edge of the terrace where he was soon served with a glass and plate of small cakes. The wine was drier, with a hint of the taste of resin in it, much more suited for this climate than the heavy port of the toasts. He soon felt refreshed and looked about, hearing a string ensemble strike up a lilting tune in the ballroom, but he had no desire to participate in the dancing. He wondered how long the affair might endure. As he could not leave before Drury, he resigned himself to another long evening. It was a strong contralto voice that spoke his name.

"Why, Captain Merewether! I could not be sure as you came out of the door with the light at your back . . ."

Merewether rose in confusion. The woman had her back to the light now, and he could not make out her features. He was sure he knew no one in Macao, and he sidled sidewise as he bowed, trying to gain the advantage of the nearest lamp for identification. It was a needless effort, the woman spoke again.

"Creusa Hale, Captain. I could not expect you to recognize me at this distance from Bombay . . ." Good God, the drunken woman he had rescued from the equally drunken attentions of that man in Bombay last winter! He became aware that another older woman was at her side, and bowed again. "My aunt Senhora Maria Alverado, wife of the Commandant of the Garrison . . ." Merewether remembered his manners.

"Will you join me, ladies?"

"Oh, we are with a party of my husband's officers from the garrison, Captain," said Senhora Alverado in excellent English. He was startled for a moment, then remembered Mrs. Tollett's identification of the family as old Portuguese merchants in Bombay. ". . . and I am obligated to rejoin them, but I shall leave Creusa in your company. Perhaps you can console her." She turned, and went back to a large group at several tables pulled together where gold lace glittered. Merewether held the chair and seated Mrs. Hale, then resumed his own seat, as he signaled the waiter for refreshments.

"Now, Captain, I have no ties on you, and if I am an embarrassment, just say so. I am no longer Mrs. Hale, Father Roderigo serves as Papal Legate in these remote parts, and he has granted me an annulment of my marriage to Hale. He's a Protestant, and there were no children, though he tried hard enough . . ." Merewether was taken aback by these rapid revelations, though he tried to follow them, as she continued, "So, being a full-blooded woman who lives for the moment rather than the morrow, I formed a liaison with your Mister Pattie..." Who? Oh yes, the second member of the Select Committee, smoldering passion barely contained — the pair should have suited one another admirably — then heard her urgent voice continue, ".. , and it was really rather a happy affair until that Anglo-Indian came to town . . . I don't know how they met, but she mesmerized him . . . He has her in his quarters, and hang the scandal . . . Of course, Robert keeps a Chinese girl, and the others do too, though they are over at Canton right now. . ."

Merewether looked at her, trying to make some sense out of the gush of words that had imparted such diverse information. She tossed off her glass of wine and signaled the waiter for another. Was she going to drink herself into insensibility as she had that night at Bombay? The prospect of a drunken woman on his hands offended him, and he sought some excuse to leave her.

"No, Captain, I shall not drink to excess," she said as though she read his mind. "That was the first glass I have had today. I realize I am a little too full of myself, and what I just said may very well not make sense to you . . ." The waiter set the wine before her but she left it untouched, looking at him with her eyes glistening. "You're married, I take it, Captain?"

"Yes, and father of a new son." What was the woman getting at?

"Makes little enough difference out here — so are Pattie and Roberts, and all the rest — and China is a long way from England, and what the little woman at home doesn't know won't hurt her; she may even be taking a tumble of her own with the local squire . . ." Merewether was becoming restive. Sober or not, he wished she would come to her point, whatever it might be.

"My dear," he said gently. "I gather that an affair of the heart has gone awry, and you are understandably upset. Who is this woman, and what service may I perform?"

"Why, Pattie called her 'Tulsi', she's a half-caste Indian, landed here late last month . . ." It was impossible. Had Madame Bai anticipated him here? What was her mission? It was entirely possible, however, that what with his stops at Goa and Penang, the exercises underway, and the poor sailing qualities of the transports, she might very well have made her way from Bombay to arrive ahead of him.

Creusa was still talking. ". . . I only saw her the once, she had an introduction to the Judge of the High Court of Macao. He is said to deal in opium . . . A beautiful enough woman, if you fancy the type . . ." There were tears trickling down her cheeks now, and she dabbed her handkerchief at her eyes. "My uncle says you are the representative of the Governor-General . . . I thought you might have influence . . ." She looked at him hopefully.

"I am sorry, but no, the Supra Cargoes are supreme out here. Even Admiral Drury has no authority over them."

An expression of disappointment crossed her face, but her tears had ceased. He sought to change the subject. "Tell me something of this place. My experience has been almost entirely with Canton . . ." The spirit of reckless abandon she had displayed in Bombay appeared to be entirely lacking.

"Well . . . It is a much quieter place than Bombay, especially at this season when the Supra Cargoes and their staff are all over at Canton, and the ships ready to discharge. We have few social events, the one tonight is the second since I have been here . . . I met Pattie at the first . . . It really is rather dull, but since my mother died I have no ties in England . . ." This was not the type of information Merewether desired, and he intervened with a question.

"Have you heard your uncle say anything about the military and diplomatic situation?"

"Very little. He does not discuss such matters with his family. Oh, I know he has orders to resist any landing, and there are eighty Mandarin War Junks up those creeks not fifteen miles from here with five thousand men in them, but I doubt the Viceroy of Canton would send them to our aid — he fears the loss of his customs duties — and Roberts and Pattie already have threatened that the cotton will not be landed . . ." A morsel of intelligence as to the proximity of the Chinese naval force but little else.

Merewether saw Marlowe appear in the doorway scanning the terrace anxiously, and raised his hand in acknowledgment. "I think my party is ready to take its leave," he told Creusa. "I am delighted to have seen you again . . ." She looked up with a changed expression, more the devil-may-care attitude she had worn in Bombay, and reached across the table to grasp his arm.

He remembered the parting at her door that early morning, and then the note, and undertook to back away, disengaging himself from the woman. He had no intention of betraying Caroline with her, if that was what she had in mind. He rose.

"Shall I escort you back to your party?" He offered his arm, and they made their way through the clustered tables and hum of unintelligible conversation to the Commandant's group.

He bowed to Senhora Alverado, then to Creusa, and took his leave. Outside, his party was already formed up to enter the carriages, and Drury soon appeared. As they alighted at the landing, the flag lieutenant approached.

"Admiral wants you on board *Russel* by eight bells of the morning watch, sir."

Back in *Comet* he found Sangh at his door with a sealed missive in his hand. "It was delivered by a Chinese boat, sah." The letter read:

> My dear Captain Merewether:
> I shall call upon you in *Comet* tomorrow afternoon.
> s/Dawson

The schoolmaster of his youth! Merewether had last seen him two years ago in Canton, and then Percy had let drop the fact that he was the agent in place for British Intelligence out here. Well, Merewether would be glad to renew acquaintance with the man, but he was startled that his arrival had been reported so promptly. He retired, with a call for four bells in the morning watch, to lie awake nearly an hour with thoughts not of the pending meeting with Drury, possibly the Governor of Macao, and Dawson, but of Creusa Hale. At this juncture, in his single cot far away from Caroline, a possible bit of dalliance with a beautiful woman was by no means as unthinkable at it had been even an hour ago. He strove to put her out of his mind, then tormented himself with the vision of the splendid torso she had displayed at Bombay. Good God, in this course lay madness! He got off the cot and went out on deck in the sultry night, cadged a cup of coffee from the officer of the watch, and came back to his room to fall asleep until he was awakened by the knock and call of the messenger just as four bells sounded.

Drury was drinking tea when the flag lieutenant ushered Merewether into his cabin. Drury waved him to a chair, swallowed, and pushed the cup aside to assume his cloak of dignity, then picked up a letter from his desk.

"This came from Roberts before daybreak. He's changed his mind again. He wants no negotiation with the Governor: simply commence landing the troops. Of course, I shall do nothing of the kind. My audience with the Governor is at ten this morning. I shall keep the appointment, make a full disclosure of the situation, and request his consent to the occupation. If it is not forthcoming, then I shall consider more extreme measures. I do not intend to take the Supra Cargoes to the meeting. Do you disagree?"

"No, sir. And I am of the opinion that the Viceroy of Canton must be informed in advance. What he tells the Emperor is then his own affair." Merewether paused to try to put his thoughts in order. "I picked up two items of interest last night. First, the Viceroy has eighty Mandarin War Junks between here and Canton with a reported five thousand men in them. Second, I have a note from the agent of British Intelligence in Canton that he will call upon me this afternoon . . ."

Drury showed immediate interest. "Five thousand! And how are they armed?"

"Rather lightly by our standards. None of them could stand against even a sloop. But of course the massed fire power if they decided to seal off the Bogue would be substantial."

"Very well, another factor to keep in mind. Now, we shall embark."

They were met at the landing by Consul Wickham and a captain, aide de camp in the Portuguese garrison, wearing a gold bullion aiguillette. The carriage took them past the offseason quarters of the East India Company, and Merewether wondered if Madame Bai might be sojourning there as Pattle's *chère amie* for the time being. They pulled up at the Governor's Mansion, and shortly were ushered into an ornate chamber where the Governor stood behind his desk to greet them. There was a man in the robes of a Catholic priest standing to one side and behind him.

"Good morning, gentlemen," said the Governor in a strong accent. "My English is limited, and Father Roderigo will serve as my interpreter."

They were seated in hard gilded chairs in front of the desk, and Drury commenced his exposition of the situation and of intelligence that had come to the attention of Government. Father Roderigo, hand cupped beside his mouth, put the words into Portuguese almost as fast as the admiral could utter them. Governor de Lemos listened attentively without interruption as Drury concluded.

"And so, Your Excellency, in order to counter this infamous plot by Bonaparte, we have no alternative but to demand that we be allowed to land and reinforce your garrison. The Viceroy of Goa is fully acquainted with the matter, and it is no more than a matter of time before his order to this effect reaches you, but I am under the necessity of proceeding without delay."

The admiral leaned back and fixed the Governor with a keen gaze. Senhor de Lemos, eyes averted, lips pursed, finally looked up and out the window towards the anchorage. When he looked back at Drury, his expression had hardened, and Merewether braced himself for the rebuff, as the Governor began to speak with Father Roderigo almost simultaneously delivering the English translation. Wickham apparently was content with the priest's version.

"Senhor Admiral, I am without power to grant your request until such time as the Viceroy shall authorize me so to do. Also, under the terms of the treaties between Portugal and China, I must inform the Viceroy of Canton before permitting foreign troops to land in Macao. I sincerely regret that I am powerless to accommodate you."

Drury now spoke forcefully, punctuating his remarks with a finger jabbed towards the Governor. "Your Excellency, I thought I had made myself clear. I am under the most imperative of orders, and am compelled to land my forces regardless of whether you consent or not. If there is bloodshed, it will be upon your head . . ."

The expression on the Governor's face altered and he appeared to hesitate before he spoke again. "Senhor Admiral," he began in a conciliatory tone. "Surely you recognize my position. I request of you at least twenty-four hours to enable me to consult with my people. This comes as somewhat of a surprise, and I must not act hastily . . ."

"Very well," Drury said. "Twenty-four hours, Your Excellency, but I shall expect your reply at the end of that period without further delay." He looked at Merewether with a signal that he considered the interview concluded, then heard the Governor's invitation for refreshments. It was an hour past noon when they embarked again for *Russel.*

"Since you are expecting a visitor, I shall drop you by *Comet,"* said Drury as they pulled away. This was certainly the most considerate flag officer he had ever encountered, Merewether decided, in spite of his exaggerated opinion of the dignity of the office he held.

As they pulled under the stern of the ship, he saw a Chinese boat lying off the starboard gangway. Dawson must already be on board.

"Mister Dawson!" he said, seizing the man's outstretched hand, remembering the long ago days as a ship's boy in the Indiaman, *Dunvegan Castle,* when Dawson had taught him enough to enable him to rise above the stigma of his illegitimate birth, and eventually achieve a captaincy in the Bombay Marine. "I am delighted to see you again!"

"Maybe not so much when you hear what I have to say." Merewether ordered Sangh to bring refreshments.

"And what may I do for you, Mister Dawson?"

"I'll be as brief as I can, Captain," said Dawson pleasantly. "But I think a bit of a background is in order to acquaint you with the current situation here. I am rather familiar with the Chinese attitudes, particularly towards the Company and the Crown. The Emperor regards King George with about the same degree of respect as he does the chief of a small tribe in Borneo, and the Company as a nuisance to be tolerated only because it enriches a few of his kinsmen. He is extremely jealous of his possessions, desires no intercourse with the foreign devils, and given provocation, would expel the British and Portuguese from their concessions in a moment —"

"The Select Committee professes to believe otherwise —"

"The Select Committee is a pack of fools, and corrupt as well. I thought when Elphingham and his crew were recalled, things might improve. They have worsened. The members are not content with the very ample commissions they already receive, but have established an agency under the name of "Baring and Company" to handle the opium trade —"

"But Baring is a member of the Committee, and the Company has absolutely forbidden the trade, as has China —"

"Precisely, but money accomplishes many things. A Hong Kong merchant, Manhop by name, was induced by Roberts and Baring last year to undertake the distribution of the contraband through Canton. He made his arrangements with the servants of the Hoppo, and they pay the same fees as for the landing of legitimate merchandise. Officially, the Hoppo knows nothing. Actually, his share of the customs is substantial, as is that of the Viceroy —"

"But who brings it in? Surely not in Company ships?"

"Country ships, usually. There are fifty-seven bottoms at Whampoa now, of which twenty-seven are country ships from Bengal, Penang and Bombay. My informant tells me that several of the ships have already landed their consignments, openly and with the payment of duty to the officials, though the Supra Cargoes have held up the landing of other goods in furtherance of their design to coerce the Viceroy into not opposing the landing of troops at Macao . . ."

At least the Indiamen were clean, if not the Select Committee, Merewether thought with a sense of relief. Every sailing order issued by the Company contained the proviso, read out to the crew at the commencement of each voyage, "You will take the most particular care that no opium be laden on your ship by yourself, your officers, or any other person, as the importation of that article at China is positively forbidden and serious consequences may result from your neglect of this injunction."

"But what has this to do with the mission to Macao?"

"A great deal. Over three hundred chests of Malawan opium passed through Macao into China last winter. The Company, of course, maintains a market for the legitimate sale of Bengal opium at Calcutta. This operation competes with it, though it is the produce of northern India, and of lesser quality than the southern product. The Hoppo and Viceroy received no customs, and the Select Committee no commission on the shipment, which was reportedly managed by one of the highest officials of Macao. The profit was five hundred dollars, net, per chest. Is this not a powerful inducement to urge the immediate occupation of the town?" It made sense. With the town occupied by troops under the control of the Supra Cargoes, it should be relatively simple to stop off any further smuggling of the drug.

"I understand. Now, what is your suggestion?"

"Inform Admiral Drury of the motives of these gentlemen. I do not believe it will make any difference, he is going to give in to them in spite of his high-flown rhetoric as to obtaining consent from the Viceroy, but he is entitled to this information." Dawson looked out of the port at the town of Macao in the distance with his near-sighted gaze for a moment, then continued, "I am not a military man, but I fail to see the necessity for an actual occupation of Macao at this time. With a mobile squadron at his command, able to oppose the French at any point they may appear, I would think him to be in a better position than with a few hundred troops ashore. If the Emperor learns of a *fait accompli,* I am certain that the wrath of China will be visited upon all of us, and the Company will lose its trade at Canton." He shook his head. "But, for reasons that I am not at liberty to divulge just now, I am content to let the Select Committee and Drury make this blunder . . ."

Merewether was surprised at the statement. Dawson had just outlined motive and probable consequences of the operation, and then expressed satisfaction in the course pursued. He looked sharply at the man and concluded that Dawson must have his reasons, though he would have preferred to know them. It appeared that the interview was over. But then Dawson spoke again.

"You remember Wong, of course?"

"Certainly, and how is the young man?"

"He is now the Mandarin. His grandfather died last winter, and being four months older than his cousin he succeeded. He possesses much wisdom for his years, as well as ambition. I expect great things of Wong, though his title derives from the old dynasty of China, and not the Manchus. If all goes well, I hope you may renew acquaintance with him."

"I regret the news of the Mandarin's death. He did me a great service three years ago."

"And now, I should be on my way back to Canton. If you need to communicate with me, entrust your message to Mister Wickham, the Consul . . ."

Merewether saw Dawson to the gangway for the weary voyage back to Canton, as the officer of the watch called away the gig for his visit to the flagship. He trusted Dawson implicitly, but was a bit bemused as to his motives in making the call, imparting the intelligence, and then indicating satisfaction in letting the Supra Cargoes achieve their ends. Time would no doubt solve the mystery.

"No," said Drury in his pleasant manner a quarter of an hour later. "I am interested, of course, in the suspect motives of those gentlemen, but your informant's report does not authorize me to ignore explicit orders. I shall expect to receive permission at noon tomorrow from the Governor to commence the landing. I shall at that time also urge him to petition the Viceroy, but in any event, Macao shall be occupied." He sat back and looked speculatively at Merewether, who gained the distinct impression that the admiral did not believe a word of the intelligence. "Very well, I shall want you present when we call on the Governor tomorrow," he continued in dismissal just as his flag lieutenant knocked and entered.

"Sir, Mister Roberts is coming aboard. Shall I send him in?"

"Yes. Wait a moment, Merewether." The tall Supra Cargo entered in his languid gait.

"Good afternoon, gentlemen. I understand you gave the Governor twenty-four hours to think over our demands." The drawl was still negligent in tone, but the words were accusatory, and Drury stiffened as he met Robert's gaze.

"Yes, it is only common courtesy to permit the man to confer with his senate and advisors. After all, his career may hang on the decision he makes now . . ." The expression on the Supra Cargo's face hardened and his eyes glittered a moment, but his tone was unchanged.

"The members of the Select Committee are somewhat disappointed at this delay . . ." Merewether sensed Drury's hackles rise, but the man retained his poise and bland expression as Roberts continued, ". . . since it is a matter of serious inconvenience to our trade here. The Indiamen have not yet begun to discharge cargo, and I shall not permit them to do so until the occupation is complete . . ."

"Is this still part of your scheme to coerce the Viceroy?" demanded Drury.

"Term it that if you will," replied Roberts lightly. "I prefer to call it a mere *quid pro quo.* Now, sir, we shall acquiesce in this 'common courtesy', but with the clear understanding that there be no further delay . . ." Drury turned a little red in the face, but clung to his composure.

"Do you have some motive for this extraordinary haste?"

"None but the interests of King and Company."

"The opium trade through Macao is no factor then?" It was Robert's turn to look startled. His hooded eyes opened wide for an instant, then narrowed to slits.

"I do not know what you are talking about. The laws of China and the ordinances of the Company forbid such traffic."

"Quite. I have apparently well-founded reports that it flourishes both through Canton and Macao . . ."

Roberts looked down at his interlaced fingers. "The subject is irrelevant at this time. Now, sir, under the orders for this operation, the Company troops are under the sole command of the Select Committee. I serve notice upon you that after the expiration of your 'common courtesy' they shall move ashore . . ."

"If I refuse to provide the boats?"

"I have enough lighters and hands at the Canton Factories to accomplish the task." Drury sat back, only the flush in his cheeks betraying the fury that boiled in him.

"Very well, then. The blood will be on your heads. I shall keep my appointment with Senhor de Lemos at noon tomorrow. I trust you will take no action pending the result of our conference."

Merewether was surprised at the capitulation. He had braced himself for the grinding head-on collision between the Royal Navy and the senior Company official in China. Roberts rose, inclined his head, and departed.

"What an insufferable ass!" exploded Drury after a moment. "In my short tenure out here I have already formed a most disagreeable opinion of the Honorable Company's senior officials . . ." He looked at Merewether and added hastily, ". . . its mercantile officials, I mean, not the officers of its Marine." He drummed his fingers on the desk a moment, then continued, "I shall call upon the Governor precisely at noon tomorrow."

Back in *Comet,* Merewether tried to sort out the situation. He was inclined to agree with Dawson's assessment of the matter. An attack overland on Macao was unlikely, there were no convenient landing points south of the city. There was sufficient naval force present to make an amphibious frontal assault all but impossible. The time of the occupation appeared not to be critical, the nine hundred troops could be ferried ashore in a day. And yet the Select Committee insisted upon immediate occupation of the town without the consent of the Governor or notice to the Viceroy. He was convinced that the Supra Cargoes had other motives, and Roberts's recent reaction to the suggestion corroborated the charge. The orders from the Governor-General, however, gave Drury small discretion. He was still turning the matters over in his mind when he joined MacRae in the cabin for dinner.

"Slow start," commented the small Scots officer. "I expected the troops to be ashore by now."

"No, Drury gave the Governor twenty-four hours until noon tomorrow to consider the matter, and Roberts is a bit miffed . . ." He gave a desultory account of the day's developments during the leisurely meal.

"Sma' doot in my mind, Captain," said MacRae at the conclusion. "I ha'e small regret that I have not had the pleasure of their acquaintance."

Drury and Merewether, accompanied by Lieutenant Colonel Patrick Kelley and Major Silas French, marched into the Governor's anteroom on the stroke of twelve. The secretary ushered them immediately into the chamber where Senhor de Lemos stood behind his desk flanked by Father Roderigo on his left and a swarthy sharp-faced European to his right.

"Good morning, gentlemen. May I present the Honorable Miguel de Silveria e Arriaga, Judge of the High Court of Macao." The man inclined his head as Drury and Merewether bowed formally. "He also holds the posts of Customs Master and Public Treasurer of the city. I have asked him to be present as my counselor . . ." Aside from the initial greeting, the statement was in Portuguese, translated simultaneously by the Padre.

Drury came immediately to the point. "Have you reached a decision, Your Excellency?"

De Lemos's face clouded as the priest translated the question. He turned to whisper urgently in the ear of the judge, listened to a reply of several sentences, then spoke.

"I am compelled to await the advices from the Viceroy of Goa, which are expected momentarily . . ."

There was a knock on the door and the secretary entered. He spoke rapidly in Portuguese. Father Roderigo gave an instantaneous translation.

"The President and Second Member demand entry to this parley." Merewether saw the flush mount into Drury's face as he opened his mouth to utter a quick refusal, then paused a moment.

"So be it," he said finally in a tone of resignation. "Let them come in . . ." Roberts and Pattle entered, their eyes searching the faces of the assemblage.

"Gentlemen," said Roberts. "In a matter of such grave concern to the Company Trading to China, it behooves the Select Committee to be heard!" His gaze passed Merewether to fix on Drury. "At what stage are your discussions, Admiral?"

"The Governor has said he is compelled to await the advices of his Viceroy, and I am about to tell him the reply is unacceptable."

"Good. Then you will immediately proceed with the landings."

"Not so fast. There must first be assurances that the landing will not be resisted, whether consent is given or not, and that the Viceroy of Canton has been informed." Roberts stared insolently at the admiral. The Governor and judge sat expressionless across the desk listening to the translation of the interchange.

"Just a moment," broke in Pattie. "Let me suggest a course of action which should satisfy all concerned." His urgent tone compelled attention. "What I propose is this: let the troops be landed under Portuguese colors —"

Drury's composure vanished. "Your proposal, Mister Pattie, is so contemptible, so unworthy of an Englishman, to land British troops in the guise of Portuguese banditti, that I shall withdraw instanter from so scandalous an act!"

"It has the added advantage of not alarming the Chinese, so that it is not necessary to petition the Viceroy," continued Pattie easily as though the outburst had not occurred.

"Never!" said Drury.

The judge whispered urgently in the Governor's ear in a moment of silence. Merewether felt that the stratagem proposed by Pattie had merit; it accomplished the practical objective of occupying Macao while being less likely to offend the territorial pride and sensibilities of China. Evidently the Governor thought so too, though it appeared from his expression and whispered remonstrances that the judge was not in agreement. De Lemos spoke in measured tones as Father Roderigo interpreted.

"Although I am without present authority to consent to any occupation of Macao, I will accept the reinforcement of my garrison, provided the troops land and remain under Portuguese colors . . ."

For a moment Merewether thought Drury might accept the compromise, but he reckoned without the fierce pride the officer felt in the flag he flew in King George's Navy.

"Never! I shall not permit Englishmen to be demeaned by any such charade!" The admiral was adamant in his position. "And now, Your Excellency, shall we take up the specifics as to the landing?"

De Lemos threw up his hands and sat back. "Your combined force is so far superior to my land and naval establishment that I am compelled to yield. I call upon all you gentlemen to bear witness that I do so under duress . . ." For a moment Merewether thought the man would weep, but then he composed himself, assuming an expression of deep dejection.

The details were soon settled: the landing to commence at daylight, all the forts to be occupied and commanded by the British with the exception of La Monte Fort, the Commandant's headquarters. The Portuguese garrisons would evacuate their barracks and be quartered on the town, but would man the new batteries to be emplaced on the land approaches from China and commanding the beaches to the south and west.

"And now, one more matter," said Drury. "I shall keep my flag in *Russel* as commander of the expedition. Of course, once landed, I realize that the troops are at the disposition of the Select Committee and I exercise no direct control of their activities. However, I designate Captain Percival Merewether of the Honorable Company's Naval Service, and the Senior Officer Present in its military forces, to be my deputy in Macao."

Merewether had no desire to exchange his relatively comfortable quarters in *Comet* for a grimy billet ashore with the inevitable turmoil and conflict to be expected when two disparate military forces without a common language met and mingled. He realized that Drury was still speaking. "Do you have suitable quarters for the captain in East India House, Mister Roberts?" It was the Supra Cargo's turn to sit up and compose his expression.

"Why . . ." Roberts paused, glanced at Pattie who almost imperceptibly shook his head, and continued, "No, sir. Every room is taken."

"I thought three members of your committee are at Canton."

“I have no right to permit their quarters to be occupied in their absence.”

Merewether guessed that the Supra Cargoes desired no close scrutiny of their activities, and was glad for the curt refusal. Perhaps it would cause the admiral to change his mind as to the assignment, but there came an intervention from an unexpected quarter.

“Sir,” said the Governor through Father Roderigo. “There are guest accommodations at the Commandant’s residence adjacent to La Monte Fort. I shall be happy to offer your deputy the use of them.” Hell! After a stiff resistance the Governor had not only capitulated, but was now collaborating with the British.

“Excellent. The captain will have to maintain a close liaison with the Commandant during the landings, and this will offer a perfect solution.” Drury looked around the gathering. “And now, we may adjourn. I trust that you will impress upon your troops that we come in peace and as allies.” He rose, bowed to the Governor, and marched out.

“I think it would be well for you to move ashore this afternoon, establish your residence and become acquainted with the Commandant. The troops will begin landing as soon as it is daylight,” said Drury as they approached East India House.

Merewether recognized the order though it was couched in the terms almost of a request. He listened to a succession of admonitions, nodding his head at intervals — most of which were superfluous — and scanned the front of East India House as they passed, wondering if Tulsi Bai might be peering out at him from one of the curtained windows. He was glad he had brought the cavalry officer’s brass-bound chests he had used last year along the Persian Road on the off-chance he might have to camp on the beach at Ras ul Khymah. They should suffice to carry his necessities for the sojourn ashore. Back aboard *Comet* he set Sangh to packing and alerted young Marlowe to prepare for the mission.

The welcome was polite enough, if not warm. The carriage with Merewether and Marlowe in the rear seat, Sangh perched on the box beside the driver, was waved by the sentry box at the gate to a walled enclosure of well-tended lawn set on a terrace below and to one side of La Monte Fort. The Commandant’s residence was substantial with the guest cottage to one side, but connected with it by a covered path which led through an octagonal summer house with pergolas supporting rose vines half-way between them. The Commandant, accompanied by Father Roderigo, met them at the entrance and the priest presented Merewether to Colonel Jorge Alverado.

The Commandant was of middle height, sturdy, ruddy of complexion, prominent nose, brown eyes and curly black hair beginning to go grey. He must be close to fifty, Merewether decided, and his expression conveyed an impression of good will coupled with the resolution required of a capable officer.

"These are your quarters, sir," continued the priest. "The pantry is stocked with provisions, and there are facilities for your servant. "Shall we inspect it now?" Merewether was agreeably surprised. He had brought a week's rations from the cabin stores, but here was a promise of fresh victuals.

"Certainly." The Commandant led the way inside through a foyer into a large drawing room, elaborately furnished, with colorful Persian rugs on the floor. There was a formal dining room, three sumptuous bedrooms, a well-equipped kitchen and both serving and storage pantries.

"The Legate of the Viceroy of Goa sojourns here when he makes his biennial inspection," explained Father Roderigo. "I think you will find your quarters entirely adequate. There is a cot for your servant and a copper tub in which you may bathe in this room off the kitchen."

"It is magnificent," said Merewether, almost overwhelmed. He had not occupied such luxurious quarters since those few weeks he had spent in Colonel Harding's mansion in Calcutta just before the expedition to Persia. He decided that he should try to establish some basis of communication with Colonel Alverado. "I am most grateful," he told Father Roderigo. "Does the Commandant speak English?"

"A little, but the Governor has assigned me to accompany you tomorrow. I also speak Chinese . . ."

"Tell him I shall be at the landing when the troops arrive in the morning, and I shall expect him to be with me. We should be mounted with sufficient aides to carry our messages, and prepared to deal with any eventuality . . ." Merewether had no concern for the

Calcutta Sepoy Battalion. They were hereditary soldiers with a deep sense of pride in their profession of arms. But the companies from Madras might well be composed of "the scum of Europe", as one anti-Company member of Parliament had termed them. He must be prepared to contain any breach of the peace instantly in this potentially explosive situation.

"He says, 'Certainly'," reported the Padre. "The horses will be outside by dawn." Evidently Alverado had received explicit orders from the Governor. On an impulse, Merewether stepped forward, extending his hand. After a momentary hesitation the colonel grasped it.

"We shall get on famously!" Merewether told him. "We must rely implicitly each upon the other." There was no hesitation in the assent, and Alverado saluted him as he and Father Roderigo departed.

Well," said Merewether, feeling himself at loose ends for the moment. "Might as well have a drink before dinner. It may be a long time before we have the opportunity for another." Sangh brought gin and Marlowe contented himself with a glass of port. "Do you ride?" he inquired of the young officer.

"Oh, yes, sir, but I haven't been on a horse since England."

"You'll be sore enough then by night tomorrow!" laughed Merewether. "And so shall I since it has been almost a year for me too." Sangh soon announced dinner, and there was indeed fresh beef and vegetables.

Tulsi Bai sat in the comfortable chamber on the second floor of Macao's East India House, the curtain a narrow space open. She had resumed her European mode of dress, not as comfortable but more becoming to her than a sari. She felt the anger that had possessed her a few moments before subside into the cold hatred she felt each time she thought of that scar-faced captain. The man had ridden by in the carriage with that pompous admiral on his way to see the Governor, and she had instantly recognized him. Pattle had not mentioned him by name, only that a Company officer was assigned as an advisor to Admiral Drury. It was an astounding coincidence: the very man who had frustrated her schemes for Malhar last summer appearing here at Macao. She would keep out of sight and it might yet be possible to repay with interest the injury he had done her.

Dispassionately she began to assess her present situation. In the beginning she had been of the opinion that Rene had overreacted in dispatching her so great a distance to escape Holkar's revenge, but now she realized he had had additional motives.

The message entrusted to her as she took ship at Goa was addressed to Miguel de Silveira, but upon her arrival she discovered that he held the office of Judge of the High Court of Macao, was second in power only to the Governor and that he was the silent partner in her brother's opium cartel. She was prepared to distrust the man, but once he had read the dispatch he welcomed her into his home where his wife made her comfortable. Madame Bai tinkled the silver bell on the taboret beside her and the half-caste Indonesian maid came in.

"A glass of burgundy, please."

She sipped the wine with pleasure, keeping a vigil through the curtain. It had been an hour since she had seen Merewether pass on his way to the Governor's mansion, and she already knew from Pattie that he and Roberts intended to intrude upon the Admiral's audience.

Pattle had been an unexpected bonus, and the thought of the man filled her with an unaccustomed warmth. The judge had managed to throw her in his way, but Tulsi had then contrived the liaison with her own wits and artifices, and her mission for de Silveira did not interfere with her enjoyment of the interlude with a young man of fiery temperament after her years of sojourning with stale men past their prime.

She thought of the woman from whom she had taken Pattie, beautiful and spirited enough, but stupid and impulsive to the point of recklessness. Confronted with a rival, Creusa had simply flown into a tantrum and flung herself out of Pattle's quarters. In the same situation, Tulsi would have maintained an icy calm and dared the man to remove her bodily, confident that he would not risk a public scandal even in the relaxed morality out here. The maid looked in, then came over to refill the glass. She was a pretty little thing and reasonably biddable.

"Your man — you said he was a gunner in the garrison?" said Madame Bai in Portuguese. She had seen him meet the girl several times and admired his dark good looks and graceful carriage. Will he be in danger if the British occupy the town?"

"I do not know." The maid shrugged and looked away. "He tells me nothing about his duties." Tulsi considered the possibility of using the man in some move against Merewether only briefly. There was no need for haste in her designs for revenge. Once the town was in British hands with the control in Roberts and Pattie, there would doubtless be other opportunities. She would bide her time, carry out her mission of keeping the judge fully informed of the Select Committee's strategies.

It was only a few minutes more before Madame Bai saw the carriage coming back towards the landing. Admiral Drury wore his usual expression of composed dignity. She could not read the outcome of the audience in his face, but he was apparently laying out instructions to Merewether who was nodding at intervals. No matter. She would learn the result of the conference soon enough when Pattie came in for his siesta. She moved to the dressing table to freshen herself with scent in anticipation of his arrival.

Here in Southern China, though almost precisely on the Tropic of Cancer, there was a distinct chill in the pre-dawn air at the end of September. Merewether could hear Sangh moving about in the kitchen, and there were footsteps and an occasional thump from the room occupied by Marlowe. Shivering, he shaved and washed himself, then worked his legs into the narrow riding breeches and thigh-high boots he had worn to Persia last year. From the waist down, he had become a cavalryman, but the addition of his uniform jacket and cocked hat created a curious hybrid appearance, and he laughed at the effect when he looked in the mirror. The pistols were already in saddle holsters with a leather box of paper cartridges and a brass flask of priming powder to serve them. He hesitated a moment over the sword, then belted it on. It would be an encumbrance, but often the sight of a naked blade proved more intimidating at close quarters than a firearm. Sangh placed a tray on the chest and he ate his breakfast standing at the window, seeing the faint glow of dawn expand to the east.

In the grey light of early morning, all his weakness, imperfections and failings came crystal clear. By noon, he knew, they would be glossed over, excused, forgotten, but at this hour they gave him concern. He harbored no particular foreboding of the day just now breaking, though it well might be one fraught with danger as two disparate military forces without a common language met and mingled. It would require only one hot-head to loose off a shot, a miscalculation of temper, an insult, or nothing at all to precipitate a pitched battle between the allies in spite of anything Drury, the Governor, the Commandant, or Merewether himself might do. He felt the nagging doubt in the back of his mind that he might panic again as he had done at Aden but resolutely put the matter out of his mind.

He tried to think of Caroline and their son back at Calcutta — the child must be nearly four months now — beginning to assume the shape in which he would grow. He intended to give the boy every advantage that he had been denied. And yet, the life of man was a chancy thing. There was no guarantee that a gentle upbringing and classical education would assure success.

It was light outside. He heard the clump of hooves on the turf before he saw the party approaching.

Colonel Alverado was accompanied by Father Roderigo, a saturnine cavalry captain wearing the aiguillettes of an aide de camp, and two young officers of about the age of Marlowe, booted and spurred, sitting their mounts in easy confidence. A groom brought up the rear leading two saddled chargers.

Merewether approached his horse with some trepidation. In spite of the long ride across Persia, he was never entirely comfortable when mounted. He measured the length of the stirrups against his arm, and shortened them one notch. The horses appeared fit, there were no fresh scars on their flanks, and he swung into the saddle and settled himself before slapping the reins against the neck to follow Alverado. It would be all right, he decided, his body had not forgotten the hard lessons of the Persian Road.

At the landing half a dozen sullen officers clustered about a pot that gave off the aroma of coffee. They snapped to attention and saluted as Alverado rode up, looking with open animosity at the two naval officers on horseback. Far out in Macao Roads, the launches and cutters from all ships present were lying off the transports, and even as he looked, Merewether saw three pull towards shore. At almost the same moment he saw Admiral Drury's barge leave the side of *Russel.* With its superior speed it was at the landing before the laden boats were halfway in. Evidently the admiral could not yet disassociate himself from the venture. There was the rattle of iron tires on stone, and a carriage rolled up with Roberts and Pattle peering out of the windows. All the elements of an explosion were converging on this spot, Merewether thought sourly, dismounting and handing his reins to Marlowe.

Drury greeted Merewether, the Commandant, then Roberts and Pattie formally, returned the salutes from the Portuguese officers, and drew Merewether to one side.

"I could not abide remaining in *Russel* while this landing is going forward," he confided *sotto voce.* "I shall not interfere, but if trouble arises it may not be amiss to have an officer of rank and experience at hand to intervene. I shall remain at this point and would appreciate reports as to progress at least hourly . . ." It was only a few minutes before the first launch began to discharge its troops, Colonel Kelley and Major French were the first to step ashore, followed by fuglemen who trotted to take position as guides and rally their men into formation.

It was an orderly operation. Evidently the company commanders had explicit instructions, and as each unit filled its ranks it marched off with a Portuguese officer to guide it to the appointed billet. By mid-afternoon, the garrisons of the three designated forts had been relieved by Company troops without incident. Merewether sighed in relief as he watched the last contingent of Portuguese troops march out of the small southern fort, and a company of Calcutta Sepoys mount the guard. He and Colonel Alverado had observed each such exchange of duty, then sent Marlowe galloping off to report success to the admiral. Now in the heat of the afternoon he was beginning to feel sore and galled. He looked forward to a gin and lemon and possible immersion in the copper tub to soothe his pain. The Commandant made a statement to Father Roderigo.

"Sir," said the Padre. "Colonel Alverado says the occupation is now complete, but the artillery is coming ashore and he wishes to visit the sites of the batteries his men are to man."

"Very well. Now, express my profound gratitude for his splendid co-operation and the exemplary behavior of his command . . ."

Drury had remained all day in a small building near the landing to receive reports as to progress of the occupation. It had been a day of alarums and excursions, every rumor unfounded, but each a cause for concern at the moment. The operation had gone smooth as silk, not even a bloody nose to mar the affair. For Merewether, it was a time to make his own final report and beg to be excused.

Merewether rode back to the landing at a leisurely pace to find Drury outside the building with his flag-lieutenant. The barge was alongside the landing stage, bow and stern hooks holding on, hands ready at the oars.

"Ah Merewether, the occupation is complete, I gather. I was about to take boat to *Russel,* but delayed in the hope you would report."

"Yes, sir. The forts are in our hands without incident. Colonel Alverado is seeing to the emplacement of the batteries, and I believe our mission is now complete."

"Quite, and my congratulations to you on a well-managed affair . . ." Little enough he had to do with it, Merewether thought, but he appreciated the sentiment. He had opened his mouth to request relief from duty when Marlowe appeared on the Praya Grande and approached them at a dead run. What now? The boy reined his horse back on its haunches.

"Sir, there's about to be a fight!"

"Where?" demanded Drury. "Speak up, young man!"

"At La Monte Fort, sir!"

"La Monte Fort? But we agreed the Portuguese would keep possession of it!"

"Yes, sir, but Mister Roberts is there with his soldiers demanding that they surrender it too, and the Portuguese have wheeled out a cannon to block the gate!"

"Good Lord!" exploded Drury. "Go and see what is going on, Merewether, and I'll follow as soon as I can get my carriage back."

It had been too good to be true. Merewether swung his sore sweaty body back into the saddle ". . . and young man, ride and see if you can find the Commandant."

The canter was an easy enough gait that the horse could just hold up the switch-back road that led up the hill to La Monte Fort. As he came to the flat crest, Merewether could see two companies of

European troops deployed a hundred feet from the main gate of the fort, standing easy. There was a little knot of men gathered midway between the troops and the open gates, most of them in Portuguese uniforms. As he pulled up beside them, he recognized Roberts, Major French, and Mister Wickham, the Consul, in heated discussion with the Portuguese officers. Roberts only threw an annoyed glance over his shoulder as Merewether dismounted from his lathered horse, and continued his remarks. Sure enough, there was a field gun, a nine-pounder of current design emplaced in the gateway with a limber to which four mules were harnessed standing in the background. The heads and shoulders of musketeers were visible in the embrasures at the top of the wall. The field-gun crew appeared to have become frozen in motion, a man on either side of the muzzle, one holding a powder cartridge, another a charge of canister, while the third balanced a rammer in his hands. All were looking over their shoulders at the parley, but it was obvious that the gun could be loaded and fired in seconds.

"Here now, Mister Roberts! What's this all about?" Roberts whirled about. There was no trace of languor in him now.

"I'll thank you to keep your nose out of this, Merewether!" He turned back to the group. "Tell them I do not care what agreement the Governor and Admiral made. They cannot bind me, and I control the troops!" Wickham spoke rapidly to the Portuguese officers, listened to a lengthy and vehement reply, accompanied by vigorous gestures from a powerfully muscled captain, then turned back to Roberts.

"He says he commands the fort, his orders are to hold it, and he will not evacuate except upon the express command of the Governor in person . . ."

It was still hot in the late afternoon this last week in September in Macao. Robert's normally pale face was flushed and gleaming with sweat. For a moment he appeared to be on the verge of losing control of himself, wearing an expression of pure fury quite at variance with his usual impassive calm. Merewether stood indecisively a few feet aside, trying to formulate some course of action which would avert the explosion. He had no authority over the Supra Cargoes — and for that matter, neither did Lord Minto, except through the roundabout expedient of representations of the Court of Directors — and he wished Drury, Alverado or the Governor would gallop up to intervene. He became conscious that Roberts was speaking again in a high but controlled tone.

"Tell that dago I give him five minutes by my watch . . ." He pulled a gold watch out by the fob and looked at it. ". . . to remove that gun and swing the gates wide for my force to march in!" He pause, then continued in a milder tone, ". . . and one hour for his garrison to march out." Wickham turned and spoke again.

The reaction of the sturdy captain was instantaneous. He turned and bellowed an order towards the fort. The gun crew resumed its drill as though the interruption had never occurred. Merewether looked about for possible cover. There was none short of the slope below this flat hilltop on which the fort stood. He looked back at the field gun, able to follow the yelped commands of the gunner even though in Portuguese.

"Charge piece!" The cartridge went into the muzzle with a wad behind it and the rammerman drove it home with three solid thumps; the canister followed. The two loaders turned to stand facing him on either side of the barrel, hands clamped over their ears, while the rammerman skipped nimbly to one side.

"Prime!" The gunner drove his vent prick through the touchhole to pierce the cartridge, then inserted a priming quill of powder.

Merewether stood bemused. It was incredible that the relentless Supra Cargo and the obdurate captain should have permitted matters to progress to this point. Of course, the Portuguese party was still in the line of fire, but the captain had effectively called the hand of Roberts, and there was now the very real danger of a misunderstood command, or even an innocent gesture to bring the glowing slow match in the jaws of the linstock held by the assistant gunner down into the priming powder.

"Take aim!" The gunner straddled the trail and sighted down the barrel gesturing with his gloved left hand to his crew to shift the trail an infinitesimal amount to the left, while with his right hand he adjusted the elevation screw to lower the muzzle. All Merewether could see now was the round black hole gaping at him. It required but the one final command: "Fire!" He became conscious that the captain was speaking in a loud harsh tone, emphasizing his points with his fist driven into the palm of his hand.

"He says," reported Wickham, "that he will give you just five minutes to withdraw your troops before he orders the gun to commence firing . . ." The captain had pulled out his own watch and now held it in his hand, aping Roberts, eyes glittering in defiance.

The Supra Cargo's own eyes blazed for a moment as he held his ground. Without artillery, it was obvious to Merewether that the Company infantry could not hope to stand against even the one field gun, backed as it was by muskets fired from the shelter of the parapet. He decided to make one more try at an intervention.

"Gentlemen!" All heads turned towards him. "Messengers are summoning the Governor and Commandant. Admiral Drury is on his way here. Can you not wait those few minutes to resolve this matter?"

"I'll not withdraw my forces," said Roberts in a hard tone. "If this dago fires, I'll see him court-martialed and shot!"

The captain strode off towards the gate, followed by his officers.

"He says," reported Wickham, "his time limit stands."

This was ridiculous. Two head-strong men willing to spill blood over a matter that could be resolved by higher authority within minutes. And if there was bloodshed here, violence would inevitably erupt throughout the city, with the distinct probability that the Viceroy of Canton would feel compelled to intervene to protect the sovereignty of China with his eighty war junks. The Company's trade here would be ended, the incident could well alienate Portugal, and England needed every friend it had in these perilous times to stand against Bonaparte. Roberts remained staring after the Portuguese officers a moment, then walked rapidly back towards his troops followed by his officers and Wickham, leaving Merewether standing holding his horse's reins. It was time to get out of the line of fire. Merewether turned remount his horse.

Why he took the action, Merewether was never able to explain, even to himself. Possibly it was the sense of guilt that yet was an indelible stain on his soul, an unbidden effort to make amends for that unreasoning panic that had possessed him at Aden. He found himself quick-stepping across the turf in the wakes of the Portuguese contingent, his sword left hanging by its belt over the pommel. He was less than a half dozen steps behind them when they reached the gun.

Merewether came to a halt a bare three yards distant from the muzzle of the gun, and held up both hands, palm out. It was one thing, he thought fuzzily, to fire a gun at anonymous ranks of soldiers at a distance and quite another to shoot an unarmed man standing in the attitude of one who comes in peace at point-blank range. And then he saw the gunner, mustachioed, handsome, lithe and agile, yellow eyes burning in his head, and was suddenly certain that this man was no lookalike. Osborne!

As the full realization of the gunner's identity sunk in, Merewether was pleased to note that he felt no panic. It was as though he stood detached to one side observing the officer in the curious hybrid garb of navy and cavalry who stood empty hands up in the age-old gesture of peace. If the fate he had escaped by a hair's-breadth at Aden had overtaken him here at Macao, so be it. In his own mind, he had lived on borrowed time since that day. He examined Osborne dispassionately at this close range, seeing the sweat rag bound about his head, the smudged soggy shirt and trousers, tucked into short boots, the stubby artillery-man's sword in its leather sheath belted on. The man's feral gaze never left his face as he stood just clear of the recoil beside the right wheel of the piece, his left hand encased in its heavy leather glove poised to stop the vent after the gun fired. He was only peripherally conscious of the assistant gunner holding the linstock with its glowing coal of fire burning in the slow match in its jaws, or the two loaders on either side of the barrel, hands over their ears in anticipation of the discharge.

The captain reached the rear of the gun and about faced, looking right past Merewether towards the Company ranks, then down at his watch. He raised his hand, still peering at the dial, looked up and brought his hand down smartly.

"Descarga!"

Discipline in the Portuguese force was excellent. The assistant gunner instantly brought the linstock down towards the touch-hole in a smooth arc. Merewether's heart leapt into his throat, he did not have time even to fall away from the muzzle so unexpected was the command. The officer had looked right past him twice, never seeing him until after he had given the command to fire. His face now was contorted, mouth opening in consternation, but it was too late to countermand the order.

Osborne's movement was deceptively deliberate. The gloved hand reached out to cover the touch-hole at the last possible instant, and the glowing coal on the slow match broke and scattered in sparks as it met the heavy leather. The captain recovered his composure enough to shout another command just as the beat of hooves echoed across the field. Marlowe and Colonel Alverado reined their sweating horses back on their haunches and leaped to the turf. Merewether was completely spent, but he forced himself to move deliberately from in front of the gun. Osborne was staring at him with a crooked grin on his face.

"We can call it quits now, Cap'n," he said in a conversational tone. "Tit for tat, you saved my life, and me yours!" Even in the throes of reaction to his escape from sudden death, the comment startled Merewether.

"I saved yours?" What was the man talking about? He had done his honest best before the Court of Inquiry at Bombay to convict Osborne, and then in *Pitt* to hang him.

"By rigging that lashup over the side in *Pitt.* You didn't exactly plan it to come out that way, but I'm still beholden to you for the favor." The hand in the leather glove remained clamped over the touch-hole, though the slow match in the linstock was now extinguished. Osborne lifted his hand, looked casually at the scorched spot on the glove, then up again at Merewether, executed an elaborate salute, and stepped back to stand at ease staring out at the new parley commencing in the centre of the field. It was only a moment later that Drury's coach came up at a gallop to disgorge the Admiral, the Governor and Father Roderigo.

"It's not that important," Roberts finally conceded after a quarter of an hour of strenuous discussion, heavily laced with references to "British Honor" between the Governor, Drury, Colonel Alverado and the Supra Cargo. La Monte Fort would remain in Portuguese hands.

Roberts was looking shaken for once, no longer angry and arrogant. The confrontation had come within a hair of spilling gallons of blood, not to mention the death of a senior Company naval officer.

". . . though I reserve the right to renew my demands to occupy the fort if the situation appears to justify it," Roberts tossed over his shoulder as the meeting adjourned. Colonel Alverado spoke up.

"I would be honored if you gentlemen will join me for some refreshments," translated the padre. "It has been a long and exhausting day, and my quarters are convenient." They were less than two hundred yards away on the bench below the fort to landward and the invitation was attractive. The Governor made a reply.

"I must regret, Colonel. I have issued a call for my senate to convene within the hour to receive a report of the day's events."

"I also must regret," said Drury formally. Hell, there was no reason for him to hang back, Merewether decided. The prospect of drink and provender after such a day was irresistible.

"I accept with much pleasure," he told the Commandant. "That is unless you have other duties for me, sir," he said to Drury a little anxiously. He could already taste the gin and lemon, the occupation was complete, Roberts was marching his force down the switch-back road in retreat and the triumphant Portuguese captain had strutted back to the fort.

"Quite all right, Merewether. I am current with the situation. Report to me in *Russel* by ten, ante meridian, tomorrow as to any developments overnight."

Merewether saw the Governor and Drury to their coach, and remounted his horse to ride with Alverado and Marlowe the short distance around the slope of the hill to the house. "If you don't mind, I shall freshen up and get out of these boots . . ." Sangh served as boot-jack for him. By the time he went through the covered walkway with Marlowe to be admitted by the Commandant's orderly, he had consumed three tots of gin and was beginning to feel human again.

The only boat at the landing was a launch from one of the transports which had just discharged round shot for the field guns. The coxswain was surly and reluctant, and the ache behind his eyes did not improve Merewether's patience. He bullied the man into going a mile out of his way to take him to *Russel.* Drury was in conference and it was nearly an hour of stumping about the deck seeing how the Royal Navy did things in a seventy-four-gun ship of the line before the flag lieutenant sought him out. He thus had full opportunity while he waited to meditate on his recent conduct.

The events of the early evening as Colonel Alverado's guest were a bit hazy. Merewether certainly had drunk too much in reaction to the horrendous confrontation of the late afternoon. Senhora Alverado, assisted by a little daughter about the age of Marlowe, and Creusa Hale, was a gracious hostess. Chinese servants glided in and out to serve the dinner with no interruption of the conversation. The Commandant with his limited English had little to say, but the two women sparkled, and Merewether had soon found himself at ease. He took only two more glasses before the repast, but bumpers of heady wine accompanied each course, and he concluded again that he had little tolerance for the produce of the grape.

"I thought I should die when I saw you walk up to the muzzle of that gun," said Creusa in a break in the chit-chat.

"I almost did." Merewether tried to keep his tone light, but the episode still sent chills up his spine. It was difficult now to justify the motives that had appeared logical at the time. "That captain just never saw me until he gave order to fire . . ."

"They tell me the gunner saved you by clapping his hand over the touch-hole . . ."

"He did." Ordinarily Merewether would not have elaborated, but the wine had loosened his tongue. "And I have no real explanation for his action. You know he was condemned to hang at Bombay last winter for mutiny in my ship . . ." Creusa cried out for attention, then translated the account of the inexplicable escape from the scaffold almost simultaneously for the benefit of the Commandant. ". . . and then he said it was 'tit for tat' and that he was 'beholden' to me for rigging the gallows out over the side. I heard that he had been an acrobat with the fairs in England before he went to sea . . ." he said in conclusion. Alverado looked at him and spoke briefly.

"Do you want him back to carry out the sentence?" translated Creusa.

Merewether hesitated a moment. The man had made a fool of him, had created a legend that would live in Marine fo'castles for generations as the man who cheated the hangman. He had no possible doubt of his guilt as the leader of the mutiny. But there was rough justice in what Osborne had said to him. Tit for tat. Quits now.

The Marine accounted him dead, and how he had survived was still beyond comprehension. He reached a decision: Taking him back to Bombay to be hanged by the neck until he was dead, dead, dead in the language of the President of the Court of Inquiry would serve little purpose now, it would never destroy the legend of his escape, and was no more than blooded revenge. Besides, Merewether was "beholden" himself.

"No," he said, conscious that he might well be accounted guilty of compounding a felony by thus obstructing justice. "Live and let live . . ."

The dinner had spun out in leisurely colonial fashion over several hours, Merewether and Creusa on one side, Marlowe and the daughter across, and Colonel and Senhora Alverado at either end of the table. At this close range he found himself covertly observing the woman in detail, conscious of the scent she wore, the smooth skin of face and shoulders, the off-hand display of cleavage, and the dark beauty of eyes and hair in the candlelight. Her mood was entirely different from the other two occasions, not sulky, demanding or reckless as she had been at Bombay, nor despondent and self-pitying as she had been the other night. The conversation was inconsequential, undemanding, a nod of assent, a chuckle of appreciation sufficed to keep up his end as she leaned towards him to underline the point of her vignette, eyes sparkling up into his. She drank the wine with each course, but sparingly, and it seemed only to increase her wit. Merewether found himself falling under the spell of this charmer as the wine added to the gin dissolved his inhibitions. He wondered that he had failed to discern Creusa's quality on two previous occasions.

After dinner, the Commandant invited Marlowe and Merewether to join him in his study, offered them long black cigars, and then lighted one for himself. Merewether only pretended to smoke — he had no taste for tobacco — and then they rejoined the ladies. Marlowe's eyes had grown heavy in spite of the proximity of an English-speaking girl his own age, and when her mother signaled it was time she retired, Merewether seized the opportunity to call the evening quits as well.

"I'm really most obliged," he told the Colonel and Senhora Alverado. "It has been a delightful interlude, and very welcome to two officers after a hard day in the field . . ."

They were ready enough to end the evening, and after only the politest of protestations, Merewether and Marlowe had bowed themselves out. The orderly was in the hallway holding the door opening on the walkway for them with a lamp to light their steps. He was halfway across to the cottage just passing the vine-covered summerhouse when he heard the call. "Oh, Captain!"

"Go ahead, Marlowe," he said brusquely. "I'll see what she wants." But his heart began to thump as he turned back towards Creusa.

He could only conclude in the sober light of day that he had been entirely mad, the wine coursing in his veins, nine months of abstinence overwhelming his scruples with never a thought of Caroline. Creusa guided him into the darkness of the summerhouse and was in his arms the next instant, but broke off the kiss after a moment and leaned back to look at him in the faint moonlight that penetrated the pergola.

"It was fated, Captain, from the first night we met . . ."

He did not dispute her, and pressed on, rough and precipitate, but there was no complaint. The fires were only momentarily quenched, and he soon sought her out again. She had matched his ardor until they crept apart as the eastern sky was beginning to grow light enough to reveal the vaulted roof above them.

Now the matter was on his conscience, but it did not weigh nearly so heavily as he had feared it would. The vision of Caroline had grown faint and distant, as though she were someone in a former life whom he had once cherished but had little cause to remember now. Merewether already anticipated the assignation Creusa had promised for this night, in a real bed instead of uncomfortably disheveled on cushions spread in a summerhouse, though he had little minded at the time. Even now, he felt a reckless disregard of consequences to career and marriage and a lunatic infatuation with the beauty combined with passion consummate the woman possessed.

What had happened to the sturdy conscience that had troubled him last year on Mauritius in his dalliance with Eleanora even before he was wed? He made an effort to rationalize his conduct, but could not keep his thoughts on the matter as they veered unbidden to Creusa. The woman had cast a spell on him, made him mad, entirely aflame with lust, impatient now of the tedious hours that must crawl by before his rendezvous.

The flag lieutenant snatched him out of his reverie. "Captain Merewether, the Admiral will see you now." He met Roberts and Pattie coming out of the flag cabin and bowed formally as they passed.

Tulsi Bai sat in her chair by the window watching the shadows of the trees shorten as the sun approached meridian. She was impatient for the return of Pattie. He had gone with Roberts almost four hours ago to call on Admiral Drury again with their newest scheme to consolidate control of Macao and suppress the illicit trade in opium that had developed here this past year. The judge already knew of the proposal, her note had been delivered by the time the Supra Cargoes took boat for *Russel.* She thought for a moment of Pattie, a magnificent bed-mate, but a man of impulse, often erratic and illogical in his conclusions, if obstinate in pursuing a course once determined. Somehow he and Roberts had received intelligence last night of the expected arrival of another shipment of northern opium, and after several discussions had settled on their scheme to demand that Drury dispatch that Company cruiser out there to intercept the ship. As an afterthought they had concluded that Merewether should be ordered in command of the expedition, thus ridding themselves of the Governor-General's observer ashore for this critical period.

Madame Bai entirely disapproved of the move, had tried to head it off, but the judge had anticipated the idea, the opium would be trans-shipped to a small junk in a lonely anchorage off the Ladrone Islands in the mouth of the Canton River before the Marine cruiser could get to sea, provided Drury favored the proposition. She saw the carriage approaching.

"No," said Pattie in a downcast tone. "That pompous popinjay says he exercises only military command in his squadron over that Company cruiser, and has no power to order it to other duty. He did say he would submit the matter to Merewether . . ." He threw up his hands in resignation, dark eyes flashing. "Except for his orders from the Governor-General, I'd send the insolent bastard out or see him broke and cashiered!" It was good news to Tulsi, but she dissembled and moved to embrace Pattie with ardor.

"Not fatal," she said lightly. "And now, siesta?"

Drury was behind his desk wearing a somewhat bemused expression. He waved Merewether to a chair, then sat silent a moment staring past him at the door before he spoke in a tone of resignation.

"I am a patient man but in the thirty-odd years that I have served His Majesty I do not recall encountering two more exasperating men . . ." He looked back at Merewether, rolled his eyes to the overhead, then back down to his desk. ". . . Oh, here is a communication for you — came over from *Comet* just an hour ago." It was a slender oilskin-wrapped packet superscribed, "To Captain Percival Merewether, Hon. Co's Marine. Private and Confidential." Merewether took it gingerly, reluctant to slit the wrapper, fearful that its contents might somehow endanger the rendezvous Creusa had promised for this evening. "Go on, open it while I order in some coffee . . ."

The message was terse in the fine handwriting of Dawson:

> Imperative you join me in Canton. The bearer of this note will bring you back. S/Dawson.

God damn! His worst fears realized, the dalliance with Creusa gone glimmering. His expression must have betrayed his emotions.

"Bad news?" Drury was looking at him with concern.

Merewether tried to analyze his emotions, then felt a sudden cross-grained sense of relief flood through him. Fate in the guise of Dawson had intervened to rescue him from his folly and further callous betrayal of Caroline. A moment more, and he was by no means certain that he welcomed the intrusion in his affairs with the memory of Creusa so fresh and vivid. Oh, well, no help for it. "I have no intimation of his motive," he said, handing the note over to Drury.

"Nor I," said Drury after a swift perusal. "And now, back to the reason I requested your presence this morning. Are there any problems with the occupation?"

"No, sir. I called around this morning at each garrison and found all quiet. Oh, there'd been a fist fight or so and bloody noses, but quickly broken up. The Portuguese seem to have accepted the situation with good grace." Merewether wondered what Roberts and Pattie had demanded of the Admiral, but surmised he would learn soon enough.

"Very good. Now, I conceive that under our respective orders I exercise military command over your cruiser as a part of my squadron in any action with the enemy, but I doubt my authority over you or *Comet* in Company affairs." What the hell? Drury continued in his unhurried didactic periods. "I therefore informed those two precious gentlemen that I should submit their demands to you for decision." This was a twist that should give the Supra Cargoes pause, Merewether thought maliciously, since Drury had given them nearly everything they desired thus far, already savoring the curt denial. "In a nutshell they desire to dispatch you and your ship to intercept an expected cargo of opium in — I am not familiar with the term - "a country ship" called the *Ganges Pilot.*"

Comprehension flooded into Merewether's head. Even in undisputed command of Macao, Roberts and Pattie possessed no control of the sea. Unless intercepted before it could be trans-shipped, the contraband would simply disappear up one of the creeks to reappear in competition with the product being imported by Baring and Company. He had the imperative summons from Dawson to Canton, undoubtedly some development in his primary mission out here, but it was also the mission of the Marine to serve the Company and *Comet* was for the time idle. It galled him to accede to the arrogant demand of the Supra Cargoes with their motive, but the laws both of China and the Company proscribed the importation of the drug. He made a reluctant decision.

"I cannot go myself, but if you can spare her I'll send MacRae in *Comet* to cruise off the Ladrones. I must respond to this summons to Canton."

"You'll violate the laws of China again?" demanded Drury in amazement. "After you were court-martialed for the same offence?"

"I must trust Dawson. He would not call for me unless the matter is of importance to the Company or Crown."

"Very well. But what of my liaison ashore?"

"Mister Marlowe can observe and report activities as well as I."

"Good lord! a stripling assuming the duties of a captain! I never heard the like. But it is your funeral," Drury added. "And you may be excused to make your arrangements."

Merewether was on deck before the image of Creusa appeared in his mind, already a bit less vivid than it had been an hour ago. Was he beginning to exorcise the infatuation that had possessed him?

There was time enough for contemplation during the long night watches as the boat worked its way towards Canton, now sliding through tortuous channels, then again traversing open water, skirting whole cities of boat dwellers where the babel of voices and flicker of lights revealed the life that continued on the river at any hour. Merewether tried to make himself comfortable in the matting shelter that protected him from the dew now glistening on the gunwales in the moonlight. It had been a hectic afternoon of preparation: orders to write for MacRae, his travelling kit to be retrieved from the guest house ashore, Marlowe instructed in his new responsibilities, and then half an hour as a Chinese servant stained his hands and face, set a black wig on his head and then drew the semblance of a Mongol fold on his eyelids.

"Not necessary to be perfect," said the laconic Fong. "Only enough to pass."

He had found Wong's cousin lounging on the quarterdeck of *Cornet* as he came back aboard with his kit, and he hastened to greet the young man he had brought back to Canton as a hostage two years ago.

"I know nothing, sah. My cousin Wong only sent me to fetch you." His English was better; probably Dawson had continued his instruction.

The journey ashore had inspired palpitations. He was under the necessity of regretting Creusa's invitation for the evening — dare he risk an hour or so now in her embrace? He dreaded the encounter, but it did not materialize. The Commandant's orderly had indicated in sign language amplified by voluble gibberish that she was absent, and Merewether was reduced to leaving a note commencing, "My love . . ." Now as the hands poled this little craft through the shallows his thoughts were not of the unknown crisis that compelled his presence in Canton, but of that ardent nymph he had bedded last night. Even now he trembled with frustration and cursed the circumstance that denied him her charms. Except for this explicit summons to duty, he should be in the very lists of love ready for the hot encounter. He moved uncomfortably to ease the pressure, and tried to divert his thoughts from this madness, falling into an uneasy series of dozes that lasted until daylight.

It was mid-morning when the boat finally came to the same landing where he had disembarked Gunny and his marines two years ago to serve as the honor guard in the triumphant return of Wong and Fong to the home of their ancestors. He climbed out stiffly, face averted, self-conscious in the blue Chinese garments, and at Fong's invitation entered the sedan chair that awaited them. There were no fanfares of bugles or ruffles of drums this time and they passed without remark through the narrow streets to the gates of the house of the Mandarin.

Wong and Dawson were in the big room where Merewether had once made his request to the old Mandarin to intervene with the Hoppo and gain Grand Chop. The elaborate lacquered desk of the scholar still stood in the corner as he remembered it, but Wong sat in the place of his grandfather. Dawson greeted him cordially, and Wong stood to incline his head with a little smile in response to Merewether's bow.

"I am sorry, Mister Wong, to hear of the death of your grandfather. He was a scholar of great distinction who did me a most important service . . ." This was wasting time, but he felt compelled to honor the amenities. "And my congratulations on your elevation in rank." His regret was genuine, as was his pleasure in the fact that Wong was now the Mandarin of Canton, though of the old Chinese Dynasty with little real power under the Manchus. He was conscious of the fact that Fong had slipped out, leaving him alone with Dawson and Wong.

He took the opportunity to examine the young man. Always assured, Wong had matured into a man of authoritarian aspect; the face was composed in harder lines than Merewether remembered, and he carried himself in an attitude of aloof dignity at variance with his manner of two years before. But the mantle of authority assuredly became him.

Dawson cleared his throat.

"Captain, since last I saw you those few days ago, the situation has altered drastically . . ."

"Yes, Roberts and Pattie hold Macao . . ."

"All to the good, I think now, as Wong will shortly explain to you." The little schoolmaster turned his nearsighted gaze to the Mandarin.

"Captain, you may have small interest in the politics of China, but I find in this situation an opportunity sent by heaven to further my own humble affairs." The man's English was much more precise, the vocabulary greater, evidence of practice and study. "I covet the post of Viceroy of Canton, now held by the corrupt Manchu, the Mandarin Vu!" He paused self-consciously. "Since last I saw you, I have taken a bride."

"Why, congratulations, and so have I!" Wong bobbed his head with a brief smile.

"She is a niece of the Emperor . . . My grandfather was a mandarin of the old order of China, conquered more than a hundred and sixty years ago by the barbarians out of the west, but he was very wise. 'If you cannot master the upstarts,' he told me, 'then mate with them. Their women are comely enough!' I followed his advice, and have no complaints."

This was an interesting commentary. Wong now possessed ties of kinship by marriage with the Emperor, as did the Viceroy and Hoppo presumably by blood, however distantly removed.

"Last spring, the Viceroy's admiral met the flotilla of Madame Ching and was most ignominiously defeated. In his shame, he died by his own hand . . ."

"Who is Madame Ching?" Merewether demanded.

"The widow of the pirate, Ching, the most bloodthirsty as well as able commander those rogues have ever had. He was killed two years ago, and she assumed command. She is as brave, ruthless and able as he, and has raided dozens of villages and taken scores of ships since his death. When she defeated the Viceroy's fleet, there was a dead calm and she sent her men over the side to swim and board our ships!" Wong shook his head in recollection of the disgrace to the navy of Imperial China, then looked directly into Merewether's eyes. "Two days ago I received the news I had expected. The Emperor in his wisdom and in recognition of our new kinship has commissioned me Admiral of the Canton Fleet!"

"Well, congratulations again." Wong appeared not to have heard the compliment, now looking down at the surface of the desk.

"The Viceroy was furious, the appointment in years past had been his. He already seeks to undermine me with my subordinates, and yesterday summoned me into his presence. He seeks to destroy me by ordering an impossible mission."

"How?" demanded Merewether, already divining the answer.

"Why, to destroy Madame Ching, of course. He directed me to set sail at dawn tomorrow, and not to return until I had done so. That is why I asked you to come to Canton. I request that you become my Captain of the Fleet during this operation!"

Merewether sat silent, looking at his fingernails while he digested the ramifications of this remarkable proposal. In the past nineteen years as man and boy in the service of the Company and its Marine, he had experienced many difficulties and some perilous assignments. But never had he dreamed that he would be requested to take command of a squadron in the Imperial Navy of China. The Royal Navy and Marine officers entertained nothing but contempt for the Chinese Navy. China was not a seafaring nation, and its war junks were clumsy, unhandy craft. Still, the pirate vessels would be no better, and it might be possible, by employing the tactics developed by a succession of British flag officers over these last three hundred years, to achieve success against them. It depended on whether those Chinese officers and seamen possessed the will to fight. Resolute men in inferior ships had often enough overcome better equipped and armed forces. He was not yet ready to make a decision as he became aware that Wong was speaking again.

"I told you at the outset of this discussion that I coveted the post of Viceroy of Canton. I have set in motion a scheme that should secure it for me." Wong's black eves glittered. "Vu fears to inform the Emperor of the British landings at Macao lest he be ordered to expel the English and lose his revenues. I have sent the news right by him to the Emperor by relays of Mongol horsemen." Merewether recalled Drury's rhetorical question put to Roberts in his first interview with the Supra Cargoes. "Is the Viceroy the only eyes or ears the Emperor possesses in Canton?" Not when it suited Wong's purposes to lend his own! He became aware that Wong was still speaking. "But I require the time for the message to reach the Emperor and for him to act upon it, and the Viceroy may destroy me in the interval . . ."

Merewether admired Wong's spirit. The Viceroy had undertaken to bully the wrong man. Wong evidently felt that he could take care of himself in the political situation, but he required technical assistance to perform his naval duties, and for the nonce was yet under the dominion of the Mandarin Vu with "do or be damned" orders to execute at his peril. This man had done him a favor two years ago, and there was no pressing need for his services at Macao, though he winced at the recollection of the entertainments he was missing with Creusa. He was about to voice his acceptance when Dawson spoke.

"And, of course, Captain, with Wong as Viceroy, the Company will have a friend at court . . ." There was even *a quid pro quo,* the profitable China trade tottered on the brink of disaster, lacking only a stroke of the Emperor's brush to push it into bankruptcy.

". . . and you will receive one-eighth of the prize money as well. . ."

"I have received instruction in the martial arts," said Wong anxiously. "And I have made three voyages as supercargo in our family's ships, but I lack experience in the art of making war at sea . . ."

"I accept," Merewether said at last. "Not for the prize money alone, though it would be most welcome to a man with a new son, but for Mister Wong and the Company. And now, may I see this squadron of yours while there is yet daylight?"

He wiped the sweat from his eyes, undid the tie strings and held the blue coat open to the fresh breeze, savoring the cooling effect on his overheated torso. His own brown hair was flying in the wind (he had abandoned the black wig the first day) and by now every seaman in the fleet must be aware that a round eye was in command of the operation. Wong, Dawson and Fong were just concluding the final phase of instruction to the commanders of the other thirteen ships lying hove to in a jumbled mass here in the approaches to the Pearl Estuary. With some four hours of daylight remaining. Merewether decided he would get the squadron underway eastward as soon as those captains regain their war junks. There should be time before dark to try out the response to the simplified direct reading signals he had devised and conduct a brief exercise in naval discipline. He refastened the jacket and walked unobtrusively forward on the poop of this wallowing war junk as Wong and Fong saw the captains over the side to rejoin their ships.

It had been a hectic three days. Out of nearly eighty war junks based on Canton, only fourteen were in a reasonable state of readiness for sea. He had cannibalized the balance of the fleet to cram these fourteen ships with some four thousand men, and all the arms they would carry. The Chinese possessed no standard system of signals to govern movements at sea, and Dawson had recruited a hundred seamstresses to run up overnight fourteen sets of direct reading arbitrary signal flags, including a Bombay Marine ensign. They had managed to get the flotilla underway just after daylight and move down the narrow channel into the open reaches of the Canton River. Once out of sight of land, they hove to and convened aboard the flagship a school of intensive instruction in naval science and tactics for the officers of the fleet. Merewether could only oversee the operation, but Wong, Dawson and Fong were articulate and forceful teachers, demonstrating turn and flank movements in response to the signal hoists with chips of wood laid out on the hatch amidships. There were gunnery drills, boarding parties were organized and rehearsed, and small arms target practice held. The second and third days, Merewether, Wong, Dawson and Fong visited every ship in the squadron to observe, criticize and correct the drills conducted by its own officers.

"God only knows how they will react in battle," Merewether had told Wong as they returned to the flagship. "But they have been exposed, certainly, to all of the art I know." There was more than just the language barrier to deal with. All but two of the captains were illiterate, unable to read the meaning of the flaghoists painstakingly drawn on rice paper opposite their definitions by Dawson, and then pasted on boards. Nine scholars had been discovered among four thousand seamen and posted to each ship, with Dawson and Fong going into the other two to interpret the signals for the commanders, and surely some of the brighter ones would soon memorize the meanings.

Now, with the conclusion of this last session of encouragement and inspiration to valor, Merewether felt that he had done as much as he could on this short notice. True proficiency would only come with the repetition of one weary drill after another, but if he could communicate with his fleet and the ships obey his signals, half the battle would be won. He decided to put the matter to its first trial.

"I suggest, Admiral, that you signal your command to get underway, course east, line ahead."

Wong consulted his table of signals then barked out an order to the petty officer who had been designated as signalman. There were some false moves, mistakes, but finally the hoists were flying, and other bits of color blossoming on the halyards of the other war junks.

"Execute!" The hoists came down, the huge slatting sails were sheeted home, and the wallow of the junk became more purposeful as she picked up way towards the east. Merewether watched anxiously as the other vessels began to fall in astern in a passable line. The intervals between ships were ragged, but he would not confuse the commanders as yet with admonitions to close up. By sunset, he had exercised the squadron with nearly every signal in the book with the exception of "Engage the enemy".

"I believe they are getting the idea, Admiral," he told Wong as they dined on a delicious mixture of pork, vegetables and bamboo shoots. "By morning, we should be southwest of the Ladrones, and that is where your last intelligence puts Madame Ching. Time enough then to consider our next course."

"Already I feel more confident, Captain. I begin to see the logic behind your tactics."

At dawn, the Ladrones were a blue smudge on the northeastern horizon. Merewether came yawning on deck, a cup of tea in hand, to find Wong anxiously searching that sector with his long glass.

"I thought I saw a sail to the east a moment ago, but I cannot find it now." Merewether wondered a moment as to the whereabouts of MacRae and *Comet.* They should be in this vicinity cruising across the approaches to Canton and Macao in search of that putative opium smuggler.

"I think, Admiral, that we may as well change course to east-northeast to weather those Islands. I lack the local knowledge to try to pass between them." He looked astern to see that the line ahead had survived the hours of darkness in reasonably good order. There were only two stragglers, and they were steering now to rejoin the formation.

The signal was soon executed, and Merewether watched to see if the lessons of the past three days had outlasted the night. The flagship made its turn and steadied on the new heading. The next ship in line held on to follow suit at the same point in the water just vacated. He breathed a sigh of relief: just one junk made a false move, and it came back quickly into position. He felt a flush of pride in his force. Now if they could only find Madame Ching, and if these buggers would fight, Wong had a chance of accomplishing his mission!

The hail from the seaman perched precariously at the masthead was unintelligible to Merewether, but Wong responded with vigor. He pointed ahead.

"Two European ships, Captain, one sailing about west and the other north. Each have two masts." Another hail floated down. "And a small junk about due north of us." That might be a picket for Madame Ching, but Merewether wished he had more information as to the European ships — one might well be *Comet.* He looked up to the masthead, and decided not. Just hold on, and they should be visible to the deck shortly.

The moment her topsails became visible, he was certain. It was another few minutes before he could make out the brig. Possibly MacRae was about to make the interception, and he silently wished him luck. He turned his attention to the small junk sailing east, but could make nothing of her. It was another ten minutes before the masthead sang out again.

"Many sails — junks — bearing north-northwest," translated Wong. "Course appears to be about east." Merewether felt a thrill of anticipation. It was unlikely to be an honest convoy so close to the Ladrones.

Merewether gauged the bearing and relative movement with his eye. If he came around to about north-northeast, he should be able to make the interception. The speeds of the two forces must be about equal. He made the suggestion to Wong to change course, then looked back to see *Comet* and the brig both come to the wind. A cloud of gunsmoke was drifting downwind from *Comet;* she must have fired her broadside to stop her prey. He shifted attention to the pirate flotilla, still pressing on in line abreast as though it were intent on reaching the two European ships, apparently oblivious to the approach of the Emperor's fleet. He tried to put himself in the shoes of Madame Ching, to fathom her strategy and tactics. First, she obviously had no fear of the Chinese Navy, having dealt with it so decisively in the past. Second, she intended to try to take those two prizes hove to over there, probably unaware that one was a Marine cruiser. Third, if the fleet came close enough to be a nuisance, she would simply execute a flank movement, square off for the wind, and sail northwardly with little chance of being brought to action. How, then, to counter this fluid situation?

The shape of the brig altered, she was paying off and heading southeast. He saw smoke erupt bow and stern from *Comet* and then the splashes in the van of the pirates. MacRae was evidently warning them off, but they sailed on. With a ship as fast, handy and heavily armed as *Comet,* Merewether had no compunction in ordering her to engage the enemy; MacRae would make the most of her speed and firepower. But even as he thought of the matter, he saw her sails fill, and she followed the brig southeastwardly. With his mission completed, MacRae did not intend to tempt fate.

"Signals, Mister Wong. 'To Number thirty one: Engage the enemy', and hoist the Marine ensign!"

In this first week of October, a cold steady rain slanted out of the night to splatter remorselessly across the deck. Captain Ian MacRae huddled in his dripping oilskins perched against the cabin skylight, arms folded across his chest for warmth, back to the chill breeze. It was still out of the southwest, but the monsoon would reverse its direction before many more days, and the weather already was becoming unsettled in anticipation. *Comet* was hove to, only two scraps of steadying sail hoisted, rising and falling rhythmically as the long rollers passed under her keel. He had not been able to get a sight today, but dead reckoning put the ship some twenty miles south of the group of tiny islands that lay in the centre of the Pearl Estuary and bore the name Ladrones in recognition of their age-old use as a haven for pirates.

"God, what a night!" The cheerful voice of Watt, the passed midshipman who had the watch, was pitched high enough to carry over the drumbeat of rain on deck, the creak of rigging and clatter of blocks, and the sigh of the wind through the shrouds. He was near twenty, a red-haired raw-boned Scot who had come late to the Marine as a volunteer but had quickly proved his worth. He was awaiting the next opening in the lieutenant's list, and in MacRae's critical judgment was entirely qualified for the commission. MacRae only grunted at the comment — no reply was expected — and decided to turn in. He could trust Watt to keep an eye on things. He was halfway to the companion when the hail came thinly down from the main crosstrees.

"Deck there! Light on the sta'b'rd quarter." MacRae checked his stride and looked aft. Nothing visible, of course, from the deck. His only real concern was whether the light was on a vessel, or the remote possibility that it was on an islet. Watt needed no prompting. He swung into the rigging and disappeared aloft. It was only a moment before his hail floated down.

"It's afloat, Captain!" MacRae resumed his interrupted journey to hang the dripping oilskins on pegs in the passage and enter his cabin.

A wild-goose chase in truth, he told himself, as he poured a dram designed to relieve the chill in his bones, and loaded his pipe. He watched the blue smoke eddy about the swinging lamp, then gave thought to his present mission. Merewether had expressed small hope of success. There was not even a reliable description of the vessel they sought other than it was two-masted and thought to bear the name *Ganges Pilot.* Whether brig, snow, schooner, brigantine or ketch, no one knew, but he would cruise out here astride the sea lanes to Macao for a few days in the forlorn hope that he might encounter such a vessel.

Now warm and relaxed, MacRae's thoughts turned again to Merewether and the long voyage that had brought them back to China. In the close confines of the ship, the man had appeared entirely his old self; the deep personality shift that had afflicted him after the action at Aden last summer vanished as suddenly as it had descended. Possibly it was no more than an aberration brought on by the enormous stresses of the chase and the bitter battle that ensued. But MacRae's tidy Scots mind still sought some logical explanation — would not accept the theory of a mental breakdown, temporary or otherwise, that Buttram had tentatively advanced over a bottle at Bombay. He would never know the truth, he decided, and the captain certainly had worn his normal countenance this commission in spite of the vexatious conduct of those gentlemen of the Select Committee.

His thoughts veered to his own situation, now nearly ten years of commissioned service in the Marine, and half a world away from his home in the West Highlands just south of Mallaig. He had never been close to his stepmother, but he could trust her to take not a groat more than her dower rights in the estate, skimpy as was the produce scratched out of the soil and the sheep pastured on the barren hillsides to be turned into wool, carded, dyed, spun and finally woven into sturdy tweed by the deft fingers of the women. Six struggling crofters occupied his lands, but two of them had been burned out last year and he had spent most of his liquid capital in rebuilding the cottages. It would be a long time returning since the families had lost their looms, tools and nearly everything else short of the clothing on their backs. He felt an unaccustomed twinge of nostalgia for the heather-clad hills that ran down to the rocky shore and the little cove only large enough to accommodate half a dozen trawlers, but his father's lifetime concern.

His father had been a rigid, precise man, taking pride in his courtesy title of "The Laird", bestowed in recognition of his ownership of nearly a square mile of bleak hills and plunging gulches that supported a sparse population of red deer and coneys in addition to the six tenants. He had quarreled at one time or another with each of them, and all of his neighbors. For more than forty years he had maintained a bitter but correctly polite feud with The MacGregor whose lands adjoined his to the east.

As an only child, and always small in stature, MacRae had never considered farming. He had early found his father's ways repressive, and even while receiving his limited schooling shipped out in the herring fleet. It was only a step to a berth in Clydeside packet, and having mastered the theory, he was soon sailing as mate. The packet accepted a charter, for Bombay and was wrecked in a typhoon off Ceylon. With another Scot, MacRae had supported himself for two years by diving for the pearl oyster before taking a berth as mate in a country ship. The officer shortage in 'ninety-eight had brought him a commission in the Bombay Marine. Now, at close to forty, and as high, he was sure, as he would ever go in the Company's Navy, he was giving sober thought to his future.

Inclined by nature to misogyny, MacRae had never had more than a passing interest in any woman, few and far between as unattached white females were out here. Occasional access to one or another of the myriad Indian maids of all work ashore at Bombay or Calcutta had sufficed to satisfy his needs. He had as a matter of principle never patronized a prostitute, though there was always *quid pro quo* for the native girl's services. Now, he must give some consideration to marriage if he decided to leave the Marine at the end of his three years' leave with pay to which he would be entitled next year. He thought briefly of Molly MacGregor, daughter of his father's old enemy, still single on his last visit to the Highlands three years ago, tied down to her querulous old father, now crippled by a stroke. They had been children together, she was intelligent, biddable, attractive enough in a fair freckled way. There would be economic advantages too, she was also an only child, and marriage would unite the holdings of MacGregor and MacRae. There might even be time for a child or two. MacRae resolved to call around on Molly when next he visited Scotland.

The clump of feet sounded overhead as the midwatch came on deck to relieve. He blew out the lamp and slid under his seldom-used blanket. Just before he dropped off, he decided to write Molly a letter — no proposal, nothing even implied, only a reminder of his existence — first thing in the morning.

At dawn the source of the light was apparent, a ragged-looking junk of small dimensions, hove to and rocking wildly with slatting sails in the chop some three miles north. MacRae examined it closely through the glass. The seas along this coast were alive with pirates who plundered mostly other Chinese vessels and the villages up the many creeks, but were not averse to taking a lightly armed European ship when the opportunity presented itself. The Viceroy had been unable to deal with them, his admirals had proved themselves singularly inept at finding or bringing to justice these corsairs, and the Empire had been reduced to offers of amnesty to lure them from the seas once they had made their pile.

"He's a wrong 'un I'll wager," said Dillon, racking the glass. "Picket for the rest of his filthy crew, no doubt, but he'll not call them down on the likes of us!" MacRae considered the matter only briefly. *Comet's* identity was apparent from the buff gun ports along her sides even though she wore no colors. Running down on the junk for a closer inspection would avail nothing. He decided to get some sail on and work to the southeast, one direction was as good as another with as uncertain an objective as he had.

"Make sail, Mister Dillon. Course southeast and by east." He went below for his porridge and tea. It was two hours before the hail came.

"Where away?"

"About north, port tack, course west." Watt had the forenoon watch again in regular rotation, the sun was still obscured, but the cloud cover was high, the rain had ceased, and visibility was good. "She's a brig, under all plain sail . . ." MacRae went on deck.

"Stand by to go about." His mind visualized the component of wind and course for an interception. "Port your helm. Your new course is nor' — nor'west. Set flying jib and stays'ls." The big schooner came to the wind, the hands tailing on to the sheets as the main and fore sails swept across the deck to the opposite tack and were trimmed against the breeze. The jib went up in rapid jerks, and *Comet* already bore a bone in her teeth, dipping and swooping across the seas as she commenced the pursuit.

"Deck there. That junk looks like it is trying to cut her off!" MacRae cursed himself silently for his earlier choice of a direction in which to cruise. If the vessel was the picket for a squadron, the pirates stood an excellent chance of snapping up the prize. He could barely make out the peaks of its brown sails above the horizon now squared before the wind. *Comet* must be logging double the speed of the junk, however, and he was sure he could come up with the pair before the brig could be looted. He made a minute course correction, and leaned against the weather bulwarks, arms folded, face impassive, to await the outcome. It was another ten minutes before the hail came down and Watt made his formal inquiry.

"Two — four — no, seven — make it ten sail of junks, bearing about west-nor'west!" MacRae stood erect. "Course about east . . ." The watch below was on deck by now as sightseers, and Watt cast an expectant glance at MacRae. He would hold on a bit longer before sending the hands to quarters, he decided, wishing that the master of that brig over there would only change course.

"Signals!" The duty quartermaster jumped for the flag bag. "Send, 'You are standing into danger', and hoist our colors." It was a direct reading arbitrary signal well known to the merchant navy, but it was yet a great distance to make out the flags and they were blowing right at the brig. In any event, she sailed placidly on towards the wallowing junks now beginning to become visible from the deck as specks on the horizon.

"Masthead makes them fourteen now, sir," reported Watt.

A sudden thought struck MacRae. This was a rendezvous! The brig intended to trans-ship her contraband into that tattered junk over there all unaware of the threat slowly coming over the horizon to the west. She then could sail on into Macao clean while the junk disappeared up one of the creeks to deliver the opium.

MacRae tried to recall what his old acquaintance, Jaimison, first in the Company transport, *Alnick Castle,* had told him over a bottle last week about this particular pirate crew. It was unique, led by a woman, the widow of their former commander, killed in action some two years ago. Ching — that was the name — Madame Ching, according to Jaimison as bloodthirsty, courageous and capable as her deceased husband. She was reputed to control some eighty sail of junks in her flotilla, divided into six squadrons, each commanded by a lieutenant, distinguished by flags of different colors. She was reputed to command the red squadron, and to be lurking in the Ladrones after pillaging a village to the north last month. It was possible that the fourteen ships over there could be honest traders sailing in company for security, but MacRae suddenly knew in his bones that it was Madame Ching about to interfere with his own mission. He must keep his options open, be prepared to rescue an innocent country ship from pirates, or capture her in spite of them.

"Send the hands to quarters! Clear for action, Mister Watts." The Marine bugles and drums sounded out. With nearly every seaman already on deck, the canvas jackets came off the eighteen-pounders in a trice. Tampions were pulled out, and rammers, sponges, buckets of sand, water and smoldering slow match, together with garlands of shot plumped down along the batteries. Gun captains secured the locks over the touch-holes and tested the spark of the flints against their cupped palms. The armory gunner's mate and his strikers filled the racks with pikes and cutlasses. Dillon came aft to report.

"Ship's cleared for action. All stations manned and ready, sir."

MacRae put the glass to his eye. The brig was still sailing on to a point of interception with the junk.

He wondered suddenly how Merewether would have handled this situation. He well understood the Captain's preoccupation with the weather gauge with all its advantages of maneuver — had seen him exploit it to win actions that otherwise might have been lost or been much more costly. He had the weather gauge on the brig, the junk and the squadron. Now, what was his objective? This was more complex than appeared on the surface. His natural instinct was to sail right to the brig, cutting off contact with the junk, and making sure of its capture. But then, what of the squadron? It would take time to put a prize crew aboard, there might be resistance to overcome, and while these details were being resolved he could be overwhelmed by sheer numbers, provided the fourteen junks were pirates.

"Ye canna' make an omelet without cracking eggs," MacRae told himself. Haul down the brig, warn off the junk, and if the pirate squadron came down upon him, he had the speed, maneuverability and fire power to deal with it. Even that fat-bellied brig should have the heels of those clumsy craft. He had no orders to take any action against Chinese pirates, and he was not a volunteer. The junks were now hull-up, lumbering through the swells in a long line abreast, and through the glass he could see that their decks were crowded with men. No honest traders these!

"Sail ho!" What, another? These waters were becoming damned crowded after several days without a sighting.

"On the port quarter, sir," Watt informed him. MacRae picked up the glass. He could see a shimmer of sails in what appeared to be a regular line ahead. Had the Chinese finally adopted the strategies of old England to sail in a disciplined formation? It was hard to believe. “Masthead makes out fourteen sail, sir.”

First things first. MacRae’s mission out here was to intercept and search that brig over there, though he felt some concern at the possibility of being trapped between two pirate fleets. He paused to reassess his position and almost instantly decided that *Comet* was in no danger yet – had the heels of any ship in sight and the eighteen-pounders to make them keep their distance.

“Steady as you go,” he told the expectant Watt, and turned to study the ships on the port quarter again. The flags exhibited were not yellow, green, black, blue or white, the colors of Madame Ching’s other five squadrons, but now looked through the glass suspiciously like the Emperor’s own device. He recalled Lieutenant Jaimison’s account of the crushing defeat suffered only last May by the Viceroy’s forces. With both pirates and Navy becalmed the ferocious woman commander had urged her sailors over the side to swim and board the ships of the Chinese Navy, capturing nearly half of the fleet. The admiral had killed himself in disgrace. MacRae shook his head. His pessimistic Scots nature would hardly accept the fact that allies might be on the horizon. Hold on and find out!

“Brig’s wearing to sta’board! “ Her master had belatedly seen the danger he was standing into and squared off before the wind.

“Change course. Steer north-northeast.” *Comet’s* speed picked up measurably as she sailed a course that would still permit her to interpose between the ragged junk and brig. There was little enough sea room to the northeast. They should be raising the Ladrones any moment now, but there was room for those with local knowledge to pass between those islands.

With *Comet* on her most favorable point of sailing, she was running down her quarry at a great rate now. The junk was less than two miles distant only a point forward off the beam, while the brig was rapidly drawing aft on the starboard bow. Time to warn off the junk!

“Pass the word to Mister Dillon to load the long nine.” There was a buzz of comment and stir of movement along the batteries. Men who had slouched in the shade a moment before stood up to assess the situation for themselves as the crew of the forward pivot gun began the ritual of loading the piece.

"Ready, sir!" Dillon's hail came aft faintly against the wind.

"Your target is the junk. Fire when ready." The platform rotated to port, was wedged in train, and the muzzle rose to maximum elevation. An instant later the spiteful high-pitched report cracked out.

The target was at least half a mile beyond the maximum range of even a long nine, but the round shot fell fortunately, sending up a plume of spray and then skipped like a flat stone flung across a mill pond for three more less spectacular but plainly visible splashes directly in line with the junk. It was only a minute before her silhouette altered as she fled northwestward. MacRae took stock of the situation again. The supposed pirate fleet was plainly visible now almost due west, holding on in a very creditable line abreast, and he could now make out what appeared to be red flags at each peak. Madame Ching in person? He looked back for the other flotilla. It was still in line ahead, steering a course that should intercept the other Chinese squadron not far from his present position. MacRae turned his attention again to the brig. She was almost abeam and in range of the long nine certainly.

"Signal: 'Heave to!' " He waited for some response, but the brig sailed on. He could make out men on her deck, most of them lascars, but at least two were European. It was apparent she would not obey the signal.

"Reload." Watt passed the word to Dillon. He intended to reel in this clumsy country ship now as though it were a salmon hooked in a Highland burn. "Put a shot across her bow!" The pivot rotated, there was an adjustment in elevation, and the report.

The splash was less than half a cable's length ahead of her bow. There was movement on her poop, she had what appeared to be about six-pounders fore and aft, probably mounted on pivots, and then smoke blossomed from both of them. The fall of shot was woefully short, but it was an affront not to be brooked by MacRae.

"Sta'board battery, stand by!" the hands were already ramming home the round shot. "Divide your battery. Forward fire ahead, after section astern." He paused only a second to see if the brig had wavered. It had not, and men were clearing out from in front of both six-pounders, evidence that they were reloaded. "Fire!"

The eighteen-pounders roared out, and the splashes almost under the bowsprit and fantail were impressive. MacRae saw movement on the poop again, the helm went over, and the brig came reluctantly around into the wind. The Ladrones were plainly visible to the north, but he could recall no report to this effect. He looked around the horizon, the pirate squadron was still almost west, closer than he fancied, paying no attention to the ragged junk, now sailing well to the northwest. The Emperor's fleet was coming directly towards him, forereaching a bit on Madame Ching. Both of those Chinese forces would have to wait. His first objective was to take possession of the brig and search her.

"Mister Barger!" The compact little second lieutenant in command of the port battery leaped across the deck to stand in front of MacRae. "You are prizemaster. Take the launch and the full Marine detachment. Get the brig underway immediately, course east. Then examine her papers, cargo manifest, everything, and while you're doing that, have Severn search her for opium. If you find any dip her flag three times . . ." *Comet* was rounding to half a cable's length from the brig and the launch was already being hoisted out. He looked across to see her master, a bulky man at the poop rail staring defiantly across at him. There were only three other white men visible, all clustered on the quarter-deck. While the launch was pulling across, MacRae looked back for the pirates. They were not intimidated by the presence of a Marine cruiser, but pressed steadily on, almost within long gun-shot by now, coming faster than junks should on their present point of sailing. Even stoic MacRae felt a pang of alarm. Best warn them off, he decided.

"Both batteries, load and stand by. Pivots, take aim to sta'board." He looked back to port. Barger was at the gangway in confrontation with the gesticulating captain, the Marines flowing past him on either side, sun glinting on their bayonets, as they drove the hands forward and took possession of the wheel and quarterdeck. All was well, no resistance.

"Pivots, commence fire!"

The splashes were right at the bow of the nearest junk, and MacRae waited a moment for the reaction, trusting Watt to keep him advised of any developments in the brig. But the pirate squadron did not waver at the show of force, it ploughed on relentlessly towards

Comet and the brig. He was going to cut this damn close. If something fouled or gave way now, he was lost.

"Brig's paying off!" It was about as fast as the maneuver could be accomplished in a strange ship, and MacRae made a note to compliment Barger.

"Get underway, course east." The schooner's sails filled and she fell in astern of the brig, the wake beginning to boil out from under her counter.

"Brig's dipping her colors! One — two — three!"

A hit? She carried the contraband. A chance in a thousand of finding an opium smuggler with only the sketchiest of intelligence. But this was somewhat beside the point at this juncture, he stood an excellent chance of losing his prize yet. *Comet* could easily sail away from the junks, but the brig was not so certain. Even now he was beginning to forereach on her, and he gave consideration to reducing sail.

"Signals!" What? Nothing on the brig. Then he saw Watt pointing aft, and whirled to look. The presumed Chinese naval squadron was much closer now, and he could see specks of color near the peak of the foremast with the naked eye that might be a flag hoist. He snatched the glass from the hand of Watt and focused it.

"I don't believe it!" He looked at Watt and saw confirmation on his countenance.

The topmast flag was the ensign of the Bombay Marine, and the flags below spelled out the arbitrary signal, "Engage the enemy!" He took the time to consider the matter. No Chinese admiral had authority under any circumstances to order a Marine cruiser into action. It was almost impossible that any such officer should even know the meaning of the signal. But Merewether had gone off to Canton last week with an urgent summons from that British Intelligence agent sojourning there, and he must be nearly the only person in China who would have the knowledge to employ such a signal. It could be a trick, but MacRae suddenly knew in his bones that Merewether was over there, for what reason he could only conjecture.

"Log the signal, and add the comment, 'By what authority, unknown'," he told Watt. This was an order he desired to obey. It had galled him to give even the appearance of flight from those pirates, but engaging fourteen ships, lightly armed as they possibly were, was not to be undertaken in a reckless spirit. He took the time to reassess the tactical situation, conscious that every eye was fixed upon him.

Two Chinese squadrons, almost equal in force, were approaching one another at approximately right angles, the pirates in line abreast, the navy in line ahead. Madame Ching could at any time turn north and probably avoid action, but with her recent resounding victory over these same ships, she evidenced no intention to do so. The pirates were on a less favorable point of sailing than the Emperor's force, which was now almost before the wind heading for a point of interception that would permit it in effect to "cross the T", engaging each ship in turn with concentrated gunfire. The tactic of itself was corroboration that Merewether must be aboard and in command. MacRae measured the distances with his eye. The line abreast was spaced in intervals of no more than a cable's length between ships. A fast, smartly handled ship might sail right across the face of such a formation, angling northeastward to allow for its speed, throw a broadside into each vessel as it passed, and have time to reload for the next junk. If his gunners made a good practice, he could very well dismast a third of them, and come back on the reciprocal of his course to deal with the survivors. There were risks, of course. He must not permit any pirate to make contact with *Comet* lest she be overwhelmed in a hand to hand combat, but with these eighteen-pounders he should be able to prevent such a catastrophe. He would take the risk.

"Stand by to jibe!" Watt looked at him in surprise, then leaped to reinforce the hands tending sheets. With the tremendous area contained in the main and fore sails, it could be a risky maneuver. He could pull the sticks right out of her in this fresh breeze if something slipped. However the elements of surprise and speed in making his move outweighed in MacRae's mind the danger to the ship. He heard the boatswain shouting admonitions to the men tailing on the lines, saw that they were ready, and gave his command. "Sta'board helm!" The rudder bit, *Comet* began to swing as the hands strained at the sheets holding them taut as the leach began to tremble then hauling in with all their might as the booms went over with a rush and the sails filled with thunderous reports on the port tack. MacRae let out the breath he had been holding, nothing had carried away. "Steady as you go. Course north."

It was only moments before Comet was within effective range of the nearest junk. He could see the eyes painted on her bluff bow, and clumps of blue-clad seamen clustered around the gun on her forecastle. It fired, but he could not make out the fall of shot, about a nine-pounder, he judged. MacRae adjusted his course, watching the relative movement closely. Now!

"Port battery. Stand by!" The guns were already loaded, and the captains were making minute corrections in elevation and train. This was well nigh point-blank range, no excuse for misses. "Commence fire!"

It was a textbook example of the best British naval strategy and tactics. Six eighteen-pound and two nine-pound iron balls crashed the length of the ship. Both masts fell in a welter of brown sail, the seamen vanished from the junk's deck, and the gun on the forecastle pointed skyward. As MacRae had estimated, there was just time before *Comet* crossed the bow of the next ship to reload the battery, and the second broadside roared out to devastate that vessel. By the time he had dealt with the third junk in line, the others had changed course and were fleeing in a disorganized gaggle northward, but *Comet* hunted them down relentlessly. As he had suspected, the pirate junks were lightly armed, many small one- or two-pounder swivels of the sort the Marine called "Coehorns", which had vanished from all but its smallest vessels, and one or two eight-to twelve-pound pieces usually mounted right up in the bows. *Comet* did not escape unscathed, but her damage was minor, and only two men suffered splinter wounds. Three of the northern-most junks escaped, having made their turn early, and MacRae went about to deal with cripples.

As his ship settled on the starboard tack, MacRae saw that there was no need for this: the Chinese Navy was systematically bombarding them, and when resistance ceased, taking possession by boarding. He saw signals on the flag junk again, and Watt read them off as each hoist climbed the mast.

"Disengage." And then, "Carry out previous orders." Finally, "Thank you!"

MacRae found the brig on the horizon to the east, and changed course to come up with her. There might be a long reach south-eastward before he could steer a course for Macao Roads unless the monsoon came in the meantime, but he would bring *Ganges Pilot* safely in as his prize.

"Tell the purser to serve out a double issue of grog, Mister Watt. And if the officers would like a wee drap themselves, they are welcome in the cabin." As he lifted the dram to his lips in a toast to the marksmanship of Lieutenant Dillon, a vagrant thought crossed MacRae's mind. He had not drafted that careful letter to Molly MacGregor.

Merewether lowered himself gingerly into the steaming wooden tub until the water reached his chin, then sat quiet for a few moments feeling the salt sweat and grime that encrusted his body begin to dissolve. Screens shut off this corner of the ground floor of the Mandarin's house to grant him privacy, but a barber with the tools of his trade squatted just outside. He must wash the grease and tangles out of his hair before submitting to the ministrations of the barber, but he was so comfortable just now that he was reluctant to begin.

Three weeks at sea with the Chinese Navy and Admiral Wong had taken its toll, not only in the lack of fresh water in which to bathe, but he had clearly lost weight. Somehow, the delicious concoctions served up by Wong's steward just did not seem to stick to his ribs. Not that there had been time for leisurely formal dining at sea; in any case; the squadron had been almost continuously underway seeking out the six squadrons of that woman, Madame Ching, bringing each to action, then systematically destroying or capturing the pirate junks. With discipline now rigidly enforced by Wong, and an effective, if limited, mastery of British naval strategy and tactics, the Canton fleet had become a force to be reckoned with. Only in that first action south of the Ladrones when Merewether had shamelessly called MacRae and *Comet* down to soften up the enemy had there been European assistance. By the third action, sagacious young Wong had grasped all but the finest points of warfare at sea, and proceeded to exploit all the advantages of the weather gauge. With Merewether hovering discreetly in the background, and with only an occasional prompting, he made his own decisions through the balance of the operation. Only three days ago they had encountered the rag-tag remnants of Madame Ching's once invincible armada off Hong Kong Island to the north, and sent the few survivors in frantic flight towards Formosa. Wong would have pursued them even then, but a courier had come on board the flag junk four hours earlier with momentous tidings above the Emperor's own seal.

"Sir, I am Viceroy of Canton!" Wong's face was creased in his deprecating smile. "The Mandarin Vu, and his Hoppo, have been degraded and removed from office for their failure to resist the British landings and their brazen attempt to deceive the Emperor." He looked back at the column of ships following his flag south before the steady pressure of the northeast monsoon, his eyes leaping from junk to junk to judge the intervals they kept. It was not yet quite a Royal Navy line ahead, but close enough. "By the day after tomorrow I shall take my oath to the Emperor before my ancestors and assume the dominion over Canton. I shall make Fong my Hoppo, and if you would consent, my Admiral of the Fleet . . ."

Another offer of high rank, Merewether thought with wry amusement, remembering that backhanded tender of a supreme command at sea in an Indian Empire ruled by Tipu Sultan almost three years ago in the blinding heat of Vellore. He must be careful not to offend the new Viceroy, but couch his refusal in delicate terms. Already he was seeking the proper words.

"Why, Admiral — more properly, 'Your Excellency' — my warmest congratulations upon a well-deserved promotion. You will rule with wisdom, honor, dignity, justice and compassion in a manner that will exalt your ancestors . . ." Was he laying it on too thick? No, he decided, it was difficult to overdo genuine praise coming from a full heart. ". . . for many years to come. I am most honored and complimented by your offer, but I am already sworn to King and Company."

In less than two hours now, the formal ceremony would commence, to be followed by a lavish entertainment in the Viceroy's palace. Merewether was summoned as a guest of honor, some Chinese order of merit to be bestowed upon him in recognition of his services, so Dawson reported. He would wear the regalia of the order for the occasion, but no other disguise, his Freedom of Canton granted by Wong's grandfather was yet valid. He sighed, ducked his head and began to work the soap into his scalp while sorting out the tangles in his hair. Once the festivities were over, there was nothing to prevent his return to Macao and Creusa. He felt a flush of heat at the thought, rinsed his hair once again, and stood up.

What had possessed the man, Merewether wondered foggily. His head was not exactly splitting, but it was sore enough to cause discomfort this early forenoon of the morning after. The Chinese wines would not of themselves cause such malaise, but Dawson had taken him to his own abode after the festivities and produced a bottle of real London gin to lubricate their discourses into the dawn hours. Only a few minutes ago a courier from the Viceroy had brought his summons, and now Merewether leaned against the rail at the stern of the flag junk clad once more in seaman's blue, wearing the black wig again, anchored in the Canton River below the city. The other ships of the victorious squadron were moored in line abreast stretching to either bank to form a barrier not to be penetrated except by small craft, and effectively denying passage either to the Indiamen moored upstream or the men-o'-war at Macao.

Drury, for some unaccountable purpose of his own, was making his way up the river in his barge, decked out in full dress, less sword. Merewether could only surmise that the officer had formed some intention of opening a parley in an attempt to crack the impasse brought on by the occupation of Macao and the failure to open the trade at Canton. The Supra Cargoes apparently yet persisted in their design to intimidate the Viceroy and Hoppo, though they must be informed by now that the men they had formerly dealt with had been broke and cashiered. Wong would be a different kettle of fish wearing the mantle of authority over this great city, and Merewether almost forgot his distress in anticipation of the resolution of the controversy.

"Sah, the Emperor has issued strict orders that the English are to be expelled," he had told Merewether at the dinner that interposed between the formal ceremony yesterday afternoon, and the entertainment last night. No more than the Company deserved, Merewether thought bitterly, remembering his investment in its soon to be worthless shares. Mayhap he could dispose of them at a discount before the news became current — if he could only get back to Calcutta! "But I know how important the Company is to you, Captain, and I choose to interpret the Emperor's order to apply only to the troops at Macao. Once the British evacuate them, I shall order the trade to be reopened at Canton, though I intend that the Company shall do penance for the sins of these willful men . . ." Merewether's heart had leaped. The Company would not be destroyed after all!

"And how do you intend to communicate these terms?" He thought sourly that Roberts and Pattie had already accomplished their purpose at Macao with MacRae's capture of the consignment of northern opium, and there was little reason now to hold the town.

"I shall summon them before me. The message goes tonight, and I think you may be interested in being present." So, there went another two or three days delay before he could rendezvous with Creusa. But the Company's fortunes were more important than his fleshly gratification.

There came the sound of gongs and drums, and Wong came over the side in formal robes, the Mandarin's ruby gleaming in his cap. The barge, under British colors, was in sight by now half a mile down the river, the oarsmen tricked out in flat straw hats and pale blue jumpers, the Admiral seated stiffly in the stern sheets, his gold lace glittering in the sunlight. To be sure the man had been entirely decent and considerate in his dealings with Merewether, but his vacillation and final yielding to the Select Committee in its every unreasonable demand had precipitated this crisis and brought the Company to the brink of ruin. He felt just enough resentment to move him to give Drury a bit of excitement for his memoirs.

"Your Excellency, would you indulge me by having those guns loaded?" He indicated two coehorns mounted in swivels on either quarter. Wong looked at him with surprise, then clapped his hands and gave the order. It was only a few minutes before the barge was within fifty yards of the junk and still pulling.

"Fire each gun to either side of the boat, but well clear." Wong's face creased in a smile of appreciation before he gave the order.

The effect was entirely gratifying, the almost simultaneous reports preternaturally loud in the still morning air. Every head in the boat snapped around, mouths and eyes wide, and two seamen jumped over the side. The splashes made by a collection of scrap iron and stones at short range were spectacular. Drury sat frozen in place for a moment as the two men overboard were retrieved, then stood a little shakily holding his hands up, palms out in the gesture of peace.

"Ahoy the junk!" he shouted. "I come in peace! Is there any one of you who speaks English?" Merewether made himself inconspicuous among the Chinese officers as Wong stepped forward. The admiral had recovered from his surprise and appeared steady enough now.

"I do. What brings you to the forbidden environs of Canton?"

"I come in peace," repeated Drury. "I desire a parley with the Viceroy . . ."

"I am the Viceroy." Drury looked at Wong with astonishment, then spoke

"I wanted . . ."

"Enough, sah," Wong interposed. "You will bear my summons to the Select Committee to appear, every one of them, before me in my palace tomorrow at noon precisely. You are dismissed!" The admiral looked unbelievingly at Wong, his eyes roving across the assemblage gathered behind him. He started slightly, and his gaze came back to fix on Merewether in the midst of the group before he spoke.

"Very well, Your Excellency, I shall convey your message . . ."

"Not message — summons!" Wong's face was set in hard lines, eyes glittering, his tone authoritarian. He turned and his entourage fell in behind him as he made his way to his barge. Drury remained standing a moment more. It had been a long time since he had been addressed in this cavalier fashion.

He resumed his seat and gave the order to the coxswain. As the hands gave way, he looked back over his shoulder for one last inspection of Merewether.

The heavy gold filigree, set with rubies encircling an enameled device, thumped on his chest as Merewether took his seat beside the Hoppo in the space allotted for senior military and naval officers serving under the Viceroy. Dawson had informed him that by his calculation the Chinese order of chivalry into which he had been inducted the night before last was at least of equal rank with a Knight of the Garter in England, and entitled him to many honors and privileges. Of course, these heathen titles meant nothing, he could not call himself "Sir Percival", but the insignia was a pretty bauble and valuable to boot. The Viceroy, preceded by his herald, made his entrance, and Merewether aped the others in making his obeisance as Wong took his seat in the elaborate chair set on the dais. There were no preliminaries.

"You have violated the territory of the Empire of China, an act of war which has caused our Emperor much distress and inclined him towards retribution," Wong said in a strong voice. The five Supra Cargoes were ranged in a line before the dais, Roberts in the centre, Pattle to his right. The other men must be Branston, Elphingstone and Baring, but Merewether could not distinguish them. The faces were impassive, but from the side he could see Roberts clasping and unclasping his hands behind his back.

"The Emperor accordingly has directed that the English shall be expelled . . ." There was movement all along the line, expressions of incredulity blossomed on the faces of Branston, Elphingstone and Baring, while Roberts and Pattie stared stonily at the Viceroy. Evidently the other three had not been fully informed of the drastic consequences attending the actions taken by them. "When he named me his Viceroy, the Emperor reposed especial trust in me to carry out his mandate in a manner to serve the best interests of China . . ." Wong ticked off his conditions.

First: Evacuation of Macao within three days.

Second: A period of two years of probation during which the Viceroy reserved the right to terminate all treaties and expel the Company.

Third: A surcharge in the nature of a fine upon the duties paid at Canton for a period of two years.

Fourth: Discontinuance of any trade in opium at Canton or Macao.

Merewether saw relief appear on the faces of the Supra Cargoes, and they were dismissed. At least they had escaped the painful duty of informing the Courts of Proprietors and Directors that the Company had lost its trade to China.

"Come," said Fong. "Wong desires to give you farewell before you depart." He led Merewether into the sumptuous private chamber of the Viceroy.

“Was I emphatic enough, Captain?” demanded the Viceroy. Tiny cups of tea and plates of cakes and sweetmeats were already set out.

“Entirely, Your Excellency. You gave those clowns the worst five minutes of their lives!” The informal audience was soon over, and Wong grasped Merewether’s hand in farewell.

“I shall send you back to your ship in the Admiral’s Barge as befits my Captain of the Fleet. My counting house has made an appraisal of your share of the prize money earned in our cruise against Madame Ching and her pirates, and the silver is in chests already loaded. My gratitude, Captain, and farewell!”

It was in the forenoon watch next day when the barge came alongside *Comet,* and the chests were hoisted out to be deposited in MacRae’s strong room. Before they went in, Merewether opened one of them to see the stacks of gleaming taels, there must be close to twenty thousand English pounds here, he estimated with a whistle. It was only fair, he decided, that Comet have a one-sixth share in recognition of its services against the first pirate squadron, but he would deal with that matter later. He had other fish to fry over in Macao. If he called away the gig now, he might intercept Creusa before siesta!

Running wing and wing before the steady pressure of the northeast monsoon, *Comet* was already nearing the approaches to the Strait of Malacca at dusk of the fourth day out of Macao. Merewether came on deck after the leisurely meal with MacRae to stand at the taffrail and enjoy the cooling breeze. He was glad to be quit of China again, though his sojourn there had been immensely profitable and his services to the Mandarin Wong, now Viceroy of Canton, had saved the Company’s trade. But there were other events of which he was not proud. He had violated his vows of a year and a half ago to Caroline, and would have done it again and again except for the fortuitous turn of events. He brushed the matter aside, he could not put the guilt out of his soul, but he might ignore it for a time until he could come to grips with his conscience and settle on the penance he must do.

His thoughts shifted to Drury, that very proper naval officer, who believed that man had no higher calling than to serve as a

King's officer and bore himself accordingly. The admiral had raised no objection to the request to proceed independently to Calcutta, the necessity of making his report to the Governor-General at the earliest possible moment being apparent. Once the order was signed, Drury had leaned back and looked at him quizzically.

"Captain, I'll be honest with you. I entertain some rather dark suspicions as to who may be responsible for giving me the fright of my life at Canton some days ago . . ." Merewether strove to keep his face impassive, remembering the admiral's expression when the charges from the two coehorns plunged into the water close aboard either side of the barge.

"Why . . ." he began tentatively, wondering if a clean breast of the matter was the best way out.

"Never mind. It's just that I saw a Chinese in the group on the junk who bore a scar greatly resembling yours. Of course, I know that you had no motive to take any such reprisal against me, so I gave the credit in my report to that harsh young man who claimed to be the Viceroy, and being fired upon while seeking a parley of peace somewhat enlivens an otherwise dry narrative . . ." Get out on this note, Merewether decided!

"I'm sure you must be correct in your surmise, sir. The new Viceroy, the Mandarin Wong, is a resolute young man of many accomplishments, and quite capable of giving such an order. And now, sir, I propose to get underway at once in the hope of getting well clear of land before dark."

"I wish you good fortune, Captain. Your services have been admirable, and while I could hardly care less about the Company's fortunes, I credit you with preserving for the time its trade to Canton." Admiral Drury had risen and extended his hand in dismissal.

Now with the sun sinking below the horizon and the second dogwatch skylarking on deck in the few minutes left before it relieved the first, a less agreeable recollection came back to haunt him as he saw young Marlowe come up the companion preparatory to assuming his duty as junior to Dillon. Merewether turned his head and stared at the horizon so as not to have to meet his gaze. It was yet painful to look upon that cherubic, downy, guileless, adolescent countenance, knowing that behind that sixteen-year-old face must lurk the sophisticated worldly experience of a Don Juan or Giacomo Casanova.

He was not proud of the part he had played that single night in the summerhouse with Creusa, but he had excused himself with the thought that she had been attracted to him, had indeed sought him out, had enchanted him, and made him forget his vows to Caroline. Now he told himself that it was no more than rough justice that he had been deprived of her charms after the one encounter, but his pride was touched none the less.

He had hurried ashore that day he returned from Canton, not even taking the time to count his prize money, arriving at the landing just after noon. With the evacuation in progress, it had taken time to commandeer transportation — he could not arrive for his rendezvous dusty and sweating — but he was at the guest house before one o'clock to be met by Sangh with a salaam at the door. He dissembled with his Indian steward, suddenly uncomfortable and a bit embarrassed, but yet intent upon the assignation.

"Mister Marlowe?" he inquired. "The occupation is over, Sangh, and you must pack for the move back aboard *Comet . . .*"

"Sah, Mister Marlowe is taking siesta . . ."

"Well, wake him up!" Astounding how quickly subordinates acquired the customs of the country if advantageous to them.

"But, sah, he takes it elsewhere."

"What?" Sangh's small sad countenance was averted, hands clasped before his chest, evidently ill at ease, reluctant to speak. "Out with it, Sangh, where is he?"

"Sah, since the day after you left, he has spent each afternoon with the woman — Mrs. Hale? — in her apartment in the Commandant's house . . ."

The news sunk in. Merewether closed his mouth, thankful that Sangh had kept his gaze averted. Then he felt a surge of raw anger rise in his throat. Pluck that presumptuous puppy up by the scruff of the neck and cast him out! He stood silent a moment as the realities of the situation sunk in. He could not create a scene, make a scandal. If nothing worse, he would be the laughing-stock of the Marine, supplanted by a beardless boy! The anger faded, leaving him limp and spent for a moment before he forced himself to speak.

"Indeed," he said, striving to keep his tone light. "We would be less than chivalrous to intrude upon Madame Hale at such a

moment. Pack his kit, and both of you be on board *Comet* tonight."
Merewether rode back to the landing, passing the field guns and cassions rattling along, feeling no particular emotion, mind almost blank, but contrarily a little thankful that the liaison had not proved out. He passed the Company Residence, wondering idly if Tulsi Bai yet sojourned there, but did not look up.

Now with only a crimson glow in the sky to mark the vanished sun, he felt embarrassed and remorseful at the recollection. He would make it up to Caroline. He would request the three years' leave to which he was entitled, and take her back to England to be reunited with that other man's child. He felt the weight lift as he went below.

The clatter of iron tires on cobblestones attracted Tulsi Bai's attention, and she left off her packing to peer again through the curtains into the street. She hoped it was not Pattle returning, for she could no longer abide the thought of the man. Another hour, and she would be quit of him forever. All her persuasion and wiles had not sufficed to divert him from his effort to intercept the opium cargo that meant another fortune for Rene and the judge. Actually she had never dreamed that Company cruiser out there would find the needle in the haystack of the approaches to Macao and Canton. But it had, and they had lost a half million counting the profit. Of course, the out-of-pocket loss was less than one-fifth of that amount, but her fortunes had not improved out here.

Any further trade was gone for the nonce as well. That young Viceroy in Canton had swept with a new broom, the complaisant functionaries who had shared in the illicit profits had been replaced with clever men who were also incorruptible. Time would probably change that, but for the present Rene and the judge must needs write off their losses and retire from the traffic.

Pattie and his amatory accomplishments had palled on Tulsi as soon as she saw his elation over the ruin *Comet* had brought to her brother's venture. A ship would depart for Goa three days hence, and her passage was already booked. Once there she might again test the political climate in Rajputana, and she doubted that Holkar's vengeance would reach so far. High time to set in motion again her intrigues to put Malhar on the throne. She pulled aside the curtain.

It was that scar-faced captain again, just passing below in his carriage, oblivious of her presence here above. Madame Bai's reaction was instinctive and instantaneous. She spat! A vagrant eddy in the still air carried the glob of spittle to land squarely between Merewether's shoulder blades, a dark spot on the blue coat, dried and nearly invisible by the time he reached the landing all unconscious of the insult. Tulsi returned to her packing in almost a cheerful humor.

Merewether sat in the rattan easy chair with his book held so as to catch the light from the lamp here in the dingy lodgings in Calcutta. He stared intently at the printed page, but his thoughts were far away. Caroline sat across the little table peering near-sightedly at the stitches she was taking in a tiny garment for Robert. She did not care for sewing, but she had felt compelled to demonstrate her maternal affection by making at least one item for her son's wardrobe. Her eyes were still a little pink from the tears of an hour ago.

He must make a decision, Merewether told himself. He had returned from Macao two days ago to find Caroline in the depths of despondency, grieving again for her son in England. He recalled the half-promise he had made her a year and a half ago when he had told her that after ten years of commissioned service he would be entitled to three years' leave with pay but he still felt a small flush of jealousy at her affection for that other man's son. And, he was finding it difficult to carry out the resolve made as penance for his misdeeds at Macao three months ago.

Still staring blindly at the printed page, his thoughts drifted back over the three-year period that had elapsed since he had been commissioned a captain in the Bombay Marine, sent out to rendezvous with that John Abercrombie who had called himself "Barbarossa", and deliver the ransom for Lynde, the Governor-Designate of Madras. He remembered the rain and then the blinding heat at Vellore during the mutiny, the bloody encounter with Tipu Sultan who aspired to become Emperor of India. He cringed inwardly as he thought of the useless deaths of Sister Jeanne and Midshipman Burcham.

The memory of the long voyage, the engagement with the Magindanao pirates at Ainoorang, and the landing in forbidden Canton to force the issuance of Grand Chop, was overshadowed by the bitter recollection of his trial before a Court of Inquiry at Bombay Castle the year before last, though he had been most honorably acquitted. Caroline made a tentative sound, and Merewether looked up.

"What did you say?"

She hesitated, eyes fixed on her work, and then said in a strained voice, "Nothing". He was sure she had started to say something and then thought better of it. Damnation! Women! He picked up the beaker at his elbow and sniffed the aroma of the Spanish brandy, took a bare sip, and looked back at the blurred page before he drifted into reverie again.

Last year had offered no surcease. The long days and anxious nights as officer in tactical command of the Bengal Squadron. The constant irritations inflicted by the unfortunate Captain Wolfe. And the fetid atmosphere of Penang. He still felt distaste for the place where he had been forced to fight a duel with that Royal Navy Captain — what was his name? Ackroyd? — though that delightful pair Livie and Tom Raffles had entertained him royally. Then he had been inept enough to be knocked on the head and marooned on the Ile de France. He wondered how Eleanora, the Creole granddaughter of old Jamie Plaintain, might be faring, and was reminded that he had not answered the letter from young Harris, posted in Boston early in the year, announcing his marriage to that proper New England maiden.

"Percival!" Caroline was looking at him, her violet eyes swimming with tears again.

"Yes, my dear?"

"I'm only being a silly woman, Percival, but do you love me?"

"Why, certainly!" Merewether was startled, this was the first such question in a year and a half of marriage. Had she somehow divined his lechery with Creusa?

"I sometimes think you love the Marine more than Robert or me."

"Nonsense!" with relief. Caroline's head was now bowed again over her sewing. He waited uncomfortably a moment to see if she had more to say, then took another sip of the brandy and looked back at his book.

A year ago, he had come back to Calcutta, thin and brown from his long ride along the Persian Road, to find Caroline expecting their child. He had been happy and proud of the event, and thought he had made this clear to her. He wondered how Rob Percy and his bride, Sally, liked London by now, and was sure that beautiful, self-sufficient little woman would manage her affairs no matter where she might sojourn.

This past year had been no better, the combined operations with the Royal Navy under the command of Commodore Dunbar, Colonel Lionel Smith and Captain Seton had degenerated into an unpleasant squabble, though it had finally ended well enough with the destruction of Ras ul Khymah. With *Rapid* decommissioned, Merewether had found himself in command of *Pitt,* a thirty-six-gun frigate, but sitting on a powder keg of mutiny inspired by a first lieutenant who understood only the cat and the rope. He winced as he remembered the men who had uselessly kicked their lives away in nooses, and finished off the brandy. Caroline remained intent on her work.

The events of the past few months were too recent to dwell on, the horrendous frigate action last summer in the Gulf of Aden when he had panicked and sought to strike his colors, and a fine young officer, John Dobbs, had died. He had come to terms with his conscience, but the event still troubled him, as did his recent adultery with Creusa Hale. The ill-advised occupation of Macao had resulted in almost the loss of the Company's China trade, and another unpleasant encounter with the Select Committee at Canton. Why, then, did he vacillate? Must he pursue the bubble reputation into yet another and another cannon's mouth until that round shot with his name etched upon it should inevitably strike him down?

Merewether sat silent, staring at Caroline's red-gold hair gleaming in the lamplight, and knew that the decision had already been made for him. He could not renege on the vow he had made as penance for his sins. He laid the book aside and rose to find paper, pen and ink.

Merewether signed his name, sprinkled sand over the wet ink, and poured the surplus back into the bowl. He looked up at the commencement again, addressed by way of the Master Attendant,

Calcutta, and the Commandant, to the Superintendent of the Bombay Marine. The first two were immediately available, Commodore Land at the dockyard, and Commodore Sir John Waldron in his flagship still anchored in the Hooghly. It would take a bit longer for the request to reach Sir James Campbell at Bombay for final action, but the deed was done. He heard the querulous wail from the next room, and the rustle as Caroline moved to the crib.

George Robert Percival at seven months did not thrive. He suffered from the prickly heat, and had scratched his tiny body into a mass of raw skin in spite of the flannel mittens now covering his hands. He heard Caroline crooning to the baby, and in a moment she brought him in, the child's yellow hair gleaming in the light.

"Hold him a moment, Percival, I must get his barley water." He took the infant awkwardly, marveling again at the bright blue eyes that peered out over the red irritated cheeks. The itch must be intolerable, though the apothecary had prepared a nostrum that appeared to give some relief. He saw Caroline's face as she brought the cup. The fair English complexion had browned and coarsened this past year in the heat of the Bengal climate, and in another year her beauty would be irretrievably lost.

"He appears more comfortable," he said tentatively. "Not trying to scratch just then." She took the boy back to his crib where he subsided quietly.

"Here it is," said Merewether, handing over the letter. He was clearly entitled to it by regulation, after ten continuous years of commissioned service in the Marine, three years' leave with pay. He had completed the ten years last September, but until now had been unable to bring himself to write the formal request.

"Oh, Percival, at last!" Caroline's face shone and she leaned over to kiss him upon the cheek. "And I shall see James again, and you will meet my family."

Last month the proceeds of the prizes taken only two years ago in the Bay of Bengal had been paid off, and only yesterday his share of the schooner in which he had escaped from Mauritius. The three French frigates taken at Aden last summer had been purchased into the Royal Navy for one hundred and seventy thousand pounds, but payment of the prize money had to come from London. He had a bill exchange drawn on the Company Treasurer for the proceeds of the taels he had received from the Viceroy of Canton. He could hardly plead poverty. When all his accounts were settled he should have enough capital to live comfortably the rest of his life, and he had been promised a substantial reduction in passage money by the master of the *Star of Greenwich* now anchored down at Budge-Budge. But the Marine had been his life. Could he retire to some peaceful spot in England? He thought not, already beginning to resent the waste of time with the operations against Mauritius and Java still pending, though postponed.

It was an awkward time to take leave. Rumor had it that three commodores would retire this year, and James had died at Surat. Attrition in the upper half of the captain's list had been even more severe, and he was almost two-thirds of the way up it by now. On leave he would stand little chance for promotion, and the two operations promised opportunities to distinguish himself and earn more prize money. But Caroline and Robert were more important, he told himself as he dropped off to sleep.

The next morning, Land looked keenly at him and endorsed the request, "Forwarded, Approved", and handed it back. "You may deliver it to Waldron."

They piped the side for Merewether in *Pitt* as he came on board, and he looked about the familiar decks. When last he saw her she was a battered hulk in the graving dock at Bombay, but Jamsetjee had made her whole again. She had a new captain and none of his officers was left aboard, but he returned the salutes of some of his old hands. Buttram, he had heard, had departed for England with his family last month, his tour of duty in the Marine ended. Archer, the flag lieutenant, took him into the cabin, and Waldron rose, extending his hand.

There was casual chit-chat while the steward poured the coffee. Merewether had not seen the Commandant since that morning in this same cabin when he was ordered to Mauritius to rescue a detachment of marines.

"Yes, I remember you went up in Persia last year with some Foreign Office bloke that lost his leg, but I haven't had the chance to read your reports since then." He looked directly at Merewether. "And now, what can I do for you, Captain?" He handed the request to Waldron.

"Well I'm damned. Has it been ten years? Seems like yesterday you were a boatswain's mate standing before the examining board trying to give an answer to 'Rhumb Line Smith!' " He laid the request on his desk and looked out the port. "Now you are entitled to this leave, Merewether, and I won't even have you wait on Bombay to act." He looked back and continued, "But I hope you have considered the fact that three retirements next month, plus the death of James, make four vacancies in the Commodore's List. You are more than halfway up the Captain's List, and the Selection Board is authorized to pass over some more senior officers and reach down to you." He was now looking intently into Merewether's eyes. "I am chairman of the Board, and I promise you will be selected if you remain on duty!"

Merewether absorbed the statement. It was a dazzling prospect. He would be the youngest permanent commodore since Jenkins over seventy years ago. Then the vision of his tortured son, scratching futilely with his mittened hands, and Caroline, her fair complexion weathered to the color and texture of saddle leather like some of those old Company widows still living out here, swam into his mind. He had promised her, and he could not renege.

"Sir, I am appreciative beyond my ability to express, but I am compelled to take this leave."

Waldron did not argue. "I'll see this taken care of at Bombay Castle. And good luck, Captain!"

The *Star of Greenwich* sailed three days later to call at Madras in spite of the fact that at this season it was a lee shore without shelter in the open roads from the north-east monsoon, and the vessel's insurance would be voided during its stay there. It was a pleasant six-day cruise. Merewether had forgotten how leisurely and comfortable life was in an Indiaman, and they had a large airy cabin on the starboard side of the main deck. Captain Allison had been third mate of the old *Dunvegan Castle,* and flattered Merewether by professing to remember him as a boy in that ship.

The prickly heat faded from Robert's small body. Caroline's complexion began to brighten in the fresh sea air. They came to anchor in the early morning of Christmas Eve in the roadstead with another anchor dropped underfoot, and then carried out a third from the stern to leeward. The fifth mate and a quartermaster were stationed at the binnacle taking continuous bearings on the tower of

Fort St. George and a spire over in the town lest the ship drag and strand on this lee shore.

"We'll not depart before late afternoon," Captain Allison told him. "I have a considerable shipment to load from lighters. Plenty of time for Mrs. Merewether to visit her aunt and uncle."

There was a stage rigged over the side with a regular staircase leading down to it. Merewether carried the child and steadied Caroline as they went down to embark in one of the shore boats.

Lady Barlow was ecstatic. She snatched the child and cuddled him in her arms. Merewether hovered in the background as the two women exchanged obstetrical details.

"I'll go and call on Sir George," he told them. "Still quite a while before lunch."

He walked over to Government House remembering the brisk young captain who had presided there during Bentinck's tenure, but Locksley was in the anteroom now, and he was greeted with professional warmth.

"The Governor will be delighted to see you, Captain," then led him into the chamber where he had met Lord William Bentinck that rainy afternoon nearly three years ago before he commenced his journey to Vellore and the confrontation with Tipu Sultan. He thought of young Burcham lying over in that grave at Fort St. George, now merely an incident of the mission.

"Why, Merewether, this is an unexpected pleasure!" Sir George rose and came around the desk to shake his hand. "It's been a year and a half, I think, and how are Caroline and George?" The three Christian names the child had been baptized with offered his relatives a choice as to which they preferred, Merewether thought with amusement.

"Fine, sir, they are with Lady Barlow now."

"What, did you come on the *Star of Greenwich?"*

"Yes, sir, going back to England on leave."

"Well, I'm damned! Oh, last October a Marine ship left some mail here to be forwarded to Calcutta for you. At this season, of course, we haven't had the opportunity." He tinkled the bell and Locksley popped in. "That mail for Captain Merewether, please."

There were three items. Two appeared to be routine Marine communiqués, but the third was wrapped and sealed for transmission by the Overland Mail. The device in the seal was somehow familiar, and then he remembered.

"Go ahead and read them. I've some dispatches I can be signing for the *Star of Greenwich* to take along." He slit the wrapper and took out a single sheet. It was dated the previous June.

> My Dear Merewether:
>
> We had a long slow passage to London with almost a month at St. Helena while a topmast was replaced. Carpenter Wiley made me a handsome peg, silver mounted, before we left *Viper*. I can now walk almost as well as before, and shall ride in the Ardsley Hunt next fall. Sally is fine and we expect a child early in the New Year.
>
> Grenville and King George's Equerry have confirmed the fact, I shall be created Baron Percy of Baku in the New Year's Honors List. I chose the title to memorialize that expensive Caspian naval engagement, and to distinguish me from the Baron Percy who is my nephew!
>
> Oh, and I have confirmed with the same authorities that you will be created a Knight of the Bath for services to Government, not Company, so you may call yourself, "Sir Percival", come January, though there will have to be a bit of ritualistic flummery at some time.
>
> If you are in London Sally and I shall welcome you, and my warmest regards to Caroline.
>
> Ever yours,
> A. R. Percy

"Well, I'm damned!" said Merewether with wonder.

"What?" Sir George looked up sharply. "Bad news?" Merewether handed him the letter, and Barlow looked first at the signature, then sniffed. "Oh, that Foreign Office fellow, lost a leg up in Persia a year or so ago, I heard." He perched spectacles on his nose and read the letter.

"Baron Percy of Baku! What did he do?"

"Stopped off Boney from invading India."

"I thought 'Boy' Malcolm did that." He read on. "Knight of the Bath! Good God, Merewether, what did you do?"

"Helped Percy, sir."

"Well, congratulations, Sir. Percival! Locksley, we have a Knight of the Bath here!"

Luncheon on a terrace overlooking Madras Roadstead was delightful, toasts in champagne to the new Sir Percival and Lady Merewether, and Sir George actually dandling the child on his knee. They came back to the *Star of Greenwich* in the late afternoon, Caroline and Merewether each a little tipsy still with the champagne they had drunk, and Master Robert asleep in his mother's arms. The stern anchor and the one under foot had been taken in, and the stream anchor was at short stay.

The ship was underway a quarter of an hour later, steering south towards the Indian Ocean and the Cape of Good Hope. Caroline was nursing the child in the cabin, while Merewether remained on the quarterdeck watching lights come on over in Madras. He had given the Crown, the Company and the Marine nineteen years of his life, and he would only be thirty-one next week. They had been good to him in their fashion, and he had tried to give value in return, but he felt somehow in his bones that he would not pass this way again.

He turned to join Caroline and their son.

Bibliography

A. L. Basham, *The Wonder That Was India,* New York 1963.

Julian S. Corbett, *Fighting Instructions,* 1513-1815, London 1905.

E. Keble Chatterton, *The Old East Indiamen,* London 1937.

H. H. Dodwell, *The Cambridge History of India,* Third Indian Reprint, 1968.

Phillip Gosse, *The History of Piracy, New* York 1934.

C. R. Low, *Famous Frigate Actions,* London 1898.
— *History of the Indian Navy,* London 1877.

H. B. Morse, *The East India Company Trading to China,* Oxford 1925.

C. Northcote Parkinson, *War in the Eastern Seas,* 1793-1815, London 1954.

United States Oceanographic Office Publication 62, *Sailing Directions for the Persian Gulf,* 1960.

Made in the USA
Middletown, DE
01 December 2019